CHANGELING'S FALL

CHANGELING'S FALL

Book I of The Eisteddfod Chronicles

SARAH JOY ADAMS
EMILY LAVIN LEVERETT

This book is dedicated to my father and step-mother, Gerald Leverett and Janice Banducci. Your love and support is fundamental to all the good in my life. Also, in loving memory of my mother Kathy, whose influence on me and my writing cannot be estimated.

-- Emily

To the librarians of the Nashua Public Library whose warmth and love of books made a safe haven for a little girl who needed one. And to the memory of my grandmother Marjorie Holmes Adams, who always protected her granddaughter's right to be left alone to read.

-- Sarah

Chapter One

A routine MRI—that's what the doctor promised. Now, the MRI was on fire. Sparks hit Deor's bare skin. More burned through her paper gown.

"Help!" she yelled. She mashed the panic button over and over until her thumb ached. Around her the MRI whirred and clunked. Something pinged, like a part coming loose, and the machine groaned.

She tossed aside the useless button and yanked at the cage that covered her face. Arching her back, she wriggled, trying to squeeze under the cage and out of the tube. Heat rolled across her skin and sparks fell like orange snow. The pain turned her fear to panic, and she shoved the cage up trying to dislodge it.

"Help!" she screamed. A rush of glittering, silver-white sparkles filled the MRI tube, rising off her skin to meet the sparks from the machine. Magic and technology collided, sizzling into steam.

Deor gasped and stopped struggling as the sparkles coalesced above her, forming a cool shield between her and the fire. The magic sparkles had been there her entire life, annoying, useless, unpredictable. They spat off her whenever she was stressed and ruined high tech things like the MRI. Now, for the first time in her life, her magic had protected her.

Hands snatched her ankles and jerked her from the mouth of the machine. The burly nurse pried open the cage over her face and scooped her up in his arms. He hurled himself through the door and down the hall, her white sparkles trailing behind like a comet's tail.

"Are you okay?" The nurse lowered her to her feet at the far end of the hall and steadied her. Sweat shone on his shaved, black head. The shoulders of his scrubs were scorched where he had reached in to get her, and the hair on his arms smelled burnt.

She curled her toes against the cold tiles under her feet. All along the beige corridor, heads poked out of doors. A small crowd of worried faces gathered around, clustering with Deor and the nurse as far from the door with the smoking MRI as they could get. Some wore paper gowns like hers; a few were in lab coats or scrubs. The small burns on her skin eased as her sparkles landed on them and vanished.

"I think I'm okay," Deor said.

Foul smoke billowed from the MRI room, rolling toward her. The nurse caught her arm and drew her back, farther away from the smoke. Her sparkles burst out again, and the smoke cloud dispersed as if blown by a fan. The nurse—all the people gathered in the hall—never saw the magic.

"I don't know what the hell happened in there." The nurse waved off the smoke around him. "I've never seen anything like it."

The MRI tech, her cheeks and clothes smeared with black soot, emerged with a spent fire extinguisher. She slid a hand over her hair trying to tuck the brown halo of wavy strands back into her ponytail. She stalked toward Deor.

"You're sure there's no metal on you?" Before Deor could answer, the tech waved her own question away. "Dumb question. It would have burned the hell out of you if you had." She sighed. "We need to get the doc to check you out."

Deor hugged herself, one arm over her chest, the other trying to hold the paper gown closed over her ass.

"Can I get my clothes? They're still in there." Trying to hold up her boobs without the help of her underwire was getting old fast.

The tech glared at the door to the MRI room like it was somehow to blame. "Yeah. Sure. But take the nurse with you, in case it catches again."

"Alright, everybody." The nurse put himself between Deor and the crowd. "Show's over." He shooed them away.

Her clothes reeked of melted plastic and burnt metal. A nurse and doctor poked and prodded her for a few minutes, finding her none the worse for wear. The hospital's legal liaison kept her for an hour filling out a slew of forms confirming over and over that she hadn't been hurt and that she wouldn't "seek financial compensation." When it was all settled, Deor bypassed the appointment desk. They couldn't afford another MRI machine, and it wouldn't help anyway.

As she dropped into the bucket seat of her so-old-it-would-soon-be-classic Trans Am, the headache she'd battled all morning crawled up from her neck, snaking its way around her temples, and binding her skull in a vise. She slipped on her sunglasses and closed her eyes against the bright sun.

She leaned her head back and whispered a small prayer to the gods of old muscle cars.

"Please, please start." She turned the key in the ignition. The engine coughed, hacked, sputtered, and died. "No, no, no!" She turned the key again. Nothing.

"Fuck." She shoved her door open for air. Not that it did much good. It was only ten a.m., but August in Bakersfield isn't known for its cool breezes. Sweat beaded on her temples and trickled down her spine to the small of her back. All around her face, her straight brown hair plastered itself to her skin. Even through sunglasses, the light pulsed with every beat of her heart, flashing in time to the pounding in her head. Her stomach rolled in response, and she leaned to the left, trying not to gag.

"Come on," she said. "I've killed one machine today. Let's not make it two."

She took a deep breath and focused on the beating of her heart, on her breathing. The magic that had blown the MRI all to hell still hugged her body. When she touched the key, her magic slid from her fingers, wrapping around the ignition like a boa constrictor. If she didn't find a way to rein it in, she'd be stuck in the parking lot for God knew how long waiting for a tow truck. The nice ladies at AAA now recognized her number. She used to go months without her magic causing trouble; now she was lucky to go a single day.

"Alright." She concentrated, took a deep breath, and thought about peas. Green peas. With butter and salt. Simple, boring peas. The other-worldly magic coating cracked and split—broken by the mundane. She drew a second deep breath and filled her mind with images of oatmeal.

Warm. Tasty. Utterly unexciting. After a final deep breath, and one last visualization of a plain baked chicken breast, the magic retreated, drawing back into her.

She turned the key. The engine purred to life.

"Yes!"

She slammed the door shut and clicked on her seat belt. Mercifully cool air drifted from the vents. She headed home, concentrating on her to do list. Sign and mail back her contract for the Assistant Professor position. Call the movers and confirm the date. Make sure her apartment deposit had arrived.

The headache had bloomed into a full-blown migraine by the time she got home. She gave off sparkles again too, one or two floating off her every second. She clicked open the door connecting the garage and kitchen as quietly as she could and listened for sounds of her grandmother. No noise upstairs and no television, no sound of her rocking chair in the parlor. Hopefully she was out doing whatever she did at her club with her friends.

Deor hung her keys on a hook by the back door and set her purse on the large island in the middle of the kitchen. The dark marble countertop was cool under her palms, and the air conditioner had chilled the air. Grandma had been up already—her teacup, saucer, and small plate were neatly stacked in the drying rack. Deor took a glass from the cabinet and filled it with water. Outside, the heat shimmered slightly around the pool, and dry grass baked in the sun. She grabbed her last two migraine pills from the windowsill and swallowed them, chasing them with the water. A sparkle fluttered away.

"So," her grandmother said from the parlor doorway, "are you going to tell me what the doctor said?"

Deor whirled and sparkles shot off her like fur puffing around a startled cat.

"Geez, Gramma!" She leaned back against the counter until her heart rate dropped to normal and the cloud dissipated. "Don't sneak up on me like that."

"Don't change the subject." Her grandmother frowned at Deor's sparkles. She flicked on the electric kettle on the counter between the fridge and the stove. She faced Deor and leaned back against the counter. Tall and lean, much more athletic than Deor's mother had been, Gramma still played tennis three times a week, as the club polo-shirt, knee shorts, and tennis shoes showed. Her short, grey hair framed her face, and her wrinkles looked more like laugh lines than heavy creases. Few people would have guessed she was in her late seventies. Deor waited for the tea making to be done—her grandmother wouldn't respond until the table was all set. Finally, she brought the steaming tea pot to the table, already set with milk, sugar, and—

"Wait. Why are there three mugs?"

"Don't be mad," a voice from behind her made her turn. Standing in the doorway to the dining room was Bill—her best friend since childhood

"Why would I be mad?" She kept her voice steady, but sparkles still flicked off her.

"You spit sparkles when you're emotional," he said catching one. It popped, vanishing like a bubble.

"Fine. I'm emotional."

"And?" her grandmother asked.

"I'm afraid of being half faerie," she finished. She rubbed a hand over her eyes. She hated everything about the word faerie: the sound, her mother's pretentious spelling of it, the invocation of tiny princesses with gauze wings.

"We already know you're half faerie. Why all the sneaking?" Bill asked.

"I think—no—I'm sure being a changeling is killing me." Panic welled in her as she said her fear aloud. A cold wave rolled down her arms, her body, all the way to her toes, whispering in her ears. Sparkles exploded again.

Bill waved his hand through them, smiling. He could touch her magic —the only one who could since her mother died, though no one knew why. Perhaps it was because he'd never given up his childhood belief in magic.

"I've had a rough day, and it isn't even noon. Why are you here?"

"I'm worried about you." Bill looked in no condition to worry about anyone else. His brown hairtoo long to be neat and too short to be fashionable—hung around his face. His eyes, bright blue when he was a kid, had faded, and dark smudges made his sallow complexion look worse. His normally square and stocky shoulders had developed a permanent stoop.

"Forget me. You don't look well." She gave him a hug. He was skinnier than his baggy clothes revealed. "Come on, sit down. How did you guys know I was going to the doctor today?"

They sat around the kitchen table, and her grandmother poured the tea. "You've been napping in the middle of the day, you just took your last two migraine pills, and you dropped this." She pulled the MRI appointment reminder card out of her pocket and slid it across the table. "So tell us, what did they find?" Her grandmother's tone was light, but her lips formed a pale, thin line.

Deor stirred sugar into her tea. "Nothing. I broke the machine." She rolled her shoulders. Her back pain had gotten worse, too. "The thing nearly blew up with me in it. There was smoke and sparks and magic everywhere."

"Wow." Bill shook his head. "You've never set anything on fire before."

A few more sparks drifted off her and landed on him. He closed his eyes, savoring them.

"I'm fine," Deor said. "You're the one who needs help."

"Since when is that news? I've been sickly since I was born." He reached for her hand and squeezed it. "There's nothing to be done about it. They keep offering to give me drugs to stop my 'hallucinations,'" he mimed the scare quotes, "but I know they're real. You're real." He chuckled. "Maybe I belong somewhere else, too."

Since preschool they had been inseparable, and Bill always seemed healthier around her family than his. Given the constant yelling and door slamming at his house, Deor hadn't been surprised. He'd practically lived with her and her grandmother through high school. They stayed close through college and grad school, leaning on each other from a distance through comps, dissertations, and hostile defense committees. When Bill's family had been "too busy" to make it to Berkeley, Deor and her grandmother had been there to see him cross the stage and be hooded as a Doctor of Philosophy. He'd driven all the way out to Ohio in his '85 Honda Civic for Deor's graduation.

In all the time she had known him, she had never seen him show even a touch of magic.

"We'll figure it out." She squeezed his hand in return.

"You haven't sparkled this much since you were a baby, and now you're breaking huge, complicated machines?" Her grandmother's deep frown and worried tone made Deor wince.

"Mom said my magic would fade as I got older." Deor pulled her hand away from Bill and sipped her tea. "I'm thirty. How much older do I have to get?"

Her grandmother sighed. "She was never happy about your magic fading. She wanted you to hang on to your faerie side."

"She never had a bad word to say about it. Even when it killed her."

"You look so much like your mother." Her grandmother blinked a few times.

"That's what they tell me."

Everyone who had known Susan Smithfield commented on how much mother and daughter looked alike, especially as Deor grew older. She had Susan's high cheekbones, her rich brown hair, her curves, her laugh, but not her brown eyes. Deor's steel grey eyes looked silver when she was happy and darkened to storm clouds when she was angry—those she must have gotten from her father. Whoever *he* was.

Deor swirled her tea. Fragmented memories of her mother surfaced in her mind. She had been eight when her mother passed—twenty-one years lost. Twenty-one years of birthdays and graduations, of choosing dresses and colleges. All without her mother.

"I wish she had chosen us." Deor looked up from her tea.

Her mother—once vibrant and strong—had faded away. She died pining for a faerie who didn't even tell her his true name.

"She would be so proud of you, of the woman you've become," her grandmother said.

She almost never compared Deor to her mother, even when she deserved it. Like the time when, at sixteen, Deor took off with a boy on a motorcycle and didn't come home for two days. She had put her grandmother through so much. Deor owed her the truth, even if she couldn't explain it.

"My back has gotten worse, too." Last year her back had broken out in what she thought was a rash—a reaction to her dissertation committee perhaps. Two columns of tiny dots appeared down the center of her back trailing from between her shoulder blades to her tailbone. The dots had melded into lines of tender, inflamed scars, like someone had slashed down either side of her spine.

"You should have told us what was going on. Whatever it is, you don't need to go through it alone." Her grandmother folded her hands on the table. Since the time Deor was a little girl, such a gesture meant no one left the table until everything was adequately explained.

"Remember when Mom died?" Deor's voice was low, not quite a whisper.

"Of course," her grandmother nodded. "We were both there."

"Right." Tears cast a sheen over Deor's eyes, blurring her vision before tumbling out.

She had climbed onto her mom's bed, and her mother had given her a hug. *You're the one bright spot*, she had whispered. *I can see you, sparkling and shining, when everything else is grey.* Her mother closed her eyes. Her grandmother, always the family's rock, took Deor's hand and led her out of the room. The next time Deor saw her mother was at the visitation, in her coffin.

"Mom said that everything was turning grey." Deor wiped tears from her cheeks. "You said it was a metaphor. It wasn't. The same thing happened to me a few months ago. At the edges of my vision at first and now everything. It isn't that I can't see in my peripheral vision; I can. But it's like the world has turned into a black and white movie."

"You should go back for another MRI," Bill said.

"There's no point," Deor said. "It won't tell me anything. Almost everything is shades of grey now. You two are the only exceptions."

"Why didn't you tell me?" her grandmother snapped at her. "You've wasted so much time."

"How so? No one can tell me what's wrong—but it sure looks like what my mom had when she died. What would telling either of you earlier have gotten me? You'd have worried more about something none of us can fix."

"Dammit, Deor," Bill snapped. "You don't know that. You don't know!" He glared at her grandmother. "I told you we should have done this at the beginning of the summer. Not three weeks before she's supposed to start her job."

"I didn't want to make a suggestion if I wasn't sure it was a last resort. I'll be right back." Her grandmother stood and walked into the dining room. Crystal and china rattled as she opened the china cabinet.

"The whole sneaking thing?" Deor pressed her toes into the Spanish tile floor, bending and flexing her feet, taking comfort in the coolness. "I guess I'd do the same for you." She brushed his hair out of his face. "Are you sure you're okay?"

He shrugged. "Fine as ever."

"That's what worries me." Up close, the circles under Bill's eyes were even darker. He looked like a corpse.

"I think you need to find your father." Her grandmother returned with a small wooden box, which she set on the table in front of Deor.

"What?" Deor snapped her attention to her grandmother. "Why in the world would you suggest that?"

"Once, when your mother was in one of her rambling moods, telling me stories about her time with your father," she settled into her seat again, "she said she worried that taking you away from him would hurt you. He wanted to take you into Faerie itself, to have you 'acknowledged' as he called it."

"Because I was a bastard?" Deor crossed her arms over her chest. "You mean legally claiming me for inheritance or something?"

"I don't know. He said it was important for you to be acknowledged—he used that word a lot, I gather—I don't think your mother knew why."

"She was so in love with him—why didn't she let him?"

"She was already planning to leave him by then," her grandmother said. "She was afraid of him. He had taken you to Faerie once without her. She knew he would do it again, and never bring you back."

Deor rubbed her temples. "So, I'm supposed to cancel all my plans, put my life on hold, and find my deadbeat dad?"

A knot tightened in her stomach. Years of work, no, years of dreams, gone. The school might hold her job for a semester, but beyond that? Not a chance.

"What color shirt am I wearing?" Bill asked.

"What?" Deor looked at the shirt—a T-shirt he'd had since forever. Purple with an ironic unicorn pooping rainbows. Today it was grey. All of it—the shirt, the unicorn, the rainbows. Her gaze travelled over the room. The floral dish towel hanging off the sink, the red Dutch oven on the stove, the green paint on the walls—all grey. She saw color only in their two faces.

"So?" Bill raised his eyebrows.

"Grey," she conceded. She flexed her fingers—her hands had become fists. "So let's make a plan. I've got to get to Faerie, find the guy, have him acknowledge me so I can be cured, slap him across the face, and come back home. How?"

"Your mother left instructions about getting into Faerie." Her grandmother pushed the wood box closer to Deor. "She always hoped you'd want to see it."

Deor opened the box. On top were a few letters with her name on them. "What's this?" She rifled through. "Mom wrote these for me? Why did you keep them from me?"

"You were so angry after she died, and you were a little girl. I thought it best to keep them back until you were old enough to understand. And then, I knew they wouldn't be any comfort."

Deor let it go. Who was she to be mad at secrets? She picked up the first letter—dated a few days before her mother died.

My brilliant daughter,

Someday I hope that you'll be as adventurous as I was and go to Caer Eisteddfod. (Don't ever call it London to a faerie—apparently that's a nasty nickname that ancient humans in the area used.) I want you to find your family. I regret taking you from your father—I would undo it if I could. He told me there were lots of ways into the Winter Court, all over the world, but I only ever saw one: the Tower Bridge in London...

"Did you read these?" Deor asked, setting down the letter.

"Yes." Her grandmother nodded. "Your mother told me to." She scowled. "She writes a lot about him—about what they did and where they went. Nothing more than a brief physical description, though, and she never calls him anything but Finn."

"How do I find him?" Deor flipped through the letters and found two Polaroids. Her mother stood in front of one of the British Museum's lions, grinning. Another picture, a close up, had her in the same place. Unsurprisingly, she held a book. "No pictures of him?"

"No." Her grandmother shook her head. "They tried, but it didn't seem to work—something about his magic. So he took pictures of your mother."

"Any pictures of her in Caer Eisteddfod?"

"No, but there is something else from him."

"What is it?" From the box, Deor lifted a small bundle and eased the decades-old tissue paper open. A silver and ivory baby rattle. It chimed one note as Deor gingerly shook it. "You kept it."

In spite of herself, she smiled and a blinked away a tear. She gave the rattle another little shake, and a single, sad sparkle floated away. The last time she'd seen the rattle was the day after her mother died. She had hurled it into a trashcan screaming that she wasn't a faerie, that she hated faeries and everything about them. Her attitude had not changed.

"It was too precious to throw away," her grandmother said. "I thought you might want it someday."

Deor tilted the rattle, examining it. She found a tiny maker's mark: a rabbit reading a book, one ear up, the other flopped over.

"If I can find who made this, maybe I can find out who bought it," she said.

"I'll go with you," Bill offered. There was a quiet hunger in his eyes that gave her chills.

"No way," she said. Humans too enamored with faeries, like Deor's mother, pined for the magic land and died. "And you look like the trip might kill you."

His face fell, fading to grey before her eyes, like he'd been refused the only thing in the world he ever wanted.

"I'll bring you something back." She touched his hand. "And, if it's safe, we can go back later."

She knew in her heart of hearts she didn't want to go at all, let alone twice, but his eyes brightened, and that was justification enough for the lie.

"So," Deor said to both of them, "what does one pack for a journey to Caer Eisteddfod?"

Chapter Two

Deor trudged up the stairs at the Piccadilly Circus Station to the surface, her suitcase bumping behind her on each step. Every time she blinked, she had to remind her eyes to open again. The painful ridges on either side of her spine and the nagging sense that she had thrown away everything on a wild faerie chase meant she'd stayed awake across a continent and an ocean.

London should have thrilled her, but her whole body ached. Dragging her bags through multiple Underground stations hadn't helped either. The grey noise of Piccadilly's constant traffic blended with the grey of the world around her, the people as flat and dull as the sidewalk. Even the continually scrolling, animated, two-story ads on every building seemed dim. Piccadilly was the flashiest place in London, but to her it might as well have been a street in Soviet Russia.

"Right. Let's start at the beginning," she said aloud and set off down the crowded sidewalk. The British Museum was to her north, St. James Park and the Palace directly to the south. And a third of a mile between herself and the Palace was Trafalgar Square, the place where her mother and father first met.

Piccadilly might be ever changing, chock-full of the latest and the trendiest, but even in mid-day, Trafalgar Square held itself still. The tap of Londoners' feet on flagstones echoed off the surrounding buildings, like footsteps in a church. Nelson stood silent on his plinth, guarded by his four lions. Tourists laughed and clicked cameras at each other or debated over maps, but their voices were swallowed up in the Square's immensity. Even the cooing of feral pigeons sounded timeless.

As she crossed Trafalgar Square, Deor's heart pounded. Her mother's letters were in her purse, but she'd already memorized what she needed.

I don't know how you will find him if you ever need him, but I'll give you all the details that might help. We first met in Trafalgar. He never told me what he was doing there. I was standing right underneath the bronze plaque with Nelson's death—the one facing Whitehall—when I first saw him. The minute our eyes met, I wanted to drown myself in those silver-grey pools. If—when—you go, be careful.

At the foot of the column, Deor took a minute to get her bearings, found the plaque she wanted, and dragged her rolling bag up the short steps. Her feet planted exactly where her mother's feet had been, she turned and looked toward Whitehall.

Pigeons. Taxicabs honking on the far side of the square. A group of schoolchildren happily ignoring their guide as she tried to interest them in the battle of Trafalgar.

"Come on, faeries. I know you're here somewhere." Maybe if she said it aloud, it would be true. She took a deep breath and scanned the Square.

Small blotches of color interrupted the grey edges of her vision. At least a dozen other blotches moved through the Square. No. Not blotches. People. Some zipped by too fast to track. Others flickered in and out. She forced herself to focus, and the colored blurs resolved into what had to be faeries. A bearded man standing in the spray of the fountain, despite the fall chill. A child, or maybe just a very short adult, dashing unnoticed from one pocket of tourists to another.

Just ten feet from her, at the base of the bronze lion to her left—a redheaded woman in an oversized sweater and leggings. It wasn't just the woman's coppery hair that glowed in the sun, but her whole body. Deor took a deep breath, fingers flexing and curling.

"Excuse me, ma'am," she said. "Are you a faerie?"

The woman jumped and turned. Their eyes met. The woman's eyes were like liquid magma, bubbling yellow, orange, and red with heat. Deor's mouth went dry. Sparkles fountained off her.

"Careful, little one," the woman said. "The humans will see you." She turned away, took two steps, and vanished.

Deor gasped. Her fingernails dug into the palms of her hands, gouging moon shaped dents.

"They're real," she said aloud.

Of course they were real. She'd always known the faeries were real. She was half faerie herself. But now they were really and truly real.

She hugged her arms tight around herself and leaned back against the column, taking slow deep breaths. She wanted to slip off her shoes and feel the comforting granite beneath her feet. But she was a grown woman in public, so she contented herself with pressing her palms into the polished stone. Eventually the blood stopped pounding in her ears.

All around her humans passed, their feet tapping across the stones. Tourists laughed and snapped pictures of themselves harassing the lions.

She didn't have to ask herself "what next?"

She knew. She just didn't want to do it.

Her stomach growled at her, and she yawned hugely. She rubbed her palms across her face, grinding them against her eyes.

"Either you go now, or get a hotel room," she said. More sparkles spat off her, like grease in a frying pan. "Now it is."

She grabbed the handle of the suitcase and yanked it after her, striding east toward the Thames and the portal into Faerie that her mother's letters said was under London Bridge.

E merging from the tunnel at London's Tower Hill tube station, Deor turned down the path toward the river. Ravens from the Tower circled in the cloudy sky. A few hundred yards away, the grey stones of the Tower Bridge were offset by the jaunty blue and white paint on the spans.

She pulled out her cell phone, her finger hovering over the call button, wanting to hear her grandmother's voice one more time. But it was one a.m. in Bakersfield, and the thought of leaving a last voicemail before heading into the unknown—it was either creepy or melodramatic.

Instead she sent a quick text to Bill.

Headed for the faerie ferry. Tell my gramma, okay? Don't worry if you don't hear from me for a bit—I'll be fine. Love you both.

She hit send and powered off the phone.

Tucking her phone into her suitcase, she made her way down the promenade and toward the bridge, her eyes fixed on the river's edge until a wooden quay appeared fuzzily in her peripheral vision. Whenever she tried to fix her eyes on it, the dock wavered and faded like a mirage, but so long as she kept it in the corner of her eye, it seemed solid enough.

"Looking for the ferry?" A tallish woman about her own age leaned against a wooden post, a duffel bag with a school crest at her feet.

Deor started. "Um, yes."

The woman wore jeans and a grey T-shirt with a lavender scarf knotted around her neck. She had golden blonde hair tied back in a low ponytail, and a smattering of freckles on her bronze skin. She was pretty enough, but she lacked the glow of the redhead at Nelson's column.

"First time?" the woman asked.

"So much for looking like a suave, sophisticated traveler. I'm Deor." She smiled and held her hand out to the woman. The moment their hands touched, a shower of sparkles blossomed off Deor.

"Wow," the woman said. "I'm Roberta. Everyone calls me Robbie."

"Shit." Deor glanced around, seeing the other waiting passengers for the first time: a woman in a suit with a potted plant, a half-sized man in full punk gear, a cluster of college students with duffels embroidered with the same crest as Robbie's bag. A few were staring and smirking.

"Sorry, sorry. Please don't disappear," Deor said waving her hands through the cloud. "They're harmless. It just happens sometimes when I'm stressed." Or in danger.

The blonde woman seemed innocuous enough. Wholesome even. Put her in the right costume and she could have sold butter.

"Good thing the humans can't see it then."

Deor automatically opened her mouth to clarify that she was human and shut it again. Getting into the fine details of her species probably didn't qualify as small talk. And flat out asking "are you a faerie?" hadn't gone too well the first time.

At the end of the dock, a flat-bottomed rowboat was being tied up, and the other passengers began moving toward it.

Robbie picked up her duffle bag and jerked her head in the direction of the boat. "Come on. Pescanus doesn't like to wait."

"Have your pennies ready," the ferryman barked. "All aboard for the Tower."

The ferryman held out a gnarled hand, tinged grey-green and half webbed. His hair hung down past his shoulders, lanky and flat like water-weeds. His face was human enough, aside from the color, but gill slits fluttered on either side of his neck.

Her knees banged into her suitcase as the students pushed past her. As they boarded, the passengers dropped silver coins into the man's palm and took their seats on the benches that lined the boat.

"Well?" he snapped at her. "You coming or not?"

"Yes. Yes, I'm coming." She fumbled in her purse. "I don't have... I mean, all my money is human money. Is that okay?"

He grunted. "Four pounds then. Three for the ride and one for the trouble of changing."

She yanked a twenty pound note out of her wallet—all she had from the airport ATM.

"Keep it," she said shoving it into his damp hand.

His kelp-like eyebrows shot up, and he folded the money quickly away, but he did have the courtesy to heave her bag into the boat for her. She stumbled her way forward to sit next to Robbie, who had seats open on either side. The other young people sat together at the back of the boat.

"We're away," the ferryman grunted.

He stood, legs wide, in the back of the ferry and spread his webbed hands out over the waters. Little waves and ripples rose up, and the boat slid back from the quay, turning without a splash toward the looming bridge ahead. The waves grew higher, and the ferry pushed forward, speeding through the water.

Around her the other passengers shook themselves, and their dull ordinariness fell away. The blonde woman's hair revealed itself as true gold and her skin glistened with same sheen. The student that she would have guessed was African darkened, his skin taking on the color of obsidian like his hair. Reds, greens, blues, and browns showed around the ferry. Hidden jewels glittered in people's hair, on fingers, and around necks. A tracksuit became a full-length skirt. Only Robbie didn't change her appearance, but even she showed the same glimmering, twilight shadow around the edges.

So that was magic.

Deor studied the others from the corners of her eyes, the way she had learned to do from years of her grandmother's admonitions not to stare. She shifted in her seat, slightly away from the magic glow and closer to Robbie's comforting humanness.

"I'm a changeling, too," Robbie said quietly as the boat picked up speed.

Deor jumped. "You are? How can you tell? About me, I mean. No, never mind. Do you know both your parents?"

Robbie stiffened, and she drew back. "Yes. One usually does."

"Oh crap, look I didn't mean to imply anything. I'm sure your family is lovely. It's my family that's a mess. I mean…ah, screw it." Deor threw up her hands. "I've never talked to another changeling or faerie before, so I'm just charging around like a cat with its head in a bag. I'm sorry. I didn't mean to hurt you."

Robbie's shoulders eased, and she smiled again. "It's okay. My dad may be just a human, but he's a good dad. And I'm a bit touchy about the 'bastard' thing. It gets old."

"Do people really call you that?"

"Not to my face. Just close enough to my back that I can hear them."

"Wow. Assholes."

There'd been a few raised eyebrows and pseudo-compassionate comments about the plight of children with single mothers when Deor was a kid, but her grandmother had been swift and merciless with any Junior Leaguer who pulled that around her granddaughter.

"It's a wise child that knows its own father," Deor said.

At Robbie's confused look, she waved her hand as if shooing away more sparkles.

"Random Shakespeare quote. It's an occupational hazard with me. Don't worry about it. You were saying?"

Robbie blinked for a second and said, "I've always known both my parents—it was part of the deal. My dad's the human. Mum let me spend the summer with him in London, sort of being human for a change, you know? But now, I'm going back for university. You?"

"I'm here looking for my faerie dad. We've never met."

"Oh. I'm really sorry. I hope it turns out okay."

"Me too, kiddo."

Before Deor could ask herself why she kept thinking of Robbie as a kid when they were plainly close in age, London Bridge's shadow loomed overhead, swallowing the front of the ferry. She had just enough time to cast her eyes up for a last glimpse of sky before the boat shot into the gloom.

A wave of cold struck her, rolled over her like crystals of ice and silver. She gasped, and at that moment, her mother's gushing praise of magic made sense. Deor held out her hand, sweeping it through the air. Magic built up on her fingers like invisible sleet, filling her palm, raw and ready to be used. Her skin tingled as if all the sparkles she'd ever thrown had grown substance and danced over her body.

On this side the bridge was all stone, and the sky was bright and clear. The roar of the human city vanished. But as they emerged from under the bridge, the waves grew, knocking the low ferry to the side.

"Woah!" the ferryman said, like he was calming a horse, and the waves around them steadied for a moment, but rose again, swelling so much that Deor seized the side and held on.

A black yacht plowed through the water behind them, churning up hard waves as it gained on the little ferry. Looming in the prow of the ship, hands braced on the rails, stood a man—tall, broad shouldered, with hair as black as his ship. His high cheekbones and dark eyes gave him a hawkish look, and his skin was pale, moonshadow blue.

The thing that made Deor blink and doubt her eyes were his wings. Huge blue butterfly wings stood out from his back. Midnight blue at the base, with black and silver veins, they lightened only slightly toward the top, like the sky at twilight.

"Are those real?" Deor said in whisper.

Beside her, Robbie giggled. "You're not the first one to say that. But yeah, completely real. He doesn't glamour them—they're just that big."

Before Deor could ask any more questions, the man looked down from the deck at the ferry sailing dangerously close to his boat. He scowled and waved his left hand, as if shooing off a bug. The ferry lurched, heaved aside by a single, bulging wave as the passengers gasped and clung to the ferry's sides. The yacht's shadow passed over them and sailed on.

"Asshole!" Deor muttered at the black ship. "Who does he think he is?"

"Rafael, Lord Farringdon, heir to the Duchy of Wellhall and the Sword of Peace and Justice to King Sweordmund the VIII," Robbie said, shaking water out of her hair.

"He should learn to drive," Deor said.

Robbie laughed, but everyone else on the ship was tittering and whispering to each other. Apparently celebrities here had much the same effect they did back home.

"Easy now," the ferryman cooed.

He gestured as if stroking the waves smooth and waters around the boat calmed to glassy stillness. He growled and spat into the water after the yacht. He was still glowering as he eased the ferry into the slips, jockeying among the other boats coming and going. Soon the passengers were clambering up the short ladder.

Deor hauled herself up onto the landing, glad to have solid ground underfoot again. Around her, passengers stretched and butterfly wings emerged on their backs, pushing through hidden slits in their clothes to flutter in the breeze. Soon the dock was a rainbow of color. None of the wings around Deor seemed as quite as large as Lord Farringdon's. Up close they looked soft, like velvet or suede. Deor stuffed her hand in her pocket before she gave in to the temptation to run her fingers along a wing and find out.

She breathed deep—the air was cool and bright with magic—washing away some of her weariness. As Deor looked around, wondering what next, Robbie nudged her.

"You go up that way." She pointed to a set of stone steps that led up the embankment to a low building marked *Immigration*.

At the foot of the stairs stood a woman in a crisp black uniform decorated at the cuffs with silver piping. Her pale yellow butterfly wings were stiff in the light breeze, and an eight-pointed crystal star gleamed over her heart. A bright sword and helmet proved that the Winter Court's military, not a civilian TSA, controlled the borders.

"I've got to meet some friends in the marketplace," Robbie said. "But look me up at the university if you like. It's always good to know another changeling."

Deor hesitated, torn between the knowledge that she wouldn't be staying long enough to be any sort of friend and the fact that Robbie was her first and only source of information.

"Thank you. I'd love to. Here, I'll give you my cell number." She stopped herself. "I'm guessing there's no cell service here, is there?"

"None. No electronics here—you might as well be carrying a brick."

"Oh, right." Deor frowned. She'd done things as a kid without cell phones. Made plans, met people. How had that worked again? "How do I look you up? What's your last name?"

"It's Roberta Gemalsdottir. Just ask at the gate and they'll mirror me. Good luck with your search!" She slung her bag over her shoulder and set off.

"Thanks." Deor gave a little wave as Robbie moved off.

She followed the be-winged, human-sized passengers to the right, away from Immigration. The guard barely glanced at Robbie as she passed. Unlike most of the other faeries, she hadn't put out any wings, if she had them. Deor made a mental note—faeries have wings. Changelings, it seemed, didn't. Her back twinged—sharp enough to make her gasp—and she wondered if Robbie lived with the same kind of back pain.

The green-skinned passenger and the short, punked-out man went to the left toward Immigration. Deor moved to follow, but the guard at the foot of the stairs blocked her with a white-gloved hand. "Faeries to the right, miss."

"I'm not a faerie," she said. "I'm human." She pulled out her American passport.

He looked skeptical for a moment, shrugged, and waved her to the left. "Have your documents ready. Welcome to the Winter Court."

She wrestled her bags up the wide stairs to where two more guards, their wings out and halberds ready, flanked the doors. Inside, at one long wooden counter, men and women in black uniforms worked behind a brass grill decorated with elaborate scrollwork. Their skin and hair colors included the full range of human tones, but they certainly didn't stop there—the entire color spectrum was present, and most had wings show-ing. A purple-skinned man with silver-white hair was apparently telling a joke to the yellow-orange woman next to him, their heads leaned toward each other until an officer said something behind them and they both snapped to attention and went their separate ways.

While she waited in line, Deor tried to categorize the people around her. There were quite a few green people in the line, but none behind the counter. So did that make them not faeries or simply foreign ones? None of them had wings that she could see.

Then there were the very short people, some bearded and some with hair like cotton candy. And fringy-looking ones that reminded her of walking seahorses or willow trees. Two places ahead of her in line, a shaggy, grey-haired man appeared to be having a conversation with the extremely large, equally grey, dog at his side.

Deor ran through all the different names for magical people she'd learned from faerie tales and wondered which, if any, applied to the people around her. If they did apply, were they the words people used to describe themselves? Better not walk up to someone and ask "excuse me, sir, are you a selkie?" only to find out the word was some sort of racist (speciest?) slur.

"Next," a guard called.

She shook her head to clear her thoughts. It didn't matter. She wasn't staying. She pulled out her passport and approached the counter, unpleasantly surprised to realize it came up nearly to her chin.

"There is a stool beneath the counter for your convenience," the young man behind the counter—his name tag said Lieutenant Bolton—droned without looking up. He took her passport and began copying information onto a sheet of paper. "Is this your first time in the Winter Court?"

"Yes, sir." As she said it, she pulled the stool toward her and stood on it. That, at least, got her a little more level. Whatever else they were, faeries were all tall.

"Race?"

"Human."

He was blond, rather pink-skinned like a man who spent time outdoors, with pretty, but bored, green eyes.

He cocked an eyebrow at her. "That all?"

"Half human, half faerie?" she tried.

That seemed better. "Changeling," he said and wrote it down. "Name, sex, and nationality of faerie parent?"

"Um…my father. He was a faerie. I'm pretty sure." It occurred to her with a sudden jolt that if there were many different types of Faepeople, Finn might have lied to her mother about his species. What if "I'm a faerie" was just a pick up line, like "I'm Italian"? But Robbie had thought she was a faerie. "Yes, my father was a faerie."

"Name?" he said in the tone of a man who'd been repeating himself all morning.

"I only know his first name."

"Miss, you can't claim Winter Court citizenship without at least one verified faerie parent."

At last. A light at the end of the bureaucratic tunnel. She breathed a sigh of relief.

"No, no. I don't want to permanently emigrate. I'm happy as an American. I just want to visit. I'll only stay as long as it takes to meet my father."

"Again, miss, you have to tell me his name. Who is your father?"

"His name is Finn. I don't know his last name."

The look Bolton gave her made Deor break out in a cold sweat. Like with Robbie, she'd stumbled into a hole she hadn't known was there, only this one had official authority and a sword. She took a deep breath to steady her nerves. Don't look nervous—they'll think you're up to something. She planted her hands on the counter, cool marble soothing under her palms.

"Miss, do you mean that as a joke?"

"No."

"So you are claiming that your father's name is Finn?"

"Yes. That's what he told my mother. She told me he had black hair and silver eyes. That's all I know about him."

She should have realized getting into Faerie wouldn't be as easy as her mother's letters made it sound.

"Is this Finn expecting you?"

Deor had been teaching long enough to recognize a loaded question when she heard one, but for the life of her, she couldn't tell where it was pointed.

"No. I haven't seen him since I was a baby. He and my mother...parted ways. That's why I'm here—to find him."

"I see. Stay there, please." He reached under the counter. A portion of the counter and grill swung open. "Come this way, please."

As she picked up the handle of her bag and came through the door, Bolton handed her passport to a soldier standing nearby. "Montjoie, notify the Tower. We have another one."

"Yes, sir." Montjoie looked Deor up and down as if memorizing her features and took off, her passport in his hand.

"Why are you doing this?" Deor said. "I didn't do anything!"

"Come this way, miss."

Bolton led her down a short, windowless hallway to a stone door that swung open at his word. He ushered her in, but kept her bags, and shut the door behind her. In the middle of the room was a stone table with two wooden chairs. Under the table was a small, square drain. There were no windows, but a harsh halo of light shone in the ceiling's center.

A lock clicked behind her, and she faced the door. After a moment, the knob faded, then the seams, until only solid stone remained. "Fuck."

Chapter Three

A s the yacht *The Duke's Pride and Joy* slid into the Sword's secure dock at Tower Landing above immigration, Rafe clapped the captain on the back. "Excellent work, as always."

"No thanks to that fool on the ferry. He ought to have his license revoked." His wind-worn features sharpened into a frown. "Good thing you spotted him in time. Shall I have the gangplank lowered for you, sir?"

"No need." He considered a second and patted the railing. "Take her into winter dry-dock after I'm ashore."

"So soon, sir?"

Rafe nodded. "I won't be needing her again this fall." With three more Adoption ceremonies to go, there'd be no time for sailing.

Not that he'd have the strength, even if he did have the time. He'd let the captain do most of the sailing on this trip, spending more time than he wanted to admit sleeping. If this weakness kept up, he'd be lucky to do the bare necessities of his job, let alone control the waves on the open ocean.

He grimaced, feeling the ache along his bones at the memory of the prior Adoption ceremonies. The bards and healers had all promised he wouldn't lose his water magic, even if he was being adopted into a family that had bred nothing but earth faeries for twelve generations. Of course, they'd also promised the Adoption would cause only "minor discomfort." So much for inviolable bardic promises.

He wouldn't even have been out on *The Pride and Joy* now if the last ceremony hadn't left him so weak that Finn insisted he take a fortnight on the sea to get his strength back. Being surrounded by that much water had always brought him strength before. He patted the ship's railing.

"See you in the spring." He gave the captain and crew a wave and vaulted over the ship's rail.

Wings spread wide, he floated onto the dock. As his boots touched the wood, the two members of the Tower guard awaiting his arrival executed perfect salutes from their posts beside the water door.

"At ease, boys." He returned the salutes.

He turned and whistled to his Molossian war dogs. Each one was half the size of a black bear with a long muzzle and jaws that could break a unicorn's leg. Their brown and black heads hung over the ship's side, faces framed in thick ruffs, tongues lolling happily. At Rafe's whistle, Jake leaped over the railing with an explosive *Woof!* The second dog, bigger than his brother, whined and danced on the deck.

"Sam, come!" Rafe shouted, and the dog leapt, landing with a *thump* and *poof* of shedding fur.

From the door of the Tower, Robbie laughed as the guards moved aside to let her through. "You're such a show off with those dogs." She came down the dock, still dressed in the plain, human clothes she favored, and threw her arms around him. "I missed you."

He returned the hug, pulling her off the ground. "I missed you too, little sister."

"Only barely!" She punched him in the arm. "You almost ran us down with that barge of yours."

"Saved your life is more like it. What were you doing on the common ferry anyway? You should have told me to come get you."

She rolled her eyes and stuck her jaw out to one side as if she'd gone back to chewing gum, a human habit that had driven her mother crazy a few years ago.

"The king doesn't even like you talking to me in public. You'll get a royal scolding if the press catches you playing chauffeur to the Consort's drab little bastard."

"Stop."

She sniffed hard and didn't meet his eyes.

He put his arm around her shoulder. "How was London?"

"All my human friends are grown-up now. They have kids and jobs and mortgages."

"What on earth is a mortgage? Just say the word and I'll get you one."

"It's a kind of debt, you idiot." She swiped at her eyes with a sleeve, and he held out a handkerchief for her. "None of my human friends had time to play. I had tea with Celia yesterday, and she asked me when I was going to stop gadding about and take things seriously. She's having babies. Maggie is a junior diplomat. Brennan's teaching at a university, and I'm just starting classes." She turned her face up to him. "They're right. I'm useless."

"Baby sister, you're twenty-nine. You're supposed to be useless at this age."

"It's not funny."

He hugged her a little closer. "They're just humans. You're a faerie, sweetheart."

She pulled back, her face set. "I'm a changeling. It's different for me. You were born with a purpose. I have to make one for myself."

"And you will. I'm sure of it. Now, where are your bags?"

"I sent them on ahead. I don't have a million flunkies to carry my things like you do," she said, the smile back on her face.

"Whose fault is that?" he teased. Robbie just laughed.

They both knew Astarte would have supplied Robbie with an entourage fit for a princess if her headstrong daughter had allowed it. For that matter, Rafe would happily pay for them himself. Robbie was painfully aware that she owned nothing and earned nothing, never allowing any of her friends to pay her way.

So instead of money, Rafe offered his sister his arm, and they walked up the dock into the Tower. The street level courtyard bustled with passing guards and the occasional raven poking about on the green lawn.

"May I take you to lunch, or are your studies already too pressing?" Rafe asked. He wouldn't mind delaying his own return to work just a little longer.

"You're sweet, but I promised Aiden I'd meet him at the marketplace, and then I have to go see Mother."

Rafe was just opening his mouth to agree when a discreet cough from the wall interrupted him.

Robbie jumped, making Rafe laugh.

"I was starting to think you were late. What is it, Arthur?" Rafe said.

His second in command stepped forward, dropping the glamour that had made him blend seamlessly with the stone of the wall. Rafe whistled.

"Impressive. You've got the texture down perfectly."

Arthur shrugged modestly. "It's almost there." He handed Rafe a sheet of Civil Patrol ground reports. "There's another Adoption protest in the marketplace. It looked pretty peaceful to start, but they've been joined by a bunch of students."

Rafe scanned the sheet, then flicked a glance at Robbie. "What were you saying about meeting friends at the marketplace?"

She crossed her arms. "Free speech is an essential Faerie right."

He grunted and turned back to the reports. "Any violence yet, Arthur?"

"Just some shoving and shouting. I sent the First Horse down. They have orders to contain, but not to escalate. Your horse is ready if you want to go with them."

"Is Michael down there?" Rafe asked.

Arthur's face assumed a blank look, his hands clasped behind his back. "His Majesty's Shield and Defender has informed the Tower that he cannot be distracted from his duty to the king's own person to deal with riffraff in the street. He bade me suggest that a few volleys with crossbows might make the rabble disperse."

"Oh, screw him sideways with his own staff of office," Rafe said. "That's his solution to everything. And people think I'm violent."

Robbie laughed. "You're the epitome of violent. You're the Sword." She pulled out her pocket mirror and squealed. "Ooh look, Aiden and Deidre are right in the front. With placards and everything. Power to the people! Hang on guys! I'll be there in two shakes."

"No, you damn well won't," Rafe snapped. "This isn't a debate club; it's a riot and you're not getting mixed up in it. Arthur, get her a cab."

Arthur saluted and strode off toward the gate.

"Rafe! Don't be such a fascist."

"I wish you'd stop using human curse words. It's pretentious, and it upsets your mother."

"You can't make me go."

"I can and I will." He leaned down so only she could hear his voice. "Do you know what kind of fodder you'd be giving the papers? Not to mention the people who think you're a threat to the kingdom and ought to be banished?"

She looked up at him, hurt in her eyes. "But it's not you I'm against."

"I know that, but they don't. Besides," he said in a gentler tone, "if I let anything happen to you, Astarte will skin me alive."

Her shoulders slumped. "People have a right to be heard, even if they are nobodies."

He kissed her on the cheek. "You're far from being a nobody, my darling sister. And I hear you."

Arthur returned, a cab drawn up at the gates.

"I told them I'd come out with them." Robbie grabbed his hand. "Don't go beat up my friends."

"I'll do my best." He squeezed her hand. "Be safe and call Astarte when you get to campus. You know she worries."

"I will." She gave him a half smile. "Be careful yourself."

The cab bowled off, careening around a corner and out of sight.

"If we ever do get a House of Commons, I wager she'll be its first Speaker," Arthur said.

"Not in Finn's lifetime," Rafe turned back toward the main keep of the Tower, stretching his legs into a fast walk. "But maybe when I'm king. We'll have an adopted king and a bastard Speaker. Won't that just set Parliament's hair on fire?"

Keeping pace beside him, Arthur laughed.

As fast as Rafe could don a uniform and get into the saddle, the two rode out of the Tower and headed for the marketplace. As they threaded their way through crowded city streets, around carriages and foot traffic, Rafe held tight to Sampson's reins, keeping the big, black horse to a brisk walk. Sampson's bulk alone was enough to clear space, and racing through the streets would only frighten people. He wanted to prevent a riot, not incite one.

Arthur rode beside him with no reins at all, his palomino responding instantly to the invisible pressure of his rider's knees. As they rode, Rafe listened to Arthur's updates, official and unofficial, on the state of things while he had been away. Most of it was routine—until Arthur came to the crime report.

"Three more assaults on changeling women reported since you left. One in Northumbria, one here in the Tanty district, and the third in London."

Rafe turned in the saddle, but Arthur didn't miss a beat.

"Don't be absurd—it wasn't Robbie. You saw her yourself. The victim's an herb merchant's daughter from Avignon—she was visiting her human grandparents. I've interviewed two of the victims myself. The third was in a human mental hospital for a week and went home with her parents, but I spoke to the grandparents under guise of being local law enforcement. A 'bobbie' I think they call them. Completely unhelpful, I'm afraid. They don't even know the girl is half faerie, only that her father is suspiciously foreign and their girl should never have gone off to live in a foreign country."

"Is the girl expected to recover?" Rafe tightened his hands on the reins, trying to keep his anger in check.

Arthur's mouth narrowed. "Hard to tell. Her parents won't let anyone near her. They say she can't speak, and they won't have her harassed. I've got Lady Penny trying to convince them to let her examine the girl, but they're stubborn."

"We've got to catch these bastards." Beneath him, Rafe's horse shivered and tossed his head, snorting sparks in his anger. Ice crystals had formed all down Sampson's gear wherever Rafe touched it. "Sorry, boy." Rafe took a deep breath for calm and melted the frost on Sampson's bridle. "We have to catch them," he said again.

"We will. I want to have a talk with them just as much as you do."

The monsters who rummaged around in girls' heads deserved a long, sharp talk with Arthur.

After a minute, Arthur cleared his throat. "Also your fiancé seems to be under the impression that I was preventing her from speaking to you while you were away."

"Were you?" In between naps and long swims in the ocean, he'd rather wondered why Lady Genevieve hadn't called his mirror. He ought to be ashamed of himself for not calling her. She'd been more than under-standing when he told her he didn't want company, even knowing that it would give the gossip columnists a tidbit to speculate about. He should have made himself remember. The strange thing was how it didn't seem to matter. Nothing seemed to matter much these days. Food, friends, entertainment—all he wanted was to sleep. And to never touch the throne again.

"Yes," Arthur said. "You needed your rest."

He sighed and rubbed his hands over his face. "Dammit, Arthur. You're my aide, not my nurse. And now I'm in disgrace with my lady. Deservedly so. Remind me to bring her something lovely to make up for it."

"No, you're not," Arthur said. "She is irritated with the officious fellow who took it on himself to interfere in his superior officer's personal life. You sent her a beautiful bouquet from the south of France and promised to see her for lunch the day after your return. Or so your valet tells me."

"Wonderful."

Rafe heard the ruckus in the marketplace before he could see it. The usual babble of buying and selling was louder, angrier, full of boos and curses. The marketplace itself was a wide, circular plaza from which eight separate streets radiated. The shops and cafes that lined the innermost circle catered to the richest clientele, with the adjoining streets carrying all sorts of goods from one of a kind magical toys to used clothes.

The whole plaza was crowded with people—faeries for the most part, but quite a few goblins, dwarves, and pixies, too. Horsemen and at least one member of the Civil Guard on foot patrol were positioned at each street entrance.

Rafe reined in Sampson beside the Lieutenant of the First Horse. Arthur had already disappeared into the crowd.

"Where's the center of the trouble?" he asked

The captain pointed to where a cluster of men and women scuffled and shouted. A good cross cut of Caer Eisteddfod society—apprentices, dock workers, high end merchants, students in university gowns, street urchins, and even a few fellows he recognized from his own club. One of the young baronets stood shouting toe-to-toe with a burly stevedore, both of them with wings flared and sharp with anger.

"Nothing like a good riot to bring people together, eh?" Rafe said to the lieutenant.

"Yes, sir. I have men covering all entrances to the marketplace. We've kept the crowd from growing, so far."

"Good. Anybody who wants to leave peaceably, let them go. No one else comes in. Hold your positions here."

Rafe nudged the horse with his foot, signaling for the lieutenant to stay back. Sam and Jake were bodyguard enough. People shrank back from the two dogs as if pushed. He eased forward, making for the center of the mess where a blue scarecrow on a stick was being waved above the crowd's head.

To his left, he caught a glimpse of blue skin. His younger brother Victor, leaning against a stall with a half-smile on his face, flicked Rafe a mocking salute. Anger, hot and acid, rolled in his stomach. Of course Victor was here. Victor didn't make trouble—he merely took advantage of it.

He swung his leg off the horse and handed the reins to a bulky man in a butcher's apron, a were-boar by the look of him. "Hold him, would you?" he said.

It never hurt to pick out the biggest, most dangerous fellows in a crowd and give them something to keep their hands full.

As people turned toward him, Rafe walked forward, one hand resting on Jake's head. Sam padded along on his other side. His two hairy body-guards didn't need to growl or bark—the crowd parted like wheat before the wind. Rafe kept moving forward until he was at the center. As he approached, even the ring leaders backed off.

"Good morning, friends," he said to the students and apprentices holding his effigy. "What is you've got there?"

The men eyed each other. One of the soldiers jerked the dummy away from the man holding it and shook it over his head. "You see, sire? You see what they've done?"

"I do." They had even made it anatomically correct.

The naked blue dummy, its tiny wings hanging limp, wore a paper crown on its head. A placard with *Pretender* hung around its neck. Adopted or not, this was how many would remember him. Forcing a smile, he raised his voice as if addressing troops.

"I am deeply offended." He pointed at the dummy, hanging by its neck from the man's hands. "The wings are far too small."

A few in the crowd giggled nervously.

He flexed the muscles of his back so that his wings flared out from the slits in his uniform, their normally soft edges tensed to be sharper than a sword. He kicked off the ground at the same time, so that he hovered, doing a slow turn to the full crowd, catching as many people's eyes as he could.

Anger—yes there was anger here, but not hatred in most faces. Fear and distrust and frustration. He'd seen the same look on his soldiers' faces when supplies were late, their requests for leave denied. After decades of bad harvests and an ever feebler king, he didn't blame them. He dropped back to his feet, but kept his wings out.

"And that dick is just sad. Come now," he said. "If you're going to burn me in effigy, make it recognizable first."

More laughs spread.

The man holding the offending dummy by the neck wore a silver star in his lapel, a veteran. A black eye swelled his face.

"Where did you serve?" Rafe asked.

Immediately the man dropped the dummy and saluted. "At Tannenberg, sir. Sergeant Tristram Gunderson, Third Foot Division."

"That was a heavy campaign. Your unit served well."

"Yes, sir," the man said. He pulled open the collar of his shirt to reveal a ropy scar across his collarbone. "I fought for you then, and I'll fight for you still, sir, retired though I may be."

An angry buzz rose from the crowd again.

"Long live the prince!" someone shouted.

"Pretender! Fake!" others shouted back.

An overripe pear arced through the air and splattered on the ground at Rafe's feet. He ignored it and laid a hand on Gunderson's shoulder.

"You didn't fight for me, Sergeant," he said so only those nearest could hear. "We fought for our country together, did we not?"

Gunderson's jaw quivered. "Aye, sir. That's right."

His friends, clustered behind him, lowered their eyes, nodding. More than a few of them wore the veteran's star as well. Rafe gave them all a smile.

"What are a few school kids with puppets to men like you?"

They gave him sheepish nods.

Rafe picked up the dummy, gave it a little shake and a rueful sigh, and dropped it on the ground where it lay like a giant child's toy.

"Sure, flatter the commoners now," one of the university students, a stripling who couldn't be more than a year older than Robbie if he was a day, shouted. "You're no more royal than I am. We need a real king!"

Others applauded.

"Do you?" Rafe turned on him. "You could do worse than men like Gunderson here, puppy-dog. When have you gotten your hands dirty with more than ink?"

The boy shrank back, but another student stepped up to Rafe, shaking his fist in Rafe's face.

"Swords don't make a king!" he said. "We want justice. We want a real Aethelwing, not a faker in a tin crown."

"Hello, Aiden." Rafe caught the boy's fist before the student could throw a punch.

Aiden let out a strangled yelp of shock, but to his credit, he didn't cower.

Rafe leaned in, his voice low. "Do you really want it to go this way? If you start a riot, these people you pretend to speak for are going to get hurt."

He eyed the crowd around him. A few yards away, armor clanked as his men shifted in their saddles and the hooves clopped as their agitated horses danced on the cobblestones.

Keeping his voice low, he said, "Thirty yards from here are the food stalls. Farmers selling to women, children, and families here to buy their evening meal. Do you really want my soldiers to march in here? Drive into them?"

Aiden shook his head.

"Now, you weren't trying to assault the king's own Sword, were you? That was just you being spirited, right?"

Aiden nodded, his face going grey around the edges.

"That's what I thought." He let go of the boy's hand, and the crowd let out a collective sigh.

Rafe glanced over his shoulder at the soldiers and shook his head. They'd pushed in closer to the crowd, weapons half-drawn. At the far edge of the crowd, Victor ducked away around a corner.

Rafe patted the boy on the shoulder. "You're a brave lad. But you're reckless."

The boy straightened his shoulders. "Bully us all you want. We deserve a king and an heir who will listen to us. All of us." He jutted his chin out like he expected Rafe to punch him.

Before Rafe could answer, a middle-aged man in a grey velvet coat pushed the students aside.

"The commons must be heard." Redfern Holman, head of the Rope-maker's Guild, drew himself up as if to make a speech.

"You too, Holman?" Rafe asked. "Don't you have better things to do than inspire students to throw punches at armed soldiers?"

"This was to be a peaceful protest." He glared at Aiden. "They got overexcited. But that doesn't change the truth." He raised his voice, his air magic sending the sound to every corner of the marketplace. "The king owes us a true heir, one of his own blood."

Shouts of approval answered him, drowning the boos from Gunderson's veterans.

"You're right," Rafe shouted. He couldn't match the air faerie's projection, but at least he could be heard. "And you shall have a true heir, one of the king's own blood. What do you think the Adoption is for?"

Holman shook his head. "A show. A pantomime to make us think everything is well."

More applause and cheers from the crowd—far louder than the few scattered boos.

His voice swelled. "Crops rot in the fields, floods and storms wash away whole rivers. It snows in June and thaws in January. The land is sick, sick in its very bones. And where is the king? Hiding in his Palace. How are we to know he's even alive?"

The crowd thundered its approval, and those with weapons shifted their grips.

Rafe waited a beat. Then another. "I spoke with him by mirror just this morning," he said. "He talked like a living man then."

A few nervous chuckles answered him.

In truth, Finn had looked haggard and frail, bundled up in robes against the early autumn cold in a way no King of the Winter Court should ever be.

"So you say!" Holman stabbed an accusing finger at him. "How are the rest of us to know? Sure the nobles meet at the throne, the bards wave their hands, and they come out and tell us all will be well. For all we know, it's just an elaborate charade."

"Believe me, it's not. The Adoption magic is very real."

What did these fools know about the Adoption? About how he'd argued with the king for weeks before agreeing to be named heir? Or how the Adoption magic scraped him raw, leaving him dizzy and aching after each ceremony?

"Why should we take your word for it?" Holman snapped.

The crowd murmured, pressing forward, closing in on Rafe. A few waved fists and cudgels. The path to his horse was still open, barely, but the soldiers he'd brought were too far away to rescue him without riding down civilians.

Damn his stupid bravado.

He forced himself to smile even as cold anger poured off him. "And why shouldn't I arrest the lot of you for disturbing the peace, Holman? I arrested Sir Gerald last week for smuggling. You think I'm afraid to take you in?"

Holman puffed out his chest as he said it. "As chairman of the Loyal Sons of London, I am prepared to sacrifice for my fellow citizens. We speak for the guilds, for the common people."

His backers, most of the crowd, cheered and whistled.

"Do you?" Rafe asked. "I thought the Master of the City did that."

"He's a noble like the rest of you!" a woman yelled from the crowd.

"Arrest me if you must, but we will be heard," Holman said. He held out his hands to be bound.

"No," Rafe said. "So long as there is no violence, you're free. But if you want to be heard, you'll stop this nonsense. Send your requests to me at the Tower. I'll see that the king hears your petition."

Holman narrowed his eyes at Rafe. "The king will allow common people to witness the Adoption? In person?"

"I can't promise that." He leaned forward. "But I swear his Majesty will hear your name and your concerns from me." Pushing downward with his wings, Rafe leaped into the air again. "Do you hear me? King Sweordmund will hear your complaints. Today. I give you my word of honor as the Sword of Peace and Justice." Amazed cheers went up from the crowd. "Now every loyal citizen," he turned in the air, "go about your business. The next person who throws a punch sees the inside of a cell."

The crowd began to fray at the edges. Rafe hovered in the air, slowly turning to watch them, making eye contact with the ones who seemed inclined to linger. The soldiers made room for people to pass between their horses.

SARAH JOY ADAMS & EMILY LAVIN LEVERETT

He dropped back to the ground, kicking the trampled and torn dummy toward Holman. "Take it with you, or I'll charge you with littering." Soon the street was nearly empty of all but the most determined shoppers.

"Your horse, sir." The were-boar stood at his back, the horse stock still, eyes sleepy.

"Thank you, my friend." Rafe reached into his pocket for a coin.

Anyone who could keep a guardsman's horse that quiet deserved more than gold. Perhaps he'd suggest the man apply at the royal stables.

"Thank you, sir." The man pocketed the crown. "I'm glad to have it."

Rafe reached for the reins, but as he did, the man's features blurred and shimmered. He shrank down to a respectable six feet, his shoulders narrowing until Arthur stood there in his uniform. A few feet away, a sad-looking carthorse tethered to a post shimmered into its proper form as Arthur's golden palomino.

Rafe let out a laugh, the tension of the last few minutes flowing out with the air. "I should have known you'd be at my back."

"You're an idiot. Walking into the crowd like that. You could have been killed."

"I kept the peace. It's my duty."

"Yes, sir, General sir." Arthur mock-saluted and held Rafe's stirrup for him to mount. "The Master of the City is going to be furious at you for encouraging Redfern's group like that."

Rafe sighed and ran a hand through his hair. "Won't he though? But they have a point. People need to know the Adoption is real. I should get back to the Palace. His Majesty will want to see me in person. You coming?"

Arthur shook his head and held up his pocket mirror.

"I'm going back to the Tower. This came while you were being princely."

Rafe read the message and rolled his eyes as Arthur mounted his horse. "Another long lost heir to throne? What the hell is wrong with people? Well, mount up and let's go."

Arthur chuckled. "You don't have to come. Go home and rest."

"I am rested. I've had all the rest I can stand. Besides, this pretender is a changeling and just the right age, too. It may be the break we've been looking for in the attacks."

"Why would they be connected?"

Rafe whirled his horse toward the end of the street and dug in his heels, the dogs and Arthur following close behind. "Why wouldn't they? Nothing else about these changeling attacks makes sense. Come on. I want to see this girl who thinks she's King Sweordmund's daughter."

Chapter Four

Cold seeped into Deor's bones and she shivered. She let her eyes drift closed as she rested her head on the stone table, arms crossed beneath her cheek. Obviously no one was coming to deal with her any time soon, though in the windowless room it was impossible to know how much time had passed. Her feet rested flat on the floor only if she sat on the very edge of the seat, so right now they dangled.

At the sound of a key, she raised her head.

The door reappeared, swinging open silently. A soldier entered. Deor's stomach flipped at the sight of him—Lord Farringdon from the ship. Up close, he was tall, a full foot taller than she was at least, but most striking was his skin—ice blue, like fields of snow at twilight. His black hair was tied back in a ponytail at the nape of his neck. He carried a sheaf of papers in his hand.

Behind him followed Lieutenant Bolton with her belongings. He settled her bags next to the table never taking his eyes off her. Like he wanted to memorize her face, just in case.

A third figure came behind them and moved to the corner of the small room. He—at least she thought it was a he—made her head hurt. She couldn't make out his face, his shape, or anything about him. He was scrambled, like two radio stations picked up at the same time, splicing together different songs. She blinked a few more times, and each time he flickered. The man, the grey wall, the man, the grey wall. The harder she concentrated, the more a small voice in her head whispered that he wasn't there—he was a shadow, a trick of the light, a figment of a vivid imagination. She shook her head and shoved the excuses out of her mind. He was there, a soldier judging by his posture, even if she couldn't see a uniform. He was brown, beautifully dark. He blurred again, grey stone swallowing him, and she let him go. A dozen more sparkles popped off her.

"You're dismissed, Lieutenant," Lord Farringdon told Bolton.

"Yes, General." He nodded at her, gave a quick salute, and left.

As the general took a seat, Deor studied him, not bothering with discreet, side of the eyes stares. His dark blue eyes and perfectly arched black eyebrows betrayed nothing. His calm smile unsettled her more than if he'd come in with a drawn gun. She wondered how many weapons he had that she couldn't see.

"So you're a general?" she asked. "Who am I to warrant that?"

He bowed slightly. "Rafael, Lord Farringdon. I am the Sword of Peace and Justice."

The title suited his sharp eyes and cheekbones. He tossed the papers onto the table as if they no longer interested him.

"So you're the king's daughter?" he said, as if they had met at a garden party.

Deor blinked hard. From his smile, she'd expected some sort of friendly "good cop" gesture, an attempt to put her at ease before the interrogation began.

"No. I didn't say that." No wonder she'd been upgraded to a private room.

"But you did claim your father was named Finn."

"I didn't claim anything." Deor drew herself up. "That's the name he gave my mother. Given that he lied to her about everything else, I wouldn't be surprised if his name was a lie, too."

"Huh." He nodded like he agreed with her. "And you don't know anything else about him?"

"Just that he had pale skin and dark hair." She made a show of looking him up and down. "Is your father missing any kids? Are you?"

"No and no." He did not seem amused. No more jokes then.

"I am not a pretender to the throne. So can I go?"

39

"No," he repeated.

In the corner, the sort-of-not-there man shifted slightly.

She stopped herself before she spoke again and offered up more information that could cause her problems. She held Lord Farringdon's gaze.

After a few moments, he broke her gaze and shuffled through a few papers.

"Tell me the truth." He smiled like someone who had heard a pleasant joke, but his words slammed into her like a fist. "Who are you and why are you here?"

She reeled slightly, the words echoing in the small room. She fixed him with a cold stare, the one that she reserved for students who thought they could argue her into changing their grade. She snatched her purse from on top of her suitcase, and the general drew one hand back as if to throw something.

"Easy!" She held up both her hands. "I'll show you my ID's."

When he nodded, she slowly pulled out her wallet and laid a series of cards on the table in front of him.

"Credit card. Blood donor card. Driver's license with date of birth. Social Security card. Here, look at this one." She slid her Ohio State University ID card across the table to him. "And you've still got my passport."

"Very convincing," he said.

He picked up the university ID card and bent it slightly, turning it over in his hands as if she'd handed him a novelty toy.

"Well," he corrected himself, "almost convincing. This says you were a faculty member at a university. Your passport says you're thirty."

"Yes." She raised an eyebrow at him. "And yes. I was adjunct faculty before I graduated with my doctorate this spring. So?"

"A doctorate?" He tossed the ID back on the table. "You're barely an adult."

Deor opened her mouth to argue and then snapped it shut again. Her mother hadn't ever told her—even in her letters—the age of her mysterious faerie lover.

"Really quick," she held up a finger, "can I ask how old you are? You seem young to be a general."

He frowned again, looking increasingly impatient. She began to suspect this was not the worst cell in the Tower.

"I will be ninety-five next year," he said.

Deor nodded. Of course he would. "Adulthood starts at thirty here?"

Lord Farringdon shrugged. "Legally, yes. I was about your age when I joined the military."

"Where I'm from," Deor countered, "thirty is often considered too old to join the military. My PhD at thirty is pretty average. Most humans die before they reach ninety-five."

"I see." He gathered up her papers and tapped them into a neat stack, her immigration form on top. "What about your mother? Where is she?"

"She's dead." Before he could speak again, she asked, "Would it be okay for a man your age to sleep with a twenty-two-year-old woman?"

"Absolutely not!" The man actually blushed.

"My mother was twenty-three when I was born." She sat back like that settled the matter. "From her description of my father, I'm guessing he was a full grown man, so between, what, thirty-five and...?"

"Some Fae live thousands of years. Historically, faeries live to around eight hundred, give or take a century."

"Oh, so between thirty-five and one thousand years old."

That narrowed it down.

"Let's try something else," he said and leaned across the table. "Hold still, please. This won't hurt."

He sketched a shape in the air in front of her face. Magic, sparks of cold electricity, flowed off his fingers and settled on her lips.

"Now, tell me again why you are here in the Winter Court."

Her skin crawled, thick with magic. She shook herself, a full body shiver, and a wave ran down her, head to toe. Small fragments of magic, like bits of colored string, flaked off her onto the table and floor.

"What did you do to me?" she demanded.

She dragged the back of her hand across her lips and shook her head to get the tingling, clinging magic off. Silver sparkles, great clouds of them, bloomed off her.

"A minor truth spell." He frowned and waved away the sparkles as they drifted around him. "It doesn't compel the truth, but it will turn red if you lie."

"Oh, hell no." She stood before realizing it didn't actually give her a height advantage.

She gripped the edge of the stone table, trying to slow her racing heart. A few more sparkles spiraled away from her. From the corner of her eye, the wall-man moved close enough to grab her, but he didn't touch her.

Across the table, Lord Farringdon leaned back in his seat and flicked a sparkle away from his face. "Are you finished?"

"Maybe." Her answer sounded like what her grandmother called "sass," but she was telling the truth, after a fashion. Who knew when she'd stop the fireworks? She flicked her hands in the air a few times, more silver sparkles fluttering away into the air.

"I see." He gestured at her chair. "Do sit down."

She swayed slightly, the magic in his voice whispering to her. Her knees shook. She stepped sideways, away from him, and away from the magic-covered man.

"I have told you nothing but the truth from the beginning. And tell your fuzzy friend in the corner to stop staring at me. It's creepy."

"What friend?" For the first time, Lord Farringdon's gaze flicked to the man who had come in with him.

She pointed straight at the man on the other side of her chair.

"Him! He's brown and blurry."

Now the man's blurred features made sense. Hundreds of fine, magical threads crisscrossing in an unreadable maze hid him, especially his face.

She squinted. "His nametag says Captain Maerhwer. Captain Horse-man?" Weird name. Maybe it meant he was half horse.

"Arthur?" Lord Farringdon seemed genuinely confused. "Did you let her see you?"

"No, not for a second." The magic covering him switched off like a light. "How did you do that, Miss Smithfield?"

"Do what?" She looked back and forth between the two men. "Oh? The *Maerhwer* thing? I studied Old English in grad school."

Captain Maerhwer stared at her like he had never met anyone so stupid.

"This is not the time to be cute," Lord Farringdon said. "Sit down." There was not a hint of magic in his voice—but there was a warning. The last chance to turn before the drop off a cliff.

"I'm not trying to be difficult." Deor sat.

The captain snorted his disbelief, and Lord Farringdon pinched the bridge of his nose.

"Let's start again from the beginning, shall we?" He slid her immigration form toward him.

"Let me help you," Captain Maerhwer said as he stepped behind her and scooted her chair closer to the table.

"Thanks," Deor muttered.

His hands remained resting on the back of the chair.

"The beginning?" Lord Farringdon asked. When she nodded, he continued. "Your name, with any relevant title."

"Deor Smithfield. No Title."

Lord Farringdon sighed and tapped the Ohio State identification card in front of him.

"Oh, that." She picked it up. "I didn't think this counted. Professor Deor Smithfield."

"Excellent. See how easy this is?" He smiled. "Now, your father is a faerie that you assume is somewhere in the Winter Court, correct?"

"Correct." She let the *assume* go for the time being.

"Again, excellent. Now your mother. She seems to be the one who encouraged your coming here, having once been here herself. She died?"

She held Lord Farringdon's gaze for a long minute. Airing her family's dirty laundry was the last thing she wanted to do, but if it would get her out of here, it was worth it.

"Yes. She died from a magical illness. When I was eight." At the look of shock on his face, she continued. "She pined for the magic, for my father, and the illness killed her."

She'd practiced the words *killed her* a hundred times a day until she had been able to say "an illness killed her" without any hint of tears. The emotions still punched her in the gut every time.

Before he could speak, she added, "The description I gave you is all I know. He called himself Finn, he was tall and pale, with silver eyes, and he had black hair. She put it more romantically, like all lovers would. I believe she used words like lily and obsidian."

He rubbed his chin and glanced at the captain behind her. "I would like very much to believe you, Miss—I'm sorry—Professor Smithfield. He slid out another page from her immigration packet and turned it to face her. "Right here, under magical talents. You marked *none*. However, in the past few minutes you've shaken off a truth spell and seen through one of the best glamours in the kingdom. Not to mention your sparkly tantrum. Help me reconcile this."

Deor rolled her eyes. He sounded nice, and with the other man at her back, what could she do but play along?

"Until I got here, the only magic I've ever done is spew useless sparkles and accidentally break machinery. I can't even control the sparkles—they show up when I'm upset or frightened." She left off the part about them coming to her rescue. "The other stuff—I have no idea what that was."

Lord Farringdon sighed. "Alright then." He nodded at the man behind her.

The captain hooked his arm around her neck, pulling her tight against the back of the chair—tight enough to keep her still, but not quite choking her—and leaned down, his mouth near her ear.

"You might want to reconsider your statement, miss," he whispered.

Deor clutched at his arm. She knew there was no chance she could break his grip. She had no leverage—her feet weren't touching the floor. She dug her nails into the meat of his forearm. He gasped, a quick intake of breath. She had hurt him at least. But his grip didn't ease.

Lord Farringdon gathered up the papers in front of him. "I am sorry that we couldn't come to an understanding. Your story—the little lost bastard—is compelling." The sarcastic edge in his voice was echoed by gust of icy, magic-laden air that blasted from him. "Perhaps we can do better at another time."

Deor bit back her urge to tell him off. It would make her feel better, but it wasn't worth a night in the Tower.

"Compelling or not, it's true," she said.

The captain tightened his arm across her throat. She dug her nails deeper into his arm.

"No permanent damage. I promise. We've got excellent healers here." The captain's breath was warm against her neck. A chill ran through her anyway.

"Well," Lord Farringdon interrupted their exchange. "I hope we will be able to talk again before the end of this week." He pushed away from the table and stood.

"Wait!" Deor gasped.

Lord Farringdon winced, and behind her the captain jerked away from her for a moment.

"This is ridiculous. You're treating me like I'm James—" She stopped herself. "Like I'm some superspy. I've never set foot in Faerie before, and I am quite in a hurry to set my feet *out* of it as soon as possible."

Lord Farringdon gave the captain another small nod and Deor was free.

She leaned forward, coughed, and drew in a few deep breaths.

"Damn," the captain said behind her. "I'm actually bleeding in one place. Don't ladies trim their nails where you're from?"

Rafe stared at her for a few moments, evaluating.

She stared back.

Truth was, even as tall, as big as he was, he didn't look healthy—he reminded her a bit of Bill. His eyes were a touch bloodshot, and she recognized under-eye circles when she saw them, no matter what color he was. The skin under his right eye seemed blurred slightly, a faint line of fuzziness that extended to the corner of his mouth.

"Are you okay?" she asked, and immediately regretted it. Why would she talk to him like he was a poor student under too much stress? He could surely take care of himself.

He blinked at her and burst out laughing. He wiped his eyes and sat back down. "I am fine, Professor." He slid the stack of papers back to her. "There is a lot missing from your story."

"I am telling you the truth. I've never done magic or seen magic before. Whatever happened earlier was, I don't know, instinct? You threw that magic on me like a net, and I..." She threw her hands up. "And I don't know what I did. I made it stop."

"No," he said. "That's not what you did. You shredded it and peeled it off. The net analogy is perfect. You clawed through it like a forest cat in a trap. That's not how magic works."

"Sorry." She shrugged. "It worked for me."

"Indeed." The captain behind her spoke, and Deor flinched. Did he have to hover? "I've never seen it work that way for anyone else."

She had been so tired when they put her in here that she hadn't bothered to notice the room's details. The stones in the wall were varying colors of jagged grey. The table was different grey stone—with pocks and small divots, rough and definitely old. The crisp black uniform Lord Farringdon wore, with its silver embellishments, made the room look dingy.

No question the man in front of her had killed people. With a title like the Sword, it was probably part of the application process. But a killer wasn't necessarily a liar—and he did not strike her as the lying type.

Frankly, he struck her as the tall, dark, and dangerous type that she'd have pursued with wild abandon just a few months ago. Oh, yes. Carrying two glasses of something hard, pricey, and poured neat, with a handful of condoms in her purse (she was a twenty-first century woman, after all), she'd burn twenty-four hours on him, well, twelve at least.

"What are you thinking?" He frowned at her, eyes flashing impatience.

Even so, she would have bought him a drink, probably two.

She was exactly like her mother.

"Nothing." When he raised his eyebrows at her, she relented. "Okay. I was thinking about my mother. And my father."

"Yes." He sat very still, like a hunter. One move and he might spook her.

What was left to lose by telling the truth?

"I'm dying," she said. She waited for a reaction but got none. "Apparently my mother passed on some kind of faerie magic to me, but my body doesn't seem to like it much. Or the magic doesn't like the human world much. It's killing me."

"Why do you think you are dying?" Lord Farringdon asked. He jerked his head at the captain behind her, who came around the table and waited by the door, blessedly far from her.

"Because I get headaches no one can explain."

"That doesn't sound magical. There could be a dozen other causes."

"Yes," Deor conceded. "Before my mother died, she told me that I was the only bright spot left for her. In the past few months, I've found she meant it literally. The color washed out of my world. By the time I left, only the faces of my family were anything but grey."

"Ah." He nodded. "And you thought a solution was here?"

"My grandmother thought that if I came back here, if I found my father and—" She broke off for a moment. "The rest doesn't matter. Just that maybe he could fix me."

"You mother died of love longing. I am sorry." He pulled the paperwork toward himself again and flipped through it. "It is possible you're right. It's possible that your father can help you. If you share more about him with us—"

"I've told you everything!" Deor snapped. "Please, let me in!"

"We can let you in," Lord Farringdon said, flinching again at her raised voice. "But you've come at a highly…political time. Your story, while not impossible or unheard of, is unlikely, but if it is true…" He signed the paper in front of him. "There. Provisional visa. You have seventy-two hours to provide evidence of your family, or, barring that, someone in the Winter Court to sponsor your continued presence."

"Sponsor? What does that mean?"

"A family member who knows you and will vouch for you. A long-term job. A paramour. Something that demonstrates you are here for the reasons you say you are, and that you are self-sufficient. I can't let you run loose without some kind of supervision."

Deor wanted to argue. She drummed her fingers on the table, her nails clicking in the silence. There was a look in Lord Farringdon's eyes that suggested further negotiation would go about as well as arguing with her grandmother about curfew on prom night.

"Fine." She reached for the paperwork and began to read it.

Lord Farringdon rose. "Alright Miss—" He caught himself again. "Professor Smithfield. This way."

"Just a moment." Deor held a finger up but kept her eyes on the paper in front of her. "Uh-huh," she muttered and turned the page over. "Fifty years in prison?" She pointed at the line. "For not returning with the correct paperwork on time?"

"Yes," Lord Farringdon said.

"That's a death sentence for me!"

"Quite possibly. Captain Maerhwer here will finish your processing through immigration. He can help you with the details: changing money, city map, means of communication." He nodded at her as he opened the door to leave. "Welcome to the Winter Court."

The door swung closed behind him, but at least it didn't vanish. She stood and gathered up the paperwork.

"Okay, Captain Horseboy, where to?"

He barked out a laugh. "You can't ever nod and smile and go along, can you?"

She thought about it. "Not usually, no."

Now that she had a chance, she looked him over. Beautiful brown skin, like she had noticed before, and brown and gold speckled eyes, with a hint of cruelty.

"You're the scary one, right? The stick to his carrot?" She packed her purse and pulled the handle out of her luggage.

"I'm sorry?" he said, the confusion in his voice very much not reaching his eyes.

Deor kicked the luggage so that it popped onto its wheels.

"Sure, he's the Sword—whatever that means—and he's tall, and coldly handsome, and looks like he'd hack a man to bits for little cause. But he won't. He's the law. You're not. If he comes after you, you know you're going to die."

"Mhmmmm," the captain said as he held open the door for her. "And me? What do you think I am?"

"The pain. You're the one with dark bloodstained rooms and bits of metal that don't quite have an obvious purpose. Sure, the general will kill a man. You'll make a man bleed, and then, only if he's lucky, he'll die."

She rolled her suitcase out the door past him.

"Thank you," she said as he held the door. There was no need to be rude.

Chapter Five

Her heart pounding and her back ramrod straight, Deor strode away from the Tower as fast as possible without breaking into an actual run. The business card-sized mirror the captain had told her to carry at all times bumped in her jeans pocket.

"Don't look back. Don't let him see you look back," she told herself.

There was no doubt in her mind that Captain Horseboy was still watching her. Whether she'd see him doing it if she looked was another question.

She kept a firm grip on her luggage and walked away—not to anywhere, just away until she was out from under the Tower's shadow. She made it a couple blocks before exhaustion and crowded sidewalks slowed her feet. She stopped, panting a little, and turned in a slow circle, trying to get her bearings.

"Hey, watch it." A short, bearded woman carrying an axe shoved Deor's purse out of her face.

"I'm sorry!" Deor called after her, but the dwarf woman stalked off muttering about faeries who thought they owned the road.

Other people, all shapes, sizes, and colors, hurried past her. Deor inched toward the curb, trying to get out of the main stream of foot traffic. She hitched her purse up on her shoulder and tucked her suitcase between her feet. No need to act like a slack-jawed tourist.

Of course, that's pretty much what she was. A tourist with no map or itinerary. Or the ability to read the local language.

Swanky shops and cafes lined the streets around her. Some shops even had the magic equivalent of lighted neon signs flashing pictures at passersby, but only half the signs were in English. She had no idea what the other languages were. A few even used runes, which she vaguely remembered from a single graduate school lecture on pre-Christian writing systems, but that didn't make them anymore comprehensible.

All around her, noontime traffic was picking up. In the busy street, a myriad of transports rolled by. Gourds the size of Volvos—summer squash and eggplant—with round windows and doors trundled along on vine wheels. Atop the carriages, drivers conducted the magic with outstretched hands. And there were carriages drawn by animals—goats, pigs, and one luxurious mahogany carriage drawn by huge white swans. Cinderella's mice paled in comparison. There was even the occasional rider on a horse.

And the people! In spite of the captain and his threats and the growing pain in her back, she smiled at the rainbow of people around her. Most were faeries—tall and elegant with their multicolored wings fanning behind them as they walked. Most of the women wore skirts that swept the ground, though some had artful slits for movement or were kilted up in elaborate folds to leave their legs free. Faeries of both sexes certainly liked their glitter, too. Neither Lord Farringdon nor the captain had worn any jewels, but most of the men she saw in the street had something sparkly tucked in their hair. If she squinted, she could see little lines of magic holding the jewels in place.

Skin colors she'd never imagined filled the world. A couple, arms intertwined, sauntered past, his deep yellow skin a lovely pair for her deep purple. His eyes were emerald circles, and hers were palest grey. The man's wings were plain and moth-like, but the woman's were a deep sulfur yellow with purple veins and frilled edges ending in a swallowtail that stuck out two feet behind her. Another passerby, his arms full of hat boxes, brushed against her wing, and the woman gasped as if she'd been groped. Her wings folded in on themselves, disappearing into her clothes, and she shrank against her companion. Only the other faerie's abject apologies and the appearance of two guards-women at the end of the street prevented the yellow-skinned man from punching him. Deor made a mental note to be extra careful around people's wings and edged around the conflict.

Nearly everyone who passed was taller than her by at least six inches. The few exceptions were the dwarves.

"Little people," she corrected herself, then corrected again. No, some of the short ones were definitely dwarves—braided beards, armor, axes, and all.

Then again there were other people who were no taller than her elbows, but beardless, with bodies like slender dancers and hair like cotton candy. They moved so fast they blurred. Faerie children, maybe? None of them had wings. Or any adult supervision. She watched as one with hair like an electric blue cloud dashed out into traffic, dodging three carts and zipping under the belly of a horse to reach the other side of the street. The horse's rider shouted a curse, and the little man with the electric hair stopped to offer a hand gesture before disappearing into the crowd. Some things translated easily here.

She yawned so wide her jaw ached. Enough staring. She needed a place to crash for the night. She damn well wasn't sleeping on a park bench, if they even had parks. And food! Her stomach growled and gurgled. Baking smells—fruit pies and breads—drifted out of a cafe across the street, and her mouth watered. She was going in there and ordering whatever they would feed her.

Getting a firm grip on her luggage, she looked up and down the street. There weren't any crosswalks painted on the cobblestones. Was she supposed to just run for it like the little man she'd seen? The street rumbled, and a beer wagon loaded with barrels and drawn by four white oxen rushed past her.

As she hesitated, torn between hunger and the impulse not to end up as roadkill, she spotted the pair of female guards coming only a few feet away. Their wings were hidden, but they wore uniforms like the ones at the Tower, and her heart beat a little faster. Was loitering a crime here? Was jaywalking? She did not need another run in with the law right now. Too late. They'd spotted her.

"Miss," one of them said. "Do you need assistance?"

"I'm fine, thank you. I just want to cross the street," she said, managing not to sound as defensive as she felt.

One of the guards, the brick-colored one, put her fingers to her mouth and whistled. Traffic in both directions screeched to a halt as she stepped into the road, her hand raised. Her cream-colored partner made a little shooing gesture at Deor.

"Thank you!" Deor yelled and ran across the street.

"You're quite welcome, young lady."

Young. The word echoed in her head as Deor settled into a table at the cafe with a tray of chicken soup, a bun the size of her face, and a fried hand-pie the man behind the counter promised was filled with "a medlar and billberry compote. Last billberries of the season." What either of those fruits were was unclear to Deor, but the filling was purple and smelled like something that would have been served on Mount Olympus.

She was three bites into the soup before she remembered. This was faerie food. Bad things happened to people who ate faerie food in stories —they forgot go home, for one thing. She took another bite of soup, closing her eyes and savoring. Yes, there was magic in this food. She could taste it, feel it in her throat. Not bad, but like a foreign spice. Nothing had tasted this good in weeks. Her mother had raved about the food in her letter. *It makes you feel more real, more alive.*

Deor picked up the bun and looked at it. Be logical. If you go back to the human world, you'll die. If you don't eat, you'll die. She thought about Bakersfield, about Bill and her grandmother. She still missed them. There was no way she wasn't going home. She bit into the golden-crusted bun and chewed, closing her eyes with satisfaction. It wasn't different from human bread—just more—more breadlike. She sighed a happy sigh and dug into the rest of her meal.

After she ate, she trudged out into the street again to find a hotel. As she walked, she gave into the tourist impulse again, enjoying the crazy mix of buildings. Just because her faerie father was an asshat didn't mean she had to hate the architecture. Built close together, houses and stores were packed in close like medieval European cities. But the styles were all over the timeline. Some of three-story buildings had steep, moss-grown roofs last seen in England during the Viking age. Around shop doors, living vines trained into elaborate *arte nouveau* arches. Victorian-style brick buildings snuggled up next to Gothic arches. A seven story, half-timbered skyscraper was going up just down the street. In Caer Eisteddfod, everywhen is now.

Deor could feel the magic all around her. The hairs on her arms prickled as if a cold breeze had blown across them. If she breathed deeply, she could even *smell* the magic woven into the thousand other smells of the city—under the scent of horses and flowers and stone and perfume and roast meat was the cold, clear scent of snow. Door handles and window latches were entwined with it. People wore it up and down their clothes, in their hair, on their wrists.

A green-skinned man with sharp cheekbones caught her staring and gave her a wink. She met his gaze and bit her lip to repress a shriek. His features were beautiful, but his welcoming smile was full of sharp, predatory teeth. She shivered as he walked by.

How would she even start to find a job here? Did papers have classifieds? Did they even have newspapers? The staff inside the cafe where she'd eaten had all been short, candy-colored people who zipped from table to table so fast they blurred. So much for waitressing. Other than teaching, what skills did she have in the real world, let alone in faerie land?

She picked up her pace, following the crowd as it spilled into a wide piazza where eight roads met. A wooden pole with street signs said this was the Marketplace. Arrows below the sign directed her toward the city center, the cultural district, the wharf, and the university.

"Yes! That's perfect," she said, turning toward the university.

A university meant a library—a place to start her search—and maybe even a job tutoring. All over the world, a university was a university, a familiar place no matter how many miles from home.

She followed the signs and the crowd going to the university until she was ready to cry with exhaustion. Finally, the street ended at a wide open gate set in a towering stone wall. Over the gate, etched in the stone: *Eisteddfod University.*

Around her the crowd thinned as most turned into the open-air food stalls opposite the university gates. On the marketplace side of the street stood an inn sporting a wooden sign of a lion, though it was more reminiscent of a kitten than the king of the jungle.

Deor squared her shoulders. Time to make a plan. She'd get a room, write out her resume, and come up with a killer job pitch. She'd tackle the university first thing in the morning.

The man behind the desk was compact, though taller than Deor by several inches, with a mane of tawny hair and a square jaw. When he asked for payment, she handed over her mirror and held her breath.

She'd paid for her food with the few stray pounds of human money—like the ferryman, the staff took it, but didn't like it. Captain Horseman had insisted she "exchange" the majority of her human money and put it on deposit.

"It's for your own protection," he said when she protested she would be fine with cash. "If you're robbed, you'll be penniless here. You're a minor, so you should have a parent or guardian co-sign your mirror account for you, but I'll override that."

"Thank you ever so much," she'd said and stuffed the mirror in her pocket. "I'm sure children everywhere sleep better at night knowing you and Blue Boy are watching out for them."

He'd looked grim as he handed her the mirror. "Don't let this out of your sight."

Now she tried to hide her nerves as she watched the yellow-maned man lay her mirror on a slab of polished granite and tapped it, read whatever appeared on the surface, and tapped it again.

"Is the second floor acceptable, miss?"

She breathed out in relief. "Yes, thank you."

The room seemed reasonable, though to be fair, she had no idea what reasonable was. It was far less than she had on her mirror, clean, not on the first floor, and came with both dinner and breakfast. Better than the Tower. The desk clerk tapped at her mirror, gave her a key, and had the bellboy carry her bags up the stairs.

The bellboy, a younger, hairier version of the man behind the desk, was shorter than the faerie men on the street. He had a broad chest that narrowed down to a lean waist and legs and a mane of tawny hair that cascaded down his back.

"First time in the Winter Court, then?" he asked as he shouldered open the door to her room.

"First time in Faerie," she said, flopping down on the single bed.

The room was clean, if plain—white plaster walls, a white coverlet on the bed. Instead of a TV, a large mirror was secured to the wall above a chest of drawers.

"Lights on," he called, and every light in the room illuminated. "The bath is this way." He pointed to the bathroom. "The shower operates by touch. Dinner is served between six and ten p.m.," he said and bowed. "Just mirror the front desk if you need anything."

"Right." She nodded, not sure how to "mirror," but too tired to ask for an explanation.

Once he was gone, she thought about a shower, but the bed was too cozy. She was asleep before she could kick off her shoes.

Chapter Six

Rafe stepped through the portal from Tower to the Palace's front entrance and saluted the two guards on duty. Jake and Sam trotted at his heels.

"Go on, boys," he told them. "Go get your supper."

They raced away to the kennels, leaping and snapping at each other like puppies. For a second he thought of following them, but instead he laid his hand on a seemingly blank space on the wall, slipping through a hidden portal to the Household, the private inner rooms belonging to the king and his family.

He paused to ease off his boots. In recent years, the king had taken to napping before dinner, and Rafe didn't want to wake him. Stepping as lightly as he could on the dark marble floor, he eased open the door to the king's parlor. "Finn?"

But this evening, the King of the Winter Court—Sweordmund VIII to his subjects, Finn to his family—was not asleep. He sat in his favorite armchair, his bare feet toward an early fire. Lord Michael Montblanc, the King's Shield, handed the king a glass of wine with an unctuous smile.

Michael's pink skin and mane of red hair glowed in the firelight, the opals fixed in his hair sending out glints with each movement. For a split second, he looked to Rafe like a creature made of fire, bending low over the ice king.

Quietly, Rafe crossed the thick carpeting to the window where Princess Consort Astarte bent over a potted rose bush. Her translucent wings flickered pale green and gold in the evening light. Her fingertips were buried in the rose's potting soil, a look of concentration on her face.

"Good evening, your Majesty," Rafe said, and bowed.

For a second she didn't respond. Then she blinked and seemed to see him. Pulling her fingers out of the soil, she squeezed his hand, turning her cheek up for him to kiss.

"Your father is put out with you," she whispered. "Michael is bearing tales again."

Rafe snorted. "What have I done now?"

But Astarte only smiled. Her golden skin, evidence of her origins in the Summer Court, scattered faint light over the table where she sat.

"What do you think of my little project?" she asked, pointing to the rose.

"It's pretty," Rafe said.

The rosebush had only three small, white blossoms. They seemed curiously mundane for one of Astarte's plants. Nothing like the Carnivorous Acanthus she'd been working on the last time he'd been in her greenhouse.

"Forgive me. I'm not sure what I'm meant to be seeing."

"I know. It's boring," she said. "Really dull to look at. But Robbie brought it from the human world for my last birthday, so I kept it, and this morning I had an idea. Now sniff them. Not too hard though."

As he leaned forward, he caught the whiff of snow, of clean air in deep forest. He breathed more deeply, and his shoulders eased, tension he hadn't realized he was carrying ebbing out of his back.

"Marvelous."

"Thank you. It is rather good, if I say so myself. I think I'll put it by Finn's bed tonight and see if it helps him sleep."

They shared a smile.

From the fireplace, Finn called, "Come over here, please Rafe. I want to have a word with you."

Rafe grimaced at the tone. "I am in trouble, aren't I?" he muttered.

"I rather think you should be, this time," Astarte said. "Go on." She shooed him away.

Taking a last sniff of the restorative rose, Rafe straightened his shoulders and padded over to Finn and Michael, bowing low before the king. "Yes, sire?"

Finn held up the newspaper, a faint tremor in his slender fingers.

"What were you thinking?" Below the top headline was a picture of Rafe in the marketplace hovering over the crowd. *Sword Averts Riot.*

"It was over in five minutes," Rafe said, ignoring Michael's smirk. "I had a few words with the protesters, and they dispersed peacefully."

"But what if they hadn't?" Finn snapped. "You could have been killed."

"By a bunch of students with pens? I could have fought my way out of that lot when I was still a squire. Barehanded. Besides, I had Jake and Sam with me."

Finn snorted and stood up.

Automatically, Rafe reached out to give him a hand, but Finn waved him away.

"I'm not that feeble. Not today anyway."

Stepping back, Rafe had to admit that the Finn looked better than he had in some time. His alabaster skin wasn't grey tinged, and he stood without his cane. He was fully dressed too, though his feet were bare as they usually were when he was at home.

Finn drummed his fingers on the mantel.

"Your safety is no longer a matter of personal choice," he said. "As the heir, you are obliged to keep yourself safe from such risks."

"But as the Sword, I am obliged to take them," Rafe said. "And since I am still the Sword and not yet fully the heir, I chose to take the risk."

"Don't get smart with me, boy." Finn's command went straight through Rafe's spine. The echo of power resonated in every order out of the king's mouth.

"No, sir."

"That's better. Be more thoughtful, next time. Besides," Finn patted him on the shoulder, "the heir ought not to be so familiar with the common people. It dulls the edge of your honor to be seen chatting in the streets with them."

Rafe stuck his tongue between his teeth. But he couldn't hold back the wave of cold that rolled off him. If it hadn't done his honor any harm to bleed with them at Tannenberg, talking with them afterward was no dishonor either.

"Yes, sir," he said.

From where he leaned against the mantelpiece, Michael offered him an avuncular smile. "Don't take it so hard, Rafe," he said. "Leaving behind the lower companions of our youth is one of the burdens of leadership that we all have to assume eventually."

"Thank you for that insight, Michael," Rafe said. At his side, he flickered his fingers, and Michael's wine froze solid in its glass.

Before Michael could say anything, Rafe turned to Finn. "While we're on the subject of the commoners, you should know that nearly all the guilds have joined—all except the Silversmiths and Artificers—to protest the Adoption."

Finn snorted. "And how is it that only those two have any sense?"

"They have the most to lose if they anger their noble clients. But it's not really the Adoption the people object to; it's the sense that they're being hoodwinked. They have no way of knowing that the Adoption isn't just for show. And they don't understand why you...Why you haven't simply taken a child bearer."

"They don't need to understand. It is enough for them to know that I am their king."

"I know, sire." He put a hand on the king's shoulder.

Finn didn't need to be reminded that his illness had taken away the ability to father a child with a child bearer, even if he could have been persuaded to do so.

"But they're afraid."

"What do they know about fear? My only child and heir risks life and limb to placate an unruly mob, but they are the ones who are afraid?" Finn pulled Rafe into a fierce, rib-cracking hug. "I couldn't bear it if I lost you."

At the fireplace, Michael turned away.

"I know, Father." Rafe's voice caught in his throat. "I'll be careful. I promise." Gently, he pulled away from the hug. "But I made a promise to Holman and the rest of them as well. Don't make me break it."

Finn sighed and laughed. "You're as single minded as your—as Edgar. So tell me, what scheme do you have in mind?"

"Allow the people to see the remaining Adoption ceremonies by mirror."

Rafe pulled a paper out of his pocket, a diagram of the throne room, and laid it on a side table. As he did so, Astarte left her work with the rose and joined them, standing close beside Finn and twining her fingers through his.

"If we put mirrors here, here, and here," Rafe said, "people can watch the whole ceremony. We don't have to let massive crowds into the Palace, but every single person who wants to can see every detail. Let one or two Guildmasters in to represent their people, and let the mirrors show the rest of the world."

"The Master of the City represents the guilds," Michael said. He pushed himself away from the mantle and came to the table, sliding his lean form between Rafe and the king and scowling at the diagram. "There's no need for anyone else to come to the ceremonies."

"The Master of the City is still a nobleman," Astarte said pulling her hand from Finn's. "The people want to see for themselves. Rafe is right—this could be just the kind of spectacle people need to have their faith in the monarchy restored." She laid her hand on Finn's arm. "Let your people see this Adoption as a triumph, not an act of desperation."

Finn gave her a smile. "What would I do without my Consort to advise me? I suppose the mirrors will be secure?"

"Completely," Rafe said. "We'll use the same magics we use to communicate in the field."

"As the King's Shield and Defender, I still advise against it," Michael insisted. "And I resent this intrusion into my area of authority. The breach of security involved in allowing the entire world to see the interior of the throne room—"

"Is minimal," Rafe said. "Arthur and I have reviewed all the manpower and the magical wards in that room. The mirrors aren't going to reveal anything that isn't already common knowledge. Besides, the Sword of the Summer Court has been in our throne room before and will be for the final ceremony. The mirrors won't show anything he doesn't already know. You'll be completely safe, sire."

Finn stepped back, chin cupped in his hand. One foot tapped the stone floor as he thought. "I like it," he said at last. "This Adoption is for all of the Winter Court, so let the entire Winter Court witness it. Excellent idea, Rafe."

"Thank you, sire." Rafe grinned at Michael, who glared back.

"And you'd better stay for dinner tonight," Finn went on. "We hardly ever see you these days."

Rafe bowed low. "I would be honored to dine with your majesties." He straightened. "I'll go dress for dinner and join you shortly."

He strode out of the room, all but dancing. He'd kept his promises, and Finn was healthy enough to sit up and eat a meal. The world couldn't offer him more.

Chapter Seven

A bright Monday morning greeted Deor as she emerged from her hotel, but there were no talking birds or woodland creatures waiting to lead her down the path to a job. Even so, the city thrummed with magic, full of bright, beautiful color.

She rolled her shoulders and stretched her arms. She luxuriated in the loosening of the muscles in her back and the easing of the tightness in her neck. She sighed, letting the last of the stiffness fall away.

"Don't get too comfortable," she warned herself. The faster she found a job and her father, the faster she could get the hell out of Faerie. She headed for the one place her skill set was useful: the university.

Like the medieval universities of Europe, Eisteddfod was walled. Glimmers of magic ran along the top of the wall as well, spiky and forbidding. In spite of that, the great gates stood wide open. "Eisteddfod University" had been etched in gold across the arc above the gates. The university crest, a crossed scroll and a sickle in a wreath of mistletoe, was carved below the name. Surrounding the top of emblem were words Deor couldn't read—Faerie perhaps—and below, a script in Latin: *Scientia super imperio.*

"Wisdom over power," she translated. What a pleasant thought.

The guard office beside the gate was empty. As she stepped from the gate tunnel into the sunshine, she paused. Inside the walls, the campus was surrounded by dense forest. A single paved path led into the trees.

"Do they issue students red cloaks and tell them to stay on the path?" she wondered aloud.

At least it wasn't made of yellow brick. She followed the path through the dense trees, a few of them already changing to fall colors.

A roar from her left froze her on the spot. A bear, teeth bared, charged through the trees. She screamed, jerking her hands up into a fighting stance. The bear skidded to a halt in front of her and raised itself up on its back feet and roared again.

The sensation of her skin rolling like waves poured over her, head to toe, and a flood of sparkles filled the air, drifting toward the bear.

He sneezed.

"Identification, miss?" a voice behind her said.

She spun around into the chest of a man two feet taller, at least, than she was, and more sparkles poured off her. A badge clipped to the green uniform read *Bernie Urson—Security*. His chin was tucked almost to his chest as he looked down at her. Brown eyes and rounded features seemed too soft for the stern expression.

"Um..." she said and fumbled in her bag for her mirror and proffered it to him, still tremblingly slightly. "Here."

The man tapped the glass and squinted to read her identification information. "Huh." He drew a mirror of his own—larger and clearly fancier than hers—and touched the two together. He read his own. "Pretty sparse information. But the Sword signed off on it." He handed back the mirror.

"Thank you." She slipped the mirror back into her pocket.

"It's okay, Bob," Bernie called over her head.

Bob the bear dropped down onto all four paws and sauntered up. Around the bear's neck hung a security badge like Bernie's. The bear gave a nod, snuffled once at Deor, and trundled away.

"There was no one—" Deor cleared her throat, trying to ease the squeak. "There was no one at the security office when I came in."

"Sorry 'bout that. What with the incoming class, the upcoming Adoption, and the protests, things have been very tense. We take security very seriously."

"Everyone around here seems to," she said, as Bob disappeared into the trees.

"What is your business here?" He looked her up and down and frowned. "Looking to enroll?"

She had showered and dressed in the best thing she'd brought—a pair of dark jeans, a black blouse, and her favorite heeled boots.

"No." She took a few steps back so she didn't have to crane her neck to see his face. "I'm new to the country, and I wanted to see if the school was hiring adjunct teachers or tutors."

The man scanned his mirror again. "It says here you only have a seventy-two-hour visa." He glanced back up. "Unless you've got quite the specialty, I doubt you'll find work here for only seventy-two hours."

Deor opened her mouth to argue, but he held up a hand.

"It's not my business." He tapped the mirror again. "You have a one day visitor's pass. If anyone asks, just show them your mirror."

"Thank you."

He pointed up the path. "Main campus is that way." He tapped his forelock and nodded. "You have a good day, Miss Smithfield."

"Where's the English or literature department?"

"The literary studies building will be on your left when you get to main campus. Just stay on the path, miss." He nodded once more and trundled away, his rolling gate exactly like Bob's.

"No shit I'll stay on the path," she whispered.

Deor emerged from the forest into the main quad and beamed at the view. *This* was a university. Huge buildings carved from stone or wood surrounded a giant circle of green. She'd come into the southern end, between two ruddy buildings, and guessed that the building directly across the quad was at least a quarter a mile away. There were buildings from nearly every style and century. The architecture of the buildings reflected all the earlier centuries, but the heart of campus was a prehistoric circle of stones.

Crowds of students and their families lugging bags and boxes followed signs saying *Student Housing This Way* with neatly scrolled arrows. Like students back in America, many seemed desperate to both herd and ignore their parents.

One girl, half again as tall and wide as Deor, hurried along in front of a tiger who carried a sheaf of paperwork in its mouth. "Really, Dad!" the girl hissed over her shoulder. "You could have stayed a man."

Deor squeaked, somewhere between a laugh and a scream, and clapped her hand over her mouth.

On the quad, students lounged and talked. A group of young faerie men of all colors played some sort of air sport. She stopped at the edge of the path to watch one man toss the ball to his airborne teammate, held aloft by fluttering brown wings. A member of the opposite team leapt up, purple wings spread wide, and snatched hold of his legs, dangling a foot off the ground until, wings vanishing, both collapsed in a heap. She hesitated, about to run over if someone had been hurt, but they popped up, laughing.

The Department of Literary Arts, housed in Hrofstag Gwythrerth Hall near the university's North Gate, turned out to be a five-story fieldstone building with a giant arched entrance.

She trotted up the wide stone steps and through the open set of heavy wooden doors. In the main lobby, two staircases swept up in wide curls to the second floor. Between them were two bricked-up doorways. Odd in such a beautiful building. On a large board to her right hung a list of faculty and staff and their offices.

She skimmed the list of professors—all called bards—and their specialties, everything from Modern Faerie to Ancient Zarthrusian, and Goblin, Pixie, and Werecreature. Only one person listed *Human Studies* in his interests, and he was labeled as *on Sabbatical*.

"Maybe they could use a temporary replacement," Deor said under her breath.

The head of the department was Bard Ama Nefasta, her office 428 D. A note next to her name read *By Appointment ONLY*.

"Well, we've got an appointment now," Deor said shouldering her bag. There didn't seem to be an elevator, so she followed a huge stone staircase as it spiraled up the center of the building. At least she didn't have to go all the way to the top floor.

By the time she reached the fourth floor, she had to pause and catch her breath. Across from the stairs was the main office numbered 428. The large room had a receptionist's desk in front and rows and rows of cubbyhole mailboxes on the right. A sign on the hallway to the left read

Faculty Lounge: NO UNACCOMPANIED STUDENTS! A sign on the right read *Offices B-D.*

"Right it is." No one sat at reception, nor at the desk in room B. Room C turned out to be a small, empty conference room. Room D's door was shut, with *Bard Ama Nefasta, Chair* in a neat sign. No voices sounded on the other side, so she knocked.

"Come!" The voice was from a person who didn't have time for prepositions.

Deor pushed open the door.

At the end of a long, narrow room, past bookshelves reaching the nine-foot ceiling, was a gorgeous mahogany desk. Neat, precise stacks of paper covered the entire surface. Behind it sat a woman in yellow trimmed, black academic robes, a bit like a well-educated bee. Her lavender hair was pulled back in a tight bun that matched her lilac skin and hard amethyst eyes.

"Good morning," Deor said.

"Who are you?" The woman frowned, drawing her severe features into sharper lines. "The list of advisors is on the window outside."

Deor tried for a smile but was pretty sure it didn't make it through. "I am not a student." Deor crossed the remaining space between them and held out her hand across the desk. "I'm Doctor Deor Smithfield, a professor of—" She paused, mind racing. Medieval wouldn't mean the same here. "—of Human English Literature."

Ama glanced down at her hand like it might be lethal, but shook it. "Bard Ama Nefasta," she said. "I am busy. What do you want?" She did not gesture for Deor to take a seat in one of the hard uncomfortable looking wooden chairs in front of her desk.

"A job." She pulled a sheaf of papers from her satchel. "This contains my resume, teaching philosophy, list of courses I've taught and am qualified to teach, sample syllabi, and summary of my research interests. I know this is very short notice, but I am new to the Winter Court and would love the opportunity to tutor students in human literature. I noticed that your regular human literature professor is on sabbatical."

"The Ohio State University?" Professor Nefasta looked up at her over the papers. "Where is that?"

"The United States of America." Deor shifted her bag on her shoulder to keep from fidgeting. "The New World?" she hazarded.

"I am aware of the Americas." She flipped a few more pages. "You've taught Shakespeare?" The hard edge of her voice softened slightly.

"Yes, ma'am." *Ma'am?* She chastised herself. The woman didn't look old enough to deserve that. "Several times."

"Sit." The woman gestured at the chair, and Deor sat. "There is not much interest in human literature, and certainly not New World literature. But, we keep one course of England's literature on the schedule. This is the university, after all."

"I understand." Deor gestured to her resume on the top of the stack. "You'll see my doctorate is in the literature of England. Medieval and Renaissance England."

She set down Deor's packet. "What would you teach in a Shakespeare course?"

Deor pursed her lips, considering. "The majority of the students are faeries?"

"Yes," Nefasta nodded. "But we do have a significant minority of other Fae, too.

"Of course." What kinds of other Fae were there? "I'd start with *Midsummer Night's Dream*. The human world meeting the Faeworld would give us a place to start a conversation. I'd teach the big plays, of course, like *Hamlet* and *Henry V*. They might also appreciate the *Tempest*. Three papers per semester and a comprehensive final exam, at least."

"I suppose that is acceptable." Nefasta studied her for a few moments. "What brings you to the Winter Court?"

"Family emergency." Deor offered a small smile. "I was given a seventy-two-hour visa. It doesn't give me enough time to do what I need to do, so I need a job. And, frankly, teaching is the only thing I'm qualified to do. I am happy to run study sessions, grade papers, lead mini-discussions, whatever you need."

"Perhaps you might have planned ahead." Nefasta held out her hand. "Mirror?"

"Right! Sorry. Still getting used the that." She pulled it out of her pocket and handed it over.

Frowning, the professor tapped it. The more she read, the deeper her frown got. "Are you a criminal?"

"Of course not." Deor shoved a hand through her bangs. "But I am a changeling. For some reason, that alarmed the soldiers at immigration."

She took a deep breath and steadied her voice. "Look, I have a PhD. I have experience. I'm a *good* teacher. My teaching evaluations were always near the top of my class."

Bard Nefasta scanned the piles on her desk and looked back at the mirror. She stood.

Deor stood, too.

"Don't get up." Bard Nefasta waved her down. "I will be back. Stay here."

When the door closed behind the bard, Deor stood. She looked around and leaned slightly forward, doing her best to make out the upside down papers on the bard's desk. Most were in what looked like the same language as the crest.

Behind the desk was a huge window. Various plants rested on the wide sill. Deor stepped around the desk. She glanced again at the papers. From this point of view, a framed picture of the bard with someone else— a man with features almost as sharp as hers, but with a shock of red hair, a red beard, and sideburns streaked white. They were both smiling.

Deor turned to the window and braced herself on the sill, leaning forward. Outside, on the smooth green, quad people of all shapes and sizes walked about. No matter what else they were, they were all in academic robes. She hadn't even brought a long coat.

From the window, she could see the whole of the campus green. An island surrounded by a ring of trees obscured all but the top of the university's imposing walls. Beyond the walls was the city, and beyond the city, on a small hill, was a massive castle. If she really looked, she could make out the soldiers moving along the top walls.

When she leaned closer, she could glimpse the spiked bridge and turrets of the Tower to her right. She was certain something hung from one of the turrets. She moved to brace herself against the window for a better look. The glass was clear as any she had ever seen—it didn't even catch the light. As soon as her fingers brushed the window, it popped like a bubble.

"Crap."

She reached out the window, trying to gather up the magic strands as they drifted into the air. She should have known. The iridescent wisps of magic must have covered the opening like the magic on Captain Maerhwer. There was no fixing it now.

Deor hurried back around the desk and sat down in the chair. The office door opened behind her, and the bard returned to her seat. She didn't seem to notice the window.

"Professor Smithfield," she said handing the mirror back to Deor. "As you noted, our human literature professor is on sabbatical." From her tone, whoever he was he might be safer if he never came back. Nefasta drew herself up, mouth pinched. "I can offer you two classes—full time employment. I will attend your classes and, so long as I find your teaching satisfactory, the job will be permanent."

Deor held her breath as the bard turned and opened a drawer under the window. "Classes officially start tomorrow." She turned back with a few sheets of paper. "Shakespeare meets on Tuesday and Thursday. You will be prepared?"

"Absolutely." Deor blew out a sigh of relief.

"Excellent. Fill these out with your mirror and send them on." She handed over the paper.

"Thank you so much, Bard Nefasta." Deor took the papers and glanced through them.

"Call me Ama," she said. "We can offer you faculty housing as well."

"That would be perfect." Sweet heaven, a university with faculty housing! She wouldn't have to waste time or money finding a place to live.

Ama gestured at the papers. "Take those out to our secretary PhiPhi— she'll help you get settled and tell you where to go." She turned around again and pulled out a stack of papers and a book. "Here is the textbook I ordered and the syllabus. It might be easier to teach from this, rather than creating a new one."

"Thank you again." Deor slid the materials into her bag and stood.

"One thing before you go," Ama added as Deor started to turn away. "You have a Lecture Tutor. He cannot be fired, though he is a student in every other sense."

"I'm sorry," Deor said. "A Lecture Tutor?"

"Oh." Ama looked surprised. "Do you not have these? Bardic study students who give some lectures, grade papers, meet with students?"

"Oh, a teaching assistant." Deor nodded. "Absolutely. Same thing, different name."

"Good. Next time I see you, you will be wearing your university robes?"

"No. I didn't bring them with me." Deor shook her head. Those things cost almost a thousand dollars, and most people rented them.

Ama was not impressed.

"Do you suggest shopping somewhere in particular?" Deor asked.

"I believe students get their robes in the marketplace. Bardic student robes will have to suffice."

"I might not be able to get them by tomorrow," because God knew how much they cost, she added to herself, "but I will have everything else prepared."

"That will have to do."

"Thank you again."

Ama nodded but said nothing, already engrossed in her paperwork.

Chapter Eight

At his desk in the Tower, Rafe gritted his teeth and forged on with, if not the worst part of his job, certainly the dullest—moving piles of paper from one stack to another. He dipped his pen in the ink again and scribbled his name at the bottom of yet another outpost report, denied six requests from the press for interviews, and forwarded three more to the Palace Secretary for Public Affairs.

He almost wrote, *I'd rather be demoted to private and flogged in public* on an elegantly engraved invitation to an amateur operatic performance by the second son of a Countess from the Midlands, but instead he scribbled his regrets at being unable to attend.

He was rifling through the remaining pile, backlogged from his fortnight away, and wondering how much of it he could simply ignore, when Arthur's face appeared in the large mirror above the fireplace.

"Do you remember that odd little changeling from yesterday?"

"Of course I do. Is she making trouble?"

"I don't know." Arthur's voice was bland, but the little crease in the corner of his eyes betrayed his frustration. Arthur *always* knew. "I lost track of her mirror about half an hour ago when she crossed the university threshold."

"Robbie?"

"She's safe in her university flat—rather annoyed that I woke her up, actually, but she promised to let us know when she goes out."

Rafe laughed. "I hope she doesn't have any early morning classes this semester. But what about the Smithfield girl? What is she doing—trying to enroll?"

"I told you, I don't know. University security refuses to answer my questions beyond confirming that she's on campus and citing bardic law about sanctuary space."

Rafe drummed his fingers on the desk, torn between the impulse to have the young woman escorted across the border the moment she reappeared in the city and concern for her safety.

"She's exactly what our mysterious changeling attackers have been targeting," Rafe said.

"I know."

"Whatever she's up to, she's going to cause trouble. I can feel it."

"Yes, I know."

Rafe paced back and forth, his feet automatically falling into a military cadence as he thought. She might only be thirty years old, but she was more like a woman in her nineties than one of Robbie's friends. There was nothing naive about the way she'd carried herself in their interview the day before. At the same time, she'd seemed so genuinely confused by magic. From their place by the fire, Jake and Sam watched him with half-raised ears.

His face still showing on the mirror, Arthur cleared his throat. "I've located our wayward changeling. And Ama wants to talk to you about her."

"Oh…" His favorite curse word escaped his lips just as Ama Nefasta's pinched face replaced Arthur's on the mirror.

"I beg your pardon?" she said.

Rafe bowed toward the mirror. "I was thinking of something else. What can I do for you, Bard Nefasta?"

"Who is Deor Smithfield and why does she have your signature on her seventy-two-hour visa?"

"Is she trying to enroll in classes?"

"No. Answer the question."

Rafe rubbed his chin, picking his words. Just talking to the bard in charge of the Adoption made his bones ache with the memory of the marrow-scraping pain of each ceremony. Jake, the larger of his two dogs, got up and trotted over, leaning his shoulder against Rafe's hip. A low growl rumbled through his frame as he fixed his eyes on the mirror. Rafe dropped his hand to the dog's head, burying his fingers in Jake's thick fur.

"Deor Smithfield is a bit of a mystery," he said, "but Arthur and I are concerned for her safety. She's parentless, claims to have no prior experience with the Faeworld, and she's looking for her father, who she was led to believe is named Finn. I'd appreciate it if you wouldn't hide her on Eisteddfod's campus."

"Sanctuary is always granted to those who ask. But," she held up her hand before Rafe could object, "she's not asking for sanctuary. Yet. She wants a job, and I'm inclined to give it to her. Permanently, if she's any good. It would serve Dell right for skulking off to the human world and leaving me to cover his classes."

"Far be it from me to tell you how to do your job, Bard Nefasta."

"Indeed."

He let that slide.

"But perhaps I can suggest a compromise that benefits us both? If you're going to hire her, house her with Lady Penelope."

Ama narrowed her eyes.

"I am not one of your spies. And I resent you co-opting one of the college's finest healers for your police work." The word "police" came out much the way she might have said "sewer cleaning."

Rafe gritted his teeth and bowed again, reminding himself that it didn't pay to anger bards. They lived too long for one thing, and this particular bard would be standing over him with a mistletoe branch in less than a week's time.

"Of course not, ma'am. I wouldn't dream of asking you to compromise bardic space in the interest of national security. But if you house Dr. Smithfield on your campus, you can ensure her safety. Again, she has no parents to look after her, and she fits our victim profile. She'll be safe with Lady Penelope."

Nefasta heaved a sigh.

"I suppose you're right. Very well. Thank you for your time, Lord Farringdon."

"You're quite welcome, Bard Nefasta."

She laughed once, more a bark than anything. "Whoever said you weren't cut out for politics was obviously a fool."

She disappeared, and once more the mirror showed only his own office. From the fireplace, Sam barked at the mirror and Jake joined in.

"Couldn't agree more, boys." He looked back at his desk, then at the clock. Screw it. The papers would wait. "Come on," he said to the dogs. "Let's go do something more interesting. Arthur! We're going to field practice."

He had been too idle in the last few weeks. Time to sweat out the laziness before he turned as spongy and useless as Michael.

He laid his hand on his office door and whispered. The door vanished, revealing the Palace's largest gymnasium on the other side. He stepped through the portal, the usual small rush of magic tingling on his skin.

He took a deep breath, savoring the smell of polish and leather. Suits of mail hung on frames along the walls. Beside each man's gear stood a chest for smaller personal items and a wooden bench. Weapons and shields hung on racks that divided the room down the center.

"Good afternoon, sir." Gordie, his squire, was already there, laying out his armor on the bench. The kid had the big hands and gangly limbs of one who hadn't yet grown into his height, but he worked hard and he paid attention. Once Gordie's wings finally came in, he'd be a force to be reckoned with.

"Captain Arthur said you were coming," Gordie said.

"Good lad. Had your lunch yet?"

"Just a bite, sir. I'll eat after practice."

Rafe nodded. "Smart move. Is it lance practice today?"

"Mounted swordplay, sir," Gordie said, climbing up on a bench so he could put on Rafe's chainmail. Rafe could do most of the arming himself if need be, but a squire needed to practice. And Gordie would be hurt if Rafe didn't let him do his job.

Rafe stripped off his uniform jacket and shirt, replacing them with a quilted tunic. He held his arms over his head so that Gordie could slide on his chainmail shirt. A clink of armor sounded. Arthur, already put together, came around the corner. His eyes twinkled.

"It's mounted swordplay today," he said. "Are you leading, or just coming along for the ride?"

"Oh, I'll be leading," Rafe said.

"Left arm, sir," his squire said, and Rafe raised his arm. Gordie hopped off the bench to buckle on Rafe's greaves.

"Is Michael joining us?" Rafe said.

Arthur snorted and rolled his eyes. In Ancient Faerie, he said, "He didn't come back last night from his mistress's, so I doubt it."

"No need for that," Rafe replied in Ancient. "I think Gordie's old enough now that you don't need to spare his delicate sensibilities. Besides, he probably understood every word." He winked at Gordie, who blushed.

"Most of it, sir. I've been practicing my verbs."

"Watch out, there," Arthur said. "You get any smarter and I'll have to recruit you to the intelligence service."

A look of real alarm spread across the boy's face.

"Relax, lad," Rafe said. "He's joking. Go on now and see that Sampson is ready. I'll be out in minute."

Gordie took Rafe's long sword off the rack and scampered off toward the stables.

"You shouldn't scare the kid with jokes like that," Rafe said, pulling on his coif and tucking his helmet under his arm.

"I don't know that I was joking," Arthur said. "He's got a good head, and he knows when to keep his mouth shut. Good things for a spy."

"But he's bound and determined to be a knight and lead death or glory charges. What good's an adventure if you can't impress girls with the story afterward?"

Arthur chuckled and the two of them walked out through the gymnasium where a squad of foot soldiers ran hand-to-hand combat drills. In the practice fields, a cluster of the Household Guard waited with their horses. Gordie had a death grip on Sampson's bridle. The black horse drummed its dinner plate-sized feet and tossed its head, jolting Gordie with each move. Arthur's palomino charger Goldbug stood a few feet away, placid as a sleepy plow horse, letting his groom scratch his neck. When Rafe entered the field, Sampson reared up on his hind legs, snorting fire, but Gordie hung on, even as his feet dangled and sparks showered down around him.

"Hey, whoa old boy. Easy there. What's wrong with you?" Rafe hooked his fingers through the underside of the bridle and pulled Sampson back to earth.

The horse stopped snorting and bashed his wide forehead against Rafe's shoulder, begging to be scratched.

"That horse is a spoiled brat—that's what's wrong with him," Arthur said for the hundredth time, as he strolled over to his own quiet mount. Rafe ignored him and spent a minute cooing and patting Sampson until the horse calmed.

"I've been trying to exercise him while you were gone, sir, really," Gordie said. "He didn't take to it well though. The stable master had to put him on the longe line and run him around, sir." The boy blushed and dropped his gaze toward the ground. "I couldn't stay on him. I'm sorry."

"No wonder he's so chippy, then," Rafe said. "You just hate the longe line, don't you? Yes, I know you do. It's okay, boy. I'll let you eat a stable hand later."

Sampson bobbled around like a colt and snorted happily. A few stray sparks fizzled in the grass at his feet.

Rafe gave Sampson one more pat and sprang into the saddle. "Thank you, Gordie. You can go off and get your lunch now."

"I'd rather stay and watch, if I can, sir."

"If you like, but don't be late to your own lessons."

"No sir." Gordie saluted and raced off the field to join a small cluster of squires at the fences.

Rafe braced his feet against the stirrups and stood up, breathing in the smell of the field. Grass in damp earth, pine groves in the far distance. Here the city sounds were muffled by the Palace walls. Grey mist rose on the river, and little gleams from the noonday sun struck off the silver armor of the men in front of him. Tack clinked as horses shifted.

He surveyed the men in front of him. No wonder the cheekier papers had started referring to the Household Guard as "Montblanc's House-boys." They were meant to be the best of the best—hardened veterans, utterly loyal to the king and the only ones in the larger Palace Guard trusted with access to the Household within the Palace. Application to the king's private guard unit was open to any man who could show the skill and a record of extraordinary military service. More than one noble house had its origins in a peasant who'd worked his way up through the ranks to the king's personal guard, but Michael had a lot of political friends and too many of their sons were showing up in the Palace's halls.

These days they looked more like a batch of dandies playing soldier at a fancy dress ball. Silver lace at their cuffs, more jewels in their hair than anyone with sense would wear to a hard day of field practice. And bells. Dammit. More than one of these popinjays had little silver bells on his thrice-damned tack. What did they think this was, a parade? Sampson shivered as Rafe's anger cooled the air around him. These "men" knew more about card parties and fashion than they did about dirtying their swords.

"Aren't they adorable?" Arthur said, easing Goldbug in next to Rafe. "Let's run them through the mud."

"Good idea." Rafe raised a gauntleted hand. "Company, form up! We'll start with a close quarters charge and regroup," he said, pointing down the field to the cluster of standing targets. "Flying V formation, then Double Round and repeat. Five times. Ready!"

He turned Sampson to be at the head of the charge.

"Steady!" He drew his sword. Behind him blades whispered as they slid out of their scabbards.

"On!" With a roar, he spurred Sampson.

The great horse, muscles bunching, leapt forward, all four feet off the ground. Men roared in answer behind him. Hooves pounded the turf. Horseflesh jostled as the wedge formed, a living, straining mass of teeth and hooves and muscle and weapons too tight for the enemy to splinter. He swung his blade, bright in the morning, and whooped.

The wedge of men hit the targets and split smoothly around them like a wave against a rock. Swords flashed. Bits of straw and padded dummy heads flew off even as they whirled into the retreat, back to the starting point and their formation.

"Again!" Rafe shouted. "For king and country!"

"For king and country!" the men behind him shouted as they plunged into the charge again. His muscles burned, the good old heat of work, a good horse under him, and a weapon in his hand.

He swung at a lance-bearing target, and his sword wedged hard in the wooden frame. He checked the reins, and Sampson whipped his head around, biting the offending warrior as Rafe yanked his sword out.

"Good boy, let's go." He turned into the mass of men, taking a place in the tail, but pushing Sampson to catch the leader and take back first place. The war horse dug in his feet and overtook the Houseboys, then Arthur on Goldbug.

But Arthur glanced at Rafe through the slit in his helmet and spurred Goldbug forward. Rafe gritted his teeth and bent low over Sampson's neck, racing for first. They pounded toward the far end of the field, so evenly matched their stirrups scraped. He spurred Sampson again. On the fences, squires and page boys whooped and cheered, shouting for their favorite.

They passed the starting mark neck and neck, charging straight toward the high fence rails. At the last second, Rafe peeled left, Arthur right, and they skimmed away, the horses' hooves scattering turf across the onlookers, who only cheered louder.

"Three more," Rafe shouted, his grin so wide it threatened to break his face in half, and the wedge formed up again. He gestured for Arthur to take the lead this time and rode at the rear so he could watch the rhythm of the charging men.

He had to rein Sampson back tight to keep the big horse from biting the horse in front of him out of pure spite at being last in anything. What he saw made him want to bite someone, too. The Houseboys held their formation well in the charge downfield, but the minute they hit the turn, the pattern fell apart. The retreat was meant to be a smooth, swirling interlace of horses to confuse and evade the pursuing enemy, not a chaotic rout.

"Keep your rhythm, men," he called just before one rider clipped another with his horse's shoulder, sending both horses off at an angle from the main group. Improperly balanced blades wobbled in men's hands. A few of the Houseboys were reining in, holding their horses back from a full-speed gallop so they could manage the abrupt turn at the end.

On the fences, the pages and squires were cheering, but Rafe wanted to clout half of the men around the head and shoulders with his gauntlet. His old drill master Brownie would be apoplectic at the sight.

"That could have gone better," he muttered as Arthur reined up next to him.

Arthur snorted. "Brownie would have them weeding the paddock on their hands and knees until dark for that mess."

It was a satisfying thought, but these were Michael's men. The harder he came down on them, the more Michael would find reason to complain about him to the king. Michael could always find something to complain about.

Rafe stood in the stirrup. "Gentlemen, as you know, these formations are crucial to the king's safety. There is a pattern for a reason."

Men shifted in their saddles. A few had the decency to look abashed, but most just scowled.

"Now, we are going to do that again. And again, until we all remember it. Company, form up!"

After an hour, Rafe dripped with sweat and panted hard. His sword arm trembled, and he lowered it, resting the sword across the saddle bow as he nudged Sampson into the briefing circle. As the horses formed a tight circle, heads inward, he pulled off his helmet and looked the men over. Sweat marked the horses' flanks, and a few of the men leaned back in their saddles. All were breathing hard, but their eyes were bright and they sat easily. Some of them were three times his age, but they weren't fully winded. He, on the other hand, could have happily rolled out of the saddle and slept on the wet grass. His bones ached.

"Good effort, men," he said. "Well done."

"Yes, well done all of you," Michael said from the field's entrance.

His tack jingling, he pranced his horse into the circle of men. Like Sampson, Michael's horse was all black. It was a decent enough horse for the job—if Michael hadn't felt the need to cover the animal in silk barding embroidered with his family crest and silver bells that jingled and jangled with every step.

"Though you lost ground on the final return, Rafe."

"Good of you to join us, Michael," Rafe said. "But this is lance practice, not parade drill."

Michael's eyes narrowed as he leaned forward toward Rafe. "I was leading charges while you were still in leading strings, little boy."

"The only thing you've lead in the last fifty years was the line to dinner," Rafe said. Before Michael could respond, he added, "Gentlemen, the king may not have traveled much in the last few years, but that's no reason for us to fall out of practice. We'll do the Center Man formation left round the field, past the pine spinney, and back. Who wants to attack?"

Arthur's hand went up with six others. "Right, you seven be our ambush." Rafe gestured them off toward the spinney. "The rest of you form up behind me."

Instead of moving back, Michael nudged his horse forward. "In light of his Majesty's instructions to you last night regarding your new role as heir, I think it might be to all our advantages to practice with you in the center instead of the vanguard. You should get used to letting us protect you."

The breeze drying the sweat on Rafe's brow went icy cold. But the men in the circle were nodding.

"Yes," Rafe said slowly. "You make a good point." Damn Michael to hell. The lowest hell where ash-grey demons could stab him with fiery pokers for days on end. "Let's go."

He slammed the helmet back on his head and sheathed his sword hard enough to make the scabbard bump against Sampson's side. As Arthur led his band of pretend ambushers away, Rafe let the remaining guard form up in a protective circle around him, the emptiness in the pit of his stomach only partly from hunger.

Chapter Nine

Deor finally laid her hand on the gate of faculty housing at twilight. The gate's magic tingled against her skin like static electricity, and she snatched her hand away. The jolt hadn't hurt—and the gate swung open at her touch—but the magic of Faerie crowded her, demanded her attention every second. Sure, the first breaths of it on her face had been glorious, but now it was like being out in the sun too long. The gate shut on its own behind her.

She dragged her suitcase over the rounded cobblestones that lined the street. From shoulders to waist, her back ached. A day traipsing hither and yon in heels left her feet screaming. At least here the houses were real houses, not dorms. Semi-detached, three-story brick townhouses lined the street, each with its own little garden front and back. Some gardens were just what she would have expected from trim English cottages, but others ran rampant or were all stones. In one, blue flames ran down the bowl of a fountain. From another, sweet smelling vines beckoned her, curling and stretching.

Number 405 Faculty Circle was a normal enough looking home, even if the front was dark. No reason to leave a light on since her housemate didn't know she was coming. She passed through the hedge lining the yard and walked up the stone path to the porch. She had been given a key, but it seemed rude to simply let herself into someone else's home. As she reached for the knocker, something in the yard on her left caught her eye. A small squirrel, no doubt out for a twilight snack, crept up near the porch and eyed her. With its deep brown eyes and mottled brown fur, it reminded her of the almost-tame squirrels she'd seen on campus back in Ohio.

"Hello there." Deor crouched down for a closer look. "You're a cute fell—"

The squirrel bunched up like it would spring, and then a blast of orange flame shot from its mouth.

Deor screamed and rocked backwards, landing on her ass. A small, charred patch of grass was all that remained as the squirrel scampered away up a tree in the yard.

"Fire breathing squirrels? Seriously?" she said to no one as she pushed herself to her feet and collected the stuff that had fallen out of her purse when she hit the ground. She was swinging the purse back over her shoulder when the door opened.

"Hello—" Deor started and stopped. At least it wasn't a squirrel. It was a dog. It looked like an Irish setter, except for the size. Standing on all fours, its head was as tall as her chest. It did not look happy to see her.

"Good evening," she started again. "Are you Penelope?"

The dog blinked at her.

"No," said a voice in the hall from behind the dog. The porch light clicked on. "I'm Penelope." She kneed the dog to the side. "This is Rufus."

"I'm Deor." She held out her hand. "That's a lovely dog you have there."

The dog snorted and Penelope scowled. "He's a wolf," she said. "From the Ireland pack."

"Oh! Sorry."

The apology seemed to satisfy Penelope for the moment, and she shook Deor's hand. "You're the new housemate?"

"I am." She grabbed the handle of her suitcase and followed Penelope and Rufus into the house, closing the door behind her.

"Your room is on the second floor," Penelope said pointing at a narrow staircase. "It'll be the one on the left. Third floor is my lab. Please take care not to disturb it. I have important work in there." She walked a few steps farther into the house. "Parlor's through there." She pointed to an open doorway on her right. "Kitchen is back through here." The dog gave her a short nod and disappeared into the kitchen.

"This is a lovely house," Deor said, for lack of anything else to say.

"It's faculty housing," Penny said. "It is sufficient."

"Sure. The life of the academic, right? All monastic—just a girl and her books and her wolf?"

A man stepped out from the kitchen. Tall, red haired. And entirely naked.

Deor jerked back, almost falling over her suitcase.

The man kissed Penelope on the cheek. "I'm off to bed now. You holler if you need anything, okay, Penny?"

"G'night, Rufus," she said, "I'll be up soon." As he stepped past her to the stairs, she gasped. "Rufus, really! Pants!"

He shrugged at her. "I'll wear them if you insist."

"I do," Penelope said. "Go on upstairs."

Deor watched him go until she realized she was staring.

"That was the wolf?" she asked.

Penelope sighed. "Werewolf," she said. "He's my paramour." She stared at Deor like she was daring her to say something, to ask question or make a joke. And, frankly, lots of jokes came to mind.

"He's handsome." Deor smiled. Fantastic. Not only did she have a roommate, she had two, and one of them didn't wear pants. If she caught him peeing on the carpet, she'd take a newspaper to him.

Penelope laughed, her face brightening and the sternness vanishing.

"He is, isn't he?" She sighed. "I'm sorry he was a bit rude." She waved at Deor's bags. "Why don't you leave those there and come on into the kitchen. Would you like some tea?"

"I would love some." Deor dropped her purse on her suitcase and followed the woman into the kitchen.

"Lights on," Penelope commanded as she walked into the kitchen. She went to the sink and filled an earthenware kettle with water, lit a burner, and set the water to boil. Now, in the light of the kitchen, Deor got a good look at her housemate. Penelope wore her dark, waist-length hair curled back from her face with little golden hair clips and braided down her back. Her dress was simpler than most of the women Deor had seen on the street, but still floor length. Her grandmother's training told Deor that this style was severe, not plain, and not poor quality. Tailored probably. Its deep green complemented her olive skin perfectly.

Penelope turned around and leaned back against the sink. "You can't be more than thirty." Penelope gave her a forced smile. "Why didn't they put you in student housing?"

"I'm not a student," Deor said. "I'm a professor. I'm working here while I research my family. I promise you, Lady Penelope, I won't be a problem."

"Of course. I'm sorry." The woman seemed to relax a bit. "Call me Penny, please." She gestured to a large earthenware pot on the stove near the kettle. "There's some stew if you would like some."

"I'd love some," Deor said and took a bowl from her. "I haven't eaten since breakfast."

"Help yourself."

Deor scooped out some stew and sat at the table. "So, are you a werewolf, too?"

The hard look returned to Penny's eyes. "We Irish aren't all werepeople and pookas, you know. I'm as much a faerie as you."

"I'm not much of a faerie." Deor shrugged and made herself smile. "No offense meant. I grew up in the human world, so I have no idea who or what I'm dealing with yet."

Penny thought about that for a moment, finally sitting down across from Deor. "I'm down here doing my post-doc study in bimorphic medicine. Most of the time I'm in the dissecting room at the college of healers, but I've done some work with the authorities on criminal cases. You?"

"I teach Shakespeare. He's a human author."

Deor took a bite of the stew, and the same flash of pleasure that had followed her first bite at the cafe hit her again. The stew was warm and thick with tangy, slightly salty gravy, crisp, bright vegetables, and chunks of savory meat that fell apart in her mouth. "This is amazing."

"It's nothing. Just throw the stuff in the pot in the morning and eat it in the evening. So you're a changeling?"

"Yes. My mother raised me in the human world. I've come back to see what the Winter Court is like." She rubbed the nape of her neck. She didn't want to go over the whole sordid tale of her mother's affair again, but the truth seemed better than lying. "My mother died when I was a child, and I never met my faerie father. I've come here to look for him because I think there's something wrong with me—I mean medically, with magic and stuff."

"You picked quite the time to come," Penny said.

"So I've heard. The people at immigration said stuff was political?"

"You could say that." The kettle whistled and Penny made the tea. "It is the most significant event in the Winter Court since the king's marriage nearly five centuries ago. Every monarch in the history of the Winter Court—in all of Faerie, actually—has had a child of their own body as heir. Now, for the first time, the king is adopting. It's unprecedented. Not to mention the level of magic involved in systematically rewriting Lord Farringdon's genetic structure so that he's literally a member of the Aethelwing line."

So the general was the heir. No wonder he and his captain were so testy about some "girl claiming to be the king's daughter."

"The king can't have children?" Deor asked as she took a sip of tea.

"No." Penny shook her head. "He's been wasting away for years. His weakness is our weakness. The kingdom is sick."

"That's very sad…" Deor said, imagining what her mother's illness would have been like on a national scale. "So this adopting an heir? Everyone thinks that will help him get better?"

"We hope so," she added. "It should matter to you, too. He's your king as well."

"No," Deor said. "I'm an American; we don't do kings. Plus, I'm just visiting."

"Of course." Penny stood up and picked up their bowls. "I could talk your ear off about the Adoption—the medical aspect fascinates me, of course. Thanks to Rufus, I'll get to attend the last ceremony, though he gets to attend them all. He's the son of the Ireland pack's alpha. He'll be alpha one day, and this is a diplomatic practice run." She smiled. "He's not always as diplomatic as he could be."

"I did see that." A blush crept up Deor's cheeks. "I wasn't trying to see it. I mean…"

Penny laughed. "They have a very different relationship to clothing. They consider it far more optional than faeries do."

"Do you want me to do the dishes?" Deor finished the last of the tea. "I'm happy to help clean up."

"Oh, no. That's fine." Penny put the dirty dishes back into the cupboard and closed the door. Before Deor could think of something to say, Penny opened the cupboard again and pulled one of the bowls out. "All clean," she said. "Magic."

"Awesome. I'd have killed for one of those in grad school."

"It's a convenience," Penny agreed. "It is getting late, and I should let you get to bed. Do you want help with your things?"

"No, thanks." Deor stood. "I can get it. Have a good night."

Supper had cheered her, but her back still ached as she dragged her luggage up the stairs. Though a bit small, her bedroom had a large window and a wardrobe, a chest of drawers, and a desk. All in all, not bad. She sat down on the bed. Sheets had been provided, and a pillow, but the bed was unmade, the linens folded neatly in a stack at the foot. As she made her bed up for the night, she heard the sounds of Penny and Rufus chatting—though she couldn't quite make out what they were saying, which was probably for the best, she did think she heard her name.

She sat down on her newly-made bed and pulled her purse onto her lap. She'd worry about the rest of the unpacking later. She examined the mirror that the captain had given her at immigration. It looked very much like a regular compact, something she would keep in her purse, except the case was wood instead of plastic. Besides functioning as her ID and bank card, she could use it to speak to anyone else with a mirror, according to the captain.

She opened it and touched the glass. Her name came up, along with a picture the captain had taken without telling her. It looked pretty much like every DMV photo she'd ever taken. She poked the glass and information scrolled by. Her new address. Her appointment at the university. Her bank account balance. All perfectly normal, working just like he said it would.

She closed it and let it rest in her palm. A second later, her hand began to tingle again as the magic from the mirror rubbed against her skin. She poked and prodded, until her finger caught a small bump on the compact's smooth back. She picked at it, like she would a small knot, until a thread appeared. A crisscross of magic lines came into view. Whatever magic it was, she got the sense it was meant to be hidden. She tugged on another thread and it snapped back into place when she let it go.

Leave it alone, she thought to herself. *It's probably what makes it work, and if you break it, you'll have to go back to the captain to get it fixed.*

She set it down on the bed next to her and kicked off her shoes.

"Nope." She couldn't let it go.

She picked it up again, tugging and pulling at the irritating threads until they loosened. She wedged her index finger under one thread and jerked up. With a small *twang* the thread snapped and the rest popped off like elastic bands. She brushed the few remaining threads away.

"I hope that wasn't important," she said. When she checked the mirror, it still worked and showed all her information.

She scooped up some of the magical threads and rolled them between her fingers. What little magic they had left chafed. When she held the mirror in her other hand, no magic pricked at her. Whatever it had been, and whatever its purpose, the spell was broken now.

She set the mirror aside, unpacked a few things, and gathered up her belongings for class tomorrow.

Chapter Ten

The next morning, the sun shone, the air was bright and crisp. Deor shivered in the autumn chill even as she enjoyed the sunshine. If the Winter Court was this cold in the first week of September, she didn't want to stay through December.

As she walked through campus housing on the way to her office, the confused parents had been replaced by students rushing to class. They ran the gamut from small to huge, from midnight black to so pale that veins showed through their skin, with a whole rainbow in between.

A shaggy golden dog bolted past her up the path, pack strapped to its back. He reached the steps of a building and leaped toward the porch, hair receding, limbs stretching and cracking, and landed as a tall, blond man, naked but for the backpack. The other guys on the porch simply waved or raised beer glasses in greeting.

She trudged up to the fifth floor of the Literary Arts building and found her office, five hundred fifty-five. Its door swung open in a smooth, squeakless glide. Heavy, brown wool curtains hung over ceiling-high windows. She dragged back the curtains, flooding the room with light. Five file cabinets had been built in under the windowsill. Each window was set far back, with a ledge deep enough to sit on.

The windows had no glass. After the incident in Ama's office, she recognized the taut, saran wrap-like magic that glittered like a silver cobweb. She traced her finger along the copper glow edging the window, feeling for a latch. No such luck. The magic broke under her touch.

"Shit," she said as a cool breeze came through. Small bits of magic clung to her finger, and she flicked them off, no idea how to fix the spell.

The wall behind the desk was a single, massive, built-in bookshelf, and the shelf immediately behind the desk formed a small table. Two chairs stood ready for visitors, and on the opposite wall, two ceiling-high cabinets made of wood framed a large mirror above a fireplace. In the light from the window, dust motes swirled in the air. On her desk was her office key, a box of stationery supplies, and a stack of papers with a note. *Deor: Here is our Employee Handbook. If you need anything, PhiPhi will assist you. Ama.*

She put the handbook on the shelf behind her and put away the office supplies after spending too much time playing with a stapler that used small winding threads of magic rather than metal brads. She scanned the class rosters, mentally practicing student names. In the human world, first day nerves had made her mispronounce names like Jim and Annabelle. She didn't have a chance in hell with Gwybbllwyx.

She settled into her chair, her first moment of peace since she had boarded the ferry. Tears welled, blurring the names on the roster. She should be organizing her office and reviewing her roster in North Carolina at her tenure-track, full-salary job—there had been twenty tenure track jobs in the world and five hundred applicants for every single one. She would never get another opportunity like that again.

She snorted at her weakness and forced herself to concentrate on the syllabus. She put a red line under the "clothing is REQUIRED" clause.

Ama had given two or three class periods to discuss each play, complete with dates. "Week One: First Day of Class and the first two acts of *Midsummer Night's Dream.*"

"Let's see what the textbook says."

On the first page, it became clear that this book had been compiled by a faerie. The introduction spoke of the "brief reign of Elizabeth the First," and the "even shorter life of the poet and playwright" contributing to the melancholy tone of many of the plays, especially the later ones.

She turned to Ama's lecture and found it similarly confused about human culture. Ama indicated that Shakespeare had "likely never met faeries," given his characterization of Puck as whimsical rather than psychotic, and remarked on the "high number of children—three—" Shakespeare had.

Deor grabbed a brass-nibbed pen and a blank journal and began to scribble her own lecture, referring to the text for dates, but little else. She started with a discussion of London itself, of humans and their lives, before moving to the specifics of Renaissance England. Hopefully some of her students had been out of Faerie. As she wrapped up the lecture and opened the textbook to begin rereading *Midsummer*, someone knocked at her door.

"Come in!" Deor called from her desk.

As the man stepped in the room, Deor choked back a laugh. He was in heavy black motorcycle leathers, right down to the steel-toed boots. His ruddy complexion suggested Eastern European heritage, and the chest hair poking out of his black v-neck shirt made him look like a movie thug. His walnut-colored braid fell halfway down his back.

It would have been an elaborate joke, a play on an early nineties Hollywood vampire, except for the very real fangs visible in his mouth. And his eyes. Cold and haughty, the brown irises were ringed with black. He took in the room and settled his gaze on her. She put on a professorial smile.

"And who might you be?"

Instead of answering her, he stepped to one side of the door and jerked his head at someone outside. "It's clear."

A tall, pale green man, his angular face topped by a halo of golden waves, entered. As he smiled and said something in a foreign language, Deor gasped. His hair contrasted rather prettily with his skin, but his grin made her think of things hiding under the bed. He had more teeth than a humanoid mouth ought to hold, each more pointed that normal. And his eyes were golden with slit pupils, like a cat's.

"I'm sorry," she said forcing herself to smile again. "I don't speak that language. Can I help you?"

"My apologies," he said, switching to English. He bowed slightly. "I am Geoff, Professor Smithfield's new TA. Is she in? I was hoping to catch her before class."

He dropped into one of the chairs across from her desk and lounged, almost posed. His black robes fell open to reveal clothes that didn't scream expensive; they murmured it in cultured undertones. His brown linen pants, ironed to a razor line in the front, draped precisely over the instep of his supple leather shoes. His crisp, button-down shirt had to have been tailored—probably handmade.

She glanced down at her own jeans and simple blouse. No wonder Ama demanded she get academic robes. If the graduate TA was dressing that well, she was in serious trouble.

She cocked one eyebrow at him. "Yeah, she's around." Playing with a grad student was cruel, but this guy needed to be knocked down a peg or twelve.

"What about you? Who are you, you naughty girl, sitting behind the professor's desk?" He grinned again, and the too many teeth sent the *Jaws* theme running through her head.

Naughty girl? Oh *hell* no.

"I'm Deor."

"After the Anglo Saxon poet? You certainly don't look like a man."

"I don't look like a lot of things," she said.

He laughed, and it danced through the room, tempting her to join him, promising whimsy and delight, and underneath, the whisper of hysteria.

"What do you study here?" he said. "Need any tutoring?"

"I think not." Whatever game he wanted to play had to end here, or it would look too much like flirting. Even though he looked like a lot of fun. She stood and held out her hand. "I'm Professor Smithfield."

"Are you, now?" Geoff stood and shook her hand, cackling and throwing his head back. "Professor Smithfield," he smirked, all teeth again. "You almost had me there. You're what? Barely thirty? And what professor wears"—he waved a dismissive hand at her general attire—"that sort of thing? Aren't those pants used for heavy work in the human world?"

"Denim is acceptable for all sorts of things," she snapped. This too young to be a professor crap was getting old, fast. "I got my Ph.D. in the spring, from *the* Ohio State University in the United States."

"You're serious?" Geoff's cheery expression vanished and he studied her face for a moment. "I thought you were a faerie," he said. "You're a human?"

"Changeling." She waited for whatever insult came next.

His eyes narrowed, and a small frown curled his mouth as he tilted his head, eyeing her up at down. After a second, he seemed satisfied and his smile popped back.

"My sincere apologies, Professor Smithfield." He gave another bow, slightly exaggerated.

When no snicker or snort came, she took a deep breath and shoved down her defensiveness.

"Apology accepted. Several people have made the same mistake. Have a seat."

He sat.

"Now, explain to me who your leather-clad friend is."

Geoff waved a lazy hand. "He's with me."

"If he's your boyfriend, why don't you introduce him?"

The vampire stiffened and narrowed his eyes at her, but Geoff guffawed again.

"No, no, he's my bodyguard. My father insists on it."

Deor raised an eyebrow at Geoff and shifted her gaze to his vampire until Geoff began to shift in his seat.

"And who is your daddy, exactly?" she said. Nefasta's condition that the TA could not be fired began to make a horrible sort of sense.

Geoff coughed as if embarrassed to admit it and said, "My father is Gregory, King of the Goblins."

"Ah." Deor shuffled the papers on the desk. Of course she couldn't fire him. He was a prince. And a goblin—that might explain the teeth. "But I still don't know his name," she said, "unless he simply goes by 'bodyguard'?"

The vampire bowed. "Vlad Drogos Rodzevrah. But everyone here calls me Donovan." His voice was like the gravelly purr of some big cat.

"Why Donovan?" She stood and extended her hand to him, and he shook it. "Never mind, forget I asked. It's nice to meet you."

His grip was firm, not too tight, and certainly not painful. The grip of a man who didn't need to demonstrate his strength. She took her hand back and gestured at the other empty chair.

"So," she said, sitting back down, "why don't we go over what I expect?" She handed them both copies of the syllabus.

Geoff nodded and scanned the first page of the syllabus.

Donavan let his lie on the desk.

"You'll need to keep up with the reading, help me with grading, keep office hours, and help students with papers."

"I can do that," Geoff said.

"Good. And one more thing. I will be asking you to do some readings aloud in class. Shakespeare should be experienced in performance. Can you handle that?"

"I'd love to. If you like, I could perform some scenes together with you. Perhaps something romantic?"

The giggle sprang back in her chest, and he caught her eye, a grin spreading across his face again. She swallowed hard.

"You'll need to sit in on both of my classes, so the second lecture of the day will probably be a bit of a bore, but I'm sure you'll survive."

"Certainly." He stood and nudged his bodyguard. "Come on. Let's get out of the nice professor's way. See you in class." He winked at her, and a blush began to creep its way up from her throat to her cheeks.

The door closed behind them, and she fanned herself with a copy of the syllabus. "Get a grip for God's sake. He's a student, a prince, and a serious distraction."

Whatever she was feeling was magical. The moment he left, the desire to giggle and get into trouble vanished.

Then again, a prince would have connections, would know people. Maybe having him as a TA would be bonus after all.

At five minutes to the hour, she gathered her things and paused to touch up her face in the mirror. Her eyes were iron grey—unusual for her. Normally they were much softer and only turned harsh when she was angry. She shook her hair out of her eyes, and a small shower of sparks flew away from her. She sighed and waved them away.

Donovan and Geoff were just arriving at the third floor lecture hall as she did.

"Hello again," she said, walking straight through the door as Donovan pulled it open for Geoff.

She set her books down on a lectern at the front of the four-tiered hall. Students already filled the room almost to capacity. Donovan and Geoff took a seat in the far right of the front row where Ama was already seated, a slate on the table in front of her, stylus poised.

Deor cleared her throat. "Good morning class, and welcome to Shake-speare. As many of you have noticed, I am not Bard Nefasta. I am Professor Smithfield." She turned and wrote her name on the board behind the lectern. "I'll be teaching Shakespeare this semester."

She stepped up to the lectern and found, even in heels, she needed the stool tucked under it. She tugged it out with her foot and stepped up.

"Why don't we start with the roll?"

From the back of the room, a few students outright laughed.

"Where's the real bard, sweetheart?" a rather green student yelled.

"I am the real professor." Deor stared at him, and the laughter died on his lips. "Anyone else have any questions?" When no one responded, she continued. "My specialty is medieval human literature, and I received my Ph.D. from an American university in Ohio. Have any of you heard of that?"

Students stared back and forth at each other mostly shaking their heads.

"Is that in the United States?" a familiar young woman in the fourth row asked.

"Robbie, right?" Deor said. "Good to see you again."

Robbie gave her a little wave and students turned to see who among them knew this strange new professor.

"Yes," she said, nodding. "Ohio is in America, across the Atlantic." At their blank stares, she added, "It's a human country."

The class rustled with hushed conversation, enough that Donovan moved from his slouch and scanned the room before settling back down again.

"Now, I am going to take roll while my teaching assistant, Geoffrey, passes out the syllabus."

Geoff dutifully rose and took the stack of papers from her.

She read the roll, full of ordinary enough names like William and Aidan, but also Lignite, Moss, Saxifrage, Zephyr, and Guthgar, not to mention Wham, Bam, Blurt, and Smacko. This last set belonged to the cluster of petite, cotton-haired students. The tiniest of the group, when answering to "Deidre," apologetically explained that her parents liked human names. There were also a few who resembled Donovan in fangs and fashion choices.

"Now that we've gotten the housekeeping taken care of," she said, "let's get to the good stuff." She pulled out her textbook. She flipped a few pages in her text, saying, "Page one thousand sixty-six."

She waited a second for the page rustling to die down, sneaking a glance at Ama as she did so. The woman wore her robes today, but the bun and the expression were as severe as ever.

Deor took a deep breath and read, "Doubt thou the stars are fire. Doubt that the sun doth move. Doubt truth to be a liar. But never doubt I love." The class watched her intently. "This is just one passage—just four lines—from Shakespeare. And in those four lines we see why, nearly four hundred years after his death, we in the human world still read, perform, and watch his plays, and believe him to be one of the greatest authors of all time.

"Now if you'll turn in your syllabus to the daily schedule, you'll see we're going to start *A Midsummer Night's Dream*, which is about faeries. If you stick with me through the semester, we'll end with *Hamlet*, Shakespeare's great masterpiece and the play from which I read."

She shut the textbook and set it aside. "How many of you have never been in the human world?" About half the class raised their hands. "Okay, keep your hands up. How many of you have rarely been?" About forty percent more raised their hands. "That's what I expected." She flipped to the daily schedule. "The schedule says that we've got to start *Midsummer* next class, so take out your notebooks, and we'll lay down some basic context for the play."

She gave her brief lecture on Shakespeare's life and times, along with some details of human technology and politics. "Alright, that does it for today. Have a good rest of the day, and I look forward to Thursday."

The class gathered their books and made for the door *en masse*.

Geoff and Donovan took their time, with Geoff lounging by the window watching her watch her students go.

Ama didn't move at all except to close her textbook and make a few notes.

"Professor Smithfield?" Robbie asked, coming up to the lectern. Her smattering of freckles still dotted her face, the only freckles Deor had seen in the Winter Court. Her golden hair was pulled back and held in place with a plastic hair clip.

"Hello," Deor said. "What can I do for you?"

"I just wanted to say 'hi' again. I didn't know you were going to be my professor. I hope I wasn't rude to you on the ferry. You know, offering to help."

"Not at all," Deor said. "I appreciated the offer."

Robbie didn't need to know she'd had no plans to work here either.

"Since you're an American, can we talk about democracy and how Parliaments work in the human world this semester?" Robbie said. "I was hoping for an American literature class, but this was the only human lit they had. I wish that the Winter Court had a House of Commons—"

"Yeah," a young man standing next to her cut her off. He had skin the color of a plum and raven hair that shot up in short, spiky points. "Robbie's told us stories about humans. Is it true you fired your king?"

"Um," Deor said glancing past the students to Ama, who watched intently, a small smile curling the edges of her lips. "Sort of," she said, looking at the young man again. "It was more like a complicated break up."

"There was a revolution!" His eyes were bright, and he quivered with excitement. "I was at the marketplace yesterday," he added.

"Oh?" Deor said.

"I was there when the Sword came and shut down our demonstration."

"He stopped a peaceful protest?" Somehow, she wasn't surprised.

"Not exactly," a different student, a girl with pale pink skin and deep red hair interrupted. "He dispersed it before it could turn into a riot," she said. Her eyes took on a dreamy gaze. "But he told the people he'd take their message to the king and make sure the commoners were heard." She sighed, and Deor barely kept from rolling her eyes.

"Did he actually do it?" Deor asked.

"He wouldn't lie. He never lies," Robbie said quickly. She grimaced. "But who knows what the king will say."

Behind the students, Ama was tapping her feet. She arched an eyebrow at Deor.

"Why don't you guys see if the library has human authors," Deor said. "Try Alexis de Toqueville's *Democracy in America*, and we'll chat later. I need to speak to Bard Nefasta, but you can always come by my office hours."

"Okay," Robbie said for her friends. "Thanks." She grabbed the boy's arm and led him from the classroom.

"Wow," Deor said to Ama as the door shut behind the students. "They're avid."

"It's a passing fashion."

96

"You don't agree with representative government?" Deor strove for a neutral tone and failed.

"There is no Winter Court without its monarch," Ama said as though that settled the matter. "Overall, a reasonable first day performance, though I notice you didn't use the material I provided you. That smart-mouthed boy at the start of class was just the beginning. Unless you can command their respect and attention, you'll be useless here." She waved her stylus at Deor's jeans. "And this? Not acceptable."

"I'll get academic robes before the next class."

"Good. Then I will see you on Thursday."

Deor breathed a sigh of relief that Ama didn't seem to notice. She gave a little wave, like an idiot beauty queen on a float, and smiled painfully until Ama was out the door.

When she was gone, Deor looked at Geoff and Donovan. "Stayed for the whole show, then?"

Geoff laughed. "There's another one at one o'clock, right?"

"Absolutely. So, how'd I do?"

"Honestly," Geoff said, a serious expression crossing his face for once, "I thought they'd be a lot harder on you."

"You're a novelty," Donovan said, eyeing her. "It'll wear off."

She pulled out a blank sheet of paper and wrote Lord Farringdon's name on it.

"Here." She handed it to Donovan. "You've got questions about me, go see him. He's the one who gave me my visa. I'm sure he'll have loads of stuff to say. Now if you'll excuse me, gentlemen, I'm going to find lunch. I'll see you in an hour or so."

She gave Geoff a companionable grin and strode out of the class, despite a strong urge not to turn her back on either of them.

Chapter Eleven

None of it made sense. Rafe drummed his fingers on the broad table where papers lay dealt out like playing cards. His opponents were invisible and unknown, but the stakes were clear —five separate changeling girls, all in their late twenties, had been attacked. Others were sure to follow. Who would be next and where and when—that he couldn't say.

He ran his fingers from one page to the next. Victim statements. Healers' reports. A map of times and locations where attacks had occurred, overlaid with the addresses of known changeling women and girls.

There had to be a pattern in all of it. Something that would tell him why someone was grabbing changelings and wiping short pieces of their memories. He picked up a piece of mirrored glass no bigger than an inch on each side and touched it to the frame of larger mirror on his wall.

A young woman appeared, a memory embedded in glass. The girl's long, curling hair hung all around her face and shoulders like a curtain. Lady Penelope's back was to the recording mirror as she held the girl's hands in her own. Rafe had watched this interview a dozen times, but he studied it again hoping for new insight.

"I'd like to try something a little different," Lady Penelope said. "May I touch your mind?"

The girl trembled, but she nodded and closed her eyes, bracing herself.

"This shouldn't hurt," Lady Penelope said. "Let me know if you feel any pain."

The girl nodded but kept her eyes closed as the healing magic flowed from Lady Penelope's hands. Rafe recognized the tints of consensual will magic even though he couldn't have managed the spell's full details. Most healers weren't licensed to use that kind of magic on patients—the potential for damage was just too high. As the spell spread over the girl, some color returned to her cheeks.

"You're free to talk," Lady Penelope said. "Go ahead when you want to. Tell us what you're seeing. Tell us what happened to the girl when she went riding."

"She went riding." It was a clever spell, letting the victim detach and temporarily become a witness to events instead of a participant. Arthur and Lady Penelope had worked it out together, modifying and refining an old dream spell used by healers on men suffering battle fatigue.

"Yes," Lady Penelope said.

"It was a damp day." The girl paused. "The horse threw her."

"Do you know why?"

"She bumped her head. She can't remember because she bumped her head."

The medical report said the girl had no physical injuries or signs of a fall. She had simply returned home an hour late, claiming her horse had stumbled and thrown her. If it weren't for a sharp-eyed and sharper-tongued groom protesting that the horse was as sound as a nut and the girl must be lying to cover up some misdeed, no one in the family would have thought to question it, let alone contact the Civil Patrol for help.

"Did you see her bump her head?" Lady Penelope kept her voice carefully neutral, avoiding implanting a story on the girl's mind.

"Yes. That's what they told me I... she... I saw."

"Who told you that?"

"The man by the tree. He grabbed her bridle and..." The girl's eyes flew open, pupils dilated as she clawed at her own throat, her breath ragged. Air whistled in her constricting throat.

Lady Penelope seized the girl's wrists, pulling them away. The spell disappeared. An air spell pushed into the girl's mouth and nose. A flurry of skirts blocked the recording mirror as someone unseen shouted for help.

Sighing, Rafe pulled the mirror chip away from the large mirror and tossed it back onto the table. He knew the rest—the girl's mother and step-father shouting at Lady Penelope to get out while a footman carried the unconscious girl out of the room. They were getting nowhere.

He planted his palms on the table and surveyed it as if it were a tactical map and he were planning a military campaign. There were too many gaps in the line—that was the problem—too many places the enemy could slip through undetected.

He couldn't put a hidden guard on every changeling around age thirty —there were just too many of them, especially in the last twenty odd years. He'd known fertility numbers had declined with the king's health, but he'd never imagined how many Winter Court faeries, men and women, had gone into the human world seeking child bearers until this changeling crisis had erupted.

Absentmindedly, Rafe dipped a finger in a nearby water glass and drew on the table with damp fingers. His magic froze the water into ferns and crystal roses as he doodled, trying to find new ideas. Whoever was working those will spells was not only a magic user of incredible power, but a genius. Most types of Will Magic required the caster's continued presence or at least some enspelled object to work for long. Abused spouses often carried a jewel of some sort tucked into their hair or dangling on a chain under their clothes. Remove the spell source and the spell's power disappeared, even if the damage did not.

These poor girls—their mental blocks were invisible and buried so deep in the victim's psyche that even he, Arthur, and Lady Penelope together couldn't find a way to fully reverse them. None of the girls bore signs of a physical assault. None had been robbed. All had simply disappeared for an hour or more and then just reappeared—some more disheveled and confused than others—with a powerful magic compulsion to not talk about where they had been.

Arthur was right. They needed a changeling they could use as bait. And even then they had no idea where to dangle that bait or what would happen to the bait once it was taken. *She*—once *she* was taken.

Even if Robbie weren't too well known to make an effective decoy, putting her in danger was out of the question. He certainly couldn't ask it of any other family in the kingdom.

"It's not happening," he said aloud.

"Oh, but it is," Arthur said, from the doorway.

Rafe jumped, startled out of his thoughts.

"Or did you mean something other than the announcement?" Arthur went on. "Because that is happening in the next ten minutes. The Princess Consort hinted that you seemed distracted at breakfast, so I came to fetch you."

Rafe shook his head, clearing the cobwebs. "Of course. How stupid of me. I forgot the time." He brushed his fingers over the table, gathering all the ice back into a liquid ball that spun in his hand. "Here, Sam, catch." He tossed the ball, and the dog leapt from the hearth rug to snatch it out of the air. Half the water sprayed across Jake, who snapped at the droplets as if they were flies.

On the dais beside the throne, Rafe stood with his feet braced and his hands resting on the hilt of the Sword of State. Used only on the most solemn occasions such as the dubbing of new knights and the execution of traitors, it stood upright before him on its point, a small piece of felt keeping the tip from scraping the stone. Only the king, his heir, or the Sword of Peace and Justice himself could touch the Sword of State. The magics woven into the blade would kill anyone else. It was a not so subtle reminder of the king's power to execute those who opposed him, even as he made a concession to the protestors.

"Are your majesties ready?" the Master of Ceremonies called. He peered out from behind the giant mirror that had been brought into the throne room. Finn was already seated. To the right of the throne, Astarte stood, one hand on Finn's shoulder. The faint golden light that she gave off warmed Finn's face.

"We are ready," Finn said.

The mirror's silver surface rippled and went black. Every enchanted mirror in the country would be dissolving into a view of the throne room at the same time.

From behind the mirror, a herald called, "Hear ye, hear ye. Be upstanding for his Majesty, Sweordmund VIII of the House of Aethelwing. His Majesty speaks."

Rafe straightened his shoulders, locking his eyes on the mirror.

"My beloved people," Finn said. "Do not be alarmed. Today, I bring you happy news. We have heard your petitions and your fears regarding this Adoption. At the urging of our beloved son and chosen heir, we have decided to grant the Common's request. To that end, the Master of the City of London will bring with him three guildmasters to witness the final three ceremonies in this hall."

Rafe imagined eminent men and women across London hurling themselves at their stationery. The Master of the City's desk would be snowed under by the end of the day.

"Moreover, we have decided," Finn continued, "to allow the remaining three ceremonies to be witnessed throughout the country by mirror. Let the Winter Court see, let the entire world see the making of an heir."

Years of stone-faced parade drill practice kept Rafe from snickering at that. But only just.

"Then you will know that this kingdom is secure, now and to the next generation." Finn lifted his hand in blessing. "Be well, my people."

The mirror rippled and the reflection returned.

Finn slumped back against the throne, panting.

"Are you well, darling?" Astarte asked.

He took her hand and kissed it. "Quite well." He got to his feet, offering her his arm. "Better than I have been in some time."

As the two of them walked away, Astarte looked over her shoulder. "Are you joining us for lunch today, Rafe?"

"Yes, Mother. Just as soon as I put this monster away." Rafe sheathed the Sword of State and headed for the armory, whistling a marching tune as he went.

Chapter Twelve

Deor sighed and chose another robe off the rack of gently used academic gowns, pulling it on over her head. The fabric puddled around her feet. At least this one seemed broad enough in the chest and hips to fit her. In nearby aisles, a few students, mostly pixies, giggled and shuffled through the racks of used human clothes. She shook out the giant, bell-shaped sleeves trying to find her hands. The robe smelled faintly of wet dog. At least Penny could probably help her with that.

"Finding anything, dear?" The dwarf woman who ran the shop came over. Her head didn't clear the top of the rack.

"I don't suppose you sell safety pins?" Deor said. She'd need to pin up at least ten inches of fabric if she was going to walk in this, even in her highest heels. Or maybe she could just borrow some scissors and hack off the extra.

"You mean human pins? No, I'm sorry. Those are contraband. Sometimes we find them in clothes from the human world, but we have to turn them over to the civil patrol."

The woman rubbed the black cloth between her fingers. "This one's in lovely shape. Summer weight woolsey-linsey's very hard wearing. I can let you have it for a hundred and fifty crowns. You'll need a hood, too. I think I found one we can cut down a bit for you. Hemming is extra."

A hundred and fifty crowns—she tried to calculate the exchange rate in her head. That was… worth five nights in the hotel she'd stayed at? She still wasn't sure how to check the balance of money on her mirror yet. She sighed. It didn't matter. No robe, no job. No job, no visa.

"Okay. I guess this will work."

"Wonderful dear. I won't be a minute." The dwarf woman whipped out a piece of chalk, slashed it across Deor's ankles, and had the robe off Deor's shoulders before she could answer.

"Thank you!" Deor called after her.

She stuffed her hands in her pockets, jiggling the rattle, and looked around her, disconsolate. She should be out there looking for her father, starting with the rattle maker. Instead, she was stuck here cooling her heels with thrift shopping undergrads. A few rows away, a faerie boy about ten was arguing with his mother about trying on a sweater. Some pixie girls were *oohing* and *aaahing* over a pair of very hard used Doc Martins that would have fit two of their feet per boot.

She wandered toward the door and almost bumped into Robbie coming in.

"Oh. It's you! I mean, hello, Professor. How are you? What are you doing here?"

"Shopping," Deor said. "They aren't paying me enough to justify buying brand new robes, so I came here. How about you?"

"I'm just here to poke around. My brother says it's pretentious slumming, but I kind of like it in here. They have a good used book section in the back. And my human father has been teaching me about budgets. You know, how to manage your own money? I, uh, tend to use up my allowance before the end of the month." She blushed. "I don't like to ask for more."

"Oh. Yes, that's a useful skill to have." What were faerie families like that a twenty-nine year-old woman would have an allowance but no idea how to manage it? On the other hand, who was she to throw stones? She'd been pissed off and confused when she realized that making only the minimum payments on her first credit card wasn't ever going to pay off the balance. Of course she'd been twenty-two at the time. She shook off the recollection.

"It was nice to see you in class," she said. No need to mention that calling Robbie and asking to crash on her floor had been one of her more desperate options had she not been able to find a job.

"Oh yes!" Robbie lit up, hands pressed together in excitement. "I was so disappointed when I found out the human professor wasn't teaching the class that I almost dropped it. At least now it's being taught by someone who's been in the human world."

Deor smiled. There was something about Robbie so earnest—no, naive—but still willing to try hard. Deor wanted to hug her. And pick her brains, mercenary as that sounded even to her own ears. Robbie clearly wanted to talk to her. It wouldn't hurt to ask her a few questions in the process about how the faerie world worked.

"Why don't you come to my office hours?" she said. "We can chat. I bet your human experience will give you interesting ways to read the texts."

"I'd love that. Thank you! When are your hours again?'

Before Deor could answer, her pocket trumpeted a royal salute. So did Robbie's. All around the shop people pulled out their mirrors so, after a second of confused looking around, did Deor. It had gone black. She poked at the surface.

A voice, repeated in stereo around the shop wherever people held mirrors in their hands, said, "Hear ye, hear ye. Be upstanding for his Majesty, Sweordmund VIII of the House of Aethelwing. His Majesty speaks."

"What the…"

The blackness cleared. A pale man in black, his body swathed in black and silver-grey furs sat on a throne. To one side, her hand resting on the man's shoulder stood a tall blonde woman with golden skin. Her translucent wings moved in a soft, breathing rhythm, scattering gold tinted rainbows across the grey stone and the ice pale man sitting on it.

"Mother?" Robbie said in a confused voice, but the king on the throne spoke.

"My beloved people. Do not be alarmed."

From the reactions around the shop, this did nothing to un-alarm people. Gasps and squeaks of "it's the *king!*" and "oh mercy, let it not be another war" sounded around the shop.

The king went on speaking, explaining the plan to broadcast the Adoption ceremonies. On his right, Lord Farringdon stared straight ahead, his hands on the hilt of the giant phallic symbol. Deor couldn't help a snicker. Still, he did look sexy in a stern, statuesque sort of way.

When the king finished the shop was silent. No one spoke. The woman with the son who hated itchy sweaters was wiping her eyes.

Robbie burst into a high-pitched squeal and danced around, hugging her mirror. "He did it! He kept his promise! I can't believe it. I have to call Aiden and Roseleaf and... No, I have to call Mother first, she'll know what happened. No! She's probably still with him. I'll call Aiden."

Robbie's fingers shook so hard the mirror bobbled out of her hand. Deor scooped it out of the air before it could shatter on the floor. She put a hand on Robbie's shoulder as she handed back the mirror.

"Take a deep breath, honey. Why don't we go sit down before you call anyone?" She led Robbie over to a set of mismatched chairs in the window. "So this is big, huh?"

"So big. You don't know. So huge!"

"So... the king is your stepfather? And he made you a promise?" Deor asked, fitting pieces together at last.

"No! He'd never let himself be called that." Robbie shook her head hard, and the puzzle pieces fell apart again. "I'm not even allowed on the Palace grounds. No, no. But did you see the Sword? He told me he'd be nice to my friends, and then when he stopped their protest, he promised to talk to the king about them seeing the ceremony. He actually did it!"

"Not usually good at keeping his promises, is he?"

"Rafe? He's the best. He never breaks his word. But the king is..." She lowered her voice. "I really shouldn't say political things. People might hear. You might tell the papers. I'll be in so much trouble."

"I'm not telling anyone." Deor laid her hand on Robbie's arm. "I promise. We're not responsible for our parents. And you don't have to tell me things that make you uncomfortable."

She had plenty of memories of her own from grade school of other kids, even teachers, asking, *So, where is your father? Why don't know you know who he is? Does he ever visit you?* and later, *What was your mom? Some kind of slut?*

Robbie's smile blossomed again. "Thank you. I probably should get a cab and get going. If any reporters see me, they'll hound me all the way to the university gates for a quote." She stuffed her mirror in her purse and stood, her face radiant. "Just think. This could be the first step to a House of Commons."

So rule was by the nobles only, but there was some sort of Parliament-like arrangement for the nobles. Good to know. Deor filed the information away in case it mattered later.

"Are you going to be safe getting home?" she asked.

"Me? Oh sure. I'll just put a little glamour on to look more faerie. No one will recognize me." She headed toward the shop door, then turned back. "Speaking of safe, did anyone warn you about your own safety?"

"What do you mean?"

"Someone's been grabbing changeling women and putting spells on them," Robbie said. "Nobody knows why."

"That's terrible."

"It's probably some random psycho, but," Robbie leaned forward, "the thing is, they all look like us. I mean like you and me—same age, height, hair color. There was one noble victim I know of, but most were commoners."

"What happened to them?" Deor shuddered.

Robbie pursed her lips. "Nobody's really sure. Whoever did it used will spells to wipe their memories. A couple said they were asked questions, but they couldn't remember what they were. They weren't physically hurt. No, you know, um..."

"Sexual assault," she finished for the girl.

Robbie nodded. "Though I think I'd rather someone attack my body than my mind. If I had to choose."

Deor squeezed her hand. She hoped the girl never had to experience either. Maybe the Winter Court was safer than the human world in that way.

"Does being back on campus really make us safer? It sounds like they were all college age."

Robbie nodded vigorously. "Campus is sanctuary space. No one would dare try anything there—the bards would get to them before the Civil Patrol did—and probably be worse. Plus, campus security is really tight, especially after they close the gates at night. But I thought I should warn you, too. Just in case. "

"Thanks for the heads up."

"You're welcome. Good luck finding what you need." With a wave, Robbie was gone.

Deor sat back down in the not-too-lumpy chair and drummed her fingers on the armrest. Maybe she wasn't the only one trying to hunt down a particular person. That didn't give her any more of a clue who her father was, but maybe it was one more clue about why her mother had left him. She sat and drummed and thought until the dwarf came back with her hemmed academic robe, a black hood with yellow lining just like Nefasta's, and the bill.

Her new robe and hood stuffed in a shopping bag made of an artfully folded leaf with stem handle ("Only one crown more, dear, and you're sure to use it again. You don't want to be dragging your nice robes in the dust do you?") Deor walked through the crowded streets hunting for the Artisan's Avenue.

When she'd asked the dwarf at the thrift store if she'd ever seen a baby rattle like Deor's, the woman had handled it reverently, admiring the fine handiwork until Deor was ready to snatch it back from her, yelling "Mine!" But the woman had at least told her where to find someone with the skill to make something like that. So Artisan's Avenue it was.

All around her people were doing late afternoon shopping. Grocery stall barkers shouted over the crowd.

"Flash frozen wyvern! Get your flash frozen wyvern all the way from Barizan!"

"Fresh fruit! Any season, any kind! You come to us and we'll get what you need!"

Live poultry in cages, piles of vegetables (were the blue spiky things vegetables, too?), clothes on street side racks—everything around her bustled.

Eventually, she pushed out of the narrower, crowded streets into posher territory. Here, clothes were artfully displayed in windows. Carriages passed and no one shouted.

There were shoe shops, lingerie shops, dress shops. Shops catering to the whole family and shops for a very narrow clientele. Shops just with hats and gloves, even one, *The Discerning Gentleman*, devoted entirely to ties. A display in that window had rows of beautifully patterned ties wound round and round themselves in elaborate Gordian knots. A hand-printed sign read, *Let us show you the Phipps Phlop!*

"Phipps Phlop?" Deor asked the girl polishing the display window.

"Oh, that's all the rage in ties now. He's the leader in male fashion."

"The style seems complicated," Deor said.

"Oh it is," the girl assured her. "That's its charm."

She passed at least a dozen women's clothing shops, but she had no idea which, if any, would have been remotely affordable. Besides, she needed to see the maker of the rattle more than she needed a new suit.

She hitched her new bag higher on her shoulder. At least that was one good thing about her robe. If she wore it closed, no one would know the difference.

At last, after pushing through crowds of shoppers for nearly an hour, straining to see street signs, she popped out into a square at the intersection of Smithy Street and Artificers' Lane. Casting a glance down Smithy Street, she spotted a gaggle of young soldiers emerging from a shop, one holding a brand new sword as his friends *oohed* and *ahhed*.

"Artificers' it is," she said.

She drew out the rattle and held it before her like a wand, comparing the tiny, precise mark on the handle to the signs hanging outside the shops. She prowled down one side of the street past jewelers and makers of fine kitchenware. When she had exhausted that side of the street, she crossed and began again.

Midway up the second side of the street, she found a single green door so discreetly set beside a plain, curtained window that she almost passed it by. The window displayed one item only: a centaur no bigger than her fist, his horse body carved of gold and his human torso a single, perfectly molded pearl. As she peered at the display, the centaur moved. He drew his bow, shooting a golden arrow into the air. The centaur jumped in triumph as the arrow hit its invisible target. The centaur trotted in a circle, leapt, pivoted, and was still again.

As he turned, Deor caught a glimpse of the same maker's mark as the one on her rattle: a rabbit, one ear cocked upright, one flopped over, sitting on his haunches, reading a book.

She turned to the door and there, larger, was the same rabbit engraved on the door handle. Painted on the door in gold lettering was the following: *Consultations by Appointment Only. Showroom open Thursday from ten to four.*

She frowned at the sign. She didn't have time for courtesies. Tucking the rattle back in her bag, she pounded on the door. No one answered. She tried again, hammering on the door and shouting, "Hello? Anybody home?"

"Can I help you, miss?" She almost jumped out of her skin when a civil patrolman appeared at her elbow.

"I need to see… whoever works here. It's urgent."

The guardsman eyed her up and down and pointed at the sign. "Why don't you move along, miss?"

"Er, yes. I guess I can come back later." Defeated, she strode away, aware of the guard's eyes on her as she went. Great. She'd have to teach at least one more class without getting fired. Which meant she should probably buy some groceries for the next few days.

"Once I find this *Finn*, I'm going to hand him a bill for expenses," she muttered, stalking back toward the food stalls.

Chapter Thirteen

T rapped behind his desk at the Tower again, his backside and brain going numb with boredom as Michael waxed poetic about yet another applicant to the Palace Guard, Rafe drummed his fingers on his desk. Ice crystals like tiny needles formed wherever his fingertips struck. The crystals grew longer as he considered the double layer of silver lace Michael had thought fit to add to his uniform cuffs. More lace bulged like a goiter from his jacket collar. Why even wear a uniform if he was going to deface it like that? As bad as the Phipps Phlop.

Arthur sat to one side, playing the dull and dutiful secretary with his meager captain's bars and complete lack of service medals affixed to his uniform, his face bland as day-old bread. A stack of application forms sat on the desk in front of him. Beside the current applicant's file, the magically conjured image of Viscount St. George Overton, of the Caer Eisteddfod Overtons, hovered over Rafe's desk for all of them to examine.

Outside the sun was setting. Dammit, if this went on much longer, he'd be late to dinner with Lady Genevieve. He slouched back in his leather chair, uniform jacket hanging open, and let his mind wander. He could just go straight to Genevieve's house the way he was, but she'd be better pleased if he was out of uniform. He probably ought to let his valet put some jewels in his hair too—Genevieve would likely want to go to the theatre after dinner.

"Which is why I intend to offer Viscount St. George a place among us immediately," Michael finished.

"No. Next applicant."

Arthur made a shooing gesture. The image of St. George Overton disappeared from Rafe's desk, replaced by a blond man in the uniform of the Tower Guard.

"Lieutenant Stephen Bolton," Arthur said. "Came out of a Yorkshire foot regiment. This is his third time applying for a transfer to the House-boys. His record is squeaky clean, and he's received a number of commendations, but…"

"Excuse me, Captain," Michael snarled. "I was not finished."

"I said no, Michael," Rafe said.

"I demand an explanation."

Frost ferns spread out across the desk from Rafe's fingers. "I am your prince. You are not in a position to demand anything from me."

Fire danced in Michael's eyes, and his fingers curled on the wooden arm of the chair, but he kept his voice even. "As the king's Shield, I am entitled to an explanation for the Sword's veto of my candidate."

"You need an explanation? George's greatest accomplishment with a blade is what he can do to a roast goose at Yule. He's a fop, an incompetent, and a would-be politician without the wit for the position. I doubt he's ever seen blood spilled, let alone spilled any himself."

Michael breathed heavily. "He's the younger brother of a personal friend of yours, and his father is the Master of the City."

Rafe shrugged. "If that's our criteria, I nominate my dog Jake for immediate promotion to Field Marshal. His pedigree is at least as long as George's."

From the hearth, Jake sat up and barked. Arthur frowned hard, suppressing a smirk. Michael's already flushed face turned bright red. Heat shimmered in the air around him. Rafe laughed and cupped his hand, pulling the heat to himself.

"Relax, Michael." The room cooled in spite of Michael's rising rage. Rafe pushed back his chair. "The rest will have to wait, gentlemen. I have a social engagement."

Arthur rose to go, but Michael stayed planted in his chair. "I am not your junior or your lackey to be dismissed at your convenience. Let me remind you, Prince to Be, that the Shield is one of the 'Three Who Say No' to the king, and if you think I can't say no to you, then you are very much mistaken. And furthermore..."

His rising tirade was cut off by the sound of slamming doors and a voice, high pitched and hysterical, calling, "Let me go. Let me go! I need Rafe!"

It was Robbie.

Guard's voices clashed with Robbie's, but a broad, Midlands accent broke in. "Can't you fools see she's been hurt? Give her to me and get on with you."

Before Rafe could open the door, Lt. Bolton swung it open. "I beg your lordships' pardon, but the general's sister is here."

Robbie shoved past him, her hair wild, her coat clutched around her. A black line like an ink stain spread across her jaw. She threw her arms around him and burst into loud sobs.

"Arthur, Bolton—one of you call a healer. Call Lady Penelope. Michael, get out." Rafe hugged Robbie close, rocking her against him, as Arthur and Bolton escorted Michael out the door.

"Can you tell me what happened?"

"I don't know." The words came out muffled against his chest. "Don't let her touch me."

"Who?" he asked.

Robbie opened her mouth, but instead of words, she spewed her stomach onto his chest, the vomit soaking through his uniform jacket into the shirt beneath. She pushed away from him and threw up more onto the rug. Jake leaped up and barked furiously at her while Sam trotted over to sniff the mess, tail half wagging.

Rafe's own throat burned at the acrid smell, but he clamped his mouth shut. Robbie didn't need him joining her. Besides, he'd smelled worse on the battlefield. While Robbie dry-heaved over the wastebasket, he stripped off his jacket and shirt.

"Sam! Leave it. Jake, hush." He dumped his clothes onto the pile in the middle of the rug. "Come on, little sister. It'll be okay."

Scooping up Robbie, he carried her to the sofa, both dogs close at his heels. He drew her close, pressing a cold hand to the back of her neck until her dry heaves stopped.

"Don't ask me."

"I have to. Sip this first." He pulled a ball of water out of the air as he had done for Sam, but this one he gave to Robbie.

She sniffed hard and took it in her hands, his magic holding it together for her. As she drank, Rafe eyed the black line across her chin to where it went under her collar.

"Someone's been using will spells on you."

"No," she said. "I went out for a walk in the marketplace. Then I went straight home. I went shopping, and I went straight home because I'm a good, obedient girl."

"Robbie," Rafe turned her toward him, cupped her head in his hand. "Look at me. Look straight in my eyes and tell me what you did this afternoon. Tell me something that doesn't make you feel sick."

Her eyes, huge and dilated, wandered away from him. "I did everything I wanted to do and went straight home. Because I'm...."

"Stop it." He took her by the shoulders, his heart pounding. He would not let her slip away into delusions like the other girls. Not Robbie. "You are not a little girl. You hear me? Say it. Say, 'I'm not a little girl anymore.'"

Her mouth tried to form the words, but her eyes wandered, unable to track together. He pressed his hands to her head, whispering spells for clarity, words to dismiss the lingering will spell, but nothing happened. No sudden recognition in her eyes. No response. The will spell was still doing its work somehow, burrowing into her mind even though the caster was long gone.

"I have to go home," Robbie said. "I'm supposed to be in bed by now."

She tried to rise, but he grabbed her by the shoulders. Where was the damned healer? He shook her, but her head lolled, her eyes half shut. He leaned forward, gathering the only other magic he could think of—a field spell against battle shock, meant to keep a wounded man sane long enough for the healers to reach him. He blew into her face, ice crystals coalescing on her lashes and hair.

She closed her eyes and breathed deep.

"I'm not a little girl." Her voice grew louder and she straightened. "I'm not a little girl! I am a grown woman. You can't make me!"

"Can't make you what?"

She balked and clamped a hand over her mouth, body shuddering. With a flick of his wrist, Rafe summoned a wastebasket and shoved it into her hands as she heaved. He held her hair back from her face until she finished.

"There was a woman," she said, panting. "And someone with her. They asked me questions about my father."

"What kind of questions?"

"I don't know."

"Was it Professor Smithfield?"

"No," she said, hugging the wastebasket. "Yes. I don't know. She was at the marketplace. We talked about you." She threw up again.

So that was the changeling's game. He hoped she'd enjoyed rummaging around in Robbie's head because he was going to make sure she lost her own. The anger burned so fierce inside him that he lifted his hand off Robbie's back, afraid that he would give her frostbite even through her coat.

Jake and Sam whined, their eyes going from him to Robbie and back again. Jake reached out and took Rafe's wrist in his mouth with a worried snort.

"Good boy." Rafe buried his freezing hands in the dog's thick ruff.

Arthur entered with Lady Penelope, who rushed over to Robbie. "No more questions for now." She shooed Rafe off the couch and took his place. "Hi Robbie, I'm a healer. You can call me Penny. Do you mind if I touch your hand?"

Rafe retreated to the corner with Arthur, casting a privacy spell over the couch as Penny began the meticulous process of examining Robbie from head to toe.

"How is she?" Arthur said.

"Better than some of the others. She knows something happened to her."

"From the look of those marks, she fought hard."

They both glanced toward the other side of the room, though the privacy spell hid everything behind a haze of blurred colors and white noise like the rustling of aspen leaves.

Rafe turned his restless anger into pacing as he thought aloud. Frost snapped and crackled under his feet with every step. Arthur stayed still, hands clasped behind his back.

"She said she went for a walk in the marketplace where she met Deor Smithfield," Rafe said.

"Meeting her professor—sounds innocuous enough," Arthur said. "It could be the cover story they gave her in place of the real memory."

"I know. But there's at least grain of truth there. No one would dare attack her on Eisteddfod's campus itself. She must have been off campus when it happened—the marketplace would be a good place to catch her. And she defied the spell enough to come here, so perhaps she remembers more than she was meant to. Mirror, show me Deor Smithfield's location. Let's hope our changeling professor hasn't gotten back onto campus yet."

The mirror's reflection of the room rippled around the edges, but nothing else changed. Frowning, Rafe flicked a spell at the mirror. Nothing. So help him, if Michael was spying on him again and had broken the mirror, he'd chop him into mincemeat and use him for eel bait. He spun on his heel, shouting.

"Has this thing been tampered with?"

Arthur ignored him, frowning at his own pocket mirror and muttering spells.

When Rafe could stand the waiting no more, he shouted, "Well?"

Arthur looked up. "She broke the tracking spell. The little half-grown maggot found it and broke it. No one breaks my tracking spells. Hell, no one finds them!"

"Find her. I don't care what you have to do—just find out where she is and have her followed by your best. Then get back here. I'm going to need you to help me break down the magic on Robbie."

Arthur snapped into a perfect salute. "Gladly."

Rafe turned toward the window, fists tight at his sides. Someone— several someones—were going to hang for this. Whoever they were they didn't deserve the honor of a beheading. His rage built and crashed, an avalanche of magical cold that blasted the rare glass windowpane—a luxury instead of the normal window spells—and coated the wall around it in windblown ice. Glass and ice fell together, shattering on the paving stones below. The outburst of rage-fueled magic left him panting, his muscles twitching as if he had just sprinted twice around the Palace wall.

His head was clearer though, plans taking the place of revenge. He needed to think, not react. So much work to be done before dawn. Erase any lingering spells on Robbie. Learn whatever they could from her testimony to Penelope. If they could find the site where the attack happened… but that would take hours, not to mention a good dose of luck. He pressed his left hand to the ice coating the wall, drawing the magic into himself, sending the water back into the air from which it had come.

He should call Genevieve in person to apologize for abandoning her at the last minute. He turned toward the large mirror, but Jake's cold snout poking him in the ribs reminded him that he was shirtless. Perhaps he'd better find a shirt before he used the mirror. Around the room, lights came on to replace the fading sunlight.

"Lord Farringdon? I'm done with my examination." Lady Penelope appeared at his elbow, a forensic recording mirror in her hand.

Rafe jumped, startled out of his thoughts.

"Thank you. What did you find? Er—you'll have to pardon my lack of clothes."

"Have you met my paramour? Or any member of his pack? Anyway, I wasn't able to find much. Her mind is more intact than the other victims, but her memories are truly gone. I can't retrieve even fragments."

"Nothing?" He looked across the room to where Robbie slept on the couch, lulled by a soothing spell no doubt.

"Not a thing. I think these attackers are getting smarter about their approach. That, or they recognized Robbie wasn't as easy to manipulate as some of the others."

"The blood of a queen does run in her veins," Rafe said. "Do you see any sign it could be your changeling roommate at work?"

Penelope looked as if he'd suggested his dog might be a suspect. "Deor? She thinks dish-cleaning magic cupboards are impressive. There's not a chance on this Earth or under it that she has the skill to work a will spell like this."

Rafe nodded, but as he did so, he remembered how the professor had defeated his truth spell as if she were brushing away lint.

"However, I am going to hazard a guess," Penelope said. "There's a goblin involved. How much or what gender, I couldn't tell you, but I believe there was more than one person bespelling Robbie, and extra-corporal evidence tells us that one of them was a goblin."

"How sure are you?" Goblin involvement turned the case political. And Geoff was in the city, which meant he could protect this fellow with diplomatic immunity. Rafe shook his head. What if the Goblin Prince was involved—he was Smithfield's TA. He certainly had the power to use will spells if he wanted, but why take such a risk? A sinking feeling in his stomach told him that, as bad as the attacks were, they could get much worse.

She pursed her lips. "Not sure enough to swear to it on the witness stand, but sure enough to tell you what to look for."

"Good enough for now." He tapped at his mirror. "I've just sent your mirror a copy of what Robbie said so you can analyze it further. If you're done here, I'll send someone to escort you home. My apologies for not doing it myself."

"No need," she said cheerfully as she pulled on her coat. "Rufus is waiting outside. He doesn't trust you lot to keep me safe."

Rafe's eyebrows knit together. Impertinent puppy.

Penny laughed. "No need to be offended. It's just his way. Good night, General. Make sure she gets plenty of rest and has someone kind nearby when she wakes. Call if she needs me, even if it's the middle of the night." The olive-skinned healer went off, hugging her long coat close around her.

Rafe crossed the room to stand over Robbie where she slept. More black marks showed along her wrists and around her throat. She looked so small under her coat. The professor was even smaller. She wouldn't come much higher than his top ribs, if that.

Why had he thought that, at a moment like this? The image of Professor Smithfield persisted. He pictured her alone in some twilight street, beckoned by a voice that couldn't be denied, and he shuddered.

"Don't be stupid," he said aloud. Right now Deor Smithfield was his chief suspect. He ought to be hunting her, not worrying for her safety.

He lifted Robbie off the couch, her head cradled against his shoulder. She'd sleep at the Palace tonight where he and her mother could watch over her, Finn's wishes be damned. The Sword was meant to say "no" to the King from time to time. And tonight he was saying no.

Chapter Fourteen

Wednesday morning was Deor's recurring nightmare come to life and peopled by all types of fae. She struggled to get the class's attention, waving and shouting as they chatted amongst themselves. She didn't know the students' names. The chalkboard mysteriously refused to be written on, and her students laughed as she failed to make it work. She couldn't get her book open to the right page. Bard Nefasta frowned and scribbled angry notes.

The only difference from her dream was that in real life she was clothed, and the absurdly large sleeves of her academic robe snagged on the podium every time she raised an arm.

The goblins were the worst. They sat together in a group, not even bothering to whisper as she talked about Elizabethan England and Aristotelian unities. She barely stopped herself from hollering, "This is important!"

In the front row, Donovan slept behind dark sunglasses, and Geoff watched it all with a growing smirk. Robbie hadn't come back to class. Probably embarrassed to be associated with her.

"Enough!" Deor finally shouted at the chattering class. "You there—" She pointed at one of the green men.

Well dressed, like Geoff, with slick blond curls and wide, innocence-feigning eyes, he paused mid-conversation and looked at her. "Yes, Miss? Did you need something?"

"My name is Professor Smithfield. And yours?"

He glanced at an adoring girl next to him and grinned. "Simon."

"Whatever." She didn't remember a Simon from the roll sheet. "Who ruled England during Shakespeare's lifetime?"

"Some frigid human quim?" He nudged the young man next to him as several people in the class giggled.

Deor closed her eyes and took a deep breath. She glanced at Geoff, who wasn't hiding his laughter. Next to him, Donovan shuddered out a blessedly silent snore. At the back of the hall, the clock read quarter-to-twelve.

"Very well." She slammed her book shut. "Clearly you all need help recalling the material. I want a summary of acts one through three from each of you first thing next class. It counts as a quiz. That's it for today. Everyone out!"

Muttering and snickering the class shuffled out. A couple of pixie and faerie students waved goodbye.

"Have a good weekend, Professor Smithfield," Geoff called before ducking out the nearest door.

She was alone with Bard Nefasta.

"Well." Deor pulled herself a little straighter. "That didn't go as well as I had hoped, but next class…"

"Don't bother with excuses," Ama cut her off. "Your command of the room is horrible. You'd be lucky if a quarter of the students respected you at all."

Deor's squared her shoulders. "True, but as you can see, I'm dealing with a biased crowd. I deserve at least one more chance to win them over. And some of the students seemed interested in the shortness of human lifespans. That's a step in the right direction."

Bard Nefasta frowned and smoothed her bun. "I'll give you one more class to get control of the situation," she said. "I can't have them not learning."

"Of course," Deor said, leaning on the lectern. "Tuesday you'll see a radically different class. I guarantee it."

She had a whole weekend to work out the details of how that was going to happen. And, if she got very, very lucky, she'd find her father before then and the whole issue would be moot.

As Ama swept out of the room, a twinge of guilt ran through Deor; she'd never bailed on a class she'd committed to teach. She brushed the feeling away. This wasn't her world and she wasn't staying.

A footstep creaked on the floorboards behind her. "Professor?" Robbie said. "I just came to say I'm sorry I missed class today. I... I didn't mean to."

Deor looked up from where she was gathering her books. Dark purple bags sagged under Robbie's red-rimmed eyes. The collar of her coat was turned up to hide half her face. "Oh God. Are you okay? What happened?"

"I can't really talk about it..." Robbie's fingers twisted together. As she bowed her head, Deor caught a glimpse of a black smudge like ink over a bruise across her cheekbone.

"Who did this to you?"

Robbie flinched away. "Don't ask me to remember. I'll throw up again."

"Okay. Okay." Now was not the time to ask why questions would make someone vomit. "Do you want to sit down? Can you take off your coat and chat with me a little?"

When the girl nodded, Deor led her by the hand to a chair in the first row. Between the girl's Eisteddfod scarf and the neckline of her shirt, black marks swirled. Once the coat was off, the markings were visible all over her arms as well.

Robbie crossed her arms and ran her hands up and down them, shivering. "I-I-I—" she stammered on the edge of tears.

Deor grabbed packet of tissues out of her bag and handed them to her.

"Deep breaths, sweetheart, deep breaths." Deor patted the girl's free hand.

Robbie hiccuped a few times and swallowed hard. "I didn't mean to miss class," she said again. "I just can't seem to move very fast today... and when I tried to go out, I got in an argument with my mother. She doesn't want me to come back to school until they catch the..." She clamped her hand over her mouth for a minute and her stomach heaved. "The... you know." She pointed to her arms and face.

"Your attacker," Deor supplied. "Was this the attacker you warned me about?"

Robbie nodded, her mouth shut tight.

"Have you talked to the police yet?"

Robbie nodded again, a little harder this time, a little less tearfully. "Is there any way I can make up the work for today?"

Deor almost laughed. The students with the most valid excuses were always the least sure they deserved help.

"Of course. Just catch up with the reading and get the notes from one of your friends, and we'll go over them in my office hours later this week. I won't count the absence against you."

"I can get a note from the Sword. Or my healer," Robbie said.

"Honey, no." Deor laid her hand over Robbie's. "I believe you."

There was no way she was sending this poor girl to the Tower to ask that pompous bully for an excuse note.

"Do you want to sit in on the next class? It's the same lesson, just different students."

But Robbie was standing up and pulling her coat back on. "I have to get back. Mother will panic and have every tree and leaf in the city looking for me, not to mention the whole Civil Patrol if I take too long."

"Trees can look for people? No, forget I asked." It didn't matter what freaky things plants could do here. "You take good care of yourself, alright? Do you have someone to go with you?"

"Bernie walked me here. Mother's private carriage is waiting at the gate." Robbie rolled her eyes. "She thinks I'm still a kid."

Deor laughed and gave Robbie a hug. "Normally, I'd roll my eyes with you, but this once, let your mom be a little overprotective. And stay safe, okay? I'll see you during my office hours."

"Thank you!" Robbie trotted up the classroom steps and waved goodbye from the door. Bernie's massive frame loomed in the shadows just beyond.

Deor picked up her books and slung her bag over her shoulder. As she slogged up the stairs to her office, she wondered what kind of attack left black smudges on the victim and how she might defend herself. She'd do all the things any woman does—stay out of dark streets, leave information with Penny about where she was going and when she meant to be back, carry her keys between her fingers. Maybe she could borrow a kitchen knife from Penny or ask one of her dwarf students where they got their axes. If anybody came after her, they weren't going to have an easy time of it.

Chapter Fifteen

After Deor's second, equally excruciating, class of the day, she headed straight for Artificers' Street. If Ama was going to fire her on Tuesday, she'd better have found her father by Monday night.

She marched up to the shop with the green door and the rabbit on the handle, intending to walk in. But the door was locked fast. She tried the handle again. Definitely locked.

"Fine then," she said and pounded on the door as if she were raising a fire alarm.

Rapid footsteps sounded on the other side, and someone yanked the door open.

A sour-faced faerie, his face almost cadaverously thin, his nose narrow as a quill, peered down at her.

"Tradespeople go to the rear," he hissed at her and would have slammed the door, but Deor jammed her foot in it.

One foot in already, she slid her arm in, rattle held out before her. "I must see the person who made this."

He flinched back and opened the door enough for her to shove into the shop.

"Did you make this?" Deor waved the rattle in the man's face.

"Miss, this establishment does not take walk-ins. Please, you must go.

The Master is expecting a very highly placed personage on a matter of great delicacy at any minute. You must go."

"I must talk to the person who made my rattle. It has your mark on it." She pointed.

He shook his head as if to refuse, but then reached for the rattle and examined it in the light. He spoke a word over it, and the rabbit closed its book, hopped around in a circle, and returned to its original position. He handed it back to her.

"Yes, Miss. This certainly is an original piece from the Master's workshop, though who did the work, I cannot say without consulting our records. The spells on it have become sadly worn." He pursed his lips at her.

She glared back at him. "Just who is this Master and how do I get to see him?"

He leaned back, as if he were afraid to anger her, but managed a condescending smile. "One such as yourself would usually have great difficulty obtaining a meeting with the Master himself. He is not available to the public." The man's gaze flicked to a pair of tapestries hanging on the wall—the perfect size to cover a doorway.

"So he is here." Deor raised her eyebrows. "Go get him." After a brief pause, she added, "Please."

"People do not simply walk in off the street and see him!"

Deor frowned.

"However," the man conceded hurriedly, "since this is an authentic Theophilous piece, if you would care to leave it, one of the Master's apprentices will renew the spells on it and have it delivered to you in, say, three weeks?"

"That's not going to work for me." Deor closed the door behind her. "I don't want it fixed; I want to speak to the man who made it. Go get Master Theophilous." Her last words rang out in the small room, and a thrill of magic tingled in her throat.

The man cowered and stepped toward the workshop, but paused. "I …"

"Now," Deor snapped, and he cringed again as a few sparkles shot toward him.

"Yes, Miss. Right away." He bowed and disappeared behind the tapestries.

"Thank you!" she added to his retreating back.

The shop was small, laid out like a parlor that just happened to hold three display cases, one of jewelry, another of personal accessories—mirrors, combs, brushes, shaving kits—and a much larger one of beautiful toys, though they were so finely wrought and delicate that even an emperor might have second thoughts about handing them to a little prince. The rest of the space was taken up with an arrangement of couches and armchairs positioned before occasional tables spread with black velvet. She laid the rattle on a velvet table and sat.

Voices rose behind the curtain. An old man shouted, "I tell you I don't remember that damn rattle!"

The sour-faced man bleated back, "But, sir, it is clearly your work."

The tapestry was thrown violently aside and a grey-haired faerie, one of the few genuinely old-looking people Deor had seen, strode into the room. He wore a leather apron and a pair of wire-rimmed spectacles with interchangeable lenses perched on his nose.

Deor stood up and extended her hand. "I'm—"

"Not now." He waved her away and picked up the rattle. After a minute of muttering over it, while his assistant danced with anxiety in the background, the red faded from his face. His frown grew to a grim line, and he sat down heavily in the chair opposite Deor, waving at his assistant to go away. "Where did you get this, young woman?"

"My father gave it to me." Deor settled back in her chair. "Is it a fake?"

"No." He gave the rattle a shake and a single spark flew out. "It's my work alright. I just can't remember doing it."

Deor slumped back into the chair. After everything she'd done just to see this man, she was stymied by old fashioned senility.

"Are you sure?" Deor asked. "Could it be just that you've made so many baby rattles you don't remember this particular one? It was made for me thirty years ago. Could you look through your records for that year? That might turn up the name of the person who bought it, or at least narrow it down?"

"I've made five rattles in my life, all different, and I'd swear this isn't one of them. But I made it alright. The magic knows me and I know it. Watch." He laid the rattle on the velvet cloth, passed his hands over it, and sang to it under his breath. "Go ahead. Give it a shake now."

She did and sparkles flew out from it in a cloudburst. They lingered too, filling the air with a growing nimbus of light. As the sparkles flew, silver bells chimed and rang. When she flipped the rattle on end, it sang like birds in harmony, and the sparks danced to it.

"My lullaby!" Deor said. "I'd forgotten."

"That's my work." The man swelled with pride, even through his anger. "It won't be lost either." He took the rattle and tossed it across the room.

Before Deor could shriek or reach to catch it, the rattle disappeared in midair and reappeared in her lap. She clutched it in both hands.

"Thank you," she said.

"Can't think how those spells got so broken," Theophilous muttered. "It would take a lot of doing for one of my spells to wear that much in thirty years."

"It's been with me in the human world," she said.

"Shame."

"Yes. I suppose." She looked up at him. "Are you sure you can't remember anything about this rattle? Anything at all? It's the only lead I have to find my father. I'm a changeling."

He pushed his glasses back onto his forehead, studying her. "You do look familiar somehow. Could be that's what's left of my memory getting jogged by your face." He rubbed his eyes. "I'm sorry, young lady, I wish I could help you, but the memory's blocked. I can feel it. The more I push, the more I want to shout that I can't remember. Makes me dizzy thinking about it too hard. That's mind magic for certain."

He leaned forward, his voice harsh. "And I'll tell you that whoever had the ever loving stones to put a mind spell on me must be one of the most powerful people in the land. He's powerful in magic and in law to get away with it. Someone who does what he wants and doesn't fear the hand of the Sword falling on him for it." He took her hand in his, and fear flashed in his eyes. "Are you sure you want to find a man like that?"

"I am." As if she had a choice. She stood up, swallowing hard. "Thank you, sir. I'm sorry I was rude to your staff."

He waved off the apology and offered her his hand. "Come back and be rude to him any time. I'll have my clerk look through the records for that year. See if we can trace him that way." He got to his feet, knees creaking, and muttered. "By gory, he may have wiped my memory, but I'll be damned if he got away without paying."

At that Deor laughed. She left her name and address with the sour-faced assistant and tucked the rattle into her satchel.

Back on the street, the sun was already low in the sky and she didn't need to add being an assault victim to her list of problems. She buttoned her coat against the sharp autumn wind and turned back toward the university.

Chapter Sixteen

As the setting sun gilded the crowded slate roofs of the Tanty district, an area full of the kind of bars and bordellos that made more money from the crime than legal sales, Rafe and Arthur crouched behind a smoking chimney pot.

"We've been following this fellow for hours and he hasn't done anything suspicious. You don't think Penny's evidence from Robbie is wrong, do you?" Arthur asked.

"I would, except that we know the Goblin Secret Service has been walking too freely in our city for a long time. I should have pushed Finn harder to let me deal with it, but he doesn't want to upset 'our ally' King Gregory." Rafe formed the quote marks with his fingers.

In the narrow street below, their quarry stood ogling a pair of prostitutes. The goblin had led Rafe and Arthur on a maddeningly slow ramble through the city, wending his way into the most dangerous parts of town. Along the way, he'd changed glamours six different times. At the moment he looked like a slack-jawed tourist from the Underdeep, his pine-needle green skin untouched by sunlight, a young man looking for trouble but not quite brave enough to walk up and ask the price.

"I've got to admit, that guy is good with glamours," Arthur conceded. "He's pulling off the young tourist thing perfectly, even though he's ten times that age."

"Come on, fungus head, make a move," Rafe said. He flexed the fingers of his sword hand.

"He knows he's being followed," Arthur said.

Rafe flipped open his mirror and whispered into it, "Bolton, Montjoie? Let him see you going away. Make it look like you've lost him." He stowed the mirror against his skin. "Let's hope he doesn't know we're here, too."

The other two officers eased out of their hiding spots farther down the street. They stepped lightly, as if unaware of the other one's presence until Montjoie gave a signal and they both dropped their glamours, revealing their uniforms. Bolton spat on the street and cursed under his breath. Montjoie shrugged stoically. Without a glance at the young-seeming goblin, they turned and walked away.

On the roof, Rafe held his breath. Arthur's new camouflage glamour still had a half second lag, and the goblin man was staring straight up at them.

Seconds slid by. The prostitutes moved on.

The goblin was alone on the street. Looking quickly left, right, and up, he laid his hand on a ragged theatre poster glued to a wall. His hand moved through the poster without ripping it and came back with a scrap of paper.

"Let's get that paper before he has a chance to destroy it," Rafe said.

The goblin tucked the note into his clothes and set off. Rafe and Arthur followed, using their wings to hover silently just above the slippery roof tiles. The goblin turned down an alley and, checking one more time to make sure he wasn't being followed, jumped for the wall. Clinging like a lizard, he scurried up the bricks, straight toward Rafe and Arthur.

Rafe dropped to the roof, signaling to Arthur to cover the other side of the alley. He crouched, waiting for the goblin to pop up above the eaves. This was almost too easy. The goblin's head appeared and Rafe lunged for him. The goblin threw himself backward and Rafe's arms closed on empty air. The goblin dropped straight down.

"Dammit!" Rafe jumped, wings out to break his fall. The alley was too narrow. His wings scraped down the rough wall. The edges, sharpened for battle, struck sparks off the stones. He jerked his bleeding wings in and dropped the rest of the way into the stinking alley. A green flash in the dark told him where the goblin was, and he plunged after it.

He burst into the open street and sprinted after the goblin. Arthur, wings spread, landed in the street just ahead.

"Stop in the name of the king!" Rafe shouted. Others on the street froze, but the goblin spun on his heels and dashed straight into a used clothing shop. Rafe darted after him with Arthur close behind.

The goblin tossed a rack of clothes behind him, but Rafe knocked them aside. Behind the counter the pixie owner shrank back in a pink blur. Rafe vaulted the counter and ripped aside the curtain shielding the back rooms.

Nothing. The meager room was empty of life. Just a small fireplace with a low fire, a table, and a rumpled cot in one corner. Not even a window.

"Arthur! Cover the door," he shouted. He scanned the room, whispering a glamour dispeller. "Where are you hiding, you slimy son of a bitch?"

The bedclothes heaved and took on a shape. Rafe grabbed for them. Too late, he realized the illusion. The goblin shot out from under the table and straight up the chimney. Rafe threw out his hands at the fire and every drop of water in the air around him condensed onto the flames. They sent up a hiss of steam, but the goblin was gone. Rafe could barely get his head in the opening. Green skin shone in the chimney's darkness and was gone.

Rafe dashed back to the front of the shop. "King's business," he shouted at the cowering shop owner.

Arthur ran out the front door ahead of him.

"Rooftop," Rafe panted. "He's up the chimney."

"Right," Arthur said.

Both men leaped for the patch of sky between the tightly packed buildings, wings beating the air. Arthur had his mirror out, calling in the man's description to the Civil Patrol. They hovered over the rooftops, peering through the smoke of a thousand cooking fires.

"There!" Rafe said, and swooped low over the roofs.

The goblin dashed along the roofline, bent double and clinging with fingers and toes.

"Don't lose him," Arthur shouted, circling wide.

Rafe gritted his teeth and pushed. His wings stung, raw from scraping along the bricks. He flattened his arms against his body to cut through the air. The pale green glow skittered and dodged among chimney pots and washing lines. Rafe zig-zagged after him, skimming as low over the rooftops as he dared.

"He's moving toward Georges Street!" Arthur called, following a few steps behind.

"I can see that!" Rafe gritted his teeth, pouring more magic into his wings for speed.

The Goblin Embassy was on Georges Street.

The goblin leapt from a third story roof onto a fire escape and scrambled down toward street level.

Rafe tucked his wings in tight and plummeted after him. "You stay in the air," he shouted to Arthur as he hit the pavement and rolled, quickly regaining his feet.

The goblin ran into the open square at the center of Georges Street, full of people out for an evening stroll.

"Got you!" Rafe reached out with his magic for the fountain at the square's center. As he cast, a black fog of exhaustion rolled over his eyes, but he shook it off. The water surged upward in a wave. It overwhelmed the goblin, knocking him to his knees, and drenching those nearby.

"Stop in the name of the king," Arthur shouted from above.

People froze. A few put their hands up. But the goblin was on his feet and running again.

"Oh no you don't," Rafe said.

He froze the water that covered the pavements into a glass slick sheet. The goblin went down, scrambled to his feet, and fell again. Rafe slid forward, skimming across the ice. He lunged, seized the goblin's wrist.

Fire flashed in the goblin's hand. Pain. The sizzle of burned flesh. He hung on, calling the ice against the fire, but the water didn't respond. For the first time in his life, his magic failed. The black fog over his vision returned. Another burst of fire from the goblin and Rafe lost his grip.

Arthur called out from behind them and the cobblestones under the goblin's feet heaved, but he jumped forward as if given a boost by the earth.

Rafe scrambled to his feet, willing his body to move faster, but his legs shook, his lungs burned.

The goblin raced up the steps of the embassy. Rafe had one vivid glimpse of sharp yellow eyes and rows of teeth, all grinning at him, before the man folded himself smaller than a lapdog and slid himself through the tiny hole in the locked door.

"Hell and damnation!" Rafe shouted.

Arthur ran up the Embassy steps and pounded on the door, but no one answered. He kicked it one time for good measure and trotted down the stairs to Rafe.

Rafe shook himself, gasping for breath.

Arthur reached him, winded and scowling. He took one look at Rafe. "Are you alright?"

"I'm fine."

"The hell you are. Come on." Arthur jerked his head toward a side street. He kept his voice low. "Let's get out of sight of this crowd, and I'll call for a carriage. You look grey. Are you going to faint?"

"I'm fine." Rafe shook his head, knowing it was a lie. "Let's get back to the Tower."

Arthur slipped his mirror from a well-hidden pocket in his uniform as they walked. "Desk Lieutenant, this is Captain Maerhwer. Call off the pursuit. We lost the goblin at the embassy. Send a carriage to my location."

Chapter Seventeen

"Come on, Deor! It's about to start." Penny's voice echoed up the stairwell, ruining Deor's last hope for sleeping in on a Sunday. She swung her feet out of bed and rubbed her hands over her face. Penny had shaken her awake an hour ago. And half an hour ago. She had been yelling from the front parlor at five minute intervals ever since. Deor's protests that this wasn't her kingdom and she didn't care had failed to register. This was A Historic Event, and Penny wasn't about to let her miss it.

"Deor! They're starting!" Penny shouted.

"Okay," Deor said. "I'll be right down."

She yawned one more time and shuffled toward the stairs, reminding herself that if her father were powerful and noble, he might be at the ceremony. Maybe, just maybe, she'd recognize him if she saw him.

In the parlor, Penny had turned their mismatched armchairs to face the large mirror above the mantle and was settled into the floral one, her eyes riveted on the mirror. Without looking away, she passed Deor a plate of scones. A teapot of herbs and flower petals steamed on a side table.

"Thanks," Deor said, taking a scone and settling into the other chair.

The mirror showed the outer gates of the Palace where guards stood two deep in black uniforms, their wings flared out behind them. The same faint drizzle that fogged the flat's windows dampened the cobblestones. A voice described in hushed tones how a letter of protest from the southeastern duchy of Wellhall had been hand delivered only this morning to the Palace, apparently signed by a local guild coalition whose chairman was now standing with the rest of the crowd outside the gates. Deor peered at the faces in the crowd, looking for some resemblance to her own.

"We remind our viewers," the voice said, "that the ceremony will be conducted in Ancient Faerie. Please adjust your mirrors to allow translation into your preferred language."

"Done it," Penny said before Deor could ask. "It'll come through in English."

"Also," the voice went on, "since reporters are not being allowed inside the throne room, the ceremony itself will be shown without commentary. However, our editorial team will be right here discussing the ceremony afterward, so please leave your mirrors on. And now, the Adoption of Rafael Lord Farringdon, by His Majesty King Sweordmund Aethelwing VIII."

The mirror rippled, went black for a second, and rippled back to life. In a long hall, black marble pillars veined with white held up a vaulted ceiling. A chessboard pattern of black and white marble covered the floor. Tall, narrow windows whizzed by on either side as the mirror zoomed in on the cluster of people at the throne end of the hall. The mirror focused briefly on various important people in the glittering crowd, though without a commentator, the only people Deor recognized were Penny's Rufus, and Geoff and Donovan, looking as princely and fangy as ever. Any of the men, she supposed, could be her father, but there was no way to tell.

"Who are all these people?" Deor said. "And why is Rufus there?"

"His father's the alpha in Ireland. He's representing his pack. Only the heads of ducal and baronial households, and a few select representatives of foreign governments, are being allowed to attend the preliminary ceremonies. See, there's the ambassador from the Summer Court." Penny pointed to a man with pink roses in his hair. "The final ceremony will be packed though. All the members of the nobility are required to attend. I can't wait. I've had my dress ready since May."

"I'll certainly make sure I watch that." She took another bite of her scone, settled back in her chair, and propped her feet on the footstool.

The nobility stood in a cluster in front of the throne at the edge of the marble floor. The throne rose above their heads on a three-tiered dais carved out of a hill of iron-grey rock. Ama Nefasta, severe in black robes edged with scarlet velvet that clashed horribly with her lavender skin, stood on the second step, a branch of mistletoe in her hand.

The throne itself seemed made for a giant. Even accounting for the height of the average faerie, it was too large. It grew from the stone of the dais, a chair shape emerging from the rough, living rock. Its surface gleamed like hematite, or gunmetal.

Deor leaned forward. "Why..." she started to say, but Penny shushed her as the mirror's perspective shifted to a side door.

Trumpets blared. Two pages emerged from the door, stepped to one side, and bowed low, followed by a herald who announced, "His Majesty, the sovereign lord of the Winter Court, scion of the house of Aethelwing, ruler of the blessed Winter Realm by right of blood and inheritance, King Sweordmund VIII."

The herald stepped aside and bowed, bending his body in half. The entire company around the throne did so as well. Deor clapped a hand over her mouth to suppress her giggle at the sight of all those noble derrieres pointed at the watching nation. Penny leaned forward in her chair, eyes shining, her hand pressed to her heart.

King Sweordmund walked into the room.

"That crown must weigh a ton," Deor said, blinking at the platinum and diamond creation.

The king's dark hair hung down over his shoulders, blending with the black of his long coat. White streaks showed at his temples. Despite his erect posture and the smile he gave his people, lines of old pain showed around his mouth and eyes. On his arm walked his wife, a smaller crown in silver and opals on her brow. Next to her husband's black and silver, she wore a dress of twilight blue.

"The evening, walking with the starry night," Deor said aloud, surprising herself as much as Penny.

"Yes," Penny said. And then, "Oooh, there he is."

"Rafael, Lord Farringdon, Sword of Peace and Justice, chosen heir of his gracious Majesty," the herald called.

Deor sighed and reached for a cup of the flower tea. If she was honest, he was just her type—dangerous, gorgeous, and a total asshole. Her relationships might end with slammed doors and broken crockery, but they were better than her mother's pathetic, once in a lifetime love. She sipped her tea and leaned forward, studying the crowd.

To her surprise, the general went to stand among the guests, next to a man in deep blue who looked almost like a copy of him, if he was made middle aged and ferociously angry. The two of them did not look at one another.

"That's Edgar, the Duke of Wellhall, Lord Farringdon's estranged father," Penny supplied.

"Wait, his parents are alive? How do you adopt someone else's adult son?"

"You don't know anything do you?" Penny tore her gaze from the mirror to tut at Deor. "The king took Lord Farringdon as a hostage when he was only five because his parents led a Parliamentary revolt against him. No one expected him to end up as the king's favorite and Sword, let alone the heir."

"How cozy," Deor said.

Nice to know family values were alive and well in the Winter Court.

The king sat on his throne, his hands on the arms. Deor squinted at it, trying to focus properly. The throne looked just as massive as ever, but somehow it fit him perfectly.

She was about to comment when Ama spoke. "Where is your son, oh king?" she said. "Where is he who strengthens your hand?"

"I have no son," he replied. "No male child to strengthen my hand."

"Where is your daughter, oh king?" Ama said. "Where is she who delights your eyes?"

"I have no daughter," he said. His voice caught for just a second on the last word. "No female child to delight my eyes."

"Then you have no heir?" Ama said.

"I have no heir."

"Do you swear this under oath, in the sight of all these witnesses, that you have no heir of your body?"

"I swear it." As he spoke, the king winced.

Two thin lines of pain shot up Deor's back. She took another bite of scone and clenched her teeth. She'd been feeling so good the last few days. She shivered and tucked her feet under her on the chair, wondering what faeries used for aspirin.

Ama said to the King. "Do you pledge your sacred word that you have no heir?"

"On my sacred word and my honor, I swear it," he said. His hands tightened on the arms of the throne. "On my very life, I swear it."

Deor's heart raced.

Ama spun toward the assembly, her robes swirling. She raised her arms over their heads, though whether to deliver a blessing or a curse, no one could have told from her expression.

"The king is without an heir!" she declared. "Woe to the kingdom that has no heir. Woe to its people, its land, and its children. We are bereft."

"We are bereft," the assembly repeated. "Give us an heir, oh king."

The muscles along Deor's back clenched and twinged. A shudder wracked her body.

"Give us an heir," Penny whispered. Her hands were clasped to her chest as if in prayer.

In the mirror, Ama turned back to the king, her hands held in a gesture of pleading. "Your people beg you," she said. "Give them an heir. Fulfill your duty to your kingdom, to your people, your land, and its children. Give us an heir."

The king raised his left hand. "I have heard you, my people," he said. "And I will give you an heir. Step forward, my chosen son."

Lord Farringdon stepped out of the crowd and ascended the dais until he stood on the top step facing the king. The mirror angle shifted again so that the watchers could see both their faces.

"Who is this man you choose for your son?" Ama said.

Deor grimaced against the pain and rolled her eyes. Why did hyper-important ceremonies always involve some type of pretended ignorance? Cut to the chase. But the king was announcing the name of his chosen heir, and Lord Farringdon was confirming that he was indeed who everyone knew he was, going so far as to recite his ancestry back three generations. His voice rose as he recited the names.

"And are you willing to give up this name?" Ama said. "To renounce your father and mother, to take a new father and a new name?"

"I am," he said. "I renounce my father and mother." The smile faded. "I give up my name."

The mirror zoomed in on Lord Farringdon for a heartbeat. Sweat stood on his brow. Deor winced and shifted in her chair, trying to ease the spasms in her back. Her head throbbed.

"Then kneel," Ama told him.

He knelt in front of the king and stretched out his hands to touch the edge of the throne's seat.

"Embrace your son, oh King," Ama said, and King Sweordmund leaned forward to put his hands on Lord Farringdon's shoulders.

"I remove your name," Ama said. She tapped Lord Farringdon on the head with the mistletoe branch, and he shuddered. Sparks like static flickered off his hands where they touched the throne.

Deor's stomach rolled. Her back muscles spasmed. Pain shot through her head as if someone were digging their nails into the base of her skull.

"I remove your father and mother." Ama tapped him again. He closed his eyes and his jaw tightened. Lines of greasy silver light crawled out from his hands up his arms. The king's hands tightened on his shoulders.

"Be no more a Farringdon." She tapped him once more.

He gasped and bowed his head, his hair falling forward and blocking his face. The light from the throne covered him.

Deor's headache dug deeper, an iron band tightening its grip. Shards of light flashed around the edges of her eyes.

"Name your son, oh king," Ama commanded. "Call him by name and give us an heir."

"You are my son," the king said, "my heir. I give you my name and my blood." The words came out in irregular breaths. "You are Rafe, the son," he gasped, "of my body. The son of Sweordmund." The king faltered and seemed about to fall from the throne. "The only child of the house of Aethelwing."

Deor could barely hear his voice. She shielded her eyes from the light as another tremor of pain rolled across her skull.

"You are my son and my heir forever," the king said. "I have no other child but you."

Deor's gasped and gripped the arms of the chair. Her whole body shook, pain ripping through her. Something pushed her from behind, and she pitched face forward onto the floor. Everything went black.

She woke up on her back with Penny massaging her temples. All her bones felt hollow, her muscles limp. The searing pains in her back and head were gone. Penny had propped her feet on the chair and put a pillow under her head.

"How are you feeling?" Penny asked.

Deor blinked, wondering the same thing. "My head is killing me and I feel achy. I feel… bigger."

That wasn't normal for her fainting spells. Maybe she had a kind of faerie epilepsy human doctors couldn't detect. On the bright side, if she was still sick, living in Faerie probably wasn't her cure. Of course, that meant she was dying.

"You're a doctor," she said. "What's wrong with me?"

"Nothing I could find," Penny said. "No low blood sugar, magical exhaustion, tumors, stroke, nothing like that. No heart problems either. But that was one serious headache. Are those normal for you?"

"Sort of." Deor shrugged and rolled her head to stretch her neck. "I get pretty bad migraines, but they usually don't come on so suddenly." She looked up at the mirror, now back to its reflective surface. "Maybe it was the mirror. I have trouble watching hand-held video—kind of like the ceremony today—back home."

"Sounds possible," Penny said, though her frown suggested she thought otherwise. "But regardless, at least part of your problem is that your wings are having some serious growing pains, so I—"

"My what?" Deor sat up with a jerk. "I don't have wings!"

She shuddered and the feeling traveled out beyond her body. Way out. She arched her back to release the tension, but the weight dragging her backward remained.

She scrambled to her feet in front of the mirror and gaped at her reflection. Giant scarlet wings with black swirling veins sprouted from her back like she were an inkblot butterfly.

"Get it off me!" she screamed. She reached around behind her trying to get a hold on them. When that didn't work, she reached over her shoulders and grabbed them.

"Ow!" She let go. They were too tender to touch. She flailed at Penny. "Get them off me!"

"Stop! What are you doing?" Penny grabbed her wrists.

Cooling magic flowed up her arms, soothing and gentle, assuring her that she was safe.

At the touch of magic, adrenaline shot through Deor. A plume of sparkles puffed around her. She knocked her roommate's hands away and shook off the spell. "Don't you dare spell me!"

"I'm a healer." Penny held up her hands, palms out. "It's just a little anti-hysteria cantrip."

Deor took a deep breath and held it, trying not to think about Gregor Samsa. "I. Am. Not. Hysterical," she said after a minute. "I am upset because I have a giant bug on my back."

"Those are your wings. Haven't you seen wings before?"

"On faeries!"

The answer was too obvious for Penny to say out loud.

Deor took several more deep breaths. "Now what?" she said. "How do I get rid of them?"

"They're part of your body."

Deor covered her face with her hands for a minute.

"I'm not a faerie," she said into her palms. "I'm not a faerie. I'm not a faerie."

Her head throbbed. Every muscle in her body ached. Her new wings jumped and twitched with every passing breeze.

She examined herself in the mirror again. She could practically wrap herself in just one wing, assuming they were that flexible. Not that she was in a hurry to find out. Her wings were sensitive to every tiny movement and flutter of air. She shuddered, and they fanned in the mirror.

Every day she spent in this place she became a little more faerie. A little less human.

"I can't go out in public like this," Deor said. "You have to help me hide them or take them off or something."

Penny stepped forward, her hands out.

"Don't touch me." Deor jerked back. "Use your words."

"I won't. I'm sorry about the cantrip." Penny kept her voice soft, as if soothing a feral animal. "It's okay. You're too tense to pull them back in. The more you relax, the easier it will be. Try to think about something else."

"What? Like baseball?" Deor rolled her eyes.

Penny pushed the footstool toward her. "Have a seat."

The swallowtail swoop at the bottom of each wing slid over the ground as she eased on to the stool. It was like having someone run a finger over her ribs.

141

"How did this happen to me?"

Penny shrugged. "You're only thirty, right? Must be delayed puberty. Probably from magic deprivation in the human world. That's probably what stunted your growth, too."

"I am not stunted! I am a perfectly normal-sized human being! Changeling. Whatever."

"You are at least four inches shy of the faerie female average," Penny said. "Though you do seem," she eyed Deor's hips and breasts, "fully developed."

"So," Deor asked, trying to keep her voice calm, "are there any other mysterious body parts that might come leaping out of me?"

Penny shook her head. "Don't be silly."

"Thank God for small favors." Deor's head throbbed. "I'm not going to break out in zits am I?"

"No, no. Your wings are the last stage of puberty. They usually show up within a month of your first fertility cycle. Have you....?"

"Yes!" Deor snapped. "Since I was twelve." She hugged her arms around herself. "If I go to a faerie hospital, they're just going to tell me the same thing, aren't they?"

Penny nodded. "I've probably treated more human-faerie changelings than anyone else in this city," she said. "Aside from the wings, has this happened before?"

"I've been feeling off for, I don't know, about a year." Deor hauled herself up off the stool. "But if you can't tell me anything else, I'm going back to bed."

She dragged herself from the parlor and up the stairs, her wings trailing behind her like a cloak. Maybe if she lay on her stomach, her wings would fold into her back as she slept—and maybe they'd never come out again.

Chapter Eighteen

When Tuesday morning came, Deor still felt like she'd been hit by a truck. Her new wings twitched and jumped in her back and her hands shook with exhaustion. The pain in her head had settled into a dull, persistent ache, even with Penny's attempts to make it go away. No matter how much water she drank, she still felt like a wrung out wash rag. Still, when morning came, she put on her new robes and dragged herself to class. If this was her last day, she was going down fighting.

As if they knew the finale was coming, every actor was in place. All her students were present, bright eyed and bushy tailed—some literally. Even Robbie had made it, sitting toward the back in a protective circle of friends. Geoff, Donovan, and Ama were already seated in the front row when Deor walked in at three minutes to ten.

She set her book down and faced her class, one hand on the podium to steady herself. As she scanned the eager faces, sizing up the class, a last straggling student slipped in through the door. Just behind her came Lord Farringdon. He was covered in magic, fuzzy from head to foot the way the captain had been in the Tower. When she squinted, the fuzziness resolved briefly into a net of magic over his whole body, distorting the edges and forcing her eyes to look away. Not making a sound, he walked to the back of the room and leaned back in a corner, arms folded as he watched her. If anyone else could see him, they gave no sign.

The morning papers had gushed over his "heroic performance" and "princely demeanor" at the Adoption, but at the moment he looked as ragged as she felt. Dark circles marred his eyes. Pain lines etched his jawline and forehead. Or perhaps that was a glare of hatred especially for her. Fine. Let him watch. He could escort her to the border after Ama fired her. Deor squared her shoulders and smiled at the class. Never let them see you suffer.

She slid the stool out from under the lectern and stood on it. "Okay," she said the second the clock hit ten, "I asked you to read and summarize the first three acts of *Midsummer* for today. Are there any comments before we begin?"

"I don't know why we have to read this faerie crap," Simon, the goblin spoke out. His friends snickered. "If I wanted to read about faeries, I'd have taken any of the other classes offered."

"Because it's not about faeries," Deor said. "It's about people. It's universal. Besides, the faeries aren't the main characters."

"The humans are just stupid sheep," a vampire girl piped up, her eyes on Donovan.

"That's so speciest," Robbie snapped.

A faerie boy turned to sneer at her. "Touchy, touchy half-breed," he said.

"Stop right there!" Deor shouted. "You are free to dislike the plays. You're free to dislike me, but you are *not* free to insult other students! Do I make myself clear?"

The boy shrugged. "What's an elf like you going to do about it?"

A few in the class gasped at his comment, but Deor ignored them.

"I will throw your sparkly little ass out of my classroom, sunshine. And, if you don't leave on your own, I will call security and have a bear help you." She glared the boy down until he shut his mouth and shrank in his chair. "Now," she said, "someone tell us, what is the conflict at the beginning of Act One?"

Students reached for their books. A couple raised tentative hands.

In the front row, Donovan snorted awake, stretched and yawned.

The class burst out laughing, all chance of someone answering the question dashed. Chatter broke out. A few students closed their books and put them away. Even Geoff was laughing behind his hand.

Deor couldn't quite bring herself to look at Lord Farringdon—she could imagine too well the look on his face.

She flexed her fingers, joints aching. Exhaustion weighed down her shoulders. She wanted nothing more than to walk away and be done with this nonsense, but the thought of letting them win burned. Ama had gone back to poking her slate, surely calling up termination papers.

Well, if Deor had to go, she wasn't going to go gently.

"Geoff!" she said, projecting from the diaphragm so her voice hit the back wall of the classroom. The conversation stopped. People turned back toward her. Donovan gave a start and blinked a few times.

"Bring your book up here, please. I think we need a little bit of performance. Shakespeare can feel so dead on the page sometimes." She smiled at the class with all her teeth.

Donovan yawned again and slouched back down, eyes closing.

"Donovan," she snapped, and he jerked his head up. "You too."

"What?"

Deor stepped out from behind the lectern. "Come here."

He glanced at Geoff who nodded. His eyes fixed on her face, Donovan slid out of the narrow student desk and came to stand next to Geoff.

"Here you go," she handed him her book, "since you don't have yours. Act Two, Scene One. About halfway through the scene."

She stepped back to the lectern, leaving the two men in center stage. "Okay, gentlemen. You're going to do a dramatic reading." Her heart was racing, her wings straining to bust out through her bra, but she kept the tremor out of her voice. "In Shakespeare's day all the actors were men," she said, turning to the class, "so we'll have men play both Demetrius and Helena. Geoff, you be—"

"—let me guess. Helena?" He grinned at her. "If I'd known, I'd have brought a dress."

"No." Deor said. "You'll be Demetrius." She pointed at Donovan. "You've got long hair. You be Helena."

Donovan scanned the page in front of him. "Read this?"

"You can read, can't you?" Deor asked.

A few of the students snickered. Conversations died down as students leaned forward, eager for whatever drama came next.

Donovan glared at her. "I'm not reading this." He held the textbook toward, but she refused to take it.

"Yes, you are. You're reading it, or I'm throwing you out of the classroom."

Geoff coughed. "Excuse me, professor, but you can't do that."

"Can't I?" She laid her hand on her chest and feigned concern. "Why ever not?"

He at least had the grace to look slightly embarrassed. "I can't be without my bodyguard."

"Oh," she beamed. "I see." She pointed at Donovan. "He's your employee, right?"

"No." Donovan cut Geoff off.

"Then you're his servant?" she asked.

Color flushed Donovan's face and his pupils widened, filling irises with black. "I am no man's servant," he said, and his voice, eerily soft, echoed off the walls in the now silent room.

She faced him, every nerve telling her to run. She was dying anyway. It might as well be here and now, a messy, violent death by vampire better than a prolonged, grey death like her mother's.

Her mind flashed back to the image of her mother dying by inches back home, longing for a man who would never come. For a split second, memory blotted out the classroom and the fanged monster before her.

What had Shakespeare said? "My life were better ended by their hate, than death prorogued, wanting of thy love." She'd never liked that play. She put a steadying hand on the lectern and lifted her chin a fraction higher.

"Are you paid?"

"It isn't that simple," Geoff said. "Our families have ties that go back for years. And—"

"Paid?" she repeated, eyes still on Donovan.

"Yes," Geoff said. "But—"

"But nothing." She flicked her gaze to Geoff. "Either he does the reading or he goes. Either you control the servant in your employ or you go. Simple." She turned back to Donovan. "Don't worry, no one will laugh at you. Even if it is supposed to be funny."

A few nervous laughs rose from the class. Most students sat still as rabbits before a predator. Ama held her stylus and stared at Donovan, so tense that her pulse was visible in her throat. In the back of the room, Lord Farringdon pushed out of his corner, poised as if he might jump the distance between them. Donovan's irises were pure black.

"The lines aren't hard, Donovan," she said. "Just kneel and say 'I am your spaniel, the more you beat me the more I follow you. Use me as you use your dog.'"

"I am no man's dog!" Donovan spat.

Deor swayed and gripped the lectern, the force of his voice almost knocking her over. The vampire's eyes were black from edge to edge, a blood red circle where his iris should be. His fangs were as long as her pinky and his fists clenched so tightly around the textbook that his knuckles were white.

"Read!"

"No. You listen to me, you puny half-breed. I am Vlad Drogos Rodzevrah! Heir to Vlad Tertius, ruler of the vampire nation. I kneel to no one! You should kneel to me."

At the command a few students—and not just vampires—dropped from their chairs to their knees. Lord Farringdon's hands came up, cupped and holding some kind of magic.

Deor's knees threatened to buckle, but she dug her nails into the lectern's wood and refused to bend.

"I don't kneel either," she whispered.

In her back, her wings strained. Every sensible part of her brain shouted for her to run. A couple of students did just that, darting out the door at the top of the room. The movement drew the vampire's eye and he lunged slightly before focusing again on her.

She forced herself to let go of the lectern. Nothing nearby could even remotely count as a weapon. He even had her textbook, which, heavy as it was, might have had a chance of slowing him down.

Ama sat perfectly still, gaze darting back and forth between Deor and Donovan, stylus raised like a wand.

She was so going to get fired for this.

If, of course, Donovan didn't kill and eat her.

"I'm sorry," she said, her voice soft.

"What?" Donovan demanded.

The tension eased from both Geoff and Ama's shoulders. One of the vampire students chuckled.

"Everyone here has been so clear about their titles. Geoff's a prince, you're the heir to a fanged kingdom. I always said I had no title, except professor. But that's a lie." She glanced at Geoff whose eyes had grown wide, his face pale.

"Really?" Donovan scoffed. "And who might you be?"

Deor gave a small curtsy. "I am her Majesty Deor Smithfield, queen of the blessed realm of I Don't Give A Fuck Who Your Daddy Is."

Donovan charged straight at her. He knocked the podium aside with one fist, stopping inches from her, looming over her so that his body filled her vision. He growled low in his throat. His deep red irises swirled like a whirlpool of blood.

"Going to kill me? Drink my blood?" Deor taunted, even as her throat dried and adrenaline thundered through her veins.

Magic rolled down her skin in waves, the whisper of it rising in her ears. Sparks flared off her like fireworks, but she held his gaze.

"I could drain you dry in moments," he whispered. "Rip your throat out in one bite."

"Sure." Deor forced herself to smile. "But you'd be doing it in front the head of the department, the bard in charge of the Adoption. Then you'd have to go back to your oh-so-important daddy and tell him you can't do your job because you ate some half-human. And what kind of big, scary monster points do you get for eating a pathetic creature like me? In public. In this space."

Donovan's nostrils flared, and he jerked forward at her again.

Her breath caught in her throat, but she didn't flinch. Sparkles fell from her, landing harmlessly on his leather jacket.

He spun away and let out a bellow that shook the windows. He tore the textbook in half, flung it to the ground, and stormed from the room. She swallowed hard and swayed, her knees again threatening to give way. Instead, she turned to Geoff.

"Get your bodyguard under control or I'll throw both of you out and fail you. If he's in here he's a student. Am I clear?"

"Yes ma'am," Geoff said with a relieved grin. He leaned forward and whispered in a voice only she could hear, "you are so much more than I expected." He bowed slightly and left.

Deor turned to the class gesturing at the scattered pages and shattered lectern. "I seem to have lost my textbook. And my podium. So let's call it a day. I'll collect your summaries on Thursday."

The students gathered their things and did not linger.

One of the goblin boys muttered to his defiant friend, "I bet she could literally throw your ass out of class."

When they were all gone, Deor let out a long sigh. She had wood splinters embedded under her nails where she had dug them into the lectern.

"I'm sorry," she said to Ama. "I'll buy you a new textbook... and a podium."

"Don't worry about that," Ama snapped.

"I know," she said, "I'm fired." She let out a small laugh. "But it was worth it."

Ama frowned for a moment. "I realize I told you to get control of your classroom, but this?" She waved her hand at the mess. "Entirely unconventional."

"I'll get my things out of my office."

"I said unconventional. Not ineffective. Picking a fight with the biggest, strongest creature in the room? What made you think that was a good idea?"

"Prison movies?" Deor offered weakly.

Ama laughed under her breath, the first sign of amusement Deor had seen from her. "Do you know how many professors would have paid to be here for that? They'll have a chance to see it soon enough, I suppose. At least two students had their mirrors out."

"Wait, did they record it?" Deor's shoulders slumped. "I didn't mean..."

Ama raised her hand. "Stop. You won." She scribbled on her slate. "I'll give you a full year contract. I can't imagine your class not filling next semester."

"Thank you." A small pang of guilt hit her for intending to leave long before that. "I promise all the classes won't be like this."

"Indeed. I do hope at some point you get around to actually teaching the material. And perhaps next time try 'wet hen' rather than profanity."

"It's a good Old English word," she protested. When Ama raised an eyebrow, Deor nodded. "Okay, wet hen, got it." She scanned the room. "Lord Farringdon's gone. I'm surprised he didn't stay to yell at me."

"What? Here?" Anger flared in Ama's eyes. "On campus?"

Deor pointed to the top corner of the room. "He was right there through the whole class."

"Right up there? Where everyone could see him. You're sure?"

"Yes. He was covered in magic, but he was there."

Ama's frown deepened to a hard scowl. "Minions of the monarch should not be sneaking around my campus! He should have requested my permission to be in the classroom." She evaluated Deor, scanning her up and down. "Are you sure it was you he came to watch?"

"Um... maybe?" Deor hazarded. "I assumed he was here to see me get fired and then throw me out of the country."

"He could have been here for more political reasons."

Oh yes. Geoff and Donovan were foreign princes, weren't they? Great, more faerie politics for her to avoid.

Ama's tone softened a touch. "I suppose he may have been here to look after Miss Ellington. Still it's inexcusable. I will look into this." She turned and left.

Deor scanned the room. Some students had left books and coats. Donovan's leather jacket still hung over the chair. "Ha!" she said to it. "Try to fuck with me in my classroom? That's what you get. Let's see someone else try something now!"

"Indeed," a voice said from a few feet away. "You have set quite the precedent."

Chapter Nineteen

"Gah!" She jumped sideways, sure Donovan had come back to eat her in private. Instead, the general stood in front of her. No more magic covered him.

"Hello, Professor Smithfield."

"Don't you have anything better to do than harass me?" She stepped in front of him and headed up the stairs. "You should leave before Ama finds you."

He followed and caught the door, holding it open for her. Keeping his voice low, he said, "Your student Roberta Ellington was attacked."

Deor turned to face him. "I know. She told me."

A chill buffeted her.

"You were the last person that she remembers speaking to before she was attacked. I want you to come down to the Tower and give a statement."

He held her gaze, his blue eyes rimmed with ice, but she didn't flinch. After Donovan it would take more than an icy stare to shake her. Fine lines had appeared around his eyes since the last time she had been this close to him. His deep blue skin had a tint of grey. Under his left eye and across his cheek, the same small glimmer of magic she remembered from the Tower lingered. She wanted to reach up and brush it away so she could see what lay underneath.

She also wanted to stay as far from the Tower as possible, but the image of Robbie, huddled in her coat, apologizing for missing class, rose up in her mind. If her testimony could help, she had to go.

"I'll come down after my second class." When he looked about to object, she added, "I promise. Right after class."

"I'll be expecting you."

"Of course." She gave him a nod. "I'll help any way I can."

"This afternoon, then." He bowed slightly.

She waited until he had disappeared down the stairwell and made her way up to her office, thrilled to find that the vampire wasn't waiting for her outside the door.

Deor's second class was perfectly well behaved, though it lacked both the TA and the bodyguard. The class answered her questions quickly and with enthusiasm—quite possibly enthusiasm born of fear, but she'd take it. They actually made their way through the first two acts of the play before class was over.

"Alright," she said at a quarter to three, "I think we've gotten far enough. I'll give you guys until Thursday for your Acts I-III summaries, too. Have a good afternoon. Class dismissed."

Her teaching assistant Geoff should have been there to observe the class and discuss the next lesson afterward, but under the circumstances she was happy he hadn't shown up. She stuffed her academic robe in her bag and headed for the door. As she crossed the grassy oval toward the surrounding forest, she tried to remember anything she could from meeting Robbie at the shop. Had anyone in the shop seemed out of place? Had any of the other customers been watching them or perhaps listened in on their conversation?

By the time she arrived at the Tower, she was positive she had nothing useful to offer. But at least she could keep her word.

As she walked from the university to the Tower of Caer Eisteddfod, she formed a mental map of Caer Eisteddfod and London, laying one over the other. So the Tower and the river were the same in both places. The Palace, its spires visible in the distance to the west, lay roughly where Buckingham Palace now stood.

Interesting. If she could get her hands on some medieval maps of London, would they show even more similarities between the two cities? Had there been trees beside the Thames once? Trees and running water together often meant faeries in human medieval texts, and it was no surprise the door to the Winter Court was at the Tower. She dug her hands into her coat—there might be a scholarly article in all this. She could call it "Entrances to the Underworld: Traces of Fae Influence in Fourteenth Century London."

Of course, no human scholarly journal would take it. A faerie scholarly journal might. Her empty stomach clenched at the thought. Even if she found her faerie father, met him, and was cured, she didn't have a job to go back to. Academia was a small world and newly minted PhDs in English were lucky to get adjunct jobs these days, let alone full time work, even if they didn't have a reputation for quitting a job with no warning two weeks before the semester started. Working at Eisteddfod might be her only job option once this was all over.

Like its human counterpart, the Tower was a walled fortress. She walked halfway around it looking for an entrance. There was no sign of the small door Horseboy had let her out when she first arrived. Eventually, she came to a wide open pair of wooden doors with guards on either side. Overhead the spikes of a portcullis threatened to fall on the head of any invader.

What was she thinking? She'd be lucky if she got out of this place alive. Overhead, the massive grey stones loomed, the gate opening through a wall so thick that it formed a tunnel. The Tower was a prison, no matter which side of the Thames she was on. She swallowed hard and approached one of the guards on either side of the gate.

"Lord Farringdon asked me to come down and speak to him. He's expecting me."

The faerie, his skin a pale shade of pink, raised an eyebrow at this but called over his shoulder.

"Lieutenant Bolton, there's a woman here to see the General."

The same blond man she had met at immigration came out of a guardhouse set into the wall.

"Professor Smithfield? Come this way. The General said to escort you up as soon as you arrived."

If she looked closely, she could see magic around his throat—not like a collar, but like the blood in his veins made visible. She could hear it, too. Word magic, then? Was that a thing? Penny had said there were four basic types of faerie magic—did that mean he was an air faerie? She made a mental note to listen carefully and think twice any time Bolton spoke.

However, he didn't say another word as he led her into a paved court-yard. Instead of being filled with picture-snapping tourists, the faerie Tower's yard was full of people in black and silver uniforms. Off to one side, a squad was doing flying exercises—dropping to the ground as if for a push-up, but lifting themselves with their wings. A drill sergeant stood over them bellowing that he didn't want to see any pansy-ass fluttering.

"My crippled grandmother could get higher off the ground than you lot! Let's see some muscle!" he shouted.

So, some things were universal.

She followed Bolton into the main keep and down a hallway. He pressed his hand to the door at the end of the hall and spoke a language she couldn't understand. It sounded vaguely Celtic with a few Germanic gutturals thrown into the mix. A moment later Lord Farringdon's voice answered in the same language. The door swung open. Bolton stood to one side.

"Go right in, Professor. He's expecting you."

Deor paused before crossing the threshold. "I'm just curious, were you speaking Faerie?"

"Yes. Please, go in."

She stepped over the threshold, and her stomach did a back somer-sault as if she had stepped off a too high curb and been yanked up in the air by her ankles at the same time. She stopped, panting, and braced herself on the doorpost behind her. In the wall to her right was a set of windows. Two of the three windows had real glass panes, but the center one was sealed with magic like the window in her office. They looked out over the rooftops and down into the courtyard where she had just been. Somehow that single step had taken her up three stories.

"Are you well?" Lord Farringdon sounded as if he hoped she wasn't.

She took a deep breath and turned toward him where he sat behind a wide wooden desk.

"I'm fine. Thank you." Thanks for the warning, you smug aristocrat.

He smiled, leaning back in his chair. The scrap of magical fuzziness still hovered under his eye. She focused on it, imagining peeling it up to see what it hid, but the more she stared, the less substantial the magic seemed. It wriggled under her gaze and fell apart, threads of it breaking off and vanishing like spider silk. When it was gone, a thin, white scar ran from the corner of Lord Farringdon's eye to the top of his lip. It gave his stern face a rakish look. Not the sort one takes home to meet Grandmother, but then she'd never been looking for that sort anyway.

"I bet there's a story behind that scar," she said before she thought better of it.

Lord Farringdon jerked his hand to his face, then looked at himself in the mirror over the mantelpiece. He turned back to her with a glare.

"Why did you do that? It's rude, you know. And technically I could charge you with assault."

"I didn't mean to. I'm not even touching you."

"Sit down." He pointed to a padded leather chair in front of his desk.

She sat, looking at the scar again. The magic must have been cosmetic. "Battle scar?"

The temperature in the room dropped.

"I'd rather not talk about it. Again, such questions are rude." As he spoke, a cold draft blew past Deor's ankles. She shivered in her coat.

"I'm sorry." She settled her bag on her lap and held his gaze. "So shall we get started with my statement? You could have just sent for me. There was no need to spy on me in my own classroom."

He arched an eyebrow at her.

"Yes, I saw you." Deor crossed her arms and leaned back. "Though apparently I was the only one. When I told Ama you were there, she was not impressed. Were you there spying on me or someone else?"

His mouth dropped open for a second like he was about to deny that he had been there, but he seemed to think better of it, and he snapped his mouth closed. After a moment, he tried again.

"There are several students from important families in your classroom, as well as two foreign dignitaries," he said. "You yourself claim to be an unimportant changeling. So why, with the dozens of other people in the room, do you assume I was there to see you?" He smirked at her. "Are you important after all, your majesty?"

She shook her head. "Not the way you mean it. I'm just here—"

"Looking for your father," he finished for her. "Yes. That is what you keep saying. So I looked into your story." He yanked a file from a stack on his desk. "No record of a child reported missing or kidnapped in Caer Eisteddfod within three years of your birth." Before she could respond, he held up his hand. "No report anywhere in the Winter Court at all. No record of a birth, even. Nor in the Summer Court." He stared at her for a moment. "No record in London, either. I had some of our allies do some digging. There was not a single child born in those years who corresponds to your story." He flipped the file closed. The chill in the air deepened.

She folded her arms across her chest. "Theophilous…"

"Came to see me. He shows evidence of will spells—very powerful will spells—much like the young women who have been attacked."

Deor clenched her fists, her nails digging into her palms.

"You can't seriously think I put a spell on him. I was a newborn thirty years ago." She slipped the strap of her purse over her shoulder. "If that's all you need from me, I'm going." She stood up.

"Sit down!" he snapped.

She sat.

"Several women, including one of your students, have been brutally attacked. The most recent remembers speaking to you around the time she was attacked. And we have reason to suspect at least one of the attackers was female. Coincidence?"

"Yes!" she shouted back at him. "And how dare you imply I had anything to do with hurting Robbie! I would never harm a student."

"No?" he snapped. "Do you have an alibi for that time?"

"I was shopping!" Deor barked, her own breath fogging in the frigid air. "And why is it so damn cold in here?"

He ignored her question. "Can you prove it?"

"Probably. I have the robe I bought. Check my mirror—you'll see how much I paid for it." Deor tightened the belt of her coat and wrapped her arms around herself. "Stop trying to freeze me."

"Did Robbie tell you where she was going?"

"She said she was going home. Do I need a lawyer?" She shoved away the voice inside herself that pointed out she had no idea what sort of rights, if any, she had in the Winter Court. For all she knew, due process meant someone cleaned up the blood afterward.

When Lord Farringdon didn't answer, Deor stood up. "I came down here in good faith to give a statement. Unless you're arresting me, I am leaving."

In two steps, he blocked her passage. "You resisted the will of one of the most powerful vampires in the land, and I'm supposed to think you're just some helpless twit looking for her long lost daddy? Ha!" He leaned forward, looming over her. "So help me, if you had anything to do my little sister's injuries, I will find out, I will prove it, and your head will be on a pike on the Tower Bridge. Do I make myself clear?"

Robbie—his sister? How? Was she a half-, a step-? Confusion vied with the urge to lean back away from him. Defiance won out.

"Don't you threaten me." The cloud of multi-colored sparkles coming off her undermined the stern professor voice she used, but she craned her neck to look up at him, locking her gaze on his.

At the far end of the room, Lt. Bolton's face appeared on the mirror over the fireplace. "I beg your pardon, Lord Farringdon. There's a mirror call for you. Bard Nefasta demands you speak to her immediately. She intends to come here in person if you won't speak to her by mirror."

Lord Farringdon shot a glare at Deor.

"Stay there," he said and stormed over to the fireplace. "Put her through."

Nefasta's face appeared, even more pinched than usual.

"Lord Farringdon, I will not have you or any other member of the military—is that Dr. Smithfield behind you? What is she doing there?"

Lord Farringdon answered her in Faerie, or at least a language that sounded like what Bolton had used at the door. Deor dug her hands into her pockets and pretended not to be listening while the two faeries argued.

It didn't take a linguistic genius to catch the gist of their conversation. Nefasta was angry. Lord Farringdon was in no mood to placate her. The room got colder as the argument went on until Deor resorted to pulling her academic robe out of her purse and putting it on over her coat. The yellow-lined hood actually functioned, unlike the ones on human robes, so she pulled that up over her ears and wrapped the long liripipe, a sort of narrow tail hanging off the back of the hood, around her neck like a scarf. She probably looked like some sort of demented bumble-bee elf, but at least she was warmer.

Eventually the argument wound down. Lord Farringdon gave the mirror a stiff, angry bow and Nefasta's face disappeared. He was seething when he turned around.

"You are a very lucky woman," he said, striding over to his desk.

He yanked a piece of paper out of a drawer and scribbled on it with a quill pen. He then pressed a seal ring against the bottom of the page.

"There," he said. "You have your visa, signed and filed. Now get out of my office. And stay away from Robbie or so help me all the bards in the world won't be able to save you."

She gave him a short nod, held her head high, and forced herself not to run from the room.

It took her half the walk back to the university to get the feeling back in her fingers and toes. She flashed her mirror at the gate bear and stalked along the path through the woods. All around her the leaves were well into their fall turn, and the dropping sun filtered through them, setting a fire behind their already brilliant glow, but their beauty only reminded her of how little time she had left. She had her visa, but she'd wasted days getting it, and she had to keep teaching or be kicked out of the Winter Court. Lord Farringdon had saved her hours of searching public records —and crushed her hopes in the process. She was sicker than ever and no closer to finding her father.

She kicked a rock off the path into the trees, her hands deep in her pockets. What was left? As she emerged from the campus woods into the open oval, the shadow of the library's spire plummeted like an execution-er's axe across campus, splitting it in two. She gazed at it, following it back to the massive building at the heart of the university. Peerages. Histories. Information on the genetics and medical needs of changelings. Pages and pages of the bluebloods of the Winter Court.

He had to be in there somewhere, lurking. She would drag him and his family secrets out of the shadows and into the light.

Chapter Twenty

Bright and early the next morning, Deor strode across campus toward the library, filling her lungs with the clean, autumn smell. Her headache was finally gone, though she had to hold her wings in. Now that she knew they were there, every deep breath made her want to put them out. It was like walking with her arms clamped tight at her sides. Still, she walked with a spring in her step. Golden leaves crunched underfoot. Frost lingered in the shade under the trees, and a wisp of cloud tangled around the topmost spire of the library.

She climbed the four shallow library steps, the stones worn down by centuries of feet, up to three sets of bronze doors, each intricately carved. On the first, a man bearing giant stag horns on his head presented a group of robed figures with a scroll. In the second, the figures stood around a stone circle like the one at the center of campus. In the third, the horned figure presided over what she hoped was just a campfire.

Once through the doors, she stopped for a moment, overawed by the sheer immensity of it all. The central foyer went up three stories, lit by clerestory windows that cast rainbow-edged beams of light onto the blue-green slate floors. Beyond them stood rank upon rank of shelves, crammed with books. She smiled and let out a deep, stress-releasing sigh. Even in Faerie, a library felt like home.

On either side of her sprawled two curving counters, one labeled

Circulation and the other *Catalogue*. A few librarians moved behind the counters or helped people, but their movements only served to punctuate the whispery silence of thousands upon thousands of books and manuscripts. She suppressed the impulse to simply wander into the stacks, pulling volumes off shelves at random, exploring the library's hidden depths like Livingstone in Africa.

She chose the *Catalogue* counter and, ignoring the stepstool, said, "Excuse me, I'm Professor Smithfield, visiting professor in the literature department. Can you introduce me to the catalogue system?"

"Certainly," the librarian said. She was a blonde woman with a painfully tight bun, though whether she was fat or thin, curvy or straight was impossible to tell. Despite the classical beauty of her face, she wore layers of beige and grey sweaters piled over a tightly buttoned, high collared shirt, and her shoulders hunched in a way that said, loud and clear, "don't look at me." Still, she gave Deor a tight, though anxious smile and said, "I'd be delighted to help you, Professor."

"Thank you. I'm trying to research the faerie side of my family. Am I right in thinking that noble faeries are the ones with the most magical power?"

"Generally, yes that's true," the librarian said.

"Good, then I want a listing of all the noblemen in the country, preferably with physical descriptions and vital statistics like age and marital status."

"Oh yes, we have that." With a bone stylus, she jotted notes on a white marble slab set into the counter. A list of book titles appeared on the slab's surface along with catalogue numbers. She pointed to the first entry with her stylus.

"The catalogue *lingua franca* is Faerie, but you can do a direct search in English, both ancient and modern, Goblin, all three Trollish languages, Western Dragon, and Dwarvish. Most of the Indo-European human languages are searchable as well, though it has been having some trouble lately with Attic B and Gothic. There are terminals at the juncture points of all the floors so you don't have to come down here for each new search."

"So, if I understand you correctly," Deor said, "I write down what I want on the slab and the catalogue will tell me where to find it?"

The woman gave a tight, nervous laugh as if Deor had just described quantum mechanics as studying really, really little stuff.

"The conceptual mapping spells on our library are some of the most complicated in the world. They take your key terminology and cross reference it intuitively with…"

She went into a prolonged description of the magic, none of which meant anything to Deor, but which, she gathered, amounted to "write what you want on one of the slabs and the catalogue will tell you where to find it."

The librarian laid a piece of paper next to the slab and with her stylus made a little check mark next to each entry on the stone. As she did so, the entry appeared on the paper. "There you go," she said, handing the paper to Deor and explaining how each book's shelfmark would lead her to the correct floor, book stack, shelf, and exact position.

Deor thanked her and followed the list into the depths of the library. Her legs were getting stronger with all the walking she'd done lately, but even so, eight floors were a bit much. When she caught her breath, she ransacked the genealogy shelves until her arms were full. She claimed a long oak table for herself by shamelessly spreading her books all over it and surveyed their spines. *Edbert's Guide to the Noble Families of Fae* seemed like a good place to start. If Edbert didn't help, she'd try *Recent Gentry and Influential Commoners of the Winter Court* by Grimthorpe Garstein Steinbrau with *Supplementary Additions* by Grimthorpe Garstein Steinbrau, Junior. She pulled out a notepad and pen, flipped open volume one of *Edbert's Guide*, and started scanning family pages.

Four hours later, as the university bell chimed noon, she let her pen drop. She flopped forward into the open book in front of her and lay there with the cool paper cradling her face. Spots danced in front of her eyes. Even after *Edbert's* helped her eliminate every man too old or too young to be a plausible suspect, her list of possibilities was four pages long. Pictures of the nobles had done nothing for her. She had stared at one man's face after another, hunting for some resemblance to her own, until she could see them with her eyes closed. One man was pale like her but had bright orange eyes. Another had her hair, but his jaw seemed wrong. Noses, eyes, cheekbones, even quirks of expression: she had studied them all. It was useless. She couldn't tell what was a flash of recognition or simple wishful thinking.

"Admit it," she said, still face down in the book, "you have no idea what he looks like." She sat back up, scraping the hair out of her eyes. Her stomach growled and rumbled.

"Fine," she said out loud. "If you lot can't help me, I'll just move on to medical texts. If they can replace Lord Farringdon's genes, maybe they can cure being a changeling."

"Arguing with dead scholars? That's a sure sign of acute academia," Geoff said behind her. Deor started and her nails dug into the tabletop, leaving four splintered trails in the wood like a cat had been sharpening its claws there. Only the wooden back of her chair stopped her wings from puffing out in alarm. She took a deep breath and breathed out, forcing her shoulders down from around her ears.

"Good grief," she whispered at him. "What are you doing here?"

"Research." He held up a book. "Best way I know to avoid actually writing my dissertation."

She slumped back into her chair, a hand over her mouth to hold down the relieved laugh.

"Where's your fanged friend?"

"Lurking." Geoff pointed behind him. "It's one of his hobbies. So, what are you working on?" He settled onto the table's edge, book resting on his knee, and scanned the titles scattered around the table.

For a second, she considered telling him the whole story. But there was no need for her to go spilling her guts in the middle of the library, especially with Donovan listening in. Shoving her notes into her bag, she said, "Just doing a little research into my roots."

"I, on the other hand," Geoff said, "am famished and giving up for the day. It's too lovely outside to work. I don't suppose you'd care to join me?"

Her stomach gurgled an answer for her.

"It's not forbidden you know," he went on. "I checked the Faculty Handbook. And no one could accuse you of taking advantage of a younger colleague." He flashed another pointy toothed grin.

Deor laughed. He looked about thirty-five or so, which probably meant he was a hundred and fifty. And he was a prince. Totally unavailable for a long-term relationship. Plus, he had connections. Something told her he wouldn't be too reluctant to spill gossip about the faerie nobility. Definitely more promising than reading another set of faerie peerages.

"Alright," she said. "Let's play hooky together, at least for lunch."

"Excellent." Geoff hopped down from the table, his perfectly pressed shirt just inches from her chest. He whistled to Donovan, who slouched out of a shadowed alcove.

"Where shall we go?" Geoff said, leading her away from the stairwell toward a wall with a painted doorway. "The world lies before us."

"Not straight into a wall," Deor said, as she pulled back. She pointed toward the stairs. "Let's start there and then find that pixie with the food cart on the quad."

"You don't like portals?" Geoff said. "I'm far too lazy for the stairs." He tapped the painted doorway, saying, "first floor."

Deor gasped as the door dissolved, revealing the library's foyer. She could have smacked herself in the head. "Let me guess, those ugly bricked up doorways in the Literary Arts building are portals, too? And I've been hauling myself up five flights of stairs."

Geoff laughed. "No wonder you're in such lovely shape. Shall we?" He stepped through the portal and offered her his hand. Her stomach turned over at the thought of stepping down eight floors, but Geoff was standing with his arm outstretched and Donovan was beside her, arms crossed and a sneer on his face. She tossed her hair, fixed a smile on her face, and stepped through.

Like at the Tower, there was a brief, stomach dropping sensation that she had fallen off a cliff as magic rushed from the bottoms of her feet to the top of her head, and she was through, standing safely in the library foyer, facing the outer doors, which were propped open to the sunshine beyond. A faint aroma of spiced meat and vegetables wafted through them.

"Well," she said. "That was invigorating. Let's get lunch." Donovan snorted and shoved past her.

Geoff offered her his arm.

They ate a lunch on a bench under one of the giant trees on the quad. "This probably isn't what you're used to, is it?" Deor said as she swallowed the last of her grilled sausage. As with human sausages, she hadn't asked what was in it, but it reminded her of the best bratwurst from the Ohio State campus. And the grilled rampion definitely beat out bell peppers.

Geoff shrugged. "I am a student among students. I eat my humble meal alfresco and return to my garret to study by candlelight."

"Oh bull." Deor's laugh almost drowned out Donovan's snort. "Your idea of a picnic is probably a silk tent and a full kitchen staff of servants."

"And dogs and huntsmen," Geoff agreed. "With musicians, in case we get bored."

"You're ridiculous." She stood up, dusting crumbs off her lap. "So what now? Back to work, or have you got something more entertaining in mind?"

"How about a carriage ride through the city? I could show you the sights."

"Fantastic." She hoisted her satchel over her shoulder. "Let's see what this city has to offer." Her father wasn't going to be lurking around the campus, that was certain. But maybe he'd be out there somewhere in the city, enjoying the things that had charmed her mother.

Chapter Twenty-One

Once they had walked across the oval and through the campus forest to the city outside, Donovan stepped off the curb to hail a cab. The vehicle that screeched to a halt in front of them wasn't just round and orange. It really was an honest to goodness giant pumpkin—the pale orange pumpkin meat had been somehow carved, dehydrated, and lacquered.The wheels were formed from vines.

"Oh my, and me without my glass slippers," Deor said as she stepped inside. Geoff merely looked confused, and she was pretty sure the guffaw she heard came from Donovan.

As she slid across the bench seat to make room for Geoff, Deor peered at the cab's interior. It lacked seeds and pulp, thank goodness, but it was undeniably an actual gourd. Geoff slid in beside her, and Donovan swung himself up the outside to sit beside the driver, who, Deor imagined, must have been thrilled by that arrangement.

The cab whisked them away from the university and past the market- place. Geoff narrated their trip through the city's political district, past the City Hall and House of Lords. A high stone wall, wide enough for the armed guards to walk along its crenelated top, outlined the Palace grounds.

"It must be miles long," Deor said leaning out the window to crane her head upward. Geoff told her it was over a mile from the outer gate to the inner wall that enclosed the Palace itself. High as the outer wall was, the Palace's turrets and spires rose above it, visible even at that distance. Deor's heart rose at the sight—it had balconies and windows and towers, but the overall impression was of raw power, a living mountain of stone. She had a sudden overwhelming urge to reach out and touch the Palace walls, to feel its flagstones under her bare feet.

Deor leaned farther out the cab's window, trying to absorb the full scope of it until Geoff seized the back of her shirt and pulled her in.

"Do they give tours? We have to go," she said.

"For the public? Good lord, no!" A look of horror crossed Geoff's face. "Why would they do that?"

"They do in the human world. When the royal family isn't in residence, you can take a tour of Buckingham Palace." She leaned her face against the cab's window frame to catch a last glimpse of the Palace.

Geoff shuddered. "Commoners are only ever allowed into the Palace on the twice yearly Petitioner Days." He shrugged. "Besides, the king is rarely away from the Palace at this point. His illness has kept him virtually bedridden, despite what they tell the papers. I'd be surprised if he lived another year."

"You said people blamed his wife for cheating on him. Is he dying of —" What had Lord Farringdon called it? "Love longing? The same thing that killed my mother?"

Geoff shrugged. "I wish I knew. Details of his disease are very scarce, even for those of us who know him." He pointed out his side of the window. "Look—there's the Royal Park."

Deor scooted to the other side of the cab, leaning over Geoff to see. They drove past a huge open space with small rolling hills covered in thick green grass. Pathways crisscrossed it, and far back, in the middle of the field, an archway stood made of vines. It reminded her of the stone circle on Eisteddfod's campus.

"What is that vine covered thing? It doesn't look like a gazebo."

Geoff laughed. "You really are completely new here, aren't you? That's a long distance portal. Each doorway goes to a different part of the Winter Court. The king maintains it for the use of the public."

An image of the giant circles of standing stones at Stonehenge and

Avebury in human England, some with their lintels still intact, flashed in front of Deor's eyes. All that folklore she had read in college warning people away from standing stones and unhallowed doorways—no wonder humans feared them. You might step between two stones and never be seen again.

She turned to keep the park in her view as the cab passed it. One section seemed to be memorials. Small mausoleums dotted the grass around one larger building.

"This is where the great heroes of the land are laid to rest." Geoff said in a mock heroic tone. "Some were soldiers or generals. Others were great poets or painters." He pointed to the smaller mausoleums. "There are soldiers who died in every war buried here."

"It's beautiful." She had been a little girl, no more than six, when her grandfather had died. But she still remembered the folding of the flag and the way the man handed it to her grandmother.

"Oh look!" she gripped Geoff's arm. "A museum. Is it open?" She tapped on the cab's ceiling. "Can you let us off here? Thank you."

The cab dropped them at the edge of a large square in the cultural district not far from the Palace. The museums, shops, and restaurants all surrounded a large square—another, much smaller green. Couples strolled and families played in the park. There was even enough room for small carriages drawn by single horses to promenade. Donovan dropped down from the roof of the cab and scanned the area before opening the cab door.

"Why on earth do you want to see a museum?" Geoff asked. "You just escaped the library."

She pointed to the posters advertising a special Adoption retrospective—*Ancestry!* Featuring rare, never before made public paintings from the king's private Royal Gallery.

"It's cultural," she said. "And I bet there will be tons of pictures of noble people." It was a long shot, but something, somewhere had to offer a spark of connection.

Geoff laughed. "If you insist. They have some gorgeous mushroom carvings in their collection, too. Almost as fine as the ones in the Barizan museum."

Offering her his arm again, he led her to a large stone building with grey stairs up to the double doors. On each side of the stairs, stone unicorns reared and beat the air with their hooves.

They strolled through picture after picture of nobility. Names like Northfalls and Overton repeated, along with Farringdon and others. Hunting parties where each man and woman posed for maximum effect. Water faeries bathed naked with carefully placed pieces of kelp. Earth faeries surrounded by animals or holding overflowing baskets of fruit. Air faeries held aloft by winds that whipped their hair around their faces. Even one dramatic portrait of a female fire faerie, her arms dancing with tongues of flame. Wings were very much on display.

But none of the men in the pictures struck her as paternal candidates. Her shoulders drooped as she peered at the nameplate of a black-winged faerie. *Died without issue.* What had she thought would happen? That she'd wander in here and stumble upon her own face dressed up in men's clothes?

Then she saw it. A picture at the end of the hall. The flash of red among all the staid greys and blacks, yellows, browns, greens, and blues, and she left Geoff's side for a better look. The picture was massive, twice the size of most others. A man with steel grey eyes in a suit of armor, sword drawn, stood behind a woman who smiled at the infant in her lap. A faint ghost of a crown on the baby echoed the solid crown on the man's head. But what had drawn her attention were the man's wings—not the black wings her mother had described, but wings like her own. Looming behind him, massive and delicate at the same time, they were red —blood red.

"That's the king's father," Geoff said as he caught up with her. "Nuttier than a tree full of squirrels. Killed his own wife because he thought she was plotting against him. In the end, he thought the flowers were out to get him." He let out a sigh just this side of sarcastic.

"Ah," Deor said, not turning to face him. On the plaque at the bottom of the painting, it listed the date of the painting and the life spans of the subjects. The man had died over four hundred years ago.

She gazed at the infant and at the woman tending him. The woman was so focused on the child, she didn't notice the figure looming behind her. In front of the baby's face, she held a silver rattle from which a few stray sparkles flitted.

"One more picture in here," Geoff said. "This way." He led her to a portrait of two boys, and she immediately knew why he wanted her to see it—one of them was a goblin. The other was a young faerie, though his wings were in. Both of them had grins full of mischief, and the goblin, dressed in royal blue, held a lizard in his hand. They had their arms slung around each other's shoulders and seemed to have been caught laughing.

"Who is that?" Deor asked.

Geoff pointed at the plaque. "That's my father and Sweordmund," he said. "My father was fostered for a time at the Winter Court. He and the king have been fast friends ever since."

"Very handsome," she said. "Both of them."

"Of course," he said with a flirty smile.

She laughed, letting his grin, his attitude, infect her own. She needed the lift in spirits anyhow.

"One more room," she said, heading toward the gallery where the final and most recent portraits were hung. "I want to see what he looked like grown up."

Geoff caught her hand. "If you've seen one portrait, you've seen 'em all. There's only so much staring at fancy faeries I can take. Besides, I'm starving again. How about some food? With tables and napkins this time."

Deor's stomach growled at the thought. They must have walked a couple miles through the galleries by now. "Sounds good to me."

Another carriage ride took them through the city again, and, despite her disappointment, she marveled at all the people, buildings, carriages—everything she saw. The city teemed with life and magic.

They headed down a street called Georges and stopped in front of a stately, but not very large, building. "That's the Goblin Embassy," he said and hopped out to help her. "The place I'm taking you is just a few doors down."

She took his arm as he led her down the well-lit street. More goblins than faeries dotted the promenade as they walked, and Geoff often nodded as they bowed or curtsied to him. They whispered and tittered to each other after they had passed. After about a block, he turned into a small doorway, much like the door to Theophilous's store—if you hadn't known it was there, you might have missed it.

"After you, m'lady." He bowed slightly.

Deor stepped in and froze. She was in jeans and a sweater. Everyone here looked the Fae equivalent of evening dress. A maître-de, scowling, came rushing her way until Geoff stepped in behind her and the goblin's whole demeanor shifted. His frown vanished and a bright smile took its place. "Your Majesty! It has been too long! How many tonight?" He glanced again at her as if he hoped she was not one of the diners.

"Two," Geoff said taking her hand. "A quiet table, if you will."

The host gathered menus and bowed. "This way."

Deor took the seat facing the door, the one in the most shadow. Geoff settled in across from her.

Once they were alone, she whispered, "I am way underdressed for this place."

"Yes," he said, golden eyes glowing. "But the kings, or in this case, the princes make the fashion. Didn't Henry the Fifth say something like that?"

"Yes, I know—'Nice customs curtsy to great kings,'" she whispered. "But I'm not a great king."

"Nonsense," he said. "You gave your title just the other day. Students have even begun wearing your slogan in support of you."

"Very funny. Ha. Ha." She jerked her napkin off the table and slid it into her lap.

From out of nowhere, Donovan appeared at Geoff's side. She jumped, and the vampire glared at her. He whispered something to Geoff, who nodded. Geoff smiled at her and stood.

"One of my attachés is here. I need a word with him. I won't be long." He turned to Donovan. "Stay here with her."

Donovan frowned. He dropped into Geoff's chair.

Deor met his gaze. A staring contest with Geoff's bodyguard was not how she wanted to spend the evening, but if it was a contest, she certainly wasn't going to lose. She folded her hands primly in her lap and held Donovan's stare.

Seconds ticked by.

"You do have to blink eventually," he said. "I don't."

"Not with you glaring at me, I don't. I wouldn't dare." She laughed. "You know, what I did in class wasn't personal. You were undermining my authority, and I couldn't have that."

The vampire blinked, but said nothing.

"I'm not going to apologize," she added.

"Out of my seat, Donovan." Geoff was back. "This is my date."

"Right." Donovan stood. "Don't apologize," he said to Deor.

Before she could answer, Donovan melted back into the shadows. If she focused hard enough, knowing where he was, she could just make out his silhouette. He wasn't fuzzy with a net of magic the way the captain or general had been—rather the shadows swallowed him like a black fog.

After dinner, she and Geoff returned to campus and walked past the stone circle. "So where can you go from here with that thing?" she asked, pointing.

"Nearly anywhere if you have the power, but a casual user can get from the circle to the capital cities of all the Fae realms," he said.

"Good to know," she said, forcing her voice to remain steady. So, even if her father wasn't half as magically powerful as he pretended to be, he could have easily lived somewhere other than Caer Eisteddfod and lied to her mother about that as well. He could be anywhere. Her shoulders drooped as she stood in front of the doorway-shaped stones. Even her wings felt weighed down.

At her side, Geoff nudged her, and she turned to look at him.

"I need to ask you for a favor, but it's an imposition."

"Ask away," he said. "I'm intrigued."

"First you have to understand where I came from." She spun the tale out like the faerie tales she'd been told—skirting her own illness and emphasizing her desire to get back to her real home. "So, no fancy spindles or poisoned apples, no piles of flax or swan brothers. Just a missing father. And I've run out of leads. At most I know he's handsome, rich, and powerful—magically and politically. Do you think it's possible you might know him?"

"Hmmm." He narrowed his eyes and looked her up and down. "This could be quite a messy business. Long lost children popping up can be... scandalous."

"I know." She nodded. "I'm sorry, I shouldn't have asked."

"Nonsense!" He seized her hand. "Of course I'll help you. I can't think of anyone offhand, but I'm sure I can come up with some names. If not because I like you and because this man should have to face what he did, then because it will be so much fun to find out." A wicked grin lit up his face, and his eyes blurred, trembling back and forth.

Deor jolted back, startled, but laughed. She leaned in and kissed him on the cheek. "Thank you."

"Does this mean I can have another date?" he asked.

"Of course." She nodded. "And I'd have said yes even if you hadn't agreed to help me." She squeezed his hand. "Thank you, Geoff."

He raised her hand to his lips and kissed it. "Anything for my professor."

From the shadows under the trees, Donovan snorted.

Chapter Twenty-Two

The mid-morning sun warmed Rafe's back as he stood in the Palace's Amber Room waiting for Finn to take his seat for the usual Friday security briefing. As the sunlight passed through the inch-thick slabs of amber that covered the walls, it gave off an autumnal glow that warmed and softened Finn's features. Even the presence of Michael across the table couldn't check Rafe's thrill at seeing Finn healthy enough to attend to ordinary business for the first time in two years. If Finn's returning health was proof the Adoption was finally starting to take effect, it was all worth it.

Finn settled himself in his chair at the head of the table. Astarte took her place at Finn's left, between the king and Michael, and smiled at them all.

"Be seated, gentlemen," Finn said. "What do we have today?"

Rafe glanced down at the notes on his slate. "Our north and western borders remain stable. The werewolves are keeping up their end of the agreement about watching the coasts. Some suspicious movement of troops to the southeast, however. I suspect that the Summer Court is probing our defenses. I've ordered two foot regiments and one cavalry unit toward the border for training maneuvers—close enough to be ready, but not an act of open aggression."

"Overkill, my boy." Finn shook his head. "The goblins have outlets in Alsace-Lorrainne should we need help in that direction."

"With all due respect, sire, it's not safe to rely so completely on the goblins."

"You are too suspicious by half. My alliance with King Gregory is the firmest our country has had in centuries. Call back the two foot regiments."

Across the table, Michael smirked. Rafe repressed the urge to ice the floor under his chair—but he wasn't thirty anymore—and said, "As you wish, sire."

While Michael took up his own report, Rafe tapped out an order on his slate, telling the two units to return to the Midlands. Before he sent the message, though, he hesitated, stylus poised over the slate's hard surface. A good soldier doesn't just obey orders, he understands them. How many times had Drill Sergeant Brownie told him that? You want to be Sword someday, you'd better learn how to obey first.

"Yes, sir," Rafe said to himself. He added to the order, directing the troops to proceed slowly so as not to waste energy and materiel and to pause at Rouen for resupply. "If the needs of the population and the state of the roads should demand it, I give you permission to over-winter in Rouen and finish your return after the spring equinox."

Done. Their commander was a clever fellow. He would obey well.

"Well done, both of you," Finn was saying. "Is there anything more?"

"One thing," Rafe said. "Allowing the Adoption to be seen by mirror has been a great success. Two planned protest marches were called off and the Woolgrowers Guild passed a resolution indicating their satisfaction with the Adoption. I expect more to come."

Finn smiled and leaned back in his chair. "Well done, Rafe. We'll make a politician of you yet."

"With all due respect, your Majesty," Michael said. "I still maintain that this has set a dangerous precedent. We may yet regret it."

Rafe narrowed his eyes. "When I am king, it's a precedent I intend to follow, so you'd better get used to it."

Before Michael could answer, Finn held up his hands.

"Enough, both of you. For good or ill, it's done. And Rafe, you are not king yet. Don't get ahead of yourself." Both men bowed their heads. Finn began to rise, but Astarte put out her hand.

"Wait. I want to know more about the attacks on the changeling girls. How close are you to catching this monster?"

Finn put his hand over Astarte's, shushing her. "The Sword has too many other duties to attend to matters of local crime, my dear. Let the local magistrates deal with it."

Astarte shook off his hand.

"I want to know who hurt my daughter, Rafe. And I want to see him face to face."

"So do I, Mother, I assure you," Rafe said.

Finn sighed and drummed his fingers on the table, but Astarte ignored him.

"Is Robbie still in danger?"

"I don't think so, but I'm not taking chances," Rafe said. "None of the other women have been attacked twice, but I'm keeping an eye on her, and them, just in case."

Finn rose from his seat, and all the others stood immediately. "Let's keep the personal business out of this briefing, shall we, Rafe? Stick to matters of national import."

Astarte uttered an outraged gasp.

"Sire!" Rafe stood, eye to eye with Finn. "This is very much a matter of national security. I'm convinced we're not dealing with some sort of madman, but a goblin plot."

"Oh come now," Michael said. "Just because you're fond of the girl doesn't mean…"

"Do not interrupt me, Michael." He turned back to Finn. "Our chief suspect is a known goblin operative, and he took refuge in the embassy. Geoff and the university are sheltering our other suspect. This is now an international incident."

Finn studied the ceiling, mouth pursed. "Who is this other suspect?"

"A last minute hire by the university. She made a number of efforts to befriend Robbie and ask her for information. She claims to be unable to do any magic, but she's lying. And now Geoff is keeping our men from getting anywhere near her. She doesn't set foot off campus without him. It's all far too convenient to be a coincidence."

"Get her away from my daughter!" Astarte's wings flared. "How could you let this happen?"

"Believe me I've tried. Robbie is convinced Deor is her friend—the only person who understands her situation because she's a changeling herself and raised in the human world. I'm doing everything I can to keep Robbie safe, but this Deor woman saw me in her classroom, and now Bard Nefasta is threatening to have the Bardic Council sanction me for violating their sanctuary space."

Shouts of alarm erupted around the table.

"What? Why wasn't I informed of this?" Finn shouted.

"Oh, Rafe! What were you thinking?" Astarte said.

"This is just the sort of stupid, chivalric blunder I would expect from someone your age." Finn leaned forward, steadying himself on the table, and glared at Rafe. "And over a child you should never have become attached to. It's clouding your judgment."

"You know this kingdom's relationship with the bards has always been fraught. How could you take such a risk, especially now?" Astarte shook her head.

Across from Rafe, Michael merely folded his hands, an elder statesman more saddened than angry at the young upstart's blunder. He nodded gravely at every word from the king and his consort.

"Enough." Finn didn't have to raise his voice. The very walls of the Palace echoed with the king's command. Dead silence fell on the room, so still that Rafe could hear the blood rushing in his veins.

Finn raised one hand. "Rafe, you know perfectly well Geoff usually finds some faerie to keep him company when he is in our lands. That hardly makes her an international spy."

"But…"

"No! We are displeased with you, Rafe. Do not risk our further displeasure."

Rafe's mouth went dry, his wings clenching inside his back as if he were twenty again, waiting for the next blow of a beating to fall.

"No, sir," he said.

Satisfied, Finn turned toward Michael. "And have you heard of this new changeling woman…?"

"I have, sire. She's nothing."

"Are you sure?" Finn leaned forward, his face hungry.

"I am sure, Your Majesty. She claims to have a faerie father and a human mother, but it's obvious she's half pixie. She's of no concern." Michael shook his head slightly, his tone of patient disappointment deepening.

"I see." Finn breathed out, a shuddering sigh. The healthy color in his cheeks faded a bit, and he groped for Astarte's hand, squeezing it hard. "I thank you. I... I will go to my rooms now. This has been more exertion than I anticipated. Astarte, please, summon my healers."

The Princess Consort hurried to slip her arm through the king's.

"Of course, my darling. Come this way. The portal's only a few feet down the hall."

Rafe and Michael bowed as he made his way toward the door, leaning heavily on Astarte. Rafe's ears burned with humiliation, but he made one last attempt.

"Finn, this is more important than you realize. If you would listen to me for five more minutes."

Astarte cut him off with a look. "Your father is not well, Rafe. Let it go." She ushered Finn out of the room. Rafe's humiliation was complete.

Michael moved around the table to lay patronizing hand on Rafe's shoulder. "I know you hope for the best, my boy, but he's not as well as he pretends to be. You mustn't push him too far."

Rafe seized Michael by the lapels and shoved him up against the wall. He spoke through clenched teeth, his face an inch away from Michael's.

"You get this through your head once and for all. I don't care how long you've served the king or how experienced a politician you are. I am the Sword of Peace and Justice in this kingdom, not you. If you do anything to interfere with my investigation into this changeling business, I will consider you a co-conspirator. Do you understand me?"

His back pressed up against the wall, Michael's face went red with rage. He struggled against Rafe's grip, but Rafe held firm. He shook Michael, knocking his head back into the wall.

"Do you understand me?"

"Yes." The words came out strangled with fury.

"Good." Rafe let him go.

Breathing hard, Michael tugged his uniform back into place.

"Puppy dog," he spat. "That's all you are, an overgrown puppy who thinks he's top of the pack because he makes a pretty show on a horse and a rabble of peasants and soldiers cheers for him in the streets." Michael seized his own slate off the table and turned to go. "You're no more fit to be king than your horse." He slammed the conference room door behind him.

As the echoes of the slam died down, Rafe stood alone, clenching and unclenching his fists, trying to shake off the weight of Michael's all-too-accurate insult. Michael was right. He had neither the birth nor the temperament to rule. Finn would never have angered the bards and endangered centuries of carefully built alliance with the goblins for the sake of one misbegotten child. For that matter, Finn would have let Donovan eat Deor alive, not prepared to hurl himself between them like a character in an old tale.

He slumped back into a chair, his head in his hands. His ring of office dug into his finger, and he turned it slowly.

"I may not be king yet, but I am still the Sword of Peace and Justice, dammit," he said to the empty room. "And there is no peace or justice in letting innocents be hunted. Even if their hunters are our oldest allies."

He pulled out his mirror, mouth set in a firm line. Before Arthur's face appeared, he caught a glimpse of his own. Dark eyes, sharp cheekbones, his birth mother's blue-tinted skin. Tomorrow he would be a pure Aethelwing—the removal of his name complete. Today he was a Farringdon. He was still himself.

"Arthur. Update me."

Arthur's grin was maniacal. "Our changeling and her prince are finally beyond the university walls. They're in the marketplace. And our goblin spy has left the embassy and is also headed toward the marketplace."

"Keep watching them. All of them. I'll join you shortly." He pocketed his mirror, already weaving a plainclothes glamour around himself. He might not be allowed to harass Geoff, but he certainly could keep an eye on him.

Chapter Twenty-Three

In the marketplace, Deor and Geoff wandered through a stall of exotic fruits. She picked up a spiky blue fruit and sniffed it. Its aroma reminded her of lilacs and raspberries, with just a hint of honeydew. "How much?" she said.

Behind her Donovan coughed.

"I'm not..." the green woman behind the stall shot Geoff a nervous glance as she spoke. "I'm not really supposed to sell those to faeries..."

Deor turned to Geoff, eyes narrowing. "Why?"

His grin spread from ear to ear. "Because it will make you, shall we say, extremely unsavory company."

Donovan coughed again.

"You mean it would make me sick?" She set the fruit back on the stall and wiped her hands down her jeans. Hands on her hips, she gave Geoff her teacher look. "And you were going to let me eat that? What if I'd taken a bite out of it and then offered to pay?"

He laughed and tried to put an arm around her, but she stepped away.

"I knew you are too well-mannered to do something like that," Geoff said. "Besides, the skin can't hurt you. Only the flesh is poisonous to faeries. You might have been fine. You're looking particularly human today."

"And this is supposed to be a date? You better hope I've got the same twisted sense of humor you do." She glared at him for another second or two and slowly lowered her hands off her hips.

He pressed his hand to his heart and rolled his eyes sadly toward heaven.

"Ah cultural misunderstandings, how you get the best of me. Humor is so hard to translate. Would a present earn back your trust?" He waved a hand expansively at the marketplace. "Pick something out. Anything in the marketplace you like—I will give it to you."

"You are too used to buying your way out of things." Deor shook her head. "And that is what folklorists call a rash promise—if this were a faerie tale, you'd be in serious trouble, prince-boy. I think I'll take you up on it!"

He grinned back and wiggled one eye at her.

She mock shuddered and said, "It's so weird when your pupils do that. Like a cat's eyes."

He offered her his hand, and they strolled along through the marketplace stalls, Geoff explaining things as they went, like what wyvern tasted like.

"Gamy, but quite delicious if cooked right. Like spoiled mushrooms if you don't." They poked through stalls of used goods that were like the world's biggest yard sale, a concept she had to explain to him.

"It's weird," Deor said as they threaded their way from household goods into an area where children's toys filled store windows. "Every time I see a faerie man, I wonder if he's my father. As if I'm going to bump into him out grocery shopping. I spent my whole life thinking the guy is the world's biggest jackass, and now I'm obsessed with him."

Geoff squeezed her hand. "It must be difficult."

"I don't suppose you've got any candidates in mind?" she asked. Geoff shook his head. "I keep trying to think who it might be, but no one seems like a good match. I'm afraid dark hair is a fairly common trait in the Winter Court." He laughed. "From the description, it could even be Rafe."

"Ugh." Deor rolled her eyes. "Wouldn't that be all kinds of fun? But it can't be him, he's not married."

"Excellent point, dear professor," Geoff said. They stopped in front of a store window set up like a meadow with a cave. In front of the cave a green plush dragon with sparkling scales roared at a five-inch tall faerie knight in black and silver armor. *Special Adoption Sale!* a sign in the window said. *Half off all Prince Memorabilia.*

"Oh, how cute," Geoff said. "It's Rafe, his real size." He pointed at the toy knight, whose skin and wings were indeed vivid blue.

Deor rolled her eyes. "You mean his height is an illusion? What a pretentious wanker. I wonder why I didn't see through that, too."

"Well no, he really is that tall," Geoff admitted. "I meant..." He lowered his voice. "I suppose I shouldn't say this about my own godfather's chosen heir, but I'll trust you not to repeat it. Rafe has always been a bit, ahem, big for his own britches, if you know what I mean."

"You mean he gets a kick out of being called the prince," Deor said. "And all the attention he gets."

"Ever since he was no bigger than a pixie. You know the Palace people were calling him 'the young prince' long before anyone dreamed he'd be the heir. I don't think Sweordmund ever said no to him."

"That's a shame," Deor said.

A shopkeeper was lifting the doll out and demonstrating to a mother and her little boy how the wings went in and out and the helmet came off.

"Oh now, that is cute," she said as the boy came out of the shop clutching his new toy to his chest. "Though I think I'd rather curl up with the dragon."

"Shall I buy it for you? I said I'd get you a present." Geoff bowed elaborately.

Deor stared at the dragon. It was adorably ferocious. She could put it on her office shelves, right at student eye level. Her six-year-old self would have begged for the toy, but two doors down, she spotted something her inner child and outer adult could agree on. She grabbed Geoff's hand and dragged him toward the used bookstore, diving into the tight aisles stacked floor to ceiling with books.

"Now this is a magic I can get behind," she said running her fingers down gilded spines. She and Geoff lost themselves in the maze of books while Donovan stood guard in the doorway. She pulled books off the shelves at random, savoring the smell of old leather covers and fine paper. The shop ran a wide gamut—everything from books the size of a teaspoon to metal studded grimoires that would have taken all her strength to lift. History books, cookbooks, books of ancient poetry, joke books, and hand drawn atlases—the shop had everything.

Eventually her browsing led her to section labeled "Knychtespelles," which she automatically translated to "Warrior Tales," if her Middle English was any guide. She pulled out a green covered book printed on pale pink paper and settled on a footstool to read. Half an hour later, she sat cross legged on the floor, her back propped against the shelf as she finished *The Diamond Knight.*

"Enjoying yourself?" Geoff whispered in her ear.

She gasped and jumped straight up, clutching the book to her chest. "Don't do that."

Geoff only laughed and took the book out of her hand.

"Is this what you like to read? I prefer the Late Barizan lyrics myself, but to each his own. Shall I buy it for you?"

Deor took the book from him, torn. It cost a month's salary—far too much for her to pay, but nothing for Geoff. She ran her fingers over the tooled leather. Such a beautiful book and there were ten more stories in it she was itching to read. The one she had just read would make a perfect comparison to *Sir Gawain and the Green Knight.* She laughed to herself and shook her head. No human academic journal would take her seriously if she offered them an article on fourteenth century faerie literature. And a promise from a prince wasn't something to waste on a book.

"No thank you," she said and slid the book back on the shelf. "I think I'll keep your promise for a rainy day."

Geoff's eyes widened slightly, but he bowed. "Anything my lady desires."

Donovan coughed behind him. "You sure that's a good idea?"

"Don't be ridiculous," Geoff said. "She's not going to use it against me, you idiot."

She grinned at the vampire. "Don't worry, Donovan. I know how promises work."

Donovan gave her a slow and calculating nod. "I bet."

"On that note," Geoff said, "why don't we stroll along to Artificers' Street and see if they have something pretty that interests you, and then we can get dinner? There's a very cozy little pixie place about two blocks from here. You haven't lived until you've had pixie food."

"If it's anything like the pie I bought when I first got here, I'm sure it's delicious."

She took his offered arm and strolled out of the bookshop, resisting a last longing look over her shoulder at the book.

Anything from the prince himself? That was the kind of promise that ruined marriages, bankrupted knights, and even tore children in half. The kind of promise that could break her father like he had broken her mother.

Chapter Twenty-Four

✤✤✤

A rthur and two other officers were waiting for Rafe in an unmarked carriage just a block beyond the Palace.

"Where is he?" Rafe asked, dropping the glamour that disguised him as just another corporal running an errand. His own illusions would never be as complex as Arthur's, and it would take more than magic to get the military gait out of his stride, so he worked with what he had.

In reply, Arthur held up a pocket mirror. Their green quarry doddered along, magicked to look like an aged goblin, head bald and hair sprouting from his ears.

"He looks like he's just meandering around, window shopping," Arthur said, "but I'd bet my best horse he's making a connection of some kind."

"Something he couldn't do from inside the embassy?" Rafe asked. "A good sign the ambassador's not actually involved in it, though it might still be connected to their secret service."

Arthur nodded. "Geoff's still in the marketplace, too. With Robbie's changeling professor."

"I don't like it." Rafe peered at the goblin in the mirror as the carriage rattled over the streets. Arthur chuckled.

"You mean that you don't like the idea of a woman that pretty being a criminal, or you don't like Geoff getting his hands on her?"

"I don't like them being this obvious. She is not stupid. Neither is Geoff. And that makes me think we're missing something. Where is His Royal Goblin-ness exactly?" Rafe said. "Are they converging?"

Arthur fiddled with the mirror and whistled.

"He and Deor are in the fruit marketplace. Buying carambola by the look of it."

"That's goblins for you," Rafe said. "At least we'll know if he's trying to sleep with her by whether or not he lets her buy it. I doubt Geoff wants his mistress to spend the next twenty-four hours sweating and puking."

He reached over Arthur's arm and flicked the mirror's edge, dropping the perspective back to give a wider view of the district. As the image fell back, their quarry turned into a green moving dot with a faint green trail behind him to show his path.

"He's heading for Artificers' Street. That's the other direction."

They watched the man's progress in silence. Their carriage slowed and rolled to a halt. A quick glance out the window told Rafe they were at the head of Artificers' Street, only a few yards away from their quarry. The crowds were thinner here. There was less foot traffic too, though more than a few carriages lined the sidewalks outside fashionable shops. He scanned the street.

A couple of City Patrol in uniform walked their usual beat with an unconcerned air, but they were a good hundred yards away from the suspect. The only person close to the goblin was a street sweeper, his skin a dull beige. The sweeper knelt to pick up a piece of trash from the gutter, dusting his hands on his knees.

"One of ours?" Rafe said.

"Lieutenant Bolton. He volunteered—probably hoping this will get him noticed and help his promotion to the Palace Guard."

"Canny fellow."

The street sweeper was whistling, out of tune and poorly.

"The street's empty. Should we grab him now or wait?" Arthur asked.

"Hold your positions just a little bit longer, men," Rafe said into the mirror. "I want to see where he's going."

A chorus of "yes, sirs" came back to him.

At Rafe's signal, the carriage driver pulled up at the curb half a block behind their target. Any closer and he'd suspect. Bolton knelt to tie his shoe, his back half turned to the suspect. Rafe and Arthur hunched over the mirror. The goblin moved with maddening slowness, for all the world looking like a doddering old man doing some window shopping.

At last, he came to a discrete green door—Theophilous' shop. His back straightened as he glanced left and right. The two Civil Patrol officers had gone down an alley. Bolton stood picking his teeth and staring at the sky, a broom held slack in his hand. The goblin laid a hand on the shop door. Green fire glowed around the door handle, and he turned the knob.

"Now! Every man go—pick him up now," Rafe shouted.

He lunged for the carriage door. Even as his boots hit the pavement, Bolton threw the broom, entangling the goblin's feet. Wings out, he leaped on top of the goblin, knocking him to the ground. The two Civil Patrol men ran out of their ally, but Rafe pushed himself harder, and they ran neck and neck toward the suspect. Fire flashed from the goblin, but Bolton held his grip.

Rafe shouted and water from a nearby puddle dampened the goblin's fire. But it was only a sprinkling, not the deluge he should have been able to call. The two Civil Patrol officers joined Bolton, falling on the goblin so he disappeared under a scrum of bodies. By the time Rafe reached the scramble, the goblin's arms were bound and draped in damping spells. Bolton's face and hands sported nasty burns that would need a healer's attention.

"I am a Royal Attaché of the Goblin Court," the man screamed, the remnants of his glamour warping and blurring his features. "You can't do this to me."

"Shut up," Bolton said. Magic-laden air whistled past Rafe's ear, blowing into the goblin's face. The man's shouts faded to nothing, though his mouth kept moving.

Rafe jerked his head at the carriage, and the men holding the goblin dragged him, kicking and silently screaming, toward it.

"That is a clever little spell," Rafe said to Bolton. "But you'd better take it off in the carriage so he doesn't suffocate."

"No danger of that, sir. I worked out the frequency damping myself. He's still got all the air flow he could need and his vocal cords are intact—he just can't make the sound travel through its usual medium. Very demoralizing, but not dangerous."

Rafe nodded, appreciating the spell's effect even as he understood only half of what Bolton said. Air magic was not his forte.

"Excellent work," he said. "Get yourself to a healer as soon as we're back at the Tower."

He turned back toward the carriage. "Alright, Arthur. Let's get this gentleman back to the Tower and see what we can learn before his royal masters start to wonder where he is."

Chapter Twenty-Five

Artificers' Street was empty as Deor and Geoff entered it, except for a lone Civil Patrol officer and a plain carriage pulling away from the curb. Behind her, Deor heard a voice call her name.

"Professor Smithfield?"

"Yes?" Deor turned. Robbie, surrounded by three of her friends, came toward her. Deor recognized Aiden, a pale yellow faerie, and Simone, a girl with jet black skin and transparent wings, from her Shakespeare class. All of them wore shirts with the university crest, but the Faerie motto now read "Eisteddfod: we don't give a fuck who your daddy is." The Latin, "*scientia super imperio*," remained.

"What do you think?" Robbie said. "A bunch of us had them made for the next protest."

"Great," Deor said, fighting the urge to side-eye Donovan. "How are you doing? Are you feeling better?"

Robbie gave her a tight smile.

"I'm okay." She traced her fingers over a black line that lingered along her collarbone. "Lady Penny gave me something to take before bed so I can sleep." Her fingers trembled, and she clutched the strap of her satchel. "I think I might be remembering. I get flashes. Little bits of a voice and colors. Maybe a face. I can't quite tell. I'm seeing Lady Penny again on Tuesday afternoon. She's going to work with me on it."

"That's great," Deor said. "I'm glad to see you out and about."

"I'm not cowering at home." Robbie lifted her chin, squaring her shoulders as her friends murmured encouragement. "If I want to go to the marketplace, I'm going." She nodded her head as if that was the end of it.

"Good for you." Deor smiled. "I think you're right. Don't let this stop you from doing what you want." She leaned in to whisper, "And don't let it stop you from changing the world. The Winter Court is lucky to have you." She patted the girl's shoulder. "Is there anything I can do to help?"

"Yeah, actually." Robbie's smile turned bashful. "Could you help me with my paper? I'm all kind of muddled up about it. I have ideas, but I don't know how to make them come together."

Deor laughed. "Of course—it's my job. Take the weekend and think on it a bit—use it as a distraction from the other stuff. Jot down any notes or ideas you've got. Then we'll meet on Tuesday before class. I'm sure we'll come up with a good paper topic for you."

Robbie's smile blossomed into real relief. "Thank you, Professor. I'll have lots of notes by then, I promise. See you then." She gave a little wave and left. As she walked away, her friends closed ranks, their bodies a circle of protection around her.

"It's good her friends are watching out for her," Geoff said.

"Poor kid," Deor said. "I hope whoever did this to her gets caught and…" She searched for an appropriate punishment, her opposition to the death penalty warring with her outrage. "I don't know," she finished lamely.

"Oh, if Rafe ever catches them, they'll get punished alright," Geoff said, his voice dropping to a conspiratorial whisper. "You know who she is, right?"

"Oh, yes. Lord Farringdon told me she was his little sister. You know they don't look alike at all. But then, what do I know about faerie genetics? Maybe she takes after her mother. She's a changeling, like me. Does that mean she's his half-sister?"

Donovan gave Deor a pitying look and shook his head. "They have no blood in common. Rafe honors her with the title in order to protect her from meddlers who might kill the girl in order to curry favor with the king. In the Winter Court, she is nothing."

"What kind of monster is King Sweordmund?" Deor shouted. Other shoppers turned to look at her. A few glared. She lowered her voice. "Why would somebody want to kill her? Somebody explain this to me."

"There are those who blame her existence for King Sweordmund's illness, or rather they blame her mother for breaking his heart. Faeries are delicate creatures when it comes to matters of love," Donovan said. "Roberta is an unfortunate reminder of the Consort's infidelity."

In answer to Deor's raised eyebrows, Geoff picked up the thread. "Princess Consort Astarte is barred by Parliamentary Decree from bearing the king a child. So about thirty years ago, she went out and found a human to do the deed for her. Didn't even try to hide it. It's been a public embarrassment for the king ever since. I don't know why Sweordmund tolerates it, except that he's too weak to make the effort."

As Geoff said it, Donovan's brows knit, and he shook his head in disgust, but he said nothing.

"Well that's charitable of you," Deor said, crossing her arms. "Is it her bastard status you object to or her humanness?"

Geoff only laughed. "Oh no—the human part of her is just the ice on the midden in this whole mess. First Sweordmund insults every woman in the Winter Court and nearly starts a war by eloping with the Summer Court's Crown Princess, then he declares he won't insult his wife by taking a Child Bearer, and she repays him by making the beast with two backs with a human. And now Sweordmund thinks the solution to it all is adopting his beloved foster son, who everyone knows has no brain for politics, or anything much other than waving a sword and looking pretty on a horse, and who just happens to be the son of his worst enemy." Geoff blew out a sigh. "This nation's a mess."

Deor nodded as she absorbed the story, but she mentally compared Geoff's image of Lord Farringdon with the man she'd met. Certainly he would look good on a horse, she was sure of that, but stupid? No. He might have enough arrogance to fill a swimming pool, but he wasn't stupid.

"Poor girl," she said. "No wonder she's not a fan of the monarchy."

"She's a fool to wear that shirt," Donovan said. "If she's not careful, she'll become more to the king than just an embarrassment." To Deor's surprise, he sounded more pitying than disgusted.

"Why do you think Rafe cares for her?" Deor asked.

Before Donovan could answer, Geoff slipped an arm around her waist and kissed her on the cheek.

"We should get you your gift and then grab a bite," he said, leading her away. But they hadn't gone ten feet when Geoff's pocket trilled. He took out a platinum mirror case set with sapphire-eyed wyverns etched in gold on the surface.

"My apologies," he said and stepped a few feet from her. Deor turned away, offering the polite illusion of privacy.

She and Donovan stood side by side, not speaking, while Geoff frowned and spoke soundlessly at his mirror.

Finally, Deor nudged Donovan. "Is he just mouthing at the mirror or is that some sort of magic?"

"Privacy spell," Donovan said.

Silence lapsed over them again as Deor's thoughts went back to Robbie and her shirt. She and the girl—and twenty-nine years old or not, Robbie was still a girl—had so much in common. Too much maybe? Had she been thinking about her own situation all wrong, been too focused on her own father to think about who else her existence might be pissing off? Geoff closed his mirror and came back.

"I am so sorry to do this, but there seems to be a bit of a diplomatic situation brewing. I've got to go down to the Tower and remind Rafe that he can't go around chaining my people to a wall, despite how much it entertains him. Donovan, call a cab for the lady." As Donovan stepped to the sidewalk's edge to hail a cab, Geoff bent over her hand and kissed it. "Do forgive me. I wouldn't interrupt our date for anything less urgent."

She smiled at him and said, "Don't be so melodramatic. Of course you have to go. I'll be fine. I can see the university walls from here."

A cab like a hollowed out squash with a curving neck screeched to a halt at the curb, and Donovan opened the door and held it before the driver could hop down.

"I wouldn't dream of letting you walk home alone, not after what happened to Robbie," Geoff said. He ushered her into the cab and shut the door. "Give me Saturday night and I'll make it up to you. We'll go out somewhere really nice for dinner. My honor as a scholar and a student."

Deor laughed again and leaned forward to give him a quick kiss through the cab door. "Saturday sounds fantastic. I'll even dress up for the occasion. Now go. Save your fellow goblin."

Geoff hopped down from the running board and waved to the driver. As Deor leaned back in the padded seat, she sighed thinking of the few clothes she had back at the flat. She certainly wasn't going to wear an academic robe on any sort of date. She knocked on the cab roof and a little hatch flipped open.

"Yes, miss?"

"Can you take me to the second hand clothes shops? Thank you." She sat back against the cushions, wondering if she should wear her wings out like most of the faeries she saw. No—no she was not going down that line of thinking. She was a human with a faerie parent. She was not a faerie and she was not staying. Her wings ached, like limbs held in one position for too long, but she pressed her back against the seat cushions and ignored them.

Chapter Twenty-Six

The cell door clanged shut on the goblin prisoner and Rafe tapped the mirror, allowing them to see inside. The prisoner sat quietly, examining his nails.

"Let's give him a while to get bored and anxious," Arthur said. "He'll talk more that way."

Behind Rafe, Lieutenant Bolton, his hands and face smeared with a healing salve, grunted. "Is it wise to keep a goblin underground? I should think he'd have an easier time escaping that way."

"Fair point," Arthur said. "Though the Tower is not mere stone. Only the king's power could break someone out of this place."

Rafe nodded and closed the mirror. A soldier pounded down the stairs into the corridor.

"General, the Goblin Prince is here to see you. He's insisting on a personal audience immediately."

Rafe, Arthur, and Bolton swore, each with different curses, in unison.

"Sorry, sir," Bolton added. Mentally, Rafe filed Bolton's Yorkshire curse away for future use.

"Bolton, go tell the prince I'll be with him shortly. In my office. Be hospitable, but don't leave him alone there, no matter what he tells you."

"Yes, sir."

Rafe cursed again under his breath. "I thought we got the goblin's mirror off him in time. Come on. Let's go see what he wants. Arthur you stay here and see what you can learn."

Back on the first floor of the Tower, Rafe paused outside his office to straighten his uniform and put on a smile. He strolled through the door, hand out.

"Geoff, what a pleasant surprise. I didn't expect to see you before the Adoption on Sunday. How can I help you?"

From his chair, Geoff inclined his head but didn't reach for Rafe's hand.

"Not a happy occasion Rafe," he said. "You know why I'm here."

"Not the foggiest. What do you need?" Rafe waved at Bolton, who immediately stepped out and closed the door behind him. Behind Geoff, Donovan rolled his eyes, but the look he gave Rafe was more sympathetic than threatening.

"Pleased to see you as well, Vlad Drogos," Rafe said. "Won't you have a seat?"

"Thank you, Lord Farringdon. I'll stand for now."

At least he shook Rafe's hand. Rafe made a mental note to invite Donovan to a private dinner some time when he was off duty. An old friend shouldn't be ignored just because he was playing bodyguard to an asshole. Though he did wonder what game Donovan's father was playing, letting his own heir take the job.

"You know quite well why I'm here," Geoff said. "You're holding one of my people unlawfully. The man is an attaché of the Goblin Embassy and a personal friend. But, since I do understand that this is a trying time for you and you may have acted hastily, if you hand him over to me right now, unharmed, I'll say no more about it."

Rafe pulled out a file and flipped through it, as if he needed time to become acquainted with the situation.

"I don't see any reports of diplomatic staff being arrested. I do see that we have a goblin in custody who is wanted in connection with ten separate assaults by magical coercion, but I didn't see any proof of diplomatic immunity." He laid the file on the desk and drummed his fingers. Frost grew outward from his fingertips, racing across the desk toward Geoff. "Even if he was your closest personal friend, Geoff, I wouldn't let a monster like this go. He's going to tell us everything, do you understand me? Everything, including his connection to Deor Smithfield."

Geoff polished his nails against his shirtfront and flicked them outward. The frost vanished in a puff of steam. Thin blue flames flickered around his fingers as he waved off Rafe's glare.

"Whatever are you talking about? You think Professor Smithfield is involved in this somehow? You must be drunk."

"There were two magical signatures on the victims. One goblin, one faerie. And the faerie was a woman."

For split second, Geoff's golden eyes widened and his smile froze. But his lazy, mocking tone returned.

"I have to tell you Rafe, I'm very fond of Deor. She's so delightful. Intelligent, sensuous, amusing, and gifted in ways she doesn't begin to understand. I really can't have you harassing her."

"If she had any part in hurting Robbie, I'll execute her myself. Don't think you can shield her from me."

"Don't think I can't. She's not a Winter Court citizen. You've heard her say so herself. I'm sure I can find her a position on my staff if need be." He winked at Rafe. "And while we're on the subject, are you sure your 'victims' are telling the truth? We both know Robbie is a happy little agitator, always looking for more attention."

Rafe lunged and, the whole world suddenly narrowed to getting his hands on Geoff's neck. A black blur filled his vision. Donovan slammed him against a file cabinet across the room. Rafe shoved back, using his height, but Donovan caught his shoulders and held. Grappling, they each strove to gain an inch, locked in place against one another.

Donovan leaned forward, mouth open, and Rafe wrenched his neck away, but Donovan only whispered in Romanian. "Not today, my friend. *Sa se razbune dormi si sa creasca puternic.* Let revenge sleep and grow stronger."

He looked Donovan in the eye. Donovan raised his eyebrows, inquiring, and let go. He stepped back, his hands up. Rafe nodded. He lowered his hands and straightened his uniform.

"My apologies, Donovan. I shouldn't have put you in this position."

Donovan only shrugged and resumed his place behind Geoff. Geoff had not moved from his chair.

"Well, Rafe?" he said. "Now that you've got that out of your system, go get me my friend."

"Go to hell."

SARAH JOY ADAMS & EMILY LAVIN LEVERETT

"Not today, I think." Geoff rose. "But I will be stopping by the Palace. I'm sure my godfather will be very interested to hear what I have to say about your behavior and its repercussions for the alliance between our peoples. Donovan? Go fetch me a cab, will you? I don't want to arrive at the Palace dusty from the walk." He turned in the doorway of Rafe's office, a jagged smile on his face. "You're not king yet, you know. And you've never been good at this sort of thing, so I wouldn't play politics with me, if I were you."

After Geoff had gone, Rafe cursed and kicked his desk so that it slid three feet across the floor. Papers and file folders flew. Cold winds full of ice crystals whipped around him.

"Arthur," he bellowed at the mirror. "Get everything you can out of that goblin. Don't hold back on account of politics. You've got half an hour. At most."

"Understood."

Rafe swore again and yanked his desk back into its proper place. If it took Geoff ten minutes to reach the Palace, Finn would be on the mirror shouting at him about diplomatic ties in another ten at the outside. He could probably hold Finn off for eight or ten more minutes after that without crossing the line into treason. He left the mess and headed down to watch the interrogation.

Chapter Twenty-Seven

A side from the reporters holding up mirrors as they went into the restaurant, Deor's dinner with Geoff began beautifully. Crystal tinkled. Silverware clinked against bone china plates. The waiters seemed to shimmer in and out of thin air, they moved so unobtrusively. Donovan was off somewhere in the shadows of the restaurant, filing his teeth no doubt. So far, a perfect evening.

"Another glass?" Geoff asked, raising the bottle from the silver ice bucket beside their table.

"No, thank you," Deor said. "It's amazing, but no more for me." She took the last forkful of her fish in lemon *beurre blanc* and savored it as she sat back against the cushions of the armchair. Geoff poured himself another glass.

Too bad she had to say no. It was wine to make a connoisseur weep. Descriptors like "chewy," "ambrosial," and "rich with hints of *fraises de bois*" actually made sense for once. But a single glass hit her like no human alcohol ever had. One of the perks—or drawbacks, depending on your point of view—of being a changeling was that it took way too much to get her drunk—certainly more than a glass of wine. Faerie wine was proving to be a different thing altogether. Already she felt a pleasant glow inside her, and the little tingle between her legs told her she'd better stop unless her goal was to get hammered.

She almost suspected Geoff was trying to get her drunk on question-able wine, except that the waiter had opened the bottle at the table. Geoff had sampled it and offered her a sip for approval. He'd also had three glasses to her one without any apparent ill effect. She gave Geoff a smile and reached for her ice water.

Sipping, she eyed Geoff over the rim of the goblet. Yes, he was defi-nitely trying to seduce her. And she might let him.

"Good evening Geoff," a suave voice next to the table interrupted the moment like the breaking of a spell. A tall, blue-skinned man bowed slightly, his long black hair falling forward over his shoulder.

Geoff stood and held out his hand. "Victor! I didn't see you here. Deor, allow me to introduce Victor Farringdon, the younger brother of our mutual friend the Sword."

Victor inclined his head at Geoff's mention of Lord Farringdon, but his smile returned as he bowed toward Deor.

"You must be the famous professor who is so indifferent to parentage." He held out his hand to her. "I hope that means you won't judge me by my brother either. We have very little in common."

Deor took his hand and blushed when he kissed hers. Certainly his manners were smoother, his lashes longer than his brother's, but the family resemblance was unmistakable. If someone took Lord Farringdon and polished the soldier out of him until he was a statesman, they'd have Victor Farringdon.

"Pleased to meet you," she said. He gave back her hand and turned to Geoff.

"You simply must bring her to the club," he said.

"What kind of club?" Deor asked, despite Geoff's shake of the head. "Like a dance club?"

"No," Victor said. "A gentleman's club."

Deor's eyebrows shot up. "Like where women take off their clothes and dance naked for tips?" Geoff burst out laughing at Victor's jaw-drop.

"Good green hills no," Victor said. "Why would you think that?"

Deor laughed. "Sorry, 'gentlemen's club' is a human euphemism. I didn't realize you meant it literally."

"I see," Victor said. "No. This is a private club for gentleman who want an evening out. Members go to play cards, share a drink, gossip, exercise. Some go to hide from their wives. It is quite the social place."

"It sounds interesting. Perhaps we should go, Geoff," she said.

Cards and workout rooms didn't interest her much, but gossip among the elite and powerful did. Her father might even be a member. Maybe she'd run into him, or at least someone who might look at her and say, "'B'gad that girl looks just like old Whathisface."

"Wednesday night is my usual night, if ever you care to join me," Victor said.

Geoff frowned, but when he caught Deor looking at him, the frown morphed into a smile. "Let's make it after the Adoption, shall we, Victor? You know how busy things are now."

Victor nodded slightly again. "Alas, he is right. Our schedules are perilously full." He shot Geoff a glance before bowing to her. "But I do hope to see you soon after."

He strolled back to his table where the same man Deor had seen Rafe standing with at the beginning of the first Adoption welcomed Victor back. His wife, a pale blue woman with long black hair and sapphire eyes, sat beside him. She met Deor's eyes and her cool, calculating gaze lingered for a touch too long. Deor broke the eye contact, returning her attention to flirting with her date.

Geoff half-raised a finger and a waiter appeared out of nowhere. Their plates were whisked away in a second. Another waiter appeared bearing a hexagonal box made out of chocolate. Its sides were imprinted with a filigree of gold leaf and chocolate icing.

"*Gâteau musical au chocolat avec feuille d'or*," the waiter said, bowing as he laid it on the table. "Please enjoy."

"Take off the lid," Geoff said. "This is my favorite part."

At her touch, the chocolate lid rose up like the cover of a music box and notes poured out of the cake. Deor gasped and laughed, leaning forward to see the mechanism, but there was none. Instead, soft lines of magic spiraled around the edges, their curves harmonizing with the music. She reached for one, and it curled around her finger. She pulled her hand away, but the magic clung to her, snapping free from the cake.

The music soured. Sweet notes cracked out of tune, honking and howling as the rest of the patrons turned to stare. The magic threads writhed and twisted in on themselves, their harmony broken. With its dying moan, the entire cake exploded. All over Geoff.

Diners gasped. The waiter and maître d' clapped their hands over their mouths, eyes wide with horror. Donovan, half out of his chair, was shaking with laughter. And Geoff just sat there, blinking as cake and cream filling oozed down his cheeks.

"I'm so sorry," Deor said.

"That was the Goblin national anthem," Geoff said, staring at the carcass of the cake.

Deor pressed her lips together, trying to keep down the giggles. "Would you like my napkin?"

"No, it's fine. I'm fine." Geoff pushed away the three waiters who were babbling apologies and mopping at him with napkins. "Take your hands off me."

His cheekbones and ear tips were flushed a deeper shade of green. Deor bit her lip harder and curled her nails into her palm as blob of white cream dropped in slow motion from his golden hair, right onto the tip of his nose. He cursed and shook it off. Donovan appeared at his elbow, interposing himself between Geoff and the staff as panicked waiters cleared away the mess that had splattered all across the table and nearby guests.

"I am so sorry, your Majesty!" The maître 'd was alternately bowing, apologizing, and hitting staff members. "The pastry cook will be fired immediately."

"No, no, please don't! It's my fault," Deor blurted out. "I touched the magic."

Both Donovan and Geoff were suddenly very focused on her.

"You did that on purpose?" Geoff said.

"No!" Deor insisted. "I was just curious, but when I touched it, the thread snapped, and then the whole thing fell apart." She waved at the now empty spot where the cake had been. "I don't do well with magic. I'm so sorry. It was so lovely. I didn't mean to break it…"

Geoff blinked. And then he laughed. The same laughter that had filled her office, that made her want to giggle and find trouble, now seeped into her. Tonight, she gave into it. She let it fill her lungs. They giggled until their eyes watered and sides ached. They laughed until they slid into the carriage and snuggled together, sated even without dessert.

The carriage took them through city streets lit with hanging baskets of phosphorescent flowers until they arrived at the Goblin Embassy.

"Welcome to Barizan," Geoff said, as the carriage rolled through the silently opening embassy gates.

"Oh my," Deor said, laughing. "This isn't going to cause an international incident, is it?"

Geoff laughed and kissed her hand, eyebrows wiggling suggestively.

Instead of stopping at the embassy's wide front doors, the carriage took them around to the back of the embassy and into what Deor assumed was a sort of underground garage. The slanting floor delivered them to a doorway guarded by two of the most muscular goblins Deor had seen yet. Their crisp, royal blue uniforms did nothing to soften the look of the rapiers hanging at their sides.

"Good evening, Your Majesty," one said opening the carriage door.

Geoff hopped lightly out of the carriage and turned to offer Deor his hand. As she descended, she looked first at one guard and then the other. Their eyes registered absolutely no response. She had the sudden and unpleasant certainty that, if questioned, both men would swear to it that they had never seen her.

The carriage door slammed shut behind her and the carriage rolled away. Deor cast a look after it as it disappeared into the shadows with Donovan perched on the roof, watching her. So, at least one person other than Geoff knew where she was tonight. She took his proffered arm and followed him inside the embassy.

"So, this is goblin architecture?" she said as the corridor slanted downward, bending and twisting. They had to be at least three stories underground by now, but she had yet to see a right angle. The walls glittered white, with sinuous abstract shapes carved into walls made of solid salt.

"Not what you expected?" Geoff said, stopping in front of a brocade-covered door.

"I don't know what I expected," she said. "Certainly not to be in the world's fanciest bunker."

"You Americans." Geoff laughed. "We goblins are an underground people, you know." He laid his hand on a brass plate at the center of the door. Green fire danced around his fingers. A lock clicked and the door split open.

"When have you met another American?" Deor said, but Geoff wrapped his arms around her and danced her over the threshold into a sumptuous sitting room done in peacock and gold. She laughed and danced with him, stepping out of her shoes and sinking her toes into the living moss carpet that covered the floor.

The bedroom beyond was even more ornate. Nearly every surface that could be gilded was. The curving, asymmetrical walls melded seamlessly with floor and ceiling. Rock outcroppings that suggested couches or lounge chairs grew up from the floor or jutted out of the walls. Silks and brocades draped everywhere, the light coming from hundreds of crystals that dotted the ceiling. The bed was a sunken ovoid in the center of the room, lined and stacked with peacock colored silks. If the nineteen-seventies had shacked up for a long, drug-fueled weekend with the Baroque era, goblin style might have been the result.

"What do you think?" he asked.

"I've never seen anything like it," she said, slipping out of her coat and dropping it over what might possibly have been a couch.

As Geoff left her to pour them both a drink, she set her purse and shoes near the door. Always good to know where those were the next morning. Just in case she needed them in a hurry—as if she could find her way out of this underground maze on her own.

"Good idea," he said. "The servants will polish them for you for tomorrow."

She kissed him, laughing. "Good to know we both planned on me spending the night."

He twined his arms around her, cupping her bottom as he leaned down to kiss her. "You can stay as long as you like," he said. "All weekend. Though I will have to leave you for a few hours tomorrow to be at the Adoption. Too much of a diplomatic incident if I didn't show up. Though," he pressed in for another kiss, "with a dish like you waiting in bed for me, I don't think I'll be inclined to linger."

She kissed him, but pulled back. "You'll look for my father?"

"Of course," he said and caught her hand.

"Now what?" she said, giggling and following him as he pulled her toward the bed. In the carriage he had been a paragon of extremes, darting in for a long kiss and a questing finger down the front of her blouse, then sliding back across the bench seat with a wink and finger to his lips.

Something else nagged at her. She'd tried to say it in the restaurant, but the waiter had appeared with the check. She should have said it in the carriage, but there had been his fingers and his tongue. She pulled back against his hand. He let the motion propel him into her arms and pressed her up against the bedroom wall. This time his lips quested along her neck, her collarbone. She shivered, her nipples stiffening.

She pushed him away from her, both hands planted on his chest. He took a step back, head cocked to one side.

"Stop," she said. "Just so we're clear. We're not..." A flash of disappointment crossed his face. "We're just having a bit of fun," she said. "Both of us, right?"

"Silly professor," he said, smile returning. "Of course we're going to have fun." He pushed his hand under the edge of her blouse, ran a finger along the waistband of her slacks. "All night if you like." His leaned his hips against hers.

If he were half as good as his looks promised, this would be loads of fun, but she pushed back just a bit, holding her mouth out of his reach.

"Just so we're clear, right?" she said. "I don't want to hurt you."

He laughed and took the back of her head in his hand, pressing her mouth with his. He fumbled with the buttons on her slacks. She pressed her shoulders against the wall, arching her pelvis into his. She tugged his shirt out of his pants as his body responded to the pressure of her hips. He gave her bottom a quick pinch and withdrew his hands, laughing softly.

"Shhhh," he said. "Wait." He pressed his hand to the door, and a wriggle of flame knit the two halves together so that the wood seemed all one piece.

She twirled away from him toward the gold, scroll-worked rim of the bed, its covers already folded back for the master's return. Geoff came after her, shedding his jacket as she wriggled out of her pants and tossed them toward her coat.

"Lights lower," he said and the light in the room went from bright to mood lighting dim. He waggled his eyebrows at her and growled.

She laughed, settling onto the bed and leaning back against the edge as he came at her. Let him have the lights down if he liked.

As he reached for her, she said, "Get the condom out now, so we don't have to stop and look for it later."

"The what?" he said indistinctly, his mouth pressing against the top of her cleavage. As she fumbled with the buttons on his shirt, his teeth just grazed her flesh and she gasped, another shiver of pleasure rolling down her body.

She reached for his pants, fumbling the buttons out of their holes.

"The condom. Get it."

He'd undone the top buttons of her blouse, lifting her breasts out even as he pressed her back against the pillows with his body. He lapped his tongue over her nipple, caught her breast with his mouth, and sucked. She gasped again, urging her breast into his mouth.

"Condom. Now," she said. Words. Must use words. Be responsible. Little green baby, she told herself. She was not making the same mistake her mother did. "Go get a condom."

She slid her hands up his chest and gave him a push. Geoff held himself off her with his arms, kneeling between her legs.

"I really have no idea what you need," he said. "Is it some sort of sex toy?"

"No." She sat up with a jerk, almost bashing his nose with her head. "A condom. You know, a rubber. A prophylactic?"

He shook his head at her.

"I'm not on the pill," she said. "I wasn't planning on having sex here..." She waved her hands in vague unwrapping gestures. His face remained blank. She fell backwards onto the bed with a frustrated groan.

"Damn. It. All. To. Hell." She sat back up, tucking her breasts back into her bra and took a deep breath. "You're not kidding, are you?"

He shook his head. "Never heard of them. No idea what you want."

"It's a sock," she said, pulling her feet into a cross-legged position and pulling her blouse closed. Her panties were already wet. That would make the lonely taxi ride home extra pleasant. "It's a little rubber sock for your dick to keep the sperm from getting, well, anywhere really."

A grimace of revulsion crossed his face, "And it goes in you? On my...?"

"Yes. And I'm sorry, really, truly sorry, because my god those are some fabulous abs you have there, but I am not risking pregnancy. Sorry."

His face lit up and he laughed.

"Oh is that all?" He launched himself onto the bed beside her. He bounced twice and landed with his head propped on his hand. "No problem at all then." He curled himself around her waist and kissed his way up her ribs, pulling open buttons as he went.

"Hello ladies," he said as he arrived at her breasts again. He nibbled at her rib cage, and she shrieked and wriggled with delight.

"I'm serious," she said through the tickling. "No sex unless you can guarantee no baby."

He sat up with a jerk, his face completely solemn for once.

"So am I," he said. "Do you really think I would bring a bastard into the world? I wouldn't do that to my kingdom or my family." He reached a hand out and stroked her hair. "Trust me, lovely professor from the human world. I couldn't get you pregnant tonight if my life depended on it. Sex with me is completely safe." He wrapped his arms around her, his voice a purr. "Does that make it all okay?"

"You swear," she said. "Not a chance that I'll get pregnant?"

"Not if I tried all night long," he said. One hand eased inside the cup of her bra. "You are safe with me." He lowered her back onto the bed, his clever fingers whisking away her bra.

"Wait." She smacked at his hand—that kind of vague promise sounded too much like her father's promises to her mother. And she knew where those led. "What do you mean exactly?"

He pulled back from her. "I'm not fertile," he said.

"Oh." He had said it so chipperly, like it didn't matter. She wouldn't have wanted to be that specific either. "I'm sorry for pressing."

He smiled. "So it is okay now?"

She let her body relax, cradled in the deep cushion of his bed. "Completely okay."

She lifted her hips to pull her underwear all the way off, hurling it onto the chair in the corner. She held out her arms to him, and he whistled appreciatively and pulled off his shirt.

He gazed down at her in anticipation. She scooted back to reach the pillow and said, "I see you're ready. Come and get me, Goblin man."

He slid his hands up her thighs. "Oh, I'm going to," he said. "Lights off."

She screamed and jerked backwards so hard that her head banged into the ornate scrollwork that rimmed the bed-pit.

"What the hell is wrong with you?" she asked as she rubbed the sore spot on her head.

In the pitch black of the room, his entire body glowed bright green. His face, his hands, his neck, all were a neon, oh-my-god-is-that-radioactive green. But the glow grew brighter as her gaze traveled down his body to his erection. It stood up, light bulb bright, between them. She could see herself in the light it shed.

Geoff blanched and looked down at his erection.

"Not that," she hastened to say. "That's fine. Great in fact." She had to be encouraging, especially after the screaming. "It's the glow that's creeping me out. Stop that. It's not funny."

His grin returned, and he sashayed toward her on his knees. In the dark, the movement left little light trails on her eyes.

"Didn't you know? All goblins glow in the dark. I told you we're cave people."

She pulled the pillow out from behind her and clutched it over her chest.

"You have tan lines," she said. "You're brighter where the sun doesn't shine." She giggled. Her giggle grew into a huge rolling laugh while Geoff knelt there, his erection swaying a little.

"I did promise you a laugh," he said, though the confident grin had vanished.

"Oh," she said, wiping the tears out of her eyes. "You certainly did." She giggled again, trying to suppress the rest of the laughter. "Promise that you're not just playing a prank on me?"

"Not a bit. This is the whole goblin." He moved closer to her, his thighs pressing against hers.

She reached up and ran her fingers over his chest and down his stomach. The glow didn't rub off or recede where her fingers went. It did pulse a bit as she ran her fingers over his erection. She gave one last giggle. "Sorry. That just took me by surprise."

"We're both full of surprises tonight, aren't we?" He leaned down over her, his mouth pressing firmly against hers before traveling down her throat and across her collarbone to her breasts. He took her nipple in his mouth and pressed himself against her.

"Yes," she said, thrusting her hips up to meet his. "Yes."

Chapter Twenty-Eight

At the Palace the next morning, Rafe waited behind the throne room door, listening for his name. He'd kept breakfast this morning to tea and dry toast. Even those had been more to reassure Astarte than from a desire to eat.

"You need to keep up your strength," she'd said, shoving a plate of his favorite blood sausage at him.

He couldn't tell her that it didn't matter what she offered him. Food didn't taste the same anymore. Nothing did. At least with his stomach empty, he could be sure he wouldn't spill his guts all over the throne and Finn's feet. He grimaced. Finn anyway. The throne could go hang itself. When he was king, he'd sit on the damn thing as little as possible. And he'd have a cushion installed.

Outside the trumpets blared again. "His Lordship, Sword of Peace and Justice, Rafael, Lord Farringdon," the herald called out from the throne room. Arthur gave him a quick pat on the shoulder that was more like a shove in the right direction.

Head up, eyes forward, Rafe told himself. *Just like parade inspection at the end of boot camp. Doesn't matter what kind of hell you feel like. Head up, eyes forward.*

He marched into the throne room, hands at his side. Six feet from the dais, he turned on his heel and left the carpet runner to enter the crowd around the throne. Familiar faces bent as the crowd bowed all around him. Smiling was beyond him, but he tried to at least make eye contact. Rodney and Clarissa. Rodney's uncle Roger, Lord of Northfalls and Commander of the Navy. Delaney Overton and his father, the Master of London. Genevieve gave him an admiring smile as she bent her knees in a curtsey. There was Donovan, watching with keen eyes, just behind Geoff's usual smirk.

His boots echoed on the marble floor. He didn't bother to make eye contact with Edgar, his almost-no-longer-father, as he took his place beside him. *Head up. Eyes forward. Don't get distracted or you'll miss your call.*

The two of them stood in a discrete circle of empty space within the crowd. People nearest them were already shivering with cold as Edgar's anger pulled the heat from the air around him, leaving everyone else to freeze. Ice crystals rimed his father's boots.

At least Madeleine and Victor had refused to come back after the first ceremony. Rafe didn't flatter himself that his suffering kept them away. Victor always had been mama's little boy, and Madeleine's contempt for her eldest son and King Sweordmund were legendary.

The crowd around him spoke. "Give us an heir, oh king."

He tensed. Next came the king's concession and the call for an heir. From the direction of Edgar, a small breeze blew around his face, cold air spiraling downward, and Rafe tasted snow. A fringe of ice formed on a wisp of his hair. He shook it out of his eye with an impatient flick.

Sweordmund was calling him now. "Step forward, my chosen son."

As he reached the top step of the dais, he watched Bard Ama Nefasta for his cues. The woman had a face like an ill-tempered hatchet, but she kept the ceremonies moving as fast as decently possible, he'd give her that. A year ago, when they were planning all this, the Palace Master of Ceremonies had wanted to stretch out every ceremony into a daylong process, including things like musicians and readings from ancient texts. Ama had called the man a fool. But she hadn't told him the magic would hurt this badly.

"Who is this man you choose for your son?" Ama asked.

"He is Rafael, Lord Farringdon, heir to the Duke of Wellhall," Sweordmund answered. He was holding up well, his posture erect. He gave Rafe a little smile.

"I am he whom the king names," Rafe said. "I am Rafael, Lord Farringdon, first born to Duchess Madeline and Duke Edgar of that name, by right of birth heir to the Duchy of Wellhall. My mother's mother was Milun Farringdon, Duchess of Wellhall. Her father before her was Lucas Farringdon, Duke of Wellhall and Sword of Peace and Justice to his Majesty King Sweordmund the Sixth."

"And are you willing to give up this name?" Ama said. "To renounce your father and mother, to take a new father and a new name?"

"I am," he said. "I renounce my father. I renounce my mother." He kept his eyes fixed straight ahead as he said it. "I give up my name." A pain ran through his chest that had nothing to do with magic.

"Kneel," Ama told him.

He knelt on the rough stone of the dais. The pocks and edges of the natural stone cut into his shins. At least he didn't have to do this naked. That had been another idea from the Master of Ceremonies. It would be symbolic, the man had said. A rebirthing.

"Embrace your son, oh king," Ama said.

He shut his eyes as Sweordmund's hands closed on his shoulders, steadying him for the ordeal. He braced his palms, sweating already, against the slick stone and gritted his teeth.

"I remove your name," Ama said. She struck him on the head with her mistletoe.

Pain like iron needles shot through his hands and up the nerves of his body. He inhaled sharply, fighting every instinct that said *let go!*

"I remove your father and mother." She tapped him again. The pain grew. His bones cracked. *Don't scream,* he ordered himself. *Don't scream. Don't let go.*

He fell. Down, down into a black abyss shot through with silver lightning. A place where he had no name, no identity. Here was nothing but the pain and the lightning like swords and the stone beneath his hands.

A long way away he heard Ama say, "Be no more a Farringdon." More lightning shot across his vision. A voice deeper than conscious words demanded to know who he was. Swords flayed his skin and splintered his bones searching for the answer. *Who are you?* He had no answer. The voice in the stone sifted him down to the smallest atom. *Who are you?*

And another voice, one he thought he knew, called him from far off. "Rafe. My son."

"I'm Rafe," he told the stone darkness. The voice he loved called to him again. Yes. That was his true name. He knew it now. "I'm Rafe," he said again to the darkness.

"Aethelwing?" The darkness continued to sift through him.

"Yes," he told it. "The heir." But he was less sure.

"Liar."

Every inch of his skin burned, shot through with iron needles.

"No. I swear." He was Rafe. And Rafe was going to be the heir. "I am not a liar," he shouted at the stone around him. "He needs me."

Somewhere, close by and far away, a woman cried out in the darkness. But he couldn't let go, couldn't help her.

"Thief!" she screamed. Silver flashed through him, lines of pain like claws drawn across his flesh. He screamed and the silver slashed him again. Hot blood oozed across his chest and back.

"I am not a thief!" *Hang on*, he told himself. *Don't you dare let go. He needs you.*

The lightning pierced him again, but the voice he knew and loved came closer, drawing him from the darkness.

"You are my son and my heir forever. I have no other child but you."

The stone darkness relented and threw him back into the world of light and sound. He fell forward against Finn's knees, the king's arms around him, his head resting on Rafe's shoulder. Finn's breath was ragged in his ear.

"My poor boy," the king whispered. "Hold still. The healers will be here soon."

Behind him, Ama was ending the ceremony. Blessing. Health. Praise for both king and heir who spend themselves for their people. He had to get up and go out with Finn or no one else would leave the room.

He struggled to rise, hands braced against the throne, but his legs buckled under him. He fell heavily against Finn's knees and more pain shot across his chest.

"Easy, son," the king whispered. "Let us help you."

Other hands were lifting him to his feet. As he turned to face the crowd, people gasped. Some were crying. Blood oozed through his white shirt, though it wasn't torn. More blood ran down his back.

"I thank you, my people," Finn said. "You are dismissed."

"Hang on there," Arthur said as he slung Rafe's arm around his neck. "We've got you." On his other side, Gordie struggled to hold him up.

Rafe heaved his head up and moved his feet forward, determined not to be dragged down the dais like a corpse. He caught a glimpse of Astarte's face, wet with tears, as she joined Finn, taking his arm with a gracious little wave to the court as she always did. Rafe tried to smile and wave.

"Just a scratch," he said, but the words came out too low to be heard.

Someone in the crowd, Redfern maybe, shouted, "Long live King Sweordmund! Long live the prince!" Cheers went up.

Together they walked down the long runner to the side door. Thank Astarte's good sense for insisting they not enter and exit through the giant doors at the far end of the hall. He wouldn't have made it. As soon as the door of the antechamber closed behind them, Mac, the King's personal healer, rushed up.

"I'll take it from here," Mac told Arthur. "Just let him down onto that couch. Sitting up please." Mac held out his hands, fingers splayed and Rafe's shirt fell off him in pieces.

Rafe looked down at his own chest. Five deep gashes crossed his chest from left collarbone to stomach. From the burning pain in his back, the throne had gotten him there, too.

"You didn't tell me about this part when we were planning the Adoption," he growled at Mac.

The man grunted and knelt in front of him, concentrating on the cuts. Two other healers, a red headed woman who was Astarte's personal healer, and a young assistant were holding his wrists and head, jabbering at Mac about genetic shifts and magical flow rates.

Finn sat slumped in an armchair, Astarte beside him, holding his hand in a death grip. Arthur stood guard at the door, arms crossed over his chest. By the wall, well out of the healer's way, Gordie stood with Ama, who clutched her mistletoe branch like a sword in front of her. Gordie stood at parade attention, but he was gulping and clutching the sides of his dress pants. Poor kid. He'd never seen a man cut open before. Rafe tried to give them all a smile.

"I'm fine," he lied. "I can hardly feel it already."

"You may feel some discomfort," Mac murmured as he laid his hands over the wounds and chanted under his breath. Scalding heat knitted the wounds' edges together. Rafe gritted his teeth and breathed in short gasps.

This wasn't the usual pain leaving him hollow, as if his marrow had been scraped out, inspected, and only half put back. These were good old fashioned knife wounds, deep and vicious. He closed his eyes, remembering his training. Pain is just pain. Don't let it control you. Kill the attacker; end the pain. He tried to remember the darkness. The woman. She did this.

"Almost done," Mac said, "steady now."

Rafe grimaced and blinked. "Arthur." He jerked his head. Arthur reached him in two steps, bending over to catch Rafe's whisper. "It was a woman. You've got to…" He gasped. Mac's chant had shifted, and a new stab of pain went up his back.

Mac glared at both of them. "I am performing *surgery*! Get the hell out of my space, Captain."

Arthur backed up, mouthing "trust me" at Rafe.

Eventually, a blessed numbness spread over his torso. Mac grunted and got back to his feet, joints creaking.

"I have no earthly idea what did that to you. Half an inch deeper and it would have nicked your spine." He glared at Nefasta.

"It wasn't the incantation," she snapped.

"Are you sure?"

"Stop!" Finn raised his hands before the room could erupt into wrangling. "We will discuss it elsewhere. For now, the prince needs his rest."

"You too," Mac said reaching for his forehead. "I won't have you dropping from exhaustion."

"I'm fine." Finn held up his hand again and stood. "Study my *feorh* all you want, if it makes you happy. But not here and not now. Arthur, you look after Rafe. The rest of us are going into my workroom to find out exactly what went wrong with the magic. I will not have this happening to my heir again." Finn strode over to Rafe and laid his hands on Rafe's shoulders. "Go to bed, my boy. We'll figure out what went wrong. I promise."

Rafe nodded, his tongue too heavy with exhaustion to speak. Astarte leaned down and kissed him on the cheek.

"You are so brave," she whispered to him.

The rest of the group trailed after them, already debating. Rafe braced his hands on the edge of the couch, willing himself to rise.

"Please, sir. Let me help you." Gordie rushed across the room to duck under Rafe's arm and help him up.

"Thank you," he managed to say.

Between them, Arthur and Gordie got Rafe through the nearest portal and into his rooms. As Rafe collapsed onto the bed, he caught Gordie's sleeve.

"Go and clean up my things," he said. "Don't leave that mess for the maids."

"Yes, sir." Gordie whipped off a salute, fingers trembling only slightly, and dashed out of the room.

"Smart move," Arthur said, swinging Rafe's legs onto the bed and yanking off his boots.

"He'll sit around panicking if he doesn't have something to do," Rafe said. "I did the first time I saw Finn hurt."

Arthur nodded and chucked the boot over his shoulder.

"How are you really?" he said as he started on the second boot.

"Weak as a kitten." Rafe stared at the carved wooden canopy overhead. "Did I scream?"

"Not much," Arthur said. "I don't think they heard you all the way to the Summer Court."

Rafe groaned and covered his face with one arm. A wet tongue scraped his arm and a nose sniffed all along his torso, concentrating on the pale white lines where the cuts had been. He dropped his arm across Jake's neck, and the big dog immediately flopped down beside him, resting his head across Rafe's chest.

He closed his eyes as Arthur drew the covers up over him. The throne had questioned him before. It always questioned him. But it had never accused him of being a liar and a thief. He tried to sit up again, but couldn't assemble his limbs in the right order.

"Don't let him... he can't... he shouldn't..." He couldn't finish the thought.

Ideas, images kept slipping away from him. Silver lightning like swords. Iron needles in his blood. A woman, screaming for help. Screaming at him to stop.

"I can't..." he tried again.

"Exactly. You can't." Arthur urged Sam up onto the bed. The dog took his place by Rafe's legs, whining. "Now shut up and go to sleep. That's an order."

Rafe ran his hand over Jake's fur once more and slept.

Chapter Twenty-Nine

Her fingers like talons, like claws, Deor screamed into the abyss. Lightning split the air, flashing with its spitting heat, but it couldn't illuminate the darkness. She stretched out her arms, sure that someone was there—the thief was out there right now.

"Thief!" she screamed, stumbling forward.

A voice called through the darkness, from miles away, "Who are you?"

There came a muttered reply mere feet from her, and she spun to find the speaker, but she could not make out the words or identify the voice. Whoever he was, he sounded lost, weak, pained.

"Thief?" she asked.

"Not a thief!" the weak voice cried out, next to her. She spun again, hands raised, and clawed the air. Weak or not, he was stealing. He screamed, and Deor opened her eyes.

Dimly shining crystals threw pale light into the sunken bed. She shivered and the chill ran down her spine and out her wings. She was on her stomach, arms wrapped around the remains of a disemboweled pillow. She fluttered her wings and winced.

She was at Geoff's. She was safe. She closed her eyes and let sleep take her again.

"By the depth of the Barizan sea," Geoff snapped, startling Deor from her sleep. "What happened in here?"

Dizzy, her mouth dry, and her body aching, Deor opened her eyes to peer at Geoff. Her vision was a white blur. She shook her head, and the blur billowed in a cloud around her. She blinked a few times and sat up, rubbed her eyes. She gathered the sheet—now in tatters—to her chest. Around her feathers fluttered in the air. The pillows were slashed, the mattress too, opened in long slices. Geoff stepped into the room letting the door close behind him.

"What happened?" he repeated, gaping.

"I don't know," Deor said.

She groped for the glass of water next to the bed. When had someone left that? Had that only been this morning? Just a few hours before? She sipped the water.

"What time is it?"

"About one o'clock," he said. "Ceremony's over. I thought we might have lunch?" He came over and sat on the rim of the bed, his feet next to her on the mattress. "Are you okay?"

She shook her head. The nightmare was still vivid, lightning flashes, thief and all. "Bad dreams."

"No kidding." He picked up a hollowed out pillowcase and shook it, sending more feathers flying.

"Geoff, I'm so sorry," she started. "I don't know what happened. I'll..." She trailed off. She wanted to say she'd replace everything, but the bedding in the room probably cost more than she made in a half a year.

He reached for her hand. "Don't worry about it." He jerked his hand back. "Ouch!"

Deor followed his gaze down to her fingertips and shrieked. Where her fingers ended, silver nails, like blades, had sprouted. They glinted in the light, their edges sharp and flaked with bits of cloth and feather. She examined the nails: no blood. It had been a dream. Terrible, but only a dream. Geoff slid his fingers under her palm and raised her hand up to study it.

"Wow." He took hold of her index finger and dragged it across the mattress. It split the material like a scalpel to skin. "That's some magic."

"What the hell is wrong with me?" She held her hands up, palms facing her, fingers curled, and stared at the silver points. She pressed left index finger against her right wrist. She shoved it in and dragged it down her arm, tracing a perfect line along the vein.

"What are you doing?" Geoff grabbed her wrist.

There was no pain. No blood. There wasn't so much as a white line of dead skin. Nothing. She yanked her hand back. This time she shoved the blade of her left index finger through the center of her right palm. It slid in like a hot knife into warm butter, but still no pain. She drew it out and, again, no mark.

Had her mother known that this magic would happen if she came back to the Winter Court? Had her father ever stabbed her mother? The wings Deor knew she could keep hidden, but how could she return to the human world like this? She sagged back against the headboard.

"I'm some kind of monster."

"No," Geoff said, patting her knee. He scooted close to her and dropped his voice. "But you don't want to tell people about this. Don't tell Donovan. He'll think you're here to hurt me."

"That's stupid!" Deor said and crossed her arms over her chest.

"I know it is, but you know how he can be."

Deor rubbed her palms into her eyes. Her whole body ached. She tried to stretch her legs, but charley-horses shot through her calves and she whimpered. She flexed her feet up, down, up, down, until the cramps eased enough for her to stop panting. She arched her back, and the same cramps tore through her wings, sharp enough for her to cry out.

"Here." Geoff handed her the glass of water. "This should help."

With her back, legs, and wings still in knots, she gulped the water down as fast as possible. She forced her shoulders down, forced them to relax, and, little by little, the spasms stopped. "Thanks," she finally whispered.

"No problem." He slid up and sat next to her, careful of her wings, and leaned against the headboard. "Gorgeous wings, by the way. You were holding out on me." He gently poked her in the side.

She chuckled. She rolled her shoulders several times and arched her back before her wings slid into her body. She didn't know whether to be glad or upset that she had such control of them now. Shimmying close to Geoff, she dropped her head on his shoulder.

"I can't believe this," she said. "I think my faerie side is trying to kill me."

"Never." Geoff slid his arm around her and pulled her close. "Tell me what you dreamed. It will make it less scary."

She closed her eyes.

"Someone was stealing from me. I was lost in darkness and someone was stealing. But I attacked him. With these claws, I think." She opened her eyes and flexed her hands, straining her fingers. The blades had already shortened. "They're going away."

"Sure," Geoff said. "That's defensive magic. You're calming down, so they're going away." He caught her hand and raised it to his lips to kiss it.

"Do you know any other faeries that can do this?" She sat up and turned to face him. "That could help me find my father."

"I don't." Geoff shook his head. "I have heard of the phenomenon, but I don't know any personally."

She thought for a moment. "Maybe I should ask Lord Farringdon?"

"What?" Geoff's eyes grew wide. "Why?"

Deor ran her thumbs over her the silver tips on her fingers. "He's got connections to the police. Maybe they have records on this kind of thing."

"Bad idea," Geoff said. "Rafe already thinks you're dangerous, right? He'd just use this as one more reason to throw you out of the country—or worse, into the Tower." He grinned at her. "And I've grown rather fond of you." He beckoned to her, urging her to snuggle up against him again.

She curled up next to him and laid her face against his chest. "You're probably right."

"Of course I am," he said, wrapping an arm around her and stroking her back. "He's a bully who cares more about putting people away than he does about catching the person who actually committed the crime. You don't want it to be you."

"Ugh," she said. "I hate people like that."

"Me too. I mean, I'm a prince, I get the perks. But that's why I came here to study. There's no way Bard Nefasta is giving me a degree unless I earn it."

"Very true." She leaned up and kissed him. "Let me know if I can help with your dissertation."

"I will." He kissed her back. "I brought you something." He pulled a small box from his trouser pocket. "Here."

She undid the bow and recognized the emblem on the box from one of the shops she had seen on Artificers' Street. She opened it. A large black pearl hung on a platinum chain.

"Geoff! You shouldn't have."

"Nonsense," he said. "It makes up for my leaving you Friday and this morning." He took the box from her hands. "Here," he said, taking out the necklace. "Let me put it on you."

"Okay." She twisted away from him and gathered up her hair, letting the sheet fall. He eased the necklace over her head and fixed it closed at the back of her neck. The jewel fell just at the top of her cleavage. She turned around. "Does it suit me?"

"Perfectly," he said, fixing it in place. "It matches your eyes."

"Thank you," she said. "For everything."

She kissed him.

Deor spent Monday napping in Geoff's bed, weak and aching, as if she'd been in a bar fight, but with no bruises, scars, or cool stories to tell. Geoff came and went, checking on her. Servants left food in the outer room while she slept. By dinner time, she managed to get up, wrap herself in Geoff's robe, and come out to the parlor.

"There she is!" Geoff beamed at her. He was wearing a sky blue suit that brought out the yellow in his eyes. Donovan glanced up from a newspaper and gave her a glare.

"Anymore nightmares?" Donovan said.

"Thankfully, no."

"Come and have a seat." Geoff patted the spot next to him on the couch. He held out a paper to her. "You can read the paper and rest."

"Thanks." She sat down next to him and studied the front page of the *Caer Eisteddfod Dispatch*. The headline above the fold was all about the Adoption.

"Yes, yes," Deor muttered. "He's absolutely fabulous. Isn't the prince fabulous? Why yes, yes he is. Let's talk about it for the next week and a half. Then we can move on to talk about how fabulous he'll be." She rolled her eyes and skipped to the next article down the page.

Goblin Prince Steps Out! the headline below the fold shouted. *While our own royal prince hasn't been socializing much, the visiting prince of the Goblins isn't hiding behind his books,* the columnist wrote. *And neither is his lovely date, which this paper has been able to identify as none other than the most recent hire at our own university: Professor Deor Smithfield. She is a professor of*

"Human Literature Studies." But don't judge this tiny book by its cute little cover! Sources tell this writer that she's a giant in the classroom, including getting the prince's moody bodyguard—tall, dark, and fangy—into line with ease, even if it is from the height of a stepstool. Prince Geoffrey is sure to get a schooling from her!

Little is known about this adorable faerie. Sources tell this writer that she's actually a changeling. Whoever her parents are, they aren't talking. Makes you wonder, doesn't it?

On Saturday night, the prince and his mistress dined at L'Cirque, where they shared a bottle of Rangley's finest white. Rumor has it (from an unconfirmed source) that a carriage took them back to the prince's suite at his underground embassy—and that she has not yet emerged. Looks like the prince's favorite musical dessert did the trick again.

"Oh, God." Deor waved the paper at Geoff. "Have you seen this?"

"Of course. Though you probably should have waited until after supper to read that. Reading about yourself before eating spoils the digestion."

"Did you leak this?" she said, shoving the paper at him.

"Me? That was an unconfirmed source. I am always confirmable. Though I prefer reliable. When it says 'a reliable source inside the prince's household,' that's me."

"Jackass."

He laughed. "Come on. Playing with the press is fun. They're so easily amused by the most trivial things." He shoved the paper back at her. "But no, I did not tell the press anything about us. There are always reporters outside L'Cirque hoping someone important will show up. It's the place to be."

"Why didn't you warn me? And what about the details about my not leaving your place?" she shot back. "That wasn't random luck."

He nodded, conceding the point. "Probably a reporter, stalking me for a byline. They do that." He gave her a half smile. "Look on the bright side. Someone might be reading their paper right this moment and thinking that you look really familiar. It could be a good thing for you."

She scrubbed her hands over her face. "I suppose," she said. "Right now I'd like to slap her smirky little face."

"She is a bit too arch," Geoff agreed. "Never met an innuendo she didn't like. She's smarter than she sounds in print though. She's a devil of an interviewer."

"You've talked to her?"

"Don't worry, sweetest," he said. "I've got it under control. Hiding only makes reporters more rabid." She snorted at him, and he leaned in for a quick peck on the lips.

"I don't want to be known as your mistress. I don't want to be known as anybody's mistress." Before he could complain, she added, "But you're right. Maybe someone will see me and say something."

"That's the spirit!" Geoff stood. "I need to go out. Stay here. Rest." He pointed at the papers. "If you don't want to be in the public eye, I understand. We can just stay at the embassy most of time from now on. Lie low, as it were." He winked at her.

"I'd appreciate it. Maybe I should go talk to the reporter who wrote this. See if she has any clue who I am."

"Of course," he said. "Once you're feeling a bit better, I'll go with you." He pulled out his mirror and said something she didn't understand, though she recognized it as not being Faerie.

"We won't be long." He leaned in and kissed her.

"Bye." She waved as he and Donovan left.

She slumped back on the couch. She was an idiot. Of course reporters followed Geoff around. She was dating a prince, and she hadn't even thought about the press. She played with the pearl he'd given her Sunday night, running it back and forth on its chain as she stared into space, planning how she'd handle the class tomorrow.

Chapter Thirty

Deor drew in a deep breath as the goblin servant waited at the front door of the embassy, hand on the knob.

"Whenever you are ready, miss." His serious face suggested he did feel for her. "As His Majesty suggested, we could provide you with an escort this morning."

"No." Deor shook her head. "I'm not his. I don't need his protection." She shouldered her bag and nodded. "Okay. Go."

The servant pulled the door open, and Deor stepped out into the bright, shining morning. At the foot of the steps from the porch to the street, half a dozen reporters were gathered. All held mirrors up, and, as soon as she stepped out, they hollered out questions.

Deor paused for a brief moment, and a short faerie woman with her blonde hair in a bouffant that would do Texas proud chirped at her. "How were the last two nights, Bard Smithfield? Is the prince everything you expected?"

"It is Professor," Deor snapped. "And as for everything else, all of you, no comment."

She shoved her way through the crowd. At the street, a royal blue carriage waited for her.

A goblin guard, her uniform separating her from the servants in the embassy, bowed low. "His Majesty requested that you allow me to see you to Eisteddfod University safely."

The reporters tittered behind her, and Deor knew they'd be more than happy to follow her all the way to school.

"Thank you," she said and let the guard help her into the carriage.

After she shut the door, the goblin climbed onto the running board and nodded at the driver above. The carriage jolted into motion, and the reporters trailed after it. Until the guard blasted a plume of blue-green flame at them.

Deor shrieked and spun around to look out the back window.

"Don't worry, miss," the guard said leaning slightly in the window. "No harm done. More a light show than a painful rebuke. But I can give them a bit of pain, too, if you like. I never did care for reporters—especially that little blonde twit."

"What? No." Deor shook her head. She wasn't going to have reporters set on fire for following someone down a public street. "But thank you," she added.

The woman gave a brief nod and resumed her place watching the scenery speed by.

At Eisteddfod a smattering of reporters had congregated around the entrance. They swarmed the carriage, and Deor shut her eyes when she realized that the carriage driver was not going to stop—if someone got run over, well it was their problem for being in the way.

There didn't seem to be any bumps in the road, and Deor opened her eyes as the carriage rolled to a stop.

Bernie lumbered out of the guard post. "What's all this now?"

The goblin opened the door for Deor and helped her down.

"Thank you," she said. "It's just me, Bernie." The bear stopped and looked her up and down.

"That explains the reporters then." He snorted. "Eisteddfod does not allow government vehicles on the property without explicit permission. No one told me you were coming."

"I'm sorry," Deor said. "Geoff was trying to protect me from the reporters."

The woman moved to stand next to Deor, arms crossed in front of her. She stared down the bear, who held her gaze.

"Really," Deor said. "I will be dropped off outside the walls next time."

Bernie shifted his gaze to Deor. "Take care that you do." He gave a small nod and trundled back to his post.

"I can escort you through campus, if you like." The soldier dropped her arms to her sides. "There might be student reporters."

"No, thank you." The path to the center of campus was clear, and coming in with a looming goblin bodyguard would draw more attention. "But I appreciate the offer."

The woman nodded. "If you want me to pick you up, call for Giselle on your mirror. Anytime." Before Deor could respond, the woman turned back to the carriage. She climbed up to sit next to the driver, and they rolled off out the gate.

"Well that was fun," she said to herself.

In the middle of campus, the clock tower chimed nine-fifteen.

"Dammit!" She picked up her pace. She did not like to be kept waiting by students who made appointments, but it bothered her even more to be late herself. Hopefully Robbie hadn't given up on her and left.

Inside the Literary Arts building, she slapped the lintel on the portal. "Fifth floor." The brick facade vanished, and she stepped through and hurried down the hall. The chair outside her office was empty.

"Dammit," she said again. Robbie had taken enough crap lately, and she didn't need her teacher blowing her off—especially when it looked like she was being blown off for a princely affair. She'd mirror Robbie as soon as she got in her office.

She caught the door handle, waiting for the click of the lock recognizing her, but green magic crackled under her touch. The door was open a sliver.

"Robbie?" she called out as she opened the door.

Maybe a janitor had trouble with the lock. Or, more likely, she hadn't shut it right when she'd left on Thursday.

There was no response. Green-tinged magic trailed from the lock as the door swung, and she bent to examine it before admitting to herself that she had no idea what she was seeing. The usual winding lines of magic were a writhing mass of tangles, like pulsing veins, through which green magic coiled like a snake. A majority of the red strands were broken, jaggedly torn.

"Shit." Hopefully Geoff had done some minor prank, and it hadn't been a reporter looking for something incriminating.

When she stepped in the room, she froze. Sprawled out on the floor, body crawling with green, snaky magic, was Robbie. Her eyes were open, vacant, and her mouth was locked in a silent scream. A thin line of blood dribbled from her lips. Her arms were splayed out to her side, as if she had been flung backwards to the ground.

Behind the girl, leaning over her, a man. Green? Deor couldn't tell. His magic oozed from his fingers and crawled over the girl, wrapping her like a spider would a fly.

"Get away from her!" Deor screamed.

The man started and jerked his gaze to Deor, but she still couldn't make out a face.

Deor scanned the room for a weapon, but he was between her and the chairs, and none of the books handy would have made a dent. The man, his face a blur, stepped over Robbie's body.

No longer the focus of his magic, Robbie's eyes closed, her head lolling to one side as blood from her mouth and nose pooled on the floor. Green magic coiled around the man's fingers, the only part of him Deor could see clearly. Panic rose in her.

"Help." A strangled whisper. She shook her head. "Help! Someone help!" she screamed.

Footsteps in the hall told her people were coming. The man paused. Behind Deor, the door opened. The man jumped from the window.

Deor sprinted to the window and clung to the sill as she leaned out. Down, up, left, right. The man was nowhere to be seen. Around the edges of the window where he had broken through, thin strands of green magic waved in the wind.

"Professor Smithfield!" Ama said.

Deor turned to face her—her nails sparked silver, so she clenched her fist to hide them.

"Robbie—" Deor pointed at the girl. "I just got here. We had a meeting at nine. I was late…" She trailed off.

Ama gasped. Deor slammed her hand over her mouth, trying to hold back the wretch rising in her stomach. She stumbled past Robbie's body and collapsed over the trashcan next to her desk, emptying her stomach of the breakfast she had grabbed before she left.

She fell back and leaned against the cupboard behind her desk, swiping a hand across her mouth. A student had appeared and was leaning over Robbie while Ama talked to someone on the mirror.

"She's still alive," the student—she recognized him now—Aiden, Robbie's friend. "Bard Nefasta! She's alive!"

Ama turned back to look at the young man crouched over Robbie. "I heard you." She snapped her attention back to the mirror and barked orders for a healer. She turned away as the mirror went dark.

"Bard Nefasta?" Aiden was crying, tears streaming down his cheeks.

Deor touched her own face and found it wet with tears, too. She crawled forward to Robbie and reached for her hand. The green magic reared up and rolled toward her, crashing like a wave against her outstretched hand.

"Don't touch it!" Ama and Aiden said in unison.

But it was too late. When the magic touched Deor's hand, the same thing that happened to Geoff's cake happened again. The green strands faded to grey and black and crumbled to dust.

"The Civil Patrol is on its way. Bernie and Bob will be here momentarily to secure the area." Ama reached for Deor and put a hand on her shoulder. "Are you okay?"

"Is *she* okay?" Aiden snapped. "Who cares?" He gestured at Robbie. "She's barely breathing and now the magic is gone. How will a healer help her? How will they find the person who did this?"

"Oh God," Deor whispered and sat back on her knees. "I didn't mean to—I didn't know."

"Idiot!" The boy leaned over Robbie again and brushed a few hairs out of her eyes. "It's okay, Robbie. You're going to be fine," he said to her.

At the edges of the girl's face, crawling down her neck under her shirt, and all up and down her arms, frightening black marks swirled. Like the ones Deor had seen on Robbie after the first attack, only much darker and larger.

The girl's chest barely rose and fell, and her eyes were still open like she stared at some monster only she could see.

"Come on," Ama said, taking Deor's arm and pulling her to her feet. "Tell me what you saw. Tell me what happened."

Deor drew in a deep breath. "When I got to the office…" She shook her head. "No, before that, I got coffee." She rubbed her hands up and down her arms. "I was late…" She babbled in fits and starts, jumping from place to place in the story until she wasn't sure herself. "I just know," she said, "that the door was open when I got here."

"Wait," Ama stopped her. "The door was open?"

"Yes." Deor nodded. "And there was a man standing over her. He came at me, but you arrived. He jumped out the window." She pointed.

Ama made her way to the window and examined the remains of the magic. "Nothing here of use that I can see."

"If I had gotten here on time—"

"There would be two bodies," Ama finished for her. "Alarms should have gone off when someone tried to tamper with the door. Whoever did this is very powerful." She stepped away from the window and looked Deor in the eye. "Either that, or they had help getting in. Now come outside so you don't disturb any more evidence." Deor edged around Robbie's unconscious form, and Aiden glared at her.

"This is your fault," he whispered as she went by. "I hope the Sword makes you pay."

"Enough," Ama snapped. "You can stay with her, Aiden, but don't touch anything else."

"I'm not the idiot," he snapped back.

Ama arched an eyebrow.

The kid must have been all kinds of distraught to take that tone with her, but Ama let it go.

"Healers should be here any minute," Ama said. "I'm sure you will be able to help them when they arrive."

Aiden wiped tears off his cheeks with his sleeve and sniffed. "Right." He held Robbie's hand.

Deor followed Nefasta out. In the hall, a small crowd of students and professors, some with mirrors, had gathered. Ama dispersed them with a stern glance and a wave of her hand.

"You all have somewhere else to be."

Bob and Bernie arrived moments later, Bob as a bear. Bernie established a perimeter, growling "take the stairs" to anyone who came within a few yards of Deor's office.

Deor sat in the chair outside her office. The same chair where she should have found Robbie. She stared at her hands, fingers curled into her palms. It seemed like hours ticked by as her nails faded from silver to white.

Chapter Thirty-One

Rafe took the Literary Arts building's steps two at a time and slammed through the half open doors, Arthur close on his heels. "Where?" he shouted at the bear standing guard over the portals.

"Fifth floor, sir."

He leaped through without even a nod of thanks. Robbie. If he could just get to her in time. Get her to the healers in time. He popped out of the portal at a dead run, taking in faces and dismissing them in an instant.

Deor, face in her hands, sat in a chair like a student waiting for punishment. Nefasta, her lavender face set in even harsher lines than usual, stood before the door. She beckoned to him.

"Healer Penelope is with her," she said.

He shoved past Nefasta into the narrow office. Penny was just closing Robbie's eyes. Decaying fragments of magic still clung like fungus to Robbie's body.

"No."

"She's not dead," Penny said. "But she's lost. I can't wake her. Physically, she's fine." She paused under his cold gaze.

"But?" He tried not to freeze the room.

"But her mind isn't. She's the kind of comatose I have only ever read about. Whatever magic this person used—" Penny frowned "—I've never seen it before. Will spells, yes, but this is more than that. Whoever came after her wasn't trying to will her to do something. He was trying to obliterate her mind."

"What will happen when she wakes? Will she wake?" Rafe knelt beside Robbie, taking her hand in his.

"I don't know." Penny said and laid a hand on his shoulder. "I will do everything in my power to help her."

Rafe stared at his little sister—he'd refused to even look at her picture when she was born. He hadn't spoken to Astarte for six months, he'd been so angry that she could do this to Finn.

Astarte had forced the issue, laying the baby on his lap one evening as he read in his room. From the second Robbie had reached up to grab his hair in her pudgy little fist, he'd loved her. For the last twenty-nine years, he had tried to protect this little half-human child while the press called her the Royal Whore's Bastard, and Parliament passed resolutions banning her from ever sitting in Parliament or holding the smallest title.

"Robbie, I'm so sorry."

"It's not your fault," Arthur said.

He couldn't reply. Too many words. Too few. The answers choked him. He'd watched men die beside him in battle and fought harder for it. He'd carried the wounded to healers and gone back to battle, glad to avenge them, but now all he wanted was to fall across Robbie's body and howl.

"We have to move her, Lord Farringdon," Penny said.

"I have to take her home to her home to her mother." He reached down to scoop her up, but Arthur grabbed his arm.

"You can't do that. Rafe, look at me." He dragged Rafe to his feet. "We have to examine the evidence first."

He clenched his fists. "You cold blooded… What if that was your sister?"

"I know." Arthur stepped back and held his arms out wide. "Hit me. Do what you have to do, but snap out of it. Mourn later. Help us find out who did this first."

"We know who did this," he hissed back. They both turned to look at Nefasta, who stood with her back to the door, ears perked. She may have allowed the Civil Patrol onto campus, and she might even believe that Deor was a suspect now, but every bard in the university would stand in their way if he dragged Deor out of here without their permission. Rafe cast a privacy spell around himself and Arthur.

"Miss Smithfield can't appeal to bardic law if she doesn't know about it," Arthur said.

Rafe nodded. "You go. Get every man you can on that goblin's trail. Then help Penny with the..." The words caught in his throat. "The forensics. I'm going to have a private chat with our little professor."

Chapter Thirty-Two

At the edge of Deor's vision, a handkerchief appeared. She took it, not raising her gaze from the floor. "Thank you." Her sobs had ebbed away, but tears still ran down her cheeks.

"You're welcome," a familiar, masculine voice said.

She looked up and up, into Lord Farringdon's face. He glanced away from her and gave a quick nod.

Deor followed his gaze in time to see Captain Maerhwer and Penny—in a fitted blue lab coat over her dress—step out of her office. Deor stifled a wail. A gurney, floating mid-air, was being guided out of the portal, Maerhwer standing guard. Robbie's body, covered in a layer of magic, was followed by a pair of guards and Penny, who scribbled notes as she walked. She glanced up and froze when she saw Deor, a deep frown crossing her features.

"Do you know what did this?" Deor asked as Penny approached with the body.

Penny glanced at the captain, walking next to her, who shook his head. She refocused on Rafe.

"Can we go into Bard Nefasta's s office and talk?" he said. Deor stood. She glanced at the closed door of her office.

"Don't you want to see the scene first?"

"I already have," he said.

"Right." How long had she been sitting there staring at the floor? Going over and over and over in her mind what she'd seen, heard, when she came through the portal. Should she have noticed something? Had there been footsteps in the hall?

"Follow me," he said, leaving a trail of cold behind him. He led the way to the main office and through into Ama's office in the back. He held the door for her and came into the room behind her, shutting the door.

Unthinking, she settled into the chair across from the desk. He slipped into its companion next to her.

"Tell me what happened."

She ran through her day, the whole thing, start to finish, and as embarrassing as the reporters' attentions had been, his was even worse. He scribbled notes, nodded, waited when she had to stop to cry, and didn't say a word.

When she was finished, she finally looked him in the face. "So?"

"Do you have any idea who did this?" he asked.

She blew her nose into the hankie. "None." She balled the fine material up in her hand. "I didn't know Robbie that well." Lord Farringdon did, her conscience chimed in.

"I'm so sorry," she said. "Robbie's your sister. I'm sorry," she repeated, her tears spilling over again.

He stared at her. "You say that you saw a man?"

She nodded. "I'm pretty sure it was a man. Maybe green, but that might have been the magic. He started to come after me, and I called for help. When he heard the footsteps, he darted out the window." She met Rafe's gaze. "I don't know how he did it. I wouldn't fit through it, and he was much bigger than me."

The image of Robbie covered in black marks like they had been tattooed onto her skin made Deor tremble. She stood up and paced.

"Do you think whoever did this was coming after me, too?"

"That is one possibility." He frowned at her. "So you saw the magic when it was green?"

"Yes." She rubbed her hands up and down her arms. Just talking about it made her break out in goosebumps like the magic was touching her.

"And then you touched it and it fell apart." His voice was so low she could barely hear it. The pen in his hand was frozen and shards of ice dangled from his mirror.

"Aiden said I'd ruined any chance you had of catching him or helping Robbie. Is that true?" Her stomach turned and she held still, swallowing hard to force down the bile.

"It is possible." A look of pain shot across his face. "The spell's signature will linger, but there's no doubt you destroyed useful evidence."

He flicked his finger across his pocket mirror skimming his notes. His gaze came back up to hers, the piercing blue cold like a winter's storm.

"Would you be willing to undergo tests? To see if you have magic residue on you?"

"I guess..."

"She most certainly would not!" Geoff stormed into the room, his slit pupils wide and his mouth in a hard line. "Come here," he said gently and held out a hand to her.

Deor caught his hand and let him draw her into an embrace. He stroked her hair, and she let out another sob.

"I know." He rubbed her back. "It's going to be okay."

"It will be if you don't interfere with my investigation," Lord Farringdon said. When Deor turned around, he was already standing. "You need to let us test you"

"Not without me present," Geoff said. "And right now, not at all. You're just looking for someone to blame."

"She was found with Ro—the victim. She claims she saw the man who did this. That's pretty convenient, no?"

Deor stepped away from Geoff and stood in front of Lord Farringdon. She had to crane her neck to look up into his face. "I did not try to kill Robbie. Why would I?"

"Excellent question. Why would you? Why are changelings that look like you being attacked?"

"Just like when I came in to give my statement," she said. "You're so sure I did something, you've decided I'm guilty rather than listening to me. Rather than finding the real culprit." She looked at the crumpled cloth in her hand. "Keep your hankie." She shoved it at his chest, and he caught it, his fingers brushing hers. Shots of electricity jumped between them. The world reeled. Blackness flashed across her vision, and she wavered. She stumbled back, and Geoff caught her.

"What did you do to her?" Geoff demanded.

Rafe shook his head as if clearing his senses. "What did she do to me, you mean."

"I didn't do anything to you," she said and clutched at Geoff. The room still rocked and rolled. She leaned into Geoff, and he slid an arm around her waist. "If you put some kind of spell on me…"

"You'll hear from my ambassadors," Geoff finished for her. "Badgering witnesses might work for the Sword, or even for the Civil Patrol, but not in my political world. Not when the people you're bullying have as much power as you do."

Rafe eyed her. "Be careful. If Geoff is helping you, it's because he wants something from you." His gaze flicked to the prince. "Likely something more than merely entertaining the press with your affair."

"Shut up," she snapped.

He gave a curt nod and headed for the door. He paused and glanced back at her.

"Do stay where we can get in touch with you," he said. "In case I have any more questions." He walked off to talk to the bears.

"Come on," Geoff said. "Let's get you back to the embassy. You'll be safe from him there. You need to rest." He led her from the room. "Do you want to talk about it?"

"No." Deor shook her head, happy to let him guide her. "No. I just want to get out of here."

In the outer office, Ama was waiting. "I've cancelled your classes for the day," she said. "The officers are interviewing students." She followed Deor and Geoff out into the main hallway.

"You don't believe I hurt Robbie, do you?" Deor asked Ama.

The woman stared at her for a minute. "I haven't made up my mind."

"Nice," Geoff said to Ama. "That's the way to protect people—like bards are supposed to do?"

Ama did not respond to Geoff; instead she looked at Deor. "Be careful," she said. "You are a pawn in a dangerous game."

Geoff snorted. "Come on." He led Deor to Donovan.

"Ready to go?" Donovan stood up from where he leaned against a wall.

"Yes," Geoff said. "Cover us. I don't want any reporters, any students, anyone bothering us."

Donovan grinned, fangs bared. He glanced down at her. "You okay to walk out of here? I don't want you fainting on me."

"I wish I could faint," she said. "But I'm fine."

"Huh. I guess we'll see." He led them to the portal and down into the crisp autumn air. Once outside, he nodded to Geoff, who tightened his arm around Deor's shoulder.

"Donovan's going to cloak us," he whispered in her ear. "It will be like looking through a veil. And you'll feel the magic. Don't worry. I've got you." He gave her shoulder a rub and added, "And don't pick at the magic like you did with the cake."

She pressed herself up against Geoff and nodded.

Donovan cast his arms out to either side and brought them back in like he was gathering the air to him. He tossed his arms up like he was throwing something into the air, and a fine blackness, a shadow, fell over the three of them.

Her senses reeled. Adrenaline flashed through her body, and her nerves tingled. She drew a forced breath in and drove it out again, repeating this over and over until the pounding of her heart slowed, but every fiber of her being screamed to cast off the magic. Her wings spasmed in her back, struggling to break free. Sparkles danced in the air around her and flickered out. Chills rolled in whispering waves down her skin. At the tips of her fingers, silver blades appeared again, and she balled her hands into fists.

Geoff squeezed her more tightly to him and caught one of her wrists. He raised her hand to his lips and kissed it. Deor shuddered at the touch, but the physical sensation grounded her, and she took another breath.

"That's it," he murmured as he turned her hand over and kissed the inside of her wrist. "It's all going to be fine. We're just being discrete. The magic won't hurt you."

"The magic won't hurt me," she said aloud. "Right." Bracing herself against her own instincts to claw herself away from him, she took a step forward with Geoff, then another, and another until she was walking down the path toward the embassy.

"That's it." Geoff eased his hand from her waist and took her arm. "It's all fine," he said picking up his pace slightly.

"Of course it is," she said, and hoped the lie became true.

Chapter Thirty-Three

T he clock tower chimed the hour, and Deor left her new makeshift office—a small desk crammed into a dark corner of Ama's space. The City Patrol—the general—hadn't yet reopened her office for use. From time to time Deor caught Ama staring at her the way Lieutenant Bolton had the first day in the Tower—like she might discover Deor's innocence or guilt if she stared at her long enough.

She buttoned her bardic robes and headed for the lecture hall. A pixie student zipped in past her. Drawing a deep breath, she stopped at the classroom door a moment, steadying herself. Time to teach. She opened the door and stepped inside.

She scanned up the tiers of the lecture hall—everyone was silent. Even Geoff, with an alert Donovan at his side, had nothing to say. None of Robbie's friends had come to class.

"Are there any questions before we start?" Deor asked and immediately followed it up with, "about the readings or the assignments?"

No one asked her anything—not about her, not about Robbie, not about Geoff. How could she address the class at a time like this? What was there to say? Especially since the papers were finally reporting on the assaults and many had given out that she was a suspect. She stepped up to the lectern.

"*Richard III*," she said, "is a play about a man determined to be king."

A few students murmured at that, but they opened their books and raised quills to take notes. The students' silence continued through the whole of both classes. Machiavelli was wrong; fear was definitely worse than love, at least in terms of class participation.

As the last of the students filed out, Geoff came up to her. "You did well," he said.

"Thanks. I need to get some stuff done this afternoon. Do you want to get together later tonight?" She could barely stand the thought of going back to her own place with Penny and Rufus' accusing stares.

"No." He shook his head. "Sorry. I have an event at the embassy. Where are you headed? Do you want me to have one my people go with you?"

"I'm a grownup, Geoff. All the dull, grownup things still need doing no matter what else is going on. I'll be careful."

She let him kiss her for real, no mere peck on the cheek, before he pulled out his mirror and she headed the opposite direction.

She made her way off campus, the autumn leaves not quite so beautiful anymore. The thought of breakfast that morning had made her ill, so she stopped at a pastry shop. As she munched her scone and sipped her tea, she thought about what she'd say to the *Dispatch*. Certainly they'd want an interview with her—they'd have a million questions. So did she. She'd give that snarky reporter the personal interest interview of a lifetime in exchange for a detailed conversation about who her father might be.

She dumped her cup and pastry wrap in the trash and stepped out onto the sidewalk. The air was crisp and sharp enough that she tightened the belt on her coat. She headed down the street to a cab stand a couple blocks away.

"Professor Smithfield?" a desperate voice called from an alley as she passed. "Deor?"

She stopped and peered down the dim street. A few feet in, the darkness of the tight-pressed buildings overwhelmed the light.

"Hello?" she called.

"Help me," the voice called back. "Please."

Something in the voice made her lurch forward. Whoever it was needed help. Help only she could give. She had to help the... girl. Yes! It was a girl, a young woman, begging for help.

She darted into the alley, almost tripping on debris. Once in the darkness, she blinked, trying to focus. A figure, or maybe two, waited at the dead end. The voice called out again for her, and she took a few more steps forward.

"It's going to be okay," a voice—but not the same one—whispered so low she had to strain to hear. "You're safe here. Safe and sound."

She took another step forward. Safe. She was safe. Her hands trembled. In the semi-darkness, a glint of light flashed. Her fingertips had turned silver again.

"You're safe," the voice repeated.

She kept walking, her hands shaking. Blood rushed in her ears, its quiet roar blocking out the sounds of the street behind her. The two figures rose up in front of her, their faces a blur of magic. She strained to see them. One was darker, taller than the other.

"You're safe, Deor," the shorter one—a woman—said. "It's okay. Be a good girl. Such a pretty, good girl." The woman held out her hand. "Come here, sweetheart. There's a good girl."

Deor shook her head. People had called her clever. Sassy. Stubborn. Even a hateful bitch. No one had ever called her a good girl, not even her grandmother.

"I've never been a good girl," she said and turned to run.

Magic chains whipped around her body. She cried out, but the sound was muffled. Her scream barely rasped from her throat.

"Be still!" the voice commanded and her whole body froze.

Chills ran up her spine, and she closed her eyes, concentrated on the feel of the magic binding her. The lines on Robbie, had they been chains?

"Turn around." A honey sweet command, but underneath, an iron will crashed against her own.

She shifted, turning slowly, examining everything she saw, forcing her eyes to see past the magic. She knew the figure speaking to her was a woman. She was taller than Deor by several inches, like all faerie women. Cold eyes—colorless? No, that was the magic. She had eyes, nose, chin, but none of it made sense. Blackness around her head. Her hair or the darkness? Deor curled her fists around the magic chains binding her. They were cold to the touch, like ice. She squeezed her fists closed, driving the spiked ends of her nails into the chain. A link gave, and another and another.

The woman reached for her face.

"You look so much like him," she whispered. "I simply do not understand how no one else sees it."

"Don't touch me!" Deor jerked her chin away from the woman's grip.

The woman dropped her hand.

"Your father is such a fool." The woman laughed—a burst of power that slammed into Deor like a punch to the gut.

So this was will magic.

"You know my father?"

"Of course." Her voice was a low purr. "Come with me, and I'll tell you all about him."

Someone nearby—she had forgotten there was someone else—snickered. "There's so much to say about him."

A flare of magic illuminated the alley. The sniggering man froze. The magic dimmed until it was a small purple spark in the woman's hand.

"Quiet." There was so much contempt in her voice that Deor shrank back, tried to pull away.

The woman returned her attention to Deor. Even with her face obscured by magic, her hatred was crystal clear.

"Come with me." She reached for Deor.

"No." Deor knocked the woman's hand away. "I'm not going anywhere with you."

Another flare of purple light erupted in the woman's hand.

"It will hurt much less if you come with me now. I might even leave few pieces of you when I'm done." Adrenaline shot through Deor, and she stepped back, out of reach.

The woman hurled her magic at Deor, a physical blast of her will. Icy magic clawed into Deor's chest, curling around her innards. The woman jerked her magic back toward herself, and Deor flailed forward dragged by the magic twined around her spine.

Deor's fingertips were silver and sharp, and magic whispered along her skin. Sparks flooded the air but vanished when they hit the woman's magic. Silver light crowded the edges of Deor's vision. Her fingers tingled with magic—it pinballed in her chest, desperate for focus.

The woman dragged Deor a step closer, and she swayed, struggling to lean away. Deor's magic was nothing compared to this woman's power, even if she had known how to use it.

Her magic crawled up Deor's neck, winding around her throat. The woman was close enough that Deor could feel her breath.

"Just a little more, I think," she said and let loose another blast of magic.

The chain links that had wrapped around Deor solidified. Each link burned her with brutal cold, driving her heart into a panicked flutter. She gasped to get air into her lungs.

"That's it." The woman soothed her. "Stand still. That's a good little girl."

Deor was a lot of things—but she was not a child.

Rage drove back the pain. Her uncle's teaching on bar fights rose in her mind. If they can't see, they can't hurt you. She balled her hand into a fist and threw a left hook. Her fist flew through the magic unscathed and connected with the woman's nose. Sharp pain shot up through Deor's hand and into her wrist.

The woman reeled back, and the chains binding Deor loosened. Deor spun and bolted for the light at the end of the alley. Green tendrils coiled around her waist as another voice called, "Stop, child!"

"No!" she screamed, tearing at the magic with silver claws. The purple chains joined the green tentacles, and everywhere they alighted on her skin, they burned, searing her. She clawed at them, pushed forward, one step, another step.

"Stop!" the woman commanded.

"Nope!" Deor gasped the word out as she hauled herself forward. Another whip of magic stung her back and she cried out—another hit and she'd stumble, fall.

Her wings shot out, tearing through her bra, shirt, and coat, propelling her forward. Tears spilled from her eyes as the will magic slammed into her wings. Searing pain like a dozen daggers tore through the delicate flesh. She fluttered them, sending drops of blood in a spray of red around her, splattering her arms and her face.

"I'm. Not. Stopping," she said more to herself than to her attackers.

The light, the end of the alley, was a few steps away. Two steps. One step. She dug her claws into the magic that bound her, wrapped over and around her like a harness, pulling her backward. She drove her silver nails—long spikes now—through the magic, through her clothes, and even through her own flesh. She clenched her fists around the will magic and yanked, tearing her bra and her clothes, her touch destroying the spell.

She stumbled, bloody and ragged, into the light. She bolted in front of a yellow gourd-shaped cab, which veered and squealed to a stop. She yanked open the door and climbed in.

"Go!" she screamed at the cabbie, a small man whose face had gone deathly pale. "The university." When he just stared at her, she yelled, "Go!"

He spun around and the gourd leapt forward.

She sat back against the seat, risking a glance behind her. A crowd of onlookers watched, but no one followed. She scanned their faces. Had any of them been in the alley?

She pressed her back into the cushions, keeping away from the windows. The cab slowed to a stop in front of the campus gates.

She looked left and right, but her purse was long gone. She tugged her mirror out of her back pocket—surprisingly still in working order, though the frame had cracked—and opened it.

She paid the cabbie and ran through the university gates, stopping only when she stepped out of the tunnel into the light. The breeze hit her and she winced. Her wings were still out and were the only things holding the remains of her shirt and coat on her body. She clutched her arms around herself, ignoring the stares and gasps of people and hurried to her flat.

She slammed the door behind her and listened. Footsteps upstairs told her that Penny was in her lab. Damn! She hurried to the parlor and tapped the mirror, calling Geoff. Instead, she got Donovan.

"*Da?*" he said. He was lounging on one of Geoff's couches. When he got a good look at her, he bolted upright. "What the hell happened to you?"

The tears came then, as the adrenaline drained leaving achy exhaustion in its wake. "I was attacked," she said, trying not to sob. "Is Geoff..."

"He's in a meeting. You're at your flat?"

Deor nodded. "Could I come there?"

"Geoff wants you here, but don't come on your own," Donovan said. "Too much press. Are you safe there?"

Deor sniffled and wiped her face. "Penny's here."

"Stay put. I'll be there in a few minutes." He was tying his hair back as he spoke.

Before she could respond, the mirror went black, cleared, and showed her parlor.

Her silver spikes had receded. She trudged upstairs to the bathroom and pulled in her wings, hissing with pain as she did. Her shirt, bra, and coat fell to the ground in a tattered pile. She picked up the blood spattered remains of her OSU T-shirt—the one from her first Rose Bowl—and the tears came faster. She buried her face in the cloth and let herself sob out the pain, the fury, and the fear.

"Sweet creator!" Penny shrieked.

Deor clutched the remains of the shirt to her chest.

Penny stood in the doorway, jaw hanging open. "What happened to you?"

"Nothing, I'm fine." Deor jerked her arm away from Penny's touch.

"You most certainly are not fine!" She turned on the faucet and grabbed a washcloth.

Deor risked a glance in the bathroom mirror. Blood splattered her face and her arms. Spiraling across one jaw and down her neck, coiling between her breasts, was the same kind of dark, tattoo-like marking Robbie had. In fact, they were over her whole body, down her arms, and, from the aches she felt, covering her torso and legs, too.

"Is this your blood? How about your wings? Were they hurt, too?"

Deor nodded and put out her wings. She gasped, pain searing through them as they hit the cold air.

"You poor thing." Penny met Deor's eyes in the mirror. "Is it okay if I touch you? Let me try and stop the bleeding, alright?"

Deor nodded and braced herself on the sink, closing her eyes, and clutching the edge of the basin. She gasped, a quick intake of breath, as Penny began. The wounds were knitting, Deor could feel it, but each second was burning fire. By the time Penny was done, Deor was shuddering and sick with pain.

"That's the hard part done," Penny said.

Deor opened her eyes again. Her wings, their edges raw and torn before, were now scabbed over.

"I can't heal it completely," Penny said. "You changelings just don't heal very fast. Let me see the marks on you." Deor turned and let Penny examine her arms, her neck, her belly. "Will magic. Strong. How did you get away?"

Deor shrugged. "I don't know. I punched one of them in the face—" She bolted to the toilet and threw up. She coughed. "I can't remember the face—" She barely got the words out before she was vomiting again.

"Stop trying," Penny said and wet another washcloth. She held Deor's hair back and pressed the cloth to Deor's forehead. "The will magic is making you sick. Every time you try to remember, it will do that."

"Dammit," she said, taking the rag and wiping her face. The cool cloth eased some of the tension.

Downstairs, the doorbell rang.

"That's Donovan," she said. "Can you get it? I called him. But I want a shower."

"Sure," Penny said heading for the door. "Be careful with your wings. It would do good to wear them out for a while."

"Got it."

Deor got in the shower and let cool water wash the blood off her body. The last of the adrenaline left, and she curled up on the floor of the tub, her arms wrapped around her knees, and let herself sob. If she could just *remember*, get a hold on either of the faces. But every time she tried, she gagged and shook, images splintering before she could force them to take shape.

Chapter Thirty-Four

In the war room, Rafe paced around a large table glamoured with a three-dimensional map of the city. "Are we sure he hasn't left the city?" he asked.

"We're not sure of anything," Arthur said.

"I'll never be able to look Astarte in the face again if I don't catch these people."

"How is Her Majesty?"

Rafe just shook his head. He had found her in her rose garden. When he had broken the news, she hadn't moved. She hadn't blinked or even breathed for longer than he thought possible. Then he'd reached his hand toward her, and she collapsed against him, crying Robbie's name over and over again. With each sob, more petals and leaves fell.

He ran his fingers through his hair, slicking it back and retying it in a tight queue.

"Without starting a war with the goblins, can we do any more to see or get inside the embassy?"

"No. Vlad Tertius's people inform me that getting involved right now would 'put them in a delicate situation.'"

"They're a barely controlled blood-drinking tribe of assassins. Since when do they give a shit about delicacy?" Rafe zoomed the map in on the university.

"Since the Vlad decided to turn them into a barely controlled blood-drinking *nation* with a currency and diplomatic ties to the other kingdoms of the Fae." As Arthur rolled his eyes, the wall mirror rippled to show a worried patrolman.

"My Lord, we found the goblin."

"Excellent! Bring him in immediately."

"My Lord." The patrolman swallowed nervously. "He's dead. A shopkeeper found him like this."

The man stepped away from view, angling his mirror to show a dim, narrow alley. Their quarry lay against a wall, half-hidden behind a garbage barrel, blood oozing from his ears, mouth, and nose.

Rafe bit back a curse. There were half a dozen spells and who knew how many other ways to kill a man that would give the same result. It would be all but impossible to find the killer by trace magic alone.

"Canvass the area. Talk to everyone. Someone had to have seen something going into or coming out of that alley."

"Yes, sir. We did find this as well." The patrolman held up a familiar woman's purse. "It has a number of cards in it. It belongs to a Deor Smithfield."

"Why am I not surprised? Good work. You and the rest of the team go over that alley with a fine brush. I'll be there shortly. Arthur, get your coat. We're going to pay a condolence call on the poor professor."

He ended the call, and the mirror went black before becoming silver again. He started at the reflection. For a split second, he thought he saw his birth father in the mirror, permanent lines of anger etched into the high cheekbones and sharp eyes. He turned away. It didn't matter. Farringdon or Aethelwing, he would see Robbie's attackers dead.

Chapter Thirty-Five

Aafter her shower, Deor changed into jeans and a vented faerie shirt, wincing at the pain as her wings slid past the cloth. Though the splattered blood had washed away, the spirals from the magic hadn't.

Downstairs, she walked into the parlor expecting Donovan and Penny, but Lord Farringdon waited for her, too. He held her purse in his hand. In a corner of the parlor where he could watch both the window and the door, the captain stood, fuzzy as usual. The men's jaws dropped when they saw her. She shoved a hand through her dripping hair.

"What do you want?"

"I came to ask why your purse was found in an alley next to a dead goblin." He gestured for her to sit down in one of the chairs. "But now I want to know what happened to you."

Donovan leaned back against the mantelpiece and nodded.

Deor held out her hand for her purse. "Am I under arrest?"

"Not anymore," he said. "Were you attacked?"

"I was," she said, pressing her hand over her stomach as she broke out in a cold sweat. "Two people. They used will spells." She clamped her mouth hold back the dry heaves.

Lord Farringdon nodded. "I'm so sorry." He held out a handkerchief.

Deor took it, dabbing at her face.

"Easy," the general said. "Be patient with yourself. Can you tell me anything else?"

"I didn't kill the goblin," she managed.

"Are you sure?"

She nodded, teeth clenched. When her stomach stopped heaving, she said, "I would have killed the woman first. She—" She clamped the handkerchief over her mouth. After a few seconds, she forced out the words. "She was the dangerous one."

He pointed to her hand, bruised and puffy.

"She definitely punched something," Penny said.

"Self-defense," Deor snapped. She yanked the neck of her T-shirt aside. The deep, black lines of the magic that had held her hadn't faded at all.

"I believe you." Lord Farringdon held up his hands. "Those markings make that clear."

Deor hunched in her seat, pulling her collar closed. The sensation of chains lashing around her body and dragging her backward lingered. She shuddered as memory flickered. There had been sparks of light in the alley, silver light gleaming off her nails like knives. She curled her fingers into her palms, hiding her hands under her arms.

"Can you come down to the station and make a statement?" he asked.

As she shook her head, cold air blew from him.

"For fuck's sake," she snapped. "Why do you do that? It's bad enough that you have to bring your fuzzy little spy along, now you've got to freeze me to death? I'm not going to answer questions just because I'm cold!"

Donovan jerked upright from where he leaned against the mantle.

"There's someone else here? Where?"

Deor pointed at the room's corner. In the blink of an eye, Donovan had a knife out.

"Whoa!" Lord Farringdon stepped between the captain and Donovan. "It's just Arthur. He's here guarding me."

The captain stepped out of the corner, glamours dropping away, his hands held up to show he didn't hold a weapon.

Donovan didn't put away the knife. Instead, he dropped back to stand next to Deor. His blade was obviously steel.

She crumpled Lord Farringdon's handkerchief in her hand. "Why are you so interested in me? I don't have anything to do with Robbie."

"We believe that the man who died in that alley is the same man who attacked her," Lord Farringdon said. "You're the last one to see him alive. And Robbie was originally attacked by a woman and a goblin."

"I didn't hurt Robbie, dammit!" Deor yelled. "Why would I? It's like I said to Geoff's pet vampire over here, I don't give a fuck who your daddy is! Either of them. I just want to find mine and go home. I don't know *who* attacked me. I don't know *why* they attacked me, and I don't know *what* it had to do with Robbie! Now get the hell out of my house and stay the hell away from me!"

When he didn't move, Donovan stepped forward.

"Her pet comment aside, you heard her, Rafe. It's time for you to go."

"You stay out of this," Lord Farringdon snapped. "Why are you even here?"

"I asked him here. And I didn't ask you." Deor pointed toward the door. "I told you to get out of my house. In fact, get off my campus or I'll call security. I'll call Nefasta!" The anger eased the nausea in her stomach.

He glared at her for a moment, freezing cold rolling off him. She glared back, willing herself not to shiver. Donovan stepped in closer and crossed his arms, a wall at her back. The captain laid a hand on his boss's shoulder and murmured in his ear.

"Hide behind Geoff if you want," Lord Farringdon said. "It won't make you safer. Or stop me from finding out what's going on." He snatched her purse off the chair. "I'm keeping this for evidence."

"Fine!" she shouted. "Shove it up your ass for all I care."

She stood, quivering with cold and anger as he and the captain marched out the front door.

"Asshole," she muttered. To one side, Penny uttered a small squeak of protest, but Deor ignored her. "I'm staying at Geoff's."

Without looking to see if Donovan objected, she stomped up the stairs to her room and began throwing stuff in a bag. Five minutes later, she and Donovan were walking across campus toward Geoff's apartment.

"Why did you stand up for me?" Deor asked Donovan as they crunched through fallen leaves. "I thought you hated me."

Donovan shrugged. "It's what Geoff would have done. Right now, that's what I do—that, and keeping him safe." He glanced down at her. "Even from the likes of you."

"I just wanted to find my father, not become an international incident."

He grunted, a shrug easing the harsh lines of his shoulders. "He would give you diplomatic immunity if you asked."

"No, thanks." She studied him through sidelong glances. Away from Geoff, he lacked the tension that so often seemed to grip him. He had an easy grace, rather than militant, lock-step movements.

"Why do you work for him?" she asked.

The gait stiffened. "I don't work for him."

Deor sighed. "Fine. Why do you have the arrangement you have? He treats you like an employee—a servant."

Donovan walked in sullen silence for a while, his boots strangely silent on the cobblestone walkway. Breezes blew and eddied around them. Students hurried to or from class, the library, supper, wherever their lives led them.

"It can't go on much longer," Donovan said suddenly. "It's starting to make vampires look like lackeys."

Deor didn't deny that it was true. "Work and friendship is tough," she said, trying for neutral.

"Yes." He kept his eyes forward, never glancing in her direction. "There may come a time when the relationship between the faeries and the goblins shifts, and my family needs to decide what our relationship with both will be."

"I thought you'd been friends for centuries?"

"Political friendships are tricky." He glanced at her and smiled for the first time, his fangs taking on the red of the setting sun. "And friendship and politics inevitably clash."

She shuddered, thinking about power. Her father was powerful, that much was clear. The woman in the alley dripped with power, and obviously knew her father well. Could she be his wife?

All the while she'd been thinking about her father, she'd forgotten about the stepmother. Her mother pined away and died for the mysterious faerie that she loved. Deor stroked the lines of will magic on her throat. What might her father's wife—the woman scorned—be willing to do to his bastard?

Chapter Thirty-Six

Deor spent Thursday night curled up in bed. Her whole body ached, and the black marks were so sensitive to the touch that she could barely stand Geoff's million-thread-count sheets against her skin. Despite all this, Geoff seemed thrilled to have her around. He showered her with attention, so much so that she wished for the peace and quiet of her own flat.

Worse was the sense that she couldn't go home. Going back to the flat now would only put Penny in danger. And even if Penny believed she was innocent, Rufus would be there every second circling her like a guard dog. At least Donovan wasn't hostile, even if he was, in his own way, circling her as much as Rufus would have been.

Still, she had a job to do, so she did it. Her students' papers weren't going to grade themselves. Curled up on Geoff's rock-but-still-comfy couch in a giant bathrobe, she read essays and blocked out other thoughts as much as she could. At least the student essays weren't terrible. But when she got to a paper by one of Robbie's friends, she swiped away a tear before it could drip off her nose.

"Hello, gorgeous." Geoff bounded over the back of the couch, landing with a bounce beside her, his head almost in her lap. "How are you doing?"

"Very ill," she said.

"Still hurting from the attack? I could get a healer to come look at you again." He stroked the tender marks along her neck and collarbone, like smudged magic marker.

She shook her head. "Thinking of Robbie. I don't even know if she's dead or alive."

Sitting up, he kissed her and pulled her onto his lap.

"Enough gloom and doom. I've got something that will cheer you up." He held up a calling card with a date and time written on it. "For you, an appointment at Wham! and Thorsen for a fitting."

She wriggled out of his grasp, pushing the card away.

"I'm not your mistress. Stop buying me things."

"What?" he started.

"You heard me," she said, hauling herself off his lap and standing to face him. "I'm not even your girlfriend. You barely made it past a one-night stand."

"Technically we're at three." He gave her his best playful smile.

She crossed her arms. "This isn't *The Prince and the Showgirl*. I appreciate all your hospitality, I really do, but I am not Eliza Doolittle, so don't buy me dresses and expect to play *Pretty Woman*!"

"I—this—the shop—you—" Geoff fumbled.

"Use your words." Deor tapped her foot. "That's what your degree is in, right? Words?"

"That isn't what I meant at all!" He proffered the card at her. "And you are a pretty woman."

She rolled her eyes. "What are you trying to get from me?"

"Oh!" he said. "This is about what Rafe said about me."

She glanced away from him. "Maybe."

"I just want to help you. I do have a lot of money." He waved her over. "But I'm not trying to buy you."

She relented and sat down next to him. She rubbed her hands up and down her thighs. "I don't know who to trust. I don't know what to do. Robbie was almost killed, someone jumped me in an alley, my faerie side is freaking out and trying to kill me, I need to find my father, and Rafe may be trying to stop me." She turned toward Geoff. "Can I trust you?"

He caught her hand in his.

"Of course. I am just what I seem to be."

"A politician and prince playing hooky from his kingdom?"

"That's not fair," he said. "I do a lot of politics here—"

"I know." Deor tugged her robe tighter around her body. "I'm sorry. I don't know what anyone here seems to be." She rested her head against his shoulder. "But so far you're the only one who hasn't threatened me or accused me of anything."

He slipped an arm around her shoulder.

"Then trust me. I will help you find your father. And you're going to help me. That's what the dress appointment is for. Consider it a necessary state expenditure." His golden eyes jiggled with mischief. "Because you're going with me to the final Adoption ceremony."

"Oh hell no," she said, pushing away from him. "I'm not going anywhere near Lord Farringdon. I've already seen the inside of the Tower more than once, thanks. I'm certainly not going to line up and wish him a long and happy reign of terror. On Monday I am going to go to the press and see what they have to say about my story. My mirror is full of messages from reporters begging for interviews."

"It's not safe to go to the press," he said. "Especially since the woman who attacked you is still out there."

"What other option do I have? I can't wait around to die like my mother."

"Don't be silly," Geoff snapped. At her shocked expression, he softened. "Could your mother grade papers when she was about to die? Did she tell a prince to shut up? Tell off the Sword himself?"

"No," Deor admitted.

"Exactly." He wrapped his arms around her. "You're not dying. It's no surprise Faerie makes you feel strange. You've never been here before. Besides, getting what you want out of the press isn't going to happen. Not until after the Adoption." He kissed her cheek. "Trust me. If your father is a Winter Court noble, he, and your stepmother, will be at the final Adoption. If he's not, I promise, I'll take you to the *Times* myself. And since you'll be part of the goblin diplomatic mission, you'll be protected from arrest."

Deor sniffed and wiped her nose. "I guess I'm being melodramatic."

"Maybe a touch." He grinned at her and proffered the card again with pleading, puppy dog eyes. "Please come with me? Please? Please, oh please, oh please?" He clung to her waist, snuggling up against her ribcage. "Don't make me go to that awful boring ceremony all by myself. Your snark is the only thing that will keep me from slipping into a coma from sheer boredom."

She eyed him. "I haven't been invited."

"Bosh!" He bounced back up. "Everyone is invited—it's just that most will attend via mirror. And it would look strange if I went unaccompanied. People might start to think Donovan and I are a couple."

She rolled her eyes at him, but she took the card. It read *Wham! and Thorsen, Fashion.* Wham! was probably a pixie name, if her student roster was any indication.

"If it means that much to you. Who are these people?"

"Only the best. You'd better hurry. The appointment's at one-thirty." He pointed to the clock on the mantelpiece.

"Geoff! I've got like five minutes to get dressed." She pushed him off her and scrambled under the couch for her shoes.

He stayed lounging on the couch, watching her with a sexy grin on his face. "Well?" she said, one shoe in her hand.

"Are you coming, or are you just going to lie there staring at my breasts?"

He stretched and yawned, rising slowly to pat her on the bottom. "Much as I'd love to do both, I can't. I've got a mirror call with the homeland I have to make, all very top secret of course, though it's mostly just checking in with the parents so they know I'm still alive. Donovan will take you."

In the carriage ride across town, Donovan sat silently across from her, arms folded. Deor resisted the urge to needle him and instead stared out the window, marking where they were. Just in case.

Wham! and Thorsen's establishment, unlike Theophilous' shop, had their names in blazing chartreuse letters over the door.

"Cute," Donovan said as he held the carriage door for her.

Deor regarded the sign and turned to him.

"Is Geoff making a fool of me? Tell me if he's setting me up to look like some sort of freak."

Donovan slammed the carriage door. "Wham! and Thorsen are the freshest, most up and coming designers in the Winter Court. The Harvest Queen wore their designs for two of her three wins."

"No comment on whether or not Geoff's setting me up to look like a fool." She reached for the carriage door. "I'm thinking I should go back to my whole 'I'm not his mistress' stance and watch the Adoption from afar."

"It's your call." Donovan shrugged.

Deor stood and chewed her lip, flicking her gaze back and forth between the shop and the carriage.

"Fine." Donovan sighed and relented. "Geoff's not big on sharing his business with me, but I can tell you what I've observed."

"That might be useful, thanks." She tried to keep the sarcasm out of her voice.

Donovan looked around searching for prying eyes and ears. "You're different than the other faerie woman he's spent time with. You've spent a lot more time with him at the embassy—some never make it through the door. He's protective of you. He wants to be seen in public with you—not at fancy restaurants, but at a major political outing."

"So you're getting in line with Lord Farringdon and Ama telling me to be careful."

"From what I've seen so far, you're careful all the time." He reached out and touched one of the black marks on her arm. "And you shouldn't have survived this kind of attack. Not with your body and mind unbroken."

She fought the urge to pull her arm away from him. He was talking and she didn't want him to stop. Instead, she offered her arm up for further inspection.

"I'll admit, faerie magic isn't my thing." Donovan studied the marks. "But whoever did this could have easily killed you instead. And probably killed the goblin they found in the alley."

"I figured that much out."

"Have you figured out Geoff's role in all this?"

"What?" Deor pulled back from the vampire. "You think he let this happen to me? Or was involved?"

Donovan shook his head. "No. He doesn't hurt women. But he'd be happy to jump into the political game you seem to leave in your wake." He looked her up and down. "It's not so different from human politics, except people live longer so animosity has centuries to grow."

"But there's definitely a game?"

"Yep." The vampire nodded. "And Geoff sees no conflict in enjoying your company as a mistress—" He held up a hand before she could object. "I know you hate that word. Let it go for now."

"Fine. Make your point."

"He'd enjoy your company, genuinely like you, and still use you in his game. The problem for you is that you don't know the stakes."

"Do you?" She doubted he would tell her even if he did.

"I'll be honest, just don't tell anyone." He grinned widely enough to show fang. "I have no idea what this is all about. I know it's about something big—too many 'just checking in' calls from his parents. Too many meetings with ambassadors and others."

"So he is using me for politics." She nodded at the shop. "And my being spiffily dressed on his arm at the Adoption is not only some mischievous fun. Like some piece on a board."

"That's my guess. If I were you, I'd make damn sure I wasn't a pawn."

"Of course I'm not a pawn." Deor strode to the shop door and rested her hand on the knob. "I'm a queen, remember?" She opened the door and stepped inside.

Bolts of fabric in vivid jewel tones interspersed with framed design sketches decorated the walls. A bare dress form stood in the center of the room with the word *Desire!* blazoned across it. There were no clothes.

"This must be the faerie version of industrial chic." She approached the young woman who stood behind a silver, mirrored table that held a stem vase with a single, hot pink flower.

"Can I help you?" the woman said.

"Yes." Deor smiled at the young woman who was clearly gearing up to send her packing. "I have an appointment." She pulled the appointment card out of the back pocket of her jeans and handed it over. "The goblin prince made it for me." If Geoff wanted her to draw attention, she'd start with name dropping. Like he'd been waiting for his cue, Donovan took up a place next to Deor and smiled at the woman.

"Of course, we're always delighted to see His Majesty's friends." She tried not to look at the vampire. "Right this way, please."

The girl led the way through a door in the back into a parlor decorated in kelly green. The green was repeated as an accent color on the deep purple couches that circled the room. "Can I get you anything to drink? Water? Wine? Blood?"

"No, thank you," Deor said just as Donovan said, "I'll have a glass."

"You're staying?" Deor asked.

"I promised Geoff I'd keep you safe." Donovan dropped into an armchair that gave him a view of the door through which they had come and the door on the other side of the room. He accepted the goblet of blood being offered to him on a silver tray.

Deor gave in and sat on a couch. She had been to enough cotillion and debutante balls to know how fittings worked. In a few minutes she'd be stripped to her underwear and measured and pinned to death.

A wiry young faerie man in a chartreuse velvet coat hurried in, followed by a tiny pixie woman with hair like chrome candy floss. He looked about thirty-five, so Deor automatically bumped him up to age ninety or older. She wouldn't make a guess about the pixie.

"Professor Smithfield," he said bowing low. "We're delighted to have you in our shop. I am James Thorsen. This is my partner, Wham!" She wore silver leggings that matched her hair and an oversized fuchsia sweater that hung off one shoulder. All she needed for the perfect eighties look was a high side ponytail. "I can't tell you how delighted we both are to be dressing you for this occasion." James pulled up a chair.

"Your figure presents such unique challenges and opportunities. Dressing you will be such fun!" Wham! spoke in the same up-speak that many of her human-girl students had used. All sentences sounded like questions. The pixie added enthusiasm, too. Not only did every phrase seem to be a question, but they all also seemed followed with several exclamation marks.

"You mean compared to faerie women, I'm short, I have huge hips, and my boobs are too big," Deor said, laughing, even if the truth did sting.

"No, no, no!" Wham! zipped out of her seat and stood in front of Deor, offering her hand. "Let me help you up."

Deor let the lady tug her from the chair.

"You're perfect!" Wham! eyed her up and down. "We want to design for the whole range of sentient beings. And you have such an amazing shape, all curves and circles instead of angles. You're like a goddess. A small, compact goddess. Men will look up to you when we're done designing for you, even if they have to go to their knees to do it!"

James applauded Wham!'s speech, throwing her a look of glowing admiration.

"Exactly," he said. "You are that rarest of clients, a unique beauty. Of course we jumped at the chance to design a dress for you."

She looked back and forth between the two designers. Not a trace of irony on either face. Next to her Donovan held down a smile as he sipped from his glass.

"Alright," Deor said, "but not a dress. If you really want to make something unique, make me pants." Geoff wanted a spectacle? No problem. It would be her spectacle on her terms, including comfort. After all, the queen on the board could move however she wanted. And if she drew the newspapers' attentions, so much the better.

Wham! squealed and clapped her hands. "Yes! We must. Come, come! On the stand, please." She gestured to Deor.

"No, no!" James was scribbling on his slate but paused to look up. "Make her walk around first. I want to see how her body moves."

For the next half hour, Deor strutted, sat, pretended to take things off a tray, stretched her arms over her head, and posed on the measuring stand. She even danced around the room with a reluctant, but graceful, Donovan while Wham! and James bombarded her with questions.

"Do you have any idea of the coverage you are looking for?" Wham! asked carefully. "We are happy to do sleeves and high collars, if it suits you."

Deor's hand drifted to her throat. The marks hadn't faded at all and weren't likely to before the weekend. After a few moments of thought, Deor smiled. "Sleeves are great if they fit whatever I end up wearing. Some sleeves, all sleeves, whatever. But no high necklines or turned up collars. This is me. I have been through what I've been through, and I'm not ashamed. They can all cope."

"Of course." Wham! clapped her hands. "Now, what about your wings? What posture do you prefer for formal events?"

"I prefer to keep them in," Deor said. Both designers gave her thrilled looks. Bold. Unique. They went back to watching her move up and down.

"I'm ready!" James declared. He tapped his slate in triumph, and a life-sized, fully naked glamour of Deor, her private bits magically fuzzed out, appeared in mid-air between them.

"Now this," James said, "is what I have in mind for you." He flicked his fingers again and the image had clothes. It wore a navy blue pant with a sleek, tailored waist that opened out into deep flaring legs with deep cuffs.

"Oooh," Deor said, "I like that. Very Katherine Hepburn." Tiny sparks of silver flickered in the fabric as the image moved.

"I don't like the color," Wham! said. She flicked her fingers and the pants turned black.

"Yes," Deor said. "I want that." Faeries came in all colors, but even here, a sharp, tailored black pant was always in style.

James nodded and made a note on his slate. "And for the top," he said, flicking his fingers again. A corset top with a gauzy black undershift appeared.

"What about handkerchief sleeves?" Wham! said. She gestured and they appeared.

"No, no!" James said. "No!" He gestured again and the sleeves became caps. The shift took on ruffles around the top.

"Yuck," Deor said before she could stop herself. "Sorry, but that's just too bondage-barmaid for me." They looked at her blankly while Donovan cracked a smile.

"It's a human thing," she said. "It would look... odd, where I come from."

Wham! and James put their heads together over the slate, whispering furiously.

"I like the corset part," she said.

"Okay." James turned the corset into a red and blue brocade. Wham turned it into blue and green. They took out the shift entirely. They changed the brocade so many times Deor started to see rainbows in front of her eyes. She sat back against the couch and tried to picture the outfit on herself as the two partners bickered.

"I've got it!" Wham! shouted, jerking Deor out of her reverie. "What kind of magic do you do? Earth, air, fire, water?"

"I don't," she said with a nervous glance at Donovan. "I'm... I just don't do any."

"Oh." The pixie flopped backwards in despair, a hand over her eyes.

"I like stone," Deor said. "And metal things. Maybe my father was some sort of earth faerie."

"Perfect!" Wham! gestured at the floating image of Deor and the brocade turned black and gunmetal grey, the dark sheen of the metallic brocade echoing that in the pants. She gestured again and the glamour's hair tumbled around her shoulders in loose brown curls.

"I love it," Deor exclaimed, barely restraining the urge to clap her hands like a little girl. "Just one more thing. Make sure it's got real, usable pockets, okay?"

Wham! and Thorsen, peace restored, shook hands and the assistant whisked away the slate and swatches, promising that the entire outfit, including platform heels, would arrive at the prince's late—probably very late—the next evening.

Donovan held the door for her both at the store and as she slid into the carriage. He took his seat across from her.

"Bold enough opening play?" Deor asked.

"It certainly won't be what Geoff expects." He raised his eyebrows at her. "But I think that is what you want."

"The more people see me, the more it's possible my father will see me, or someone will recognize me."

"It's a strategy," Donovan agreed.

"Like they say back home: there's no such thing as bad press."

Chapter Thirty-Seven

"May I come in?" Rafe said softly from the doorway. Astarte nodded without turning to look at him. The healers had gone. Robbie lay motionless in the bed, the peach and scarlet bed hangings only making her pallor more obvious. Astarte sat on the edge of the bed, holding her daughter's hand and singing a lullaby. The white rose bloomed on the bedside table.

The bedroom carpet was as soft as feathers and his boots made no sound in it.

"How is she?" he asked.

"The same."

Rafe swallowed hard around the lump in his throat. Only the faint blue glow of a monitoring spell around Robbie's mouth and nose told him she was still breathing. Memories of his little sister crowded together to choke him. Robbie as a toddler, fat little legs dashing through the grass after a Molossian's tail, certain the giant war dog would never hurt her. Robbie at her sixth birthday party, doing her first proper magic, glamouring a thistle into a rose for her mother. Robbie weeping uncontrollably into his shoulder after the boy she liked called her a freak. His hand drifted to his belt. But his sword was with his armor, and there was no one here to kill.

"When do they expect her to wake?" he asked.

"I won't have you interrogating her," Astarte said.

Before he could answer, she turned to him, her eyes brimming with tears. And fear. He had never seen fear in those eyes before. Anger, sorrow, laughter, cunning, joy—many, many emotions, but never fear. Until today.

He reached out to her, and she clung to him, weeping while he patted her on the back. Where the hell was Finn? He ought to be here comforting his wife. Never mind who Robbie was or how she'd been born. Astarte had given up everything else to be Finn's wife. He ought to be here now.

Rafe fumbled a handkerchief out of his pocket and gave it to Astarte.

"I'll catch them. I will—I promise. One of them is dead already."

"No. No, you mustn't kill them." Astarte pushed away from him. "You have to catch them alive, do you hear me? We have to learn everything we can from them, or..." She gestured helplessly toward Robbie. Rafe nodded, unable to say more.

A small cough from the doorway drew his attention. He hurried to the door as fast as he could without making a sound.

"What is it, Arthur?"

"I'm sorry to disturb you, but there's... a problem." Arthur glanced past Rafe to Astarte.

"Tell me." He needed something, anything but sitting uselessly in this room.

"A group of students and professors held a vigil for Robbie in the park. Then the Anti-Monarchists showed up. And the Sons of London. And every other malcontent and troublemaker in the city. There were marches everywhere by suppertime."

"Double the patrols. So long as there's no violence, let them march."

People should be screaming in the streets. The whole city should be shaking with outrage.

But Arthur shook his head again. "That's the trouble. Michael showed up at the Tower with this."

He held up a writ of martial law, sealed with the king's insignia. He tapped his finger on a single line. Curfew to be imposed on all citizens within the city limits, effective immediately.

"They didn't go quietly, did they?"

"They didn't disperse. Rocks were thrown at the Civil Patrol. The second Michael ordered his men to charge, it turned into a full-blown riot. He's out there cracking heads now. The university has locked its gates. Half the Tanty is on fire, and I'm getting reports of brawls and looting from all over the city."

Rafe cast a desperate look over his shoulder. He couldn't leave Astarte like this. Guilt warred with relief—something to fight, something he could put right.

"One second," he said. Swiftly, he knelt by Astarte, putting his arms around her. "Forgive me, I have to go."

She threw her arms around his neck, but she didn't tell him no. Ten minutes later, he and Arthur clattered through the Palace gates, their horses' hooves striking the cobblestones like an avalanche. They made straight for Michael's last reported position. Rafe had already ordered his men to subdue and arrest anyone committing a violent crime, but to warn and release anyone who was only in violation of the curfew. Finn would have nothing good to say about that tomorrow, but tomorrow was hours away.

By three a.m., the fires in the Tanty were out, but the city was only just barely subdued. Rafe and four others, all mounted, trotted down a city street lined with shops, eyes open for trouble. Ahead of them glass shattered.

"There! Stop in the name of the king."

Looters bolted out of a broken shop window, loaded down with whatever they could carry.

He spurred Sampson into a trot, signaling his men to follow him. One drew a bow, and Rafe threw out a hand, freezing the bowstring until it shattered. "I told you! No deadly force unless we're attacked."

The would-be archer snorted and tossed away his broken weapon. He wore the insignia of the Palace Guard, not the Civil Patrol or Army.

The looters veered around a corner ahead of the chase. One stumbled and went down. "Grab him!" Two of Rafe's men reigned in hard and leaped down to arrest the thief. Rafe spurred harder. Stinging sweat dripped into his eyes. He pulled ahead of his men, wheeling around the corner at full gallop into an enclosed courtyard.

Sampson bellowed and reared. The tiny square teemed with armed men. Rafe held his seat, wings out for extra balance. As Sampson's hooves clattered back onto the pavement, Rafe struck out with his shield, knocking back a club.

Someone leaped for Sampson's bridle and was bitten for his trouble. The houses were crowded here, the eaves leaning close in over the space. The crowd surged forward, surrounding him. Sampson tried to kick, but there was no room.

"Down with him!" the mob shouted.

"Kick in his pretty lordling's teeth!"

Rafe shot a glance skyward. Only a narrow strip of pre-dawn stars showed between the roof edges. No escape that way.

Hands grappled with his legs, dragged at his shield.

"I am your Sword!" he shouted. "Lay down your arms."

The crowd jeered. Someone struck at him with a stick.

He ripped off his helmet so they could see his face. "I am the Sword of the Winter Court! Do you not know me?"

A rock struck him square in the temple. Stars exploded in his vision. Even as his consciousness slipped, he beat his wings instinctively against the air to keep upright. His shield fell from his grasp.

"Sir!" a soldier shouted.

Hands out of the crowd grabbed his reins. Fire shot from a soldier's hands into the faces crowding around him, and they howled.

"This way, sir. We've got you."

He gripped the saddle, fighting to stay upright. Blood dripped into his eyes. Sampson burst out of the courtyard into the open street, a mounted soldier dragging at his reins.

"We have to go back..." he managed. "The others..."

"Handling it, sir," the soldier said.

The ring of swords and screams of men sounded behind him. He swayed and clutched at the saddlebow, the stars swirling overhead.

On the morning of the final Adoption ceremony, Rafe stood still before his mirror as Jameson fixed the last of the diamonds in his hair. Jameson stepped down from the low stool, examining his work with a critical eye.

Rafe forced a smile. "Perfect work, as always, Jameson."

His valet frowned and stepped forward, flicking an invisible speck off the jacket's silver embroidery. "There, sir. Now you are presentable." He blinked rapidly before saying, "The next time I see you, I shall call you Your Majesty."

Rafe grinned at him. If he didn't think the impropriety would give Jameson a heart attack, he'd hug the man.

"Thank you, Jameson. I hope you enjoy the ceremony."

"Yes, sir." His eyes flicked over Rafe's shoulder. He bowed deeply. Rafe turned.

Princess Consort Astarte stood in the doorway, a dress of deep coral accenting the warm golden tones of her skin. Her hair was caught in a black net, and she wore no jewels, only a single white rose. She stood with one hand on the doorpost, smiling at him. But her eyes were liquid with tears.

"My, aren't you handsome. Jameson, will you excuse us?" She stepped into the room, laying her hand on Rafe's arm. "Your father wants to speak to you."

"What's wrong?"

She tucked her hand into his arm. "I think I'd better let him tell you."

Together they left his bedroom and went out through the spacious parlor that joined his suite of rooms to the other suite meant for a second royal child. The heir and the spare. Not that there had been a spare in seven generations, when the non-heir took her mother's name and became a Farringdon, the first Duchess of Wellhall. And now there was only him, the substitute.

"I'm glad it's almost over," he said.

"I hope so," she said.

They crossed the hall and entered the king's own parlor. Finn sat in an armchair. Beside him stood Michael in his parade dress uniform. Before Finn's chair stood Lord Overton, Master of the City, and his son Delaney. Overton wore his chain of office and ceremonial robes. Redfern Holman, the head of the Loyal Sons of London, eyes wide at his surroundings, stood just behind them. Roger, Lord of Northfalls, current Speaker for Parliament and Robbie's foster father, alone of the group wore a white rosette over his heart. He carried a rolled and sealed parchment in one hand, and his frown deepened when Rafe met his eyes. As they reached Finn's chair, Astarte left Rafe and went to sit to one side, away from the cluster of men.

"You wanted to speak to me, Sire?" Rafe eyed the cluster of men. "What is this?"

"As you know," Roger began, "today you become the Crown Prince, the king's chosen heir."

"Yes, I do," Rafe snapped. "Get on with it. We've got less than twenty minutes before the pre-ceremony reception."

Thank the Creator and Astarte's wisdom for insisting that the congratulatory reception came before the final ceremony, not after. If he was bleeding and cross-eyed afterward, at least he could go lie down and not have to dance with well-wishers.

"To be blunt, your Majesty," Lord Overton said, "we do not think it wise for you to continue in your present role."

"It's a little late for that," Rafe said. "But if you've picked a substitute heir, I'm all for it. Who is he? Delaney?"

"No!" Delaney said, a blush flaring on his cheeks. "I wouldn't try to take your throne away from you, Rafe. But we..." He straightened. "The Parliament and the people of the Royal City of London, are all in agreement with His Majesty the King that it would be unwise in the extreme for you to continue serving as Sword once you are the prince. The two offices are contradictory in their natures and their duties. We hereby request, on behalf of His Majesty and the kingdom, that you resign your office and lay aside your duties as the Sword of Peace and Justice."

The bottom dropped out of Rafe's stomach. Some distant part of himself remembered that Delaney always sounded more pompous the more embarrassed he was. It didn't matter. Rafe still wanted to punch him in the head. Roger, Overton, Holman—they were smiling and nodding too. They were saying vacuous things about protecting his safety and thanking him for his service.

"You put them up to this," he said, pointing at Finn. "This was your idea, wasn't it? And you waited until now to tell me?"

"Rafe, you could have died," Astarte said. "We can't bear to lose you."

"It was a flesh wound!" And his own stupid fault.

"Only by lucky accident!" Finn stood up. "If you will not think of your own safety, think of the country's good. My boy, you had to know this was coming."

"I'm sorry, Rafe," Delaney said. He was the only one.

Rafe nodded. He straightened his shoulders, parade erect, heels clicking together.

"Naturally, I will obey Your Majesty's wishes in all things. I shall resign first thing in the morning. As your current Sword, however, I strongly advise that you appoint Captain Arthur Maerhwer in my place." He ignored the look of pure hate from Michael and went on. "He has no connection to any particular faction in Parliament, which alone ought to make him a candidate. More than that, he's a brave man and the best damn spymaster I've ever seen. The army will follow him. They know what he's worth." He kept his eyes locked on the ornamental scrollwork just above Finn's head.

Lord Overton stepped forward before the others could say anything and bowed low. "Thank you, Lord Farringdon. With King's Sweordmund's permission, we will leave you to finish preparing for the ceremony."

At nod from Finn, the contingent trooped out, already sighing with relief.

"Son." Finn laid a hand on his arm, but Rafe shook it off.

"Mother, would you excuse us?" he said as evenly as he could manage.

She cast a troubled glance between them but gathered her skirts and left the room without a word.

"I know you're unhappy, Rafe—" Finn began.

"Unhappy? Who will find the person attacking changelings if I'm not Sword? Have you thought of that?"

Finn inclined his head. "The Civil Patrol is well able to go on solving matters of crime, with or without you as Sword."

Rafe picked up a chair and hurled into the fireplace where it splintered into kindling.

"Control yourself!" Finn snapped.

"I am in control!" Rafe shouted back. "If I wasn't, you'd be picking yourself up off the floor." He advanced toward Finn. "I've given you my name, my blood, my identity. I've spent my whole life in your service. Now you take my office—my one source of pride—away and call me unhappy?"

Finn stepped forward, too, his eyes blazing silver with anger. "Don't you dare suggest that there is more honor in the Farringdon name than in that of the Aethelwings."

"You don't understand." Rafe backed away, shaking his head. "You've never understood. I didn't fight and sweat and bleed through every test and battle to sit on a throne. I did it to become the Sword, to *bring honor back* to my family name."

"My boy." Finn laid his hands on Rafe's shoulder. "My dearest boy. You have. And you have my love. You will always have it."

Rafe wanted—how desperately he'd always wanted—to be Finn's son. He had given Finn everything he could—all the parts of him he had to give. Now Finn had taken even the title of Sword, the one name he had earned for himself.

Rafe stepped back, shaking his head. He cast a glance out the window. The sun stood almost at noon. Down below the crowds were streaming into the reception. "I will do my duty, as I promised. But this matter is not settled."

Chapter Thirty-Eight

The carriage that took Deor and Geoff to the Adoption was no ordinary street cab. Instead, it was the official goblin ambassadorial coach, complete with Royal Crest on the doors, gilded wheels as high as her head, and a team of four snarling, wild-eyed wyverns to draw it. Muzzles of magic held their jaws closed but didn't hide the sharp teeth protruding from their mouths.

Deor hid a shudder and stepped away from the carriage as soon as they alighted in front of the Palace. She slipped her hand into her left pocket and curved her fingers around her rattle. She didn't know what she'd do with it if she found her father. Wave it in front of his nose like some smoking gun and expect the man to crumble into guilty hysterics? Hope it would sparkle and play music if she got close enough to him? She squeezed it one more time and let the memory it conjured, her mother waving it and smiling, linger for a moment before she pulled her hand away and turned her attention back to Donovan.

"Is it me, or do the wyverns smell like rotten meat?" she whispered.

"What do you think they eat?" he said. His usual biker jacket had been changed for a scarlet military dress uniform. All of the trim, the buttons, ribbons, medals, and stitching were black. A black skull medal with ruby eyes and fangs adorned his left shoulder. On his right hand, he wore a heavy gold ring, like an unmelted nugget, that clutched a cabochon cut ruby the size of a quail's egg.

"You look terrifying," Deor said. "What is all this?"

"My family's formal uniform."

Deor nodded, resisting the urge to tell him he looked like the offspring of a third world military dictator and a heavy metal band.

"Do you want your wrap from the carriage?" Geoff asked, impeccable in a deep blue suit with peacock and gold accents, offered her his arm.

"No." She took his arm.

"Shall we? A little champagne, a few hors d'oeuvres, and then we'll see what happens. Stunning choice of outfit, by the way. Especially the décolletage. And you're wearing my gift! But don't you think a little glamour would better?" He frowned slightly at the swirls, the evidence of her attack, still clearly visible on her chest and arms.

"No. I like the way I look," she said, tracing her fingers along one of the many marks. "Who knows, maybe I'll catch a guilty look from one of the ladies in attendance." She took delicate steps in her sky high heels.

As Geoff led her up the broad, shallow steps of the Palace, they joined a throng of glittering nobles, all headed in the same direction. She spotted Rufus ushering Penny. He wore a kilt but no shirt, only a formal sash of green and yellow plaid, pinned at the shoulder with a giant silver wolf's head. Penny's wings were out, their olive green accenting the olive tones of her skin. A little in front of them, a male faerie with lavender hair and matching jacket and kilt was walking arm in arm with a grey-haired man who wore almost no jewels at all.

As they passed through the great doors, Deor took a deep breath, magic flowing around her. A sense of welcome caressed her face. A spell for the guests? The great pile of stone stretched over her and away from her, a labyrinth of halls and floors and under cellars, but the sense was one of safety, not oppression.

"It's beautiful," she said.

"If you like this, you should see Barizan," Geoff said.

The throng entered an expansive ballroom where servants in black and silver, the king's eight-pointed star on their shoulders, circled, handing out glasses of champagne.

Doing a quick head count, she said, "They must have drained France."

Geoff grinned at her. "Good thing France is in the Winter Court then."

Across the room, a brown-skinned woman raised her glass in a silent salute to them and Donovan cracked a smile so wide Deor thought his face might split. With a shock of the familiar, Deor realized that the woman was not a dark-skinned faerie, but a human of African descent, or she had been human at one point. White fangs glinted as she smiled back at Donovan, a come hither smile if there ever was one, and turned away to speak to the crimson-colored faerie at her elbow.

"Do you know her?" Deor asked.

"That's my wife, Chloe." Donovan beamed. "Isn't she stunning?"

"Someone actually married you? Willingly?" Deor said before Geoff could catch her and slip a glass into her hand.

"Don't drink too much champagne," Geoff said. "You'll need it for the toasts."

She was just about to say she didn't plan on drinking at all when trumpets blew from all sides. Doors opened at the far end of the reception hall and a herald announced, "My lords and ladies, His Majesty Sweordmund the Eighth and his Consort, the Lady Astarte."

Loud cheers broke out and cries of "Long live the king!"

When the cries had died down somewhat, the herald spoke again. "The Heir Elect, Rafael, Lord Farringdon." The room erupted into cheers again.

Craning her neck to scan the crowd, Deor noted that the younger people in the room and those who wore military uniforms shouted the loudest and most enthusiastically. A small crowd around Edgar and Madeleine Farringdon clapped politely, but did not cheer.

As the cheers faded, Victor Farringdon, standing beside his mother, met Deor's eyes. She waved a little at him and he smiled back. Beside him his mother's eyes widened sharply, and she clutched her son's arm. Deor turned away. His mummy probably thought a peasant had no right to be at something like this.

"Well my grandmother was president of the Junior League for six years running," she said to her champagne. She returned to scanning the crowd for faces that echoed her own.

Chapter Thirty-Nine

D oing his best not to freeze the room, Rafe stood his ground in the receiving line.

Astarte, breaking protocol, stood between him and Finn. At least the steady stream of well-wishers flowing past him made as good an excuse as any for his not saying more than "hello" and "thank you."

As Rodney, Roger's nephew and heir, approached with his paramour Clarissa Rangley on his arm, Rafe forced himself to smile. No need to cold shoulder old friends.

"I just heard. I'm so sorry, Rafe. I'd have protested if I'd known," Rodney whispered in his ear as they embraced. Clarissa kissed him on the cheek and squeezed his hand. Before he could answer, they had moved on.

"I'm surprised Geoff hasn't yet come to pay you his compliments," Arthur said quietly from behind him. "Do you think it means anything?"

"I don't care. He can mean whatever he wants." He nodded and shook hands with another couple. A black fog hung around his brain. He barely managed to smile when Lady Genevieve took his hand. Her warm smile turned into a quizzical look.

"Something the matter, darling?" she said, her voice perfectly pitched to prevent anyone near from hearing her.

"Nothing. I'm fine. Thank you for coming. I mean…"

"Of course I'm here. I know how tired you are these days. Be strong—the goblin ambassador is on his way." She squeezed his hand and drifted off.

He scanned the crowd, picking out the goblins. Sure enough, the ambassador was next in line, full of compliments and already offering to foster any children he might have in the future. As if he'd let a child of his spend a minute unguarded in Barizan. Rafe kept his answer polite, but didn't bother to pull back the chill as the ambassador shook his hand.

"There's Geoff," he said to Arthur. "He's got Smithfield with him."

The top of her head was a brown divot, constantly moving through crowd. In a room where men and women alike wore a king's ransom in gems, she wore only a single black pearl that nestled at the very top of her cleavage. Not a glamour anywhere on her, either not even to hide the will spell markings. She half turned, laughing at something.

"The most striking woman in the room," he said, realizing too late that he'd spoken aloud.

"Don't let Genevieve hear you say that," Arthur said.

He squinted, craning his head to keep an eye on Deor's movements. A smile crawled on to his face despite everything.

"You know, I do believe she's dragging Geoff around the room. And I don't think he likes it much." He didn't hear Arthur's response as the trumpets drowned out all conversation. "That's my signal," he said. "I'll see you after the ceremony."

He left the room with a forced smile and his head up, marching through the parting throng. Cheers and cries of "the Creator bless you!" and "long live the king" followed him as he fell into step behind Finn and Astarte. Men in uniform saluted as he went by. He was surrounded by friends, he reminded himself. If only it didn't feel as if they were cheering his execution.

Chapter Forty

Deor took Geoff's arm and followed him from the reception down an arched hallway to the throne room. The checkered floor, the vaulted windows, the throne itself, all of it was more massive than it appeared on the mirror. Geoff guided her, followed by Donovan, to a plush seat midway up the rows of chairs. Other goblins, including the ambassador, filled in the seats around them.

"We don't have to stand, how nice," Deor whispered to Geoff.

"The ceremony will likely be a bit longer than the others," he said. "Lot of speeches when the main part is done."

She nodded, but wondered to herself how Lord Farringdon, who barely seemed able to stand at the reception, was going to field questions or listen to speeches. Her musings were cut short as the trumpets sounded and the king, led by Lord Farringdon, made his way to the throne. She tapped her feet, drumming them on the stones, until Geoff slammed his hand down on her knee.

"Sorry," she whispered. She slipped her feet out of her shoes.

As Lord Farringdon admitted that he knew who the king was and recalled his own family, she kneaded the ground with her toes, the cool stone soothing her nerves through her stockings.

Ama made another brief speech, and Lord Farringdon knelt before the throne. The dais rose just high enough that Deor did not have to strain to see. He placed his hands on the arms of the throne. Ama raised her branch of mistletoe.

"Be no more a Farringdon."

Deor slapped her hand over her mouth as her stomach lurched and threatened to throw its contents on the people in front of her. On the dais, Lord Farringdon shuddered. Ama tapped him again, and he threw his head back, neck muscles clenched. Deor doubled over, clutching her stomach. She blinked, batting her eyes furiously, but only blackness surrounded her. She groped in her darkness for Geoff's hand, but found nothing.

A scream echoed through the darkness.

"Thief?" she called out, hoping those around her didn't hear.

"No," the voice hollered.

"Easy, easy son," another voice spoke from the void. "This shouldn't be hurting you."

Soothing, gentle, but not for her. The darkness eased and her vision cleared.

She sat back up in her seat. Geoff was staring at Lord Farringdon, a small smirk on his face. Everyone else fixated on the throne. Clearly, no one had noticed her. She shifted to see what was going on up front as the crowd was murmuring and whispering.

Lord Farringdon had put out his wings. His shirt hung in tatters. He was panting hard. The king leaned forward, cradling him, whispering to him. Nefasta waited to the side, her face lined with worry.

Lord Farringdon's wings slid in, and the linen shirt fell away.

Along his back, deep lines had been slashed. Lines dripping blood, like the ones in her dreams.

"Oh my god," she whispered. She glanced down at her hands, instinctively curling her fingers like claws. The tips were silver and sharp.

"Geoff," she whispered. "Geoff, we have to stop this."

"Shhh," he said.

"Please," she said laying her hand on his arm.

He glanced down, eyes growing wide with shock. He caught her wrist, jerking her to her feet with him and leaving her shoes behind. "Come with me."

She nearly fell over the people in their row as he dragged her to the side aisle and into a parlor off the Throne Room, Donovan following.

Once inside, he shut the door and locked it before turning to her. Two chairs and a small sofa formed a circle around a low coffee table in front of a fireplace.

She leaned on one of the wingback chairs, catching her breath.

"What the hell?" Donovan snapped. "This is not the time for pranks, Geoff." He glared at Deor when he spoke.

"No, it's my fault," she started.

"Hush!" Geoff snapped. A wave of green magic slammed around her neck.

Her throat tightened, and it was all she could do to let out a small squeak. She clenched her fists, and for the first time, she could feel the blades. They didn't cut into her, but the magic was there, pulsing. She tried to scream, but sounds wouldn't come out.

Geoff grinned, his pupils flickering.

"It won't help," he said. "Struggling, that is. It might even cut off your air." He took a step toward her and caught her fist, kissed her hand. "Relax, let it happen."

He turned to Donovan. "She started having a fit during the Adoption. I brought her here to keep her from causing a scene." When Donovan raised an eyebrow, he added, "Even I have limits."

The more she tried to speak, the more the magic tightened around her throat. She drew a deep breath and concentrated on the physical presence of the magic, wrapped around her neck like a collar. She brought her free hand up and ran her fingers along the edge.

"What are you doing?" Geoff demanded.

She tugged her other hand free of his and curled both her hands through the magic, as she had done in the alley, and yanked. The magic held, fought her, but she dug her fingernails in and it gave way as she tore through it. She coughed, gasping for breath.

"Don't you ever put your magic on me again," she panted. "We have to stop the Adoption. I'm—"

"I know," Geoff said. He reached for her again.

She dodged, putting the sofa between them. At the edge of the room, between her and the door, Donovan waited.

"You're in on it with him! You and Lord Farringdon. I thought you were protecting me from him." She backed away from him, bumping into the wall. "He wants to be king, and you're helping him!"

He moved forward, shaking his head. "Close, but no. Poor Rafe, with his devotion and knightly heart. He'd never betray the king. No, he's honest when he says he's happy as Sword. The perfect patsy. Besides, he's nothing to you. What do you care if he dies?"

"He's a person, Geoff. I don't want anyone to die. Especially not me."

"Don't be silly." Geoff chuckled. "You're not the one who's going to die."

"What do you mean?" She stepped away a few paces, keeping the sofa between them.

Near the door, Donovan looked as confused as she was.

"You're half faerie, half human," he said. "The pain you're feeling? That's just the faerie in you dying. By the end of today, you'll have exactly what you came here for."

"I came here for my father's acknowledgement."

Crossing his arms, Geoff said, "I thought you came here to get your human life back. Let the process work. When it's over, you can go home and live the human life you've always wanted."

"You're lying." Deor shook her head. "My mother came to Faerie, and she died because she left."

"She was a human, not a changeling. It was a cruel thing your father did. Humans who touch the Fae do often pine away. But that's not what you are. Let all of this go. Just sit here with me; I'll hold you until it's over, and then you'll be Deor Smithfield."

"People will die," she said.

"So what?" Geoff shrugged. "Not people you care about. People who hurt you. People who hurt Robbie. Don't they deserve what they get?"

As if on cue, blackness flashed. The ceremony had started again.

"No! Stop!" she screamed at the darkness in her mind. "You have to stop."

"Who is there?" a voice shouted.

Muscles across her body spasmed. In this space, it was death not to answer.

"It's me," she tried.

At the same time, Rafe called out, "Your son! The heir. Please!"

"No!" Tears wet her face. She had to find a way out of the darkness.

"It's not your problem," Geoff said, his voice gentle, tempting. If she let it all happen, she could walk away. Go home, forget this place like a silly dream.

"No," she said again. Geoff was wrong. It was her problem. It was *her*.

She blinked her eyes open. She gripped the back of the sofa, her silver nails slicing through the fine fabric.

"I can't, Geoff. We have to stop it."

"Sorry, professor." Geoff vaulted to the sofa to land next to her. "You're not stopping anything."

She swung her fist at him, but he caught her wrist. She swung her other hand, aiming to claw his face with her sharp nails. He caught that arm easily, too.

"Really?" He examined her fingers and waved off Donovan. "I can handle this myself."

To Deor's surprise, the vampire didn't make a move. She curled her toes on the carpet—through the lush rug, the stones of the castle called to her. The magic of the castle strove to break through and roll into her.

Geoff spun her around, pulling her back flush against his chest. He caught both her wrists again and held them, arms crossed over her body.

She tried to twist away. She slammed her heel into his instep, but her feet were stockinged and his shoes sturdy.

"Silly girl." He brushed her cheek with his. "Did you think that just because I have a bodyguard, I don't know how to fight?" He jerked her around to face the door, face Donovan. "Did you think he would help you?"

"Donovan?" she asked, but her voice was a whisper.

Around her, a web of green light formed—like the magic on Robbie. She struggled, but fire burst from both of Geoff's hands, and she screamed in pain, though it came out as a squeak. Tighter and tighter the magic wrapped itself around her torso. Soon, Geoff would be able to let go and she wouldn't be able to move. She flexed and clenched her fists, but it did nothing to help her break the spell.

"Let me go!" she demanded, her voice low. The words bounced off the parlor walls like they were in an echo chamber.

For a second, Geoff's hands loosened, and Donovan winced.

"Let me go!" she repeated, words reverberating again.

Geoff's grip tightened. "Your voice of command won't work on me. Not even in here."

A tendril of magic curled up her chest, and she yelped again when it reached bare skin, singeing her flesh. It crawled toward her throat.

"You will be quiet and stay put."

Deor trembled as his magic crept into her. Not like the will magic that wrapped around her in the alley, not trying to get her to do something she didn't want to do, but, like his laughter in her office, promising everything she wanted.

Her nails glinted.

He kept whispering, words too soft for her to hear, but the magic in them worked its way into her mind, and her vision dimmed. Her arms were so heavy; everything was so heavy. A voice told her it was time to rest, that he would watch out for her.

She dug deep, drawing magic up and around her, fighting the swirls of darkness that tugged her down, pulled her toward unconsciousness.

"I won't let him die. Not like this."

She tried to make her body work, but in the darkness was only magic —her physical body was useless. The tips of her fingers burned, and lightning raced through her wings—her magic wings. She drew a deep breath and with all the strength she could find, she thrust out her wings. A scream brought her back to the real world.

She fell forward to her hands and knees, panting. Her wings fluttered in the air behind her, the cuts from before open again, bleeding. She hauled herself to her feet and spun around. Geoff stood, mouth agape, a few feet away. Down each side of his face, down his chest, even down his thighs, ran two perfect, parallel, bloody slits.

"By the fangs of my father," Donovan said from behind her.

Geoff brought his hand to his cheek and wiped away blood. He looked at his bloody fingers and back to Donovan.

"Well?" he shouted. "Kill her!"

She spun to face Donovan, her hands outstretched.

"Wait!" she begged. Her silver nails were long, now, at least an inch. "Please."

Geoff lunged for her again. "I'll kill you myself!"

She whirled back to meet him, claws up.

Geoff reared back out of her reach.

"Sweordmund," she said, examining her fingers. "Sword-hand. Of course. I've been so stupid." She waved her hands at Donovan. "Sword hands! Look, dammit, look!"

Donovan caught her arm and ran his finger along her thumbnail. He hissed and a few drops of blood oozed from his finger. Geoff lunged at them, and Donovan hauled her out of Geoff's way.

"You knew who she was?"

Geoff held his hands up. "Easy, Donovan. It's going to be fine."

"You knew and didn't tell me?" He strode forward, dragging her and driving Geoff back until he bumped into the wall. "What were you thinking?"

"It will all be over soon," Geoff said, green magic winding itself toward Donovan. "It's all going to be for the best. Think how much stronger your father's kingdom will be with Sweordmund dead. The Winter Court will be ours for the taking."

"Don't try that will shit on me, Geoff." Donovan's own voice of command rolled over her skin and she shuddered. He yanked her in front of him again and stared at her face for a moment.

"I can't believe I missed it," he said. "You look just like him."

Deor frowned. "I look like my mother."

"You've got his glare."

"Give her to me," Geoff commanded. "Give her to me or our alliance is done."

Donovan's gaze shifted from her face to Geoff's.

"No!" She struggled, but escaping the vampire's grip was impossible. She slashed at his arm with her free hand, drawing deep lines.

"Stop that," he said, annoyed. "You'll ruin my jacket." He caught her wrist and transferred it to his other hand, easily holding both of hers. "I will deal with you in a moment." He swung her back out of his way. "I'll deal with you, now," he said to Geoff.

"We're allies!" Geoff insisted, and Deor could hear panic creeping into his voice.

"We were," Donovan said quietly, no magic in his voice.

She didn't see the punch coming, a blur of motion. Geoff rebounded off the wall and collapsed in a heap.

"Treacherous son of a bitch," the vampire said to the pile on the floor. "You were going to make me break my family's blood oath."

He leaned in toward Deor, fangs bared, and poked a finger at her chest. "You are so lucky I do give a fuck who your daddy is."

"Yes. Thanks." She nodded at her wrists. "Can you let go now?"

He released her and headed toward the door. "Let's go."

"Right. One second."

Deor grabbed the chain that held the pearl and yanked, her nails severing the strand. She threw the necklace on top of the prone goblin.

"Asshole!" She kicked Geoff in the stomach, but he didn't move. She drew her leg back again for another go.

"That's enough," Donovan said, laying a hand on her shoulder. "We have more pressing things to do."

"Right." Deor sighed and lowered her foot. "Do we have a plan?"

"First—" he pointed at her. "—you think your corset will hold?"

Her wings had torn through the back, but the boning was still mostly in place, as was the magic.

"I think so," she said. "Barring any more wing incidents."

"Leave 'em out." He nodded at her wings. "They make you look regal— and like you walked in off a battlefield. Remind folks of your grandfather."

Deor nodded.

"Alright then," Donovan said. "Stay with me. Look for Arthur. He'll be hiding somewhere in a glamour. We'll signal him, tell him who you are, and then we'll let him take it from there. We can trust him. Okay?"

Deor chewed her lip. "Can I trust you?"

"My family has sworn a blood pact not to harm the Winter Court royal family—why do you think Geoff was keeping me so close?"

Deor opened the door and stepped back. "After you."

They made their way to the edge of the crowd at the back of the Throne Room. At the dais, Lord Farringdon trembled and shook, blood leaking from his wounds. A pang of guilt shot through her. She had done that to him, and he hadn't deserved a scratch.

She scanned the room for a familiar blur.

"The captain's immediately to left of the dais." She pointed.

Donovan squinted. "I'll take your word for it," he said. "Let's go. Quietly up the side, okay?"

"Got it." She nodded. The stones were cool beneath her feet, and soft, like walking on firm carpet. She straightened her back, wings stiff behind her.

Ama spoke. "Oh king," she called out, "claim at last your heir. Call him your own. Call him your son."

The king spoke, his voice echoing in the Palace stones.

"Rafe is my own." Lord Farringdon shook under the king's hands. Hot spikes of pain shot down Deor's spine. "Rafe is—"

"Stop!" Deor screamed.

"Or you could do that instead," Donovan muttered behind her.

She bolted up the side aisle, charging for the throne itself, dimly aware that men in armor with large pikes were rushing to greet her, and, one step ahead of them, dagger drawn, was the captain.

"The king has a daughter!" she shouted.

Chaos erupted.

Chapter Forty-One

Deor braced herself as the captain caught her around the waist and tackled her to the ground. She landed softly, the stone floor catching her like a mattress. His weight drove the air from her lungs, and she cried out as her wings crunched under her. Above her, soldiers pointed pikes. Behind the ring of soldiers, Donovan was equally surrounded, his hands held over his head.

"What are you doing?" the captain said, his dagger at her throat.

She struggled slightly, but the blade nicked her and she froze.

"The king has a changeling child," she said, keeping her voice soft. "That's why the changelings were attacked. The attackers were looking for her."

Around her people shouted. Nefasta shouted for silence, but no one seemed to notice.

"Arthur," Donovan said above her. "Look at her hands."

The Captain eased up, so that she could move. Without taking his eyes off her, he said, "If this is some kind of trick, Donovan, I'll have your fangs for my trophy case."

"Her hands," Donovan repeated.

"Slowly," he said to her and eased his blade away from her throat. "Your left. Just your left," he added, his knife shifting down to poke her ribs.

She raised her left hand slowly and brought it in front of her, held it out to him.

"Sword hands," she said. "That's what the king's name means."

The captain caught her hand in his and touched the spikes at the end of her fingertips. He poked the tip with his finger and winced as a drop of blood welled there.

"Please," she said. "We don't have much time."

The captain sheathed his dagger and pushed himself off of her. He bowed low, offering her his hand. "Your Majesty," he said.

She took it and let him help her to her feet. "Thank you?"

Around them, the crowd babbled in hushed whispers. She scanned the room and caught Victor Farringdon's eye. He gave her a small smile and leaned over to whisper something to his parents. They began to move toward the exit.

"King Sweordmund," the captain called. "We need to speak with you."

The king rose, and Deor shrank back as his gaze settled on her.

"Come on." The captain nudged her forward, his hand on the small of her back. Behind her, Donovan stayed, surrounded by pikes.

Ama was glaring, arms crossed and a mistletoe branch still in her hand. By the look in her eye, she was quite ready to smack Deor with it. The Consort—Robbie's mother—watched her with warm brown eyes. Definitely not the woman from the alley. At the king's feet, Lord Farringdon knelt, sweat and blood dripping off him. His forehead rested on the edge of the throne.

"Come here, child," the king said. "What is it you have to say that is so important?"

Should she curtsey? She wasn't even wearing a dress. Her corset was torn and tattered from the wings, the scuffle with Geoff, being tackled. She tried a curtsey anyway. She managed an awkward knee bend and bob of the head.

"I'm sorry to interrupt, Your Majesty," she said.

From the side, Nefasta snorted her disbelief.

Lord Farringdon, still on his knees before the throne, turned toward her, his face a mask of pain. Their eyes met, and she had the urge to fling her arms around him, to tell him she was sorry. The king stood between them, towering over them both.

"Speak quickly, child," King Sweordmund said. He moved off the dais to stand in front of her.

"I'm not a child," she snapped.

He drew back slightly. A harshness came into his grey eyes, darkening them from clouds to steel. Eyes that she had seen before, that she saw every morning in the mirror. A burst of anger shot through her. How many times had she planned this moment? Worked out what she would say, and how? But now, all she could do was stare back into her own eyes.

"You murdered my mother."

A gasp came from the crowd around the throne.

"I have never killed a woman," the king said. "Arthur, who is this lunatic?"

The Consort gasped as a flash of recognition crossed her face. Just as quickly, she recovered and moved to the front of the dais.

"Good people, I regret to inform you that the Adoption will not be completed today. Please see yourselves out." There was a long pause as the audience stared at her in disbelief. She returned their stares with stern composure. "Now."

The audience began a polite stampede for the exits, with the slower ones receiving encouragement from the guards.

The Consort returned to the king's side, but did not take his arm. She had eyes only for Deor. "Do continue, young woman."

Deor nodded to her, but focused on the king.

"You didn't tell my mother you were married until after she was pregnant—"

"Professor Smithfield," Ama snapped.

"Not now, Ama." The king cut her off. "What is your name, child?"

"Deor," she said. "After the poet."

Lord Farringdon grabbed the edge of the throne and hauled himself to his feet.

"I thought you were dead," the king said to her. "Michael told me you were dead. He said you both died in an accident—one of those horrible iron carriages humans use."

Deor shook her head. "I'm alive, but my mother died alright. She pined for you until it killed her. Do even remember her name? It was Susan."

From beside the king, a sob burst from his Consort.

"You had an heir and didn't tell me?" Nefasta rounded on the king, mistletoe branch held like a club. "No wonder this was so hard on your Sword. The lies you spoke in the ceremony were killing him!"

Deor turned to Lord Farringdon.

"I'm sorry," she said, gesturing at the bloody lines. "I did that. I didn't know until today. I'm so sorry. You didn't deserve any of it."

As she spoke, a little of the color came back to his face. He waved her off, still leaning on the throne with one hand.

"No need. You were losing your throne, and I was a thief."

"You're no thief," she said.

He took a step toward her. "I should have seen it in you the moment you first snapped at me," he said. "That look you get when you're angry? He has the same one."

"This is all well and good," Nefasta interrupted again, "and I do see the resemblance, but we must know for sure."

"I know for sure," the king said quietly, not looking at his wife. "She is my child."

"We'll put her on the throne," Nefasta said. "Then we can all be as sure as you are."

"No!" Lord Farringdon said. He put out his hands to block her from the throne. "After what it did to me? It could kill her."

Deor stepped back. "I don't need that," she said. "He can have the king-dom. I only came to be acknowledged so my body stops trying to kill me." She turned to the king. "You acknowledge me as your child?"

"I do," he said. He reached for his wife's hand.

"Do not touch me." The Consort wrenched her hand out of the king's.

"Great." Deor closed her eyes and concentrated, burying the magic deep in her, like shoving it into the bottom of a trunk in the back of a closet—leaving her wings out to hold up her corset. When she opened her eyes, everyone gaped at her.

"You look human," Lord Farringdon said. "Completely human."

Deor shrugged. "That's what I always wanted."

The magic still thrummed inside her.

"Oh. And this."

She stepped up to the king and slapped him across the face as hard as she could.

"That's for my mother, asshat," she said and turned the Consort. "I am so sorry, Your Majesty. I know it isn't enough, especially now, but my mother always felt guilty about him. She didn't know he was married until after she was pregnant."

The woman nodded, tears running down her cheeks. "Thank you."

"I am so sorry Robbie got hurt because of me." Deor's voice broke, giving way to tears. "If there is anything I can do." She touched the marks on her neck. "I don't know if examining these might help?"

She turned away from the throne, from the father, from Lord Farringdon, from the woman who found the depths of her husband's betrayal. The ordeal was over. She wanted to go home.

Beneath her feet, the castle thrummed. It had its own gentle voice, trying to comfort her, softening its stones for her. The king was still blinking, his hand on his cheek where she'd struck him. She wondered how long it had been since that happened. From the look in his Consort's eyes, it was likely to happen again soon.

"Professor Smithfield?" Ama stepped into her line of vision. "You can't leave. Not if you are the heir."

"I'm not the heir," she said, and pointed at Lord Farringdon. "He is."

"It isn't a choice," Nefasta and the king said in unison.

"Look, I'll do whatever I have to do to hand it off to him."

"Not for all the kingdoms in the world," Lord Farringdon said. "I don't want it. I never did. I'm the Sword."

"Sit on the throne," Nefasta said. "Let's get this sorted once and for all."

The captain offered her his arm. "Here, my lady, let me help you."

She hesitated before taking his arm.

"Help you to the throne, I mean," he added.

She nodded and let him escort her to the dais, but paused before she sat.

"What happens once I sit down?"

"The throne's magic will either recognize you as heir, or it won't. Either way we'll be done fooling around," Ama said.

"And if it doesn't?" she asked.

"It might rip you apart," Lord Farringdon said. When the king glared at him, he added, "It's true. She should have fair warning. Or at least better warning than I did."

Deor stepped away from the captain and ran her hand along the stone arm of the throne. It felt smoother than it looked, and warm to the touch.

"The voice in the darkness, the one that asked the questions, that was the throne, wasn't it?"

"It will question you," the king said.

Deor turned around and faced the group. "I sit here, and if it says no, I can go?"

"Yes," the king said.

She sat. The stone seat shifted under her weight. She looked around in alarm but couldn't see any evidence of change. Still, all her other senses told her that she was sitting in a comfortable armchair, almost a recliner. A little footrest emerged from the stone and supported her bare feet.

"It never did that for me," the king said. But his voice came from the other end of a tunnel.

She sank back into the throne's embrace.

The daughter?

"Maybe," she told it.

Stone darkness wrapped around her, but it was neither smothering nor cold. Silver light probed at her, slipped tingling fingers under her skin, down along her bones and nerves. *Yes,* it said. The stone voice had a tone of satisfaction. *Daughter.*

It prodded her in the back, sending silver tendrils into her wings and drawing her magic back into the light.

"Stop that," she said, and the tendrils withdrew.

The heir. At last.

The darkness exploded into color and sound. Images flickered so fast that she couldn't grasp them. People in long robes, old fashioned clothes. Men and women with silver crowns on their heads. Some frowned. Others laughed. One lay at the foot of the throne, a pool of blood oozing from his body. Most had dark hair and silver eyes. Their wings flashed all the colors of the rainbow, but most often black, and once, scarlet red. All of their fingernails flickered silver.

Voices, chatting, arguing, reciting poetry, whispering love, pronouncing judgment swirled around her in a liquid language she longed to speak but didn't know.

"I can't understand them," she told the throne.

It prodded her like a schoolteacher with a reluctant student.

"I can't."

Suddenly, she could. Fragments of voices whipped across her consciousness.

"What will the goblins do about this? We need them on our side."

"How dare you question my judgment?"

"Send in the ambassadors."

"My darling, my sweetest flower, my angel…"

And one voice she did recognize. "She's gone, Michael! She's gone, and I can't find her anywhere."

A lump rose in her throat. The sights and sounds faded. The throne gave her a little shove out of the silver-edged darkness, and she sat once more on a stone seat in a long hall with anxious faces peering at her. Around her, sparkles filled the air.

The king held out his hand to her and she took it.

"You're a faerie again," he said.

"*I'm the heir.*" She stepped unsteadily away from the throne.

He burst into tears and laughter and threw his arms around her.

"*Don't touch me.*" She pushed away from him, struggling out of his grip. Tears streamed down her face. Her fingernails sparkled in the light. "*I'm never going to be human,*" she said. "*Never.*"

The rest of them gathered around her, their eyes wide. The Consort was the first to bow. Then Lord Farringdon and the captain. Even Ama Nefasta bent her head in acknowledgement.

Deor rounded on the king, her voice breaking. "*I'm not quitting my job at the university. And don't expect me to call you dad.*"

He sighed with relief and joy and nodded at everything she said. She flinched as he took her face in his hands and kissed her on the forehead.

"You can have anything you want. Anything. How did you learn to speak Faerie?"

"*I don't know how to speak Faerie. And I said don't touch me,*" she said, even as something clicked in her brain. "*Am I not speaking English?*" She listened to the sound, not the sense of her own words. "*Oh my God.*" She rounded on the stone chair. "*What did you do to me? I better still be able to speak fucking English.*"

The king was laughing, and her last two words came out in perfect American English. She stepped off the dais and stumbled, and the captain caught her. She swayed in his arms.

"Can I please sit down somewhere?" she said. "Not on the throne?"

Instantly, the king's wife stepped forward. Her cheeks were tear stained, but she stood tall, like an ancient and powerful queen from legend.

"Come this way," she said. "Professor Nefasta, would you be so good as to join us?" She led the way off the dais and to a small side door.

Donovan, silent and still until now, followed, offering Lord Farringdon an arm.

The Consort tapped the star on the door and said, "Household."

The door disappeared and she led them all through to a wide room full of rugs and couches, little tables and sideboards. Two footmen stood at either end of the room along with an older faerie whose hair was flecked with grey and red-headed faerie woman. Both wore the healer's blue that Deor recognized from Penny.

The captain settled Deor on the couch. She leaned back against it and caught his hand as he pulled away.

"Geoff," she said, tugging on his hand, "he knew who I was. He tried to keep me from stopping the ceremony. Donovan helped me."

"I knocked the jackass out cold in the parlor east of the Throne Room. He might still be unconscious," Donovan said.

Lord Farringdon nodded. He shook off the remaining tatters of his shirt and dumped them on the ground as he walked toward a large mirror hung on the wall. The wounds across his chest and back were already closing. He rolled his shoulders and his wings flared out from his back, silver edged. Deor couldn't hide a small smile. It looked too much like a movie—this perfectly muscled man wandering around shirtless, frowning and commanding troops.

"Montjoie," Lord Farringdon barked at the mirror. "Locate your commanding officer and arrest him for high treason."

The uniformed man on the mirror gaped at the Sword, jaw working as he struggled to get the words out.

"You heard me. On the king's authority, I order you to arrest Count Michael, the King's Shield and Defender, immediately. I want him in a cell in the Tower by the time I get there." He snapped his finger at the mirror, and the man disappeared.

The king put a hand on his shoulder. "Are you sure you're well enough, my boy?"

Lord Farringdon rounded on him, his dark hair flying.

"Don't you call me 'my boy.' I am your Sword. That is all I am. You will never call me your boy again." Lord Farringdon turned back to the room, his wings flaring behind him, a new glint in his eye. He strode over to the couch where Deor sat and bowed deeply until his back was parallel with the floor.

"Forgive me, Princess. I mistrusted you when I should have protected you. It won't happen again." He turned to Arthur and Donovan. "Let's go see if we can't find the goblin prince and have words with him."

Donovan smiled. "Yes, let's. I need to give formal notice of my resignation."

Lord Farringdon smiled at Deor. "I can't tell you how glad I am that you've come to the Winter Court." He bowed deeply to her and led the other two men out the portal through which they all had come.

Deor sagged back against the couch as the red-headed healer took her wrist and instructed her to breathe deeply.

Chapter Forty-Two

Soldiers snapped straight to attention as Rafe portalled directly into the war room.

"Good afternoon, gentlemen," Rafe said, returning their salute.

A second later every man reached for his sword as Arthur and Donovan appeared behind him.

"Swords down. The vampire is with us. Welcome to the War Room, Donovan. Tell anyone what you see here, and I'll stake you out in the sun."

"Fair enough." Donovan sat in an empty chair and leaned over the war room table.

Rafe cleared his throat. "Effective immediately, I am no longer the heir elect. Prince Geoffrey is *persona non grata* in this kingdom, and Vlad Dragos is our ally."

"For the moment," Donovan said.

"The king's Shield is to be arrested on charges of high treason." Rafe waved a hand over the table, and the city map appeared, hovering above a larger map of the entire Winter Court.

"Arthur, start shifting regiments toward our border with the goblins. I want the garrisons reinforced by thirty percent by the end of the week, but do it quietly. Bolton, seal the city gates for the next twenty-four hours. No one gets in or out without direct authorization from the king or myself. Fletcher, increase the watch on the Goblin Embassy."

Rafe turned to face Donovan. "Now that we have the preliminaries taken care of, tell me the whole story. Everything that happened, with him, her, all of it. Do you know who he was working with?"

Donovan ran a thoughtful tongue over his fangs. "Know with proof? Nope. But I'd bet my teeth it was Victor. They've been very chummy lately."

"No surprise there. Arthur!"

"I'm already sending a message to Montjoie and Fletcher," Arthur said. "If they're still in the city, we'll catch them."

Rafe shrugged. "They won't be. You know my parents wouldn't come to this city without a portal set to take them straight to Wellhall. Start sending spies into Wellhall's territory." He turned back to Donovan. "So, let's hear it."

He leaned back in his chair, arms crossed, all his attention riveted on the vampire. Whatever machinations the goblins had in store, whatever new treason the Farringdons were planning, he was still Sword and he would be ready.

Chapter Forty-Three

As the healers turned their attention to her, Deor clutched her shredded corset to her chest. The old man with bushy grey hair and the stern, red-headed woman tried to take her pulse, examine her wings, and study her wounds at the same time. Servants with towels crowded in to help. She was hedged in, surrounded, and pulled in every direction by groping hands.

"Get off me!" The stones of the room vibrated with the force of her command. The healers and servants cringed back so that she sat in a circle of wide-eyed, silent faeries.

The Princess Consort threw back her head and laughed, a choking, sobbing laugh that tore at her throat. "Well, there's no doubt she's your daughter!"

"Astarte, my love. Please…" The king reached for her, but she knocked his hand away.

"Don't you touch me. For years I've apologized. I've begged your forgiveness. For years." She backed away from him shaking her head. "You will never touch me again." She gathered up the skirts of her dress and marched out of the room.

Deor scanned the circle of faces around her.

"I'm fine," she said. "Really, I feel fine. Thank you."

If anything, she felt too good. She thrummed and buzzed with the magical power poured into her by the throne. She needed an outlet for it all. The servants' eyes all turned toward King Sweordmund.

"You heard the princess," he said, and the room cleared instantly.

Deor gave him a look. She hitched the remains of her corset a little higher on her chest and tried to pull in her wings. They were rigid and quivering with tension.

"Dammit," she muttered. She stood and closed her eyes, willing herself to breathe calmly and relax her shoulders until her wings slid into her back.

When she opened her eyes again, Sweordmund was hovering in front of her, looking worried. Seeing him this close made her wings jump and quiver in her back, trying to get out again. She glared at him.

"Don't just stand there staring at me. Do something useful."

He blinked. "I prefer that you not talk to me in that tone of voice," he said. "I am, after all, your father."

"Tough luck for both of us," she snapped. "Can you at least give me a bathrobe or a shirt or something before I end up walking around topless?"

He turned away, flailed a bit, and turned back, as if he wasn't sure where to find such a thing. Without a servant around, he probably wasn't.

"How about a towel or a blanket, then?" she said.

"Your rooms! I can take you to your rooms." He lunged for the doors opposite the ones through which the Consort had left.

"I have rooms?" she said, clutching her corset and hurrying to keep up with his long strides. She was going to have to take up running to keep up with these long-legged men. "How can I have rooms? You thought I was dead."

"There are always rooms reserved for the heir," he said.

He led her across a hall and into a giant parlor. The room was so large it had two fireplaces. Half the walls were lined with deep-set bookshelves. Recessed alcoves held suits of armor or marble busts. At the far end, French doors led out onto a balcony. To her surprise, two huge dogs lay sprawled out on a rug. They thumped their tails at the king, but the smaller and sharper-eyed dog got to his feet. He fixed Deor with a stare that clearly said, "I've got my eye on you, troublemaker."

"What are they?" she said.

"They're Rafe's dogs, Jake and Sam. They're waiting for him. His rooms are through that door." King Sweordmund pointed to the right.

Deor clutched her face with her palm for a moment. "Of course they are. He is—he was—the heir. You can't just kick him out of his apartment because I've shown up. He's been through enough today. He doesn't need being evicted to top it all off. Take me to a guest room."

The king laughed and shook his head, gesturing to the left. "This parlor is just a shared space. The heir's suite is to the left."

She followed him into a bedroom big enough to dwarf the king-sized, four-poster bed at the center. Sweordmund disappeared into a walk-in closet. Looking at the high ceilings, she felt sorry, in a vague and self-distracting way, for whoever had to climb up and dust for cobwebs. Perhaps they had magic dust cloths.

She yawned hugely and hugged her corset tighter. The room was chilly, and she shivered despite the warm light of afternoon outside. Something about the room seemed faintly goblin-like. The gaudy peacock blue of the bedspread perhaps or the amount of gilded carving.

Sweordmund reappeared with a blue bathrobe in his hand. "Will this do?"

"Why does it have Geoff's insignia on it?" Before he could apologize, she yanked it out of his hands. "Whatever. It'll work."

"I'm sorry," he said. "He often stays in these rooms when he visits…"

Pulling on the robe, she let the corset drop to the ground under it. The robe puddled and flowed around her feet, but at least it was warm.

"And I bet you never once thought of how symbolic that looked, did you?" she said over her shoulder as she shimmied out of her slacks and yanked off her stockings. "The heir to another court staying in what should have been your heir's rooms?"

"He is my godson."

She snorted and concentrated on an image of Geoff's face, her nails going silver in response. She tore off the embroidered medallion and dropped it on the floor. She moved to kick the pile of clothes out of her way, but her foot caught something heavy. She picked up her pants and fished in her pocket until her retrieved the rattle. She shook it, flipping it upside down and righting it again. Sparkles ballooned out in a larger cloud that she'd ever seen, and the music filled the room.

"You kept it." The king reached for the rattle.

Deor pulled it toward her. "It was the only thing my mother had of you. I thought it might help me find you." She set it on the bench behind her.. "Theophilus is furious, by the way, at what you did to him."

"I wanted you to have something from faerie."

Deor shook her head. "I don't even know what to call you." Before he could answer, she said, "I am not calling you daddy. Not ever." *Your Majesty* stuck in her throat, too.

"I suppose you could call me Finn," he said. "It's my at-home name, more or less."

She laughed bitterly. The name he'd given her mother. The name that had gotten Deor in so much trouble the day she crossed the border.

"Sure, that works. Finn it is," she said.

"Deor, we should talk," he said.

She rubbed her face. Yes, they should. They should sit down and have a conversation like sensible adults. She should force herself to sit down and be civil with this man, the man her mother loved so much that she died without him instead of living with her daughter.

"I can't," she said. "Not right now. Besides, shouldn't you go deal with your wife?"

Another wave of guilt crashed over her. She would never be able to make it up to his wife—and now the poor woman was probably going to have to call her "Your Majesty" and curtsy to her.

"I want to go home," she said aloud.

"You are home," Finn said. He stepped toward her, arms out for a hug, but she backed away, shaking her head.

"Again, don't touch me." Tears welled in her eyes. She hugged the robe around her. "I'm not going to be able to leave, am I?" she said, her voice cracking. "You've trapped me, just like you trapped my mother. If I leave, will I fade away and die, too?"

He dropped his hands to his side, helpless. They stood there in the center of the ridiculously giant bedroom, staring at each other.

"You don't know, do you?"

"No. I don't know. You might. If you stayed away too long. But…"

"But why would I want to live anywhere else than the glorious realm of the Winter Court? Is that what you're going to say? I have a whole other life back there, out there in the human world." She waved a hand toward the windows. "I have a grandmother and a job and friends and…"

And none of that changed anything. "Just get out and leave me alone. Go apologize to your wife."

If it were possible, he was paler than he had been before. He gave her a stiff near bow, a slight inclining of the head, and marched out of the door.

"Jackass." Her knees buckled, and she collapsed onto the padded bench at the foot of the bed, sniffling and hiccupping, wiping her face on the plush robe until the nasty, choking sobs finally stopped.

"I hate this place," she said out loud, sounding like a child. "Sorry," she said, patting the stone floor with her bare foot. "It's not your fault."

The Palace stones didn't exactly move, but she got the distinct impression that the building offered her the stone equivalent of a hug. She snorted, swiped at her face again, and stood up.

"I'm disgusting, and I need a shower," she said. If nothing else, it was something to do.

Immediately, she knew that the bathroom lay to her right through two doors. Towels were in a side closet. Was this where faerie stories of invisible servants came from? She took a deep steadying breath, dumped the robe on the bench, and followed her instincts to a long, hot shower.

The bathroom was comfortingly un-goblin in style. Plants grew on most flat surfaces, and the shower itself was a small waterfall with its own knee-deep pool that came on the minute she stepped up to it. She stood for a long time in the water until her fingernails were no longer silver and her wings stopped twitching with tension.

Once out of the shower, Deor rummaged around in the closet where Finn had gotten the bathrobe, finally selecting a pair of silk pajamas that were still wrapped in tissue paper and tied neatly with a bow. Perhaps Geoff hadn't had a chance to wear these yet. The pant legs pooled around her feet, but they had a drawstring waist and the top fit well enough. She yawned again and eyed the bed, but the thought of sleeping in what was essentially Geoff's bed made her fingernails go silver again.

Hugging herself against the chill, she wandered back out through her rooms, feeling tinier and tinier in comparison to her surroundings. She dropped onto a sofa in the shared parlor, a room big enough to hold her first apartment. And utterly empty of people. The tears threatened again.

One of Lord Farringdon's dogs got up, stretched and bowed, before walking over to her, tail wagging. He rested his giant head on her lap and looked up expectantly. The other dog remained where he was, sitting guard over Lord Farringdon's door. Deor pulled her feet up onto the couch, running her fingers through the dog's warm fur until she fell asleep and dreamed again about the darkness inside the throne and the faces of her ancestors.

She woke with a jerk a few hours later. The room had gone dark and the dogs were gone. Her feet were freezing. As she sat up, her stomach growled and gurgled.

"Lights on," she said, and they lit as she climbed to her feet. If she was lucky, there would be a kitchen or something. If not, she'd find a way to call for a servant.

Again, she had a strange knowledge of the space. The dining room was to her left, second door off the parlor.

When she reached it, she gasped. She'd been hoping for a snack. Instead she had a feast. On the sideboard, a roast waited, perfectly pink in the middle, crisp and brown on the outside, a few slices already carved. A loaf of crusty bread sat beside that. A little carousel of sauces waited, only half of which she could identify. There were three types of mustard and a horseradish sauce for certain. She dipped a finger in a brown sauce and rolled her eyes in ecstasy. It was tangy and gravy based, whatever it was. There were sautéed mushrooms and onions, still hot, in a covered dish. Beside that was a cold salad, a dish of spicy hot pickles that made her eyes water, fresh fruit, and a platter with three kinds of cheese. Under a glass dome, a pyramid of petit fours waited for dessert.

Behind her, at a table big enough to seat twelve, sat a place setting for one. Deor had a sudden flash of herself, bare feet dangling like a child's, leaning over her plate alone.

"No, thank you," she said.

Instead she assembled a sandwich and took her meal out to the balcony. The moon had fully risen and mist hung over the river. She leaned on the balustrade, chewing, trying to spot landmarks she knew. There was the Tower. And the university was over there, the spire of its library rivaling the height of the Palace.

"And I am here," she said out loud.

"May I join you, Princess?" Lord Farringdon said behind her.

He too was in his pajamas, or at least the lower half of them, black silk trousers that came to the tops of his feet. Over that he wore an open robe of the same color. The dark lines that had scored his chest and stomach were gone. He carried a plate piled high with food and a small table.

"It's your balcony," she said. "And you can call me Deor."

"If you like. And call me Rafe." He put the table down and pulled up a pair of chairs. "We didn't catch Geoff, I'm sorry to say. He's escaped over the border. We think Michael, our former captain of the guard, is with him."

She sat opposite him, picking at her sandwich. Suddenly her appetite was gone.

"Do you think you'll be able to identify the woman in the alley?" she asked. Flashes of the woman's face, too rapid to really see, flooded her mind, and her stomach lurched.

"I'd bet money that it was my mother, Madeline. One of the most powerful will spell wielders in faerie. She hates Finn. And Donovan thinks that Geoff was working with my brother Victor."

"Did you arrest her? And can you give me five minutes alone with her and a crowbar?"

Rafe shook his head. "If only I could. My family has fled back to Well-hall. It would take the entire army and a siege of months, maybe years, to get her out. Could you say under oath that you were certain it was her?"

Deor tried to match the image she had of Madeline with the flashes from the alley. All it did was make her sick.

"No."

Rafe nodded. "I doubt any of the other girls will be able to identify her. And there wasn't enough magic residue on the goblin's body either—though we know he is the one who hurt Robbie." He scowled. "Someday I will make the Farringdon name honorable again."

"I'm glad he's dead then. Do you think I can help Robbie?"

"I hope so."

"Thank you for all you've done," she said and gave him a smile.

His frown remained—the guilt and anger obvious in every line of his face.

"So," she said changing the subject. "We're roommates? Or suitemates, I guess."

"We are." His scowl broke.

"Finn actually gave Geoff rooms here?"

"Yes. Not the best choice." Rafe shook his head. "By rights these apartments belong to the royal children. The heir and the spare, they call them."

"Well, if I have to be the heir, you could at least stick around to be the spare." She nudged him with her bare foot.

"Not a chance in the seven hells." Rafe speared a mushroom as if to be sure it was dead. "I am the Sword, and the Sword I will remain."

"It does suit you." She popped a piece of meat into her mouth. "I've thought that since the moment I saw you. There's something sharp about you."

She rubbed her hand up and down her arms, staring out at the cityscape and the hills beyond them. The land seemed to go on forever, far beyond where England would have hit the sea.

Finally, he spoke again. "I'm just so disgusted with Finn. How could he do that to Astarte?"

"How could he do that to you? Put you through that when a kid could still be out there? Risk your life without telling you?" Deor shuddered at the cold coming off of him. "It makes me angry. Angry for me, my mom, my grandmother, you, Astarte. For Robbie." She frowned at her sandwich. "She should divorce him."

"She can't. They have a permanent marriage." At Deor's querying look, he explained. "Their vows are a binding magical bargain. If either one breaks the vow, the magic rebounds onto that person's head."

"Till death do us part. What's the marriage's view on murder?" Deor took a huge bite out of her sandwich.

"That's not funny," he said.

Deor shrugged as she chewed and swallowed. "I'm not sure I'm joking. I'm sorry I hurt you."

"It was self-defense. No apology necessary."

She eyed him over her sandwich as she rubbed her bare feet back and forth over the stone floor, thinking.

He caught her staring at him and smiled. "Finn does that, you know."
"What?"

"The bare feet on stone. Especially when he's troubled or working something out. He'll pace in bare feet or pat the walls."

"I can feel the Palace. All the way down to the bedrock."

It sounded silly. But it was real, she knew, as real as the way she could feel her own limbs. Rafe didn't laugh or give her the cautious look people reserve for the crazy. Instead, he nodded.

"Finn kept saying it would come to me like that, but it never did. What else can you feel?"

She put down her sandwich and stood, planting her feet on the stone. She closed her eyes to concentrate on the magic, the sensation of stone roots underneath her. Getting her bearings took some time. She'd always shoved the magic away. Trying to draw it up made her stomach spiral.

The Palace stones were founded on bedrock that spread outward for miles. Stone on stone, seams and fissures, veins of precious metal woven through the rock. Her senses spread out further, rose with mountains thrusting up through the ground, bare rock soaring into the sky. She touched the soil over the stone, a rich fertile layer binding the living rock to the fragile life that moved over it. Forests and fields, all sending their roots back down toward her in the bedrock.

And people. People moving, working, sleeping, laughing, clustering, and separating in constant motion over the surface of the land. Eyes still closed, she curled her fingers, bunching the magic, twining it around her fingers, gathering it into her. For one split second, she saw all of it, the whole kingdom rooted and centered on her.

Welcome.

Images, sensations all rushed together toward her in a great rolling avalanche, the whole kingdom embracing her at once. She fell to her knees. She was back in the stone darkness, at its center.

Welcome.

Rafe's voice called to her. Not weak this time, strong, but frightened. "Princess! Princess Deor! Come back."

She was on her knees on the balcony, and he knelt beside her, shaking her shoulders.

"What happened? Are you alright?"

She raised her face to his blue shadowed one, worry knotting his black eyebrows. With his fingertips, he brushed a tear off her cheek. A jolt arced between them, the throne's magic, but without pain, connecting them in a flash of silver light. He didn't pull away.

"Are you alright?" he repeated.

She nodded, and rolled back up to her feet. The tears wouldn't stop their streams down her cheeks. Her whole body trembled. For a moment, she thought she might collapse again.

Rafe stood and swept his arm under hers, steadying her. She swayed forward, bracing her hand on his chest to keep from falling into him. Her gaze met his, and another jolt leapt between them, one that had nothing to do with magic.

She steadied herself and stepped away from him, his hand still on her waist.

"What happened?"

The tears stopped, and she blinked the last few off her lashes.

"The whole land welcomed me." She dropped back down into her chair. "Claimed me as its own."

"Isn't that a good thing?" He knelt next to her, his face even with hers.

"I don't know." She locked her gaze on his, the blue of his eyes as deep as the grey of her own. "And..." She shook her head. "Never mind."

"No," he said and took her hand. "Tell me."

"It needs so much. I'm afraid I won't be enough."

He squeezed her hand. "You are enough," he said. The concern vanished from his face, replaced by a wry grin. "From what I've seen, you shouldn't have any problem at all."

She didn't take her hand from his, even as her pulse fluttered. The throne's magic wound around them, the twining threads glimmering in the air. For once she didn't care how spells worked or what they did.

THE END

Special Thanks

Thanks to all of the people involved in Magical Words.net and the Magical Words Betas as writers and readers. Your insights, humor, and generosity mean the world to us.

Thanks to the many other friends and family who have supported our writing, both up close and from afar.

Finally, our thanks to all at Falstaff Books, and specifically John G. Hartness, for believing in the project, and Melissa Gilbert, who should be made the patron saint of copy editors and proofreaders everywhere for her patience and skill.

About the Authors

Sarah Joy Adams writes urban and epic fantasy, and magical realism. She is also an associate professor at Azusa Pacific University where she teaches medieval literature and creative writing. Her academic specialty is Old English literature, folklore, and saints' lives all of which influence her writing. When not writing or teaching she enjoys playing Pokemon Go with her four year old, walking in the San Gabriel Mountains, and catching up on all the movies she wasn't allowed to watch as a child.

Her previous publications include short stories in *Cinched*, *The Big Bad I & II*, and *Extinct is not Forever*.

Emily Lavin Leverett is a fantasy, sci-fi, and horror writer, an editor, and an English professor from North Carolina. She teaches English literature including Chaucer and Shakespeare. Medieval literature, especially medieval English romance, is the focus of her academic scholarship and heavily influences her fiction. When not writing, editing, or proofreading, she spends her time reading and watching television and movies. As avid hockey fans, she, her spouse, and their two cats support the Carolina Hurricanes.

Recent short story publications include stories in *Athena's Daughters II* and *Cinched: An Anthology of Corsets*. Edited volumes include *The Big Bad* series with John G. Hartness and *Tales from the Weird Wild West* and *Lawless Lands* with Misty Massey and Margaret McGraw.

CPSIA information can be obtained
at www.ICGtesting.com
Printed in the USA
FFHW021932201118
49518871-53875FF

9 781946 926173